Canada's Greatest Love Story

Evangeline

THE NOVEL

Based Upon the Famous Classic

By

Richard F. Mullins

"...a perfect blending of the love story and
the history ...a triumph of creative synthesis ..."

Acclaim for *Evangeline: The Novel* by Richard F. Mullins

"Before I read this book, I thought I knew the story of Evangeline. This new version is absolutely fascinating."
Derek Mann
Editor, Toronto/ Halifax

"… simply lovely! That's all I can say. Simply lovely!"
Michele Bauwens
Librarian
Worcester Public Library

"I hated to see this novel end. When I finished it, I wanted to go back to the beginning and start all over again."
Lynn Pelham
Dartmouth, Nova Scotia

"It's all so interesting. The research, the details, the biographical information on the real-life characters…"
Roger Martin
Madawaska, Maine
Tenth Generation Acadian

Evangeline

Richard F. Mullins

To Julie,
I hope you will
enjoy this book.
Take care and stay
healthy;
Sincerely;
Richard F Mullins

Trafford
Publishing

Order this book online at www.trafford.com
or email orders@trafford.com

Most Trafford titles are also available at major online book retailers.

The Library of Congress has catalogued this book under its original title *From
Here To Avignon: The Real Story of Evangeline* by Richard F. Mullins.

Printed in the United States of America.

ISBN: 978-1-4269-4506-9 (sc)
ISBN: 978-1-4269-4507-6 (hc)

Library of Congress Control Number: 2010914486

Trafford rev. 12/17/2010

 www.trafford.com

North America & international
toll-free: 1 888 232 4444 (USA & Canada)
phone: 250 383 6864 ♦ fax: 812 355 4082

About the Book

The Acadian tragedy is arguably Canada's greatest piece of history. In 1755, Charles Lawrence, the acting British governor of Nova Scotia, ordered the arrest and deportation of over 7,000 French residents of Nova Scotia, New Brunswick, and Prince Edward Island. The deportation was a secretive, poorly planned and, in the end, a botched and hastily executed affair. As a result, many French families and lifelong friends were separated as they were indiscriminately shipped to the various American colonies all along the Atlantic Seaboard. For Charles Lawrence and the British, the mission was a triumph. For the French residents, it was a ruthless act of ethnic cleansing. For objective historians, the cruel expulsion ranks alongside the Chinese Opium War as one of the most unscrupulous events in British imperial history.

Today, 260 years later, the grievous wound still festers among the three million descendants of those French exiles. The story isn't over. It goes on and on.

Here for the first time is the complete story, a compelling fusion of the real history and the legendary love story. It's an unforgettable tale of intrigue, survival, and the enduring power of first love.

For my wife, Lorraine, the love of my life,
and for our three French-Irish-Scottish daughters,
Michele, Colette, and Nicole.

Acknowledgments

Special thanks to my wife, Lorraine, for her loving support, and for her French translations; also to Helen Sylliboy of Eskasoni, Nova Scotia, for her Mi'kmaq translations.

I want to express my most sincere appreciation to a generous, professional editor, Derek Mann, for his kind comments and for his expertise in editing my manuscript.

Special thanks also to my sister, Mary Alice, and her husband John Mac Kenzie for their research help and for their hospitality in Halifax.

Warm thanks also to the following relatives and friends who read the manuscript and gave me their honest praise: my daughters Michele and Colette; John and Julie Malia of West Peru, Maine; Robert and Louise Lagassey of Bangor, Maine; Cleve and Carol Leckey also of Bangor; Mike and Lynn Pelham of Dartmouth, Nova Scotia; John and Nancy Tapley, Brenda Sassi, Louise Smith, and Marshall Todd all of Rumford, Maine; and Christine Huckins of Canton, Maine.

I am grateful also to Leonie Lagassey, Maude Marin, and Terry Ouellette, all of St. Agatha, Maine, for their enthusiastic support of this book.

My appreciation also goes out to the following relatives who took extra time and provided me with written, chapter-by-chapter comments and suggestions: my daughter Nicole; my sister-in-law, Florence Mullins of Bras D' Or, Nova Scotia; and to my brother-in-law, Roger Martin of Madawaska, Maine.

I will always be grateful to Mr. Donald Grenier, the best English teacher in New England, for helping me to become a more creative thinker.

I also thank God for my oldest friends Peter, John, and Merle Mc Leod, Peter White, Denis Roach, and Neil Kennedy of New Waterford, Nova Scotia, for teaching me how to think in the first place.

I owe a deep debt of gratitude to Dorothea Allen and Grace Crowell of Rumford, Maine, who loved my little family and who never lost their faith in me.

I am also indebted to the Blackfoot People of Cluny, Alberta, for their friendship, and for teaching me their Native ways.

Lastly, I must acknowledge the following institutions for their generosity in sharing with outsiders like me their marvelous research materials: the Massachusetts Historical Society in Boston; the Historical Society of Pennsylvania in Philadelphia; the Gabrielle Roy Library and the Historical Society in Quebec City; the Nova Scotia Archives and the Legislative Library in Halifax; and the libraries of Dalhousie University in Halifax, the University of New Brunswick in Fredericton, the University of Moncton, New Brunswick, Harvard University in Cambridge, Massachusetts, Wellesley College in Wellesley, Massachusetts, Brown University in Providence, Rhode Island, and the University of Massachusetts at Amherst.

Preface

Very few writers are good at writing dialect, so how should I presume? I have not even tried it here because, while I may have thrown away literary opportunities to achieve "local color" and "authenticity", I thought it more important to present the Acadian-British political issues of 1755 as clearly as possible, and not have them muddled by distracting dialogue. It would not be fair to have the British side presented by articulate Englishmen in perfect English, and the French side presented by Acadian characters in fractured English thereby clouding their viewpoint, demeaning them, and making them objects of ridicule. It is of more historical interest now that the Acadians be understood for what they said in 1755 and not for how they said it.

In the later chapters, the Shawnee Native Americans are depicted with equal dignity. At times they may speak broken English but their word omissions only add a kind of poetic element to their speech.

The Mi'kmaq characters speak, with dignity, in their own language.

Richard F. Mullins

Introduction

This book is intended as both a tribute to, and an amplification of Longfellow's *Evangeline*. Longfellow published his heartbreaking tale to worldwide acclaim in 1847, and it is still lovingly read today by those daring few who are brave enough to tackle a long narrative poem. The story, which Longfellow embellished, (its having been told to him by someone else), is basically a true one. Starting in 1755, over 7,000 people of French descent living in Nova Scotia, New Brunswick, and Prince Edward Island were brutally uprooted and deported to France, and to the English colonies all along the eastern seaboard of the United States.

This version, while it is far less poetic in style, contains more historically accurate information. Why Longfellow omitted many of the fascinating, historical facts behind the tragedy is a mystery. Perhaps in his day people simply didn't know all the facts of the story; or, more likely, they didn't have access to the facts because there was a government cover-up in English-speaking areas since some - not all - of the villains in the story are Englishmen. It is also possible that Longfellow did know, but chose to reject the ugly politics in the tale in order to keep his love story as beautiful and as simple as possible.

At any rate, this book is an attempt to re-tell the famous love story, and to put it in its more politically and historically accurate context. Part One - aside from the love scenes - is the most historically accurate section. Virtually all of the action as well as the dates, the place names, the ships' names, the last names of the Acadians, and the full names of the English officials involved in the deportation are authentic. The Edwards family, the Black family, and Dr. Durveldt, who appear later in the story, are all fictitious characters.

I sincerely hope that Longfellow fans (and I am one of them) will read this book with an open mind. I intend no disrespect to that great old man, nor do I plagiarize his work. I am simply adding information that has, for years now, been offered to the general public by the many wonderful and dedicated Acadian scholars who have done the research and dug up all of the relevant facts. I am resurrecting the grand old tale, dusting it off, adding some new information, and presenting it, in a palatable way, to today's more restless and more demanding general readers.

Chapter One

The Kiss

Late May, 1754, Grand Pré, Nova Scotia.

No, it was not a *spiritual* kiss. No, no, no! What exactly is a spiritual kiss anyway? A bodiless one? Lipless? The timid touching of two cool foreheads? No, no. It was instead a long, warm, lingering, blood-stirring kiss between two young, healthy lovers. Young, healthy, French, teen-age lovers. An *unadulterated* kiss - spirited - not spiritual. What is more, it was springtime, an unusually warm afternoon under the white apple blossoms and, naturally, neither of the lovers wanted the kiss to end. Not even the steady hum of the bees fumbling from blossom to blossom above them could part Evangéline and Gabriel. They kissed on despite the bees, despite the warm rays of the sun, despite all distractions.

The apple tree under which they lay that happy afternoon stood on the edge of the great meadow known in French as Grand Pré, an expansive stretch of flat land, like a misplaced western prairie, on the picturesque shores of Nova Scotia's Minas Basin. It was a sight both strange and beautiful, strange in its Atlantic setting, and beautiful in its length, like a promise not yet fulfilled, or like a comfortable habit that just goes on and on.

Suddenly Evangéline began to giggle. She pulled herself away from Gabriel. "What are you doing?" she asked. "What do you mean 'what am I doing'? I'm kissing you, of course."

"But you are kissing only my lower lip," said Evangéline.

1

"I like nibbling on your lower lip," said Gabriel defensively.

"What about my upper lip? Don't you like my upper lip, too?"

"Certainly I do. It's just that your lower lip is plumper, like a big berry."

She pretended to frown. "And my teeth, I suppose, are like the snow? You're not very original."

"Original? What are you talking about?"

"I hope you were not planning to say that my teeth are like snow and my lips are like plump red cherries!"

"No," said Gabriel touching her lower lip like an examining doctor, "because this one is more like a blueberry."

Evangéline pushed his hand away and touched her lip. "Oh, no! You haven't made it all blue, have you? My father will notice when I get home!"

"Just a little blue. But what I meant was that it feels more like a smooth blueberry than a … a … strawberry," said Gabriel, smiling.

"So why are you interested in only one of my lips? You love just half of me, is that it?" said Evangéline with a feigned pout. "Well, I love all of you," whispered Evangéline in his ear. "I love you totally, completely."

"No, you don't! You treat me cruel. You kiss me, then you push me away, then you kiss me again," said Gabriel, pretending to be wounded. Evangéline held her hand to her mouth to stifle a laugh. "When are you going to prove that you love me completely?"

"I will prove it right now," said Evangéline, and she pressed her lips to his in another warm, lingering kiss.

"That's not what I mean. You know what I mean," said Gabriel applying some emotional pressure.

"When we're married, I'll love you completely. It would be a mortal sin to love you *that* way before we're married."

"But that's too long to wait."

"Gabriel, I don't want to be like Marie Granger, walking down the aisle big with child. I want you to be proud of the way I look on my wedding day. We'll have our whole lives to make love." Gabriel said nothing but looked down towards the Grand Pré shore. Silvery glints of sunshine danced sideways on the bright blue water. Not as upset as he pretended to be, and happy to be where he was, sitting beside his love, Gabriel wanted to be nowhere else in the world.

Across the basin to the northwest, Cape Blomidon stretched itself languidly like a faithful dog, his head resting patiently on his forepaws and his eyes eagerly scanning the horizon for the first glimpse of the ship that would bring his master home again safely from the sea.

Still, Gabriel pretended to be hurt, and put on his most pathetic face. Evangéline snuggled closer to him and asked, "Do you still love me?"

"You know I do," he said. He held her in his arms and whispered, "Evangéline, mon amour."

He loved her totally, too, and although he was a husky powerful young man, he was completely helpless around her. So beautiful was she that he went weak in the knees every time he looked at her, and he had been looking at her since she was seven. Her long, naturally curly hair had never been cut, and it gently billowed in soft auburn waves down her back almost to her slim waist, the auburn tints changing after a full summer of sun to muted topaz. Her cheeks had the natural blush that expensive make-up tries unsuccessfully to achieve in older women. On her tiny ears hung her mother's earrings, her only precious heirloom. Her eyes were the color of fresh green grass when seen through two crystal raindrops, while above them, semi-precious eyelashes curled themselves into tiny beguiling fans.

And the daily improving perfection of her young figure was an oxymoron that delighted the older and wiser men (who detected it sooner) as much, if not more, than it did Gabriel. A few of the older men clicked their tongues disapprovingly to think that all of those feminine young charms were being wasted on a sixteen-year old boy. "What a crime!" they sighed. "Quel gaspillage!"* Quite innocently, she turned all of the old men into instant sixteen-year olds whenever she passed in front of them, looked them in the eyes, smiled, and said, "Bonjour, monsieur. C'est un beau jour." That gorgeous auburn mane, those moist green eyes, those fresh pink cheeks, the perfect female form … oh, oh, oh, a beautiful day it is indeed! Then, the old men, alive again as though resurrected from their own long-dead love lives, would bombard her with questions. All at once and all together, they vied for her attention like panting, tail-wagging pups anxious for a soft pat on the head, "Comment ça va, Evangéline?" "How's your father, dear?" "Where's Gabriel today?" "Where are you going?" "Do you need some help with that basket?" anything to detain her, anything to keep her longer in their sight, anything to see those eyes again looking at them, to see the smile meant only for them. Such animated moments usually ended with the appearance of an older woman who could always be counted on to mutter, "There's no fool like an old fool!"

---

* "What a waste!"

It was not, however, only her physical beauty that made Evangéline so attractive, but the total honesty in her face. She was an open book, often playful, but never devious. Every bit of mental activity registered in her tell-all expressions. A sad thought curled her lip, childlike; a silly idea ignited her giggle; and a confusing concept brought a deciphering squint that Gabriel always found hopelessly irresistible.

Moreover, she was a virgin, which increased her irresistibility, and she was determined to remain one, which increased it even more. Her sexual reluctance, however, was not based on religious grounds, although she was as pious as any girl her age. Pious but not fanatical. She merely believed that chastity kept things simple while sex brought complications and spoiled the happy flow of innocent living. She had seen such complications in the relationships of her older relatives and friends; how love's spark and dazzle dulled and disappeared too quickly after the long-awaited wedding. *Their* spark and dazzle would not disappear if she had anything to do with it! And that, as they say, was that!

They lingered in each other's arms although they knew they had to part now. Evangéline had to go home and prepare her father's evening meal. She gazed one last time into Gabriel's eyes. Then she pressed her hands together like a nun in prayer and she asked, "How much do you love me?" Before he could answer, she parted her hands slightly and said, "Do you love me this much?"

Gabriel looked at the small separation of her hands and whispered, "More."

Evangéline parted her hands a little wider. "Do you love me *this* much?"

Gabriel hesitated a moment, teasingly, and then said, "More."

Evangéline then held her hands about two feet apart and asked, "Do you love me *this* much?"

Gabriel looked at her left hand, then at her right. He hesitated again. "I'm trying to think." Evangéline kicked his foot, and he said, "More."

She then held her arms as wide open as she could and asked, "*This* much?"

Gabriel looked at her intently, "From here to Avignon," he said.

Evangéline squinted. "Where's that? Where's Avignon?"

"My father said that Avignon's a beautiful place in France. France is halfway around the world, you know," said Gabriel, proud of his geographical knowledge.

"*Halfway?*" asked Evangéline. "So you do love only *half* of me?"

"From here to Avignon, Evangéline, mon amour! From here to Avignon and back again."

Pleased with that reply, she gave Gabriel a quick kiss, rose, and ran off through the meadow towards her house.

****

When Evangéline reached her house, the village twins, Cécile and Céleste Richard were waiting by the door, each twin with a warm loaf of bread in her hands. In another month, dozens of wild pink roses would tumble down around them from a white trellis arching the doorway. "We saw you kissing Gabriel," said Cécile.

"Cécile!" scolded Céleste. "Here," she continued, "are two loaves of bread for you and your father. Our mother made them for you."

The mother of the twins, Héloise Richard, a patronizing busybody, always helped those she thought were in need whether they were or not. Evangéline's father, since he had been a widower for the past five years, was considered a man in need. Besides, sending bread was one of the local methods - thought to be subtle - of discovering whether a young single man, or a lonely old widower like Benedict, happened to be entertaining some female visitor from the neighborhood. A single loaf of bread had been known to yield a week's worth of delicious gossip. Appearances were important to Madame Héloise and she was not shy in clucking her censure whenever a single man, regardless of his age, had an un-chaperoned visit from a single woman. "It's probably all very innocent," she would say, "but it doesn't look right to me! Of course, who am I to judge? And I'm not making any accusations, you understand, but … well, … I don't know. I just don't know!" Other people's appearances were, of course, more subject to scrutiny than her own. Her high standards didn't apply to herself because she was short and barrel-shaped with arms as big as thighs, and cheeks so plump she looked like a trumpet player puffing air into an unseen instrument.

"Thank you," said Evangéline to the twins. "Father will be pleased to have fresh bread for supper."

"Will you and Gabriel be getting married after harvest time?" asked Cécile.

"I wish we could! But my father says we're still too young even though I'm fifteen. Besides I would feel a little guilty leaving him alone," said Evangéline. "Perhaps next fall."

"And will you wear *lace* on your wedding dress?" asked Cécile teasingly. The three girls laughed spontaneously at Cécile's joke. They all knew that Father Chauvreulx, the parish priest, would be horrified to see a bride wearing lace, the trademark of jaded, aristocratic ladies and Parisian prostitutes (who were often one and the same).

Although less outspoken than her sister, Céleste also loved to tease. The twins were twelve years old and, like two old maids, they enjoyed teasing young lovers about their romantic relationships. They had no desire for romantic relationships themselves since they were devout, religious girls planning to join a convent in Québec as soon as their parents would grant them permission. The previous year, two nuns from the Seminary of the Ursulines in Québec had visited Grand Pré to encourage religious vocations among the young village girls. From that point on, the twins were committed and couldn't wait to take the veil. With their fragile, bony frames like two tiny, colorless, beady-eyed birds, meatless - all tendons and gristle - they were destined to be unfit for the marriage bed and may as well have had the words "Convent-bound Do Not Touch" stamped on their foreheads. Céleste continued the harmless teasing by bringing up another contemporary taboo. "And will you dance *alone* with Gabriel at your wedding feast?"

At this scandalous suggestion,[*] the three girls again giggled decadently. Evangéline said, "No, but I will dance with Gabriel when we're alone together on our wedding night. And with a fontange[**] in my hair!" Céleste gasped and Cécile sighed. And since that exciting remark was enough to hold their vivid imaginations for another day, the twins chirped their good-byes and scurried off to repeat every word of their private conversation to their other girlfriends.

After Evangéline and her father had eaten their meal complemented by Madame Héloise's mouth-watering bread, Monsieur Bellefontaine looked at his daughter and said, "There may be trouble ahead, Evangéline. Our good governor, Monsieur Hopson, is ill and is being sent back to England for medical treatment. It's rumored that his replacement is a man who hates the French."

"I see," said Evangéline. "And what is *this* man's name?"

---

[*]   Only group dancing was permitted in those days. Not until the waltz appeared did one man dance alone with one woman.

[**]   fontange: a knot of hair ribbon that the priests considered sexually provocative.

"Lieutenant-colonel Charles Lawrence. He came to Halifax from Louisbourg, and he was angry when Louisbourg was given back to the French in the treaty of Aix-la-Chapelle."

Although the loss of Governor Hopson was not good news, she appreciated being informed. She liked the way her father treated her as a grown-up and spoke to her about important adult matters. In their serious chats she always learned something. Benedict was patient and articulate when explaining complicated issues. Even when he was in a quiet mood, she felt she was learning something, something about stability, balance, proportion, and grace. His general air of balance and proportion was his best asset.

He was a tall man but not too tall; in fact, neighbors often described Benedict as being taller than he really was. He was handsome, too, with his blue eyes bluer because of the pure whites around them, his leathery face with the year-round tan, and his earnest look of benevolent concern. However, he was not so handsome that women thought of him passionately and were tempted to consider leaving their husbands and running away with him. His strong back and muscular arms went largely unnoticed until you focused on them; they didn't stand out in any intimidating or threatening way, and were not bulging enough to provoke defiant challenges from weaker men. Nothing about him was extreme. His attractiveness lay in a superior blend of moderate traits. His disposition was gentle but firm, and his general viewpoint was a traditional one, full of respect for the old, yet broad enough to confront and accommodate the new.

In short, Benedict was the perfect image of middle-aged fatherhood, complete with a stomach that carried a few extra pounds to give his opinions more weight. People trusted him, valued his judgment, and even went out of their way to seek his advice. Although he was no more qualified to judge than other capable neighbors, villagers often brought their handiwork to show to him. His personal stamp of approval meant something. And if their handiwork were not portable, they invited him to their work site, anxious to see his approving nod or appreciative smile. Only then did they feel that they possessed something of true value, a treasure to be more fully enjoyed, protected, and handed down to deserving heirs.

"Why, Father, do the English hate us so much? Why do they hate peaceful farmers?"

Benedict stood up and sighed. "Because they are afraid, and fear makes people act foolishly. The English are afraid that France will soon attack this province and take it away from them."

"But what does that have to do with us? We're not soldiers," protested Evangéline.

"No, dear, we're not, but we do have hunting guns. The English are afraid that when they're down at the shore fighting off ships from France we will sneak up behind them and shoot them in the back." [1]

"But we wouldn't do that, would we?"

"No, we would not because we don't trust France any more than we trust England. Many times we've asked France for support and we were always refused."

"Well, can't we tell that to the English?"

"We have, many times, but they don't believe us. They say they will believe us only when we have taken a complete oath of allegiance to the English crown. We *will* take the oath our fathers took, but we will never take the complete oath which forces us to take up arms against the attacking French. After all, our grandfathers came from France."

"Why not take the complete oath? It's only a matter of words, isn't it?"

"Well, if we give in to them on the oath, then they will want something else. Our guns, perhaps. And after that, they might demand our crops, and on and on it will go. You see, we are an occupied people, but we still must keep some pride. We can't keep giving in all the time." Benedict sat down wearily in his chair. "And an oath, dear, is not just a matter of words. It's a serious business. When you take an oath, you're asking God to support what you're saying, so it ought to be the truth."

"Oh, Father, I'm afraid. Will anything bad happen to us? Will the English kill us all?"

"No, no, no, dear, but they can, if they decide to, make our lives miserable. Just pray to God and to St. Charles* that Monsieur Lawrence will learn some kindness from Monsieur Hopson. Just pray hard, dear."

---

* The name of the local parish church was St. Charles des Mines.

Chapter Two

A Certain Status

Summer came and Evangéline and Gabriel spent warm evenings walking hand in hand, barefoot, along the Minas* Basin beach making footprints in the coppery corrugated sand. Closer to the water's edge, the sand turned to clay and Gabriel loved to squish the gooey red muck between his toes. The little boy in him still enjoyed playing in the mud. But one small frown from Evangéline sent him wading to bathe his feet clean again.

To pass the time, they'd sit on the sand and watch the crafty gulls dive, re-surface, climb skyward, and drop their catch onto the crags below; then down they'd swoop, land, and peck out the slippery clams from their shattered shells. Gabriel would pick up the violet mussel, and pink scallop shells with their lustrous insides, and for each one he handed Evangéline he received a kiss. At the end of their stroll, he always threw the shells back into the surf so that he could collect them, and more kisses, the next evening.

Evangéline grew more in love each day. She loved everything about her Gabriel. Nearly six feet tall, he had the chest, biceps, and forearms one would expect a blacksmith's son to develop. She loved his thick hair, brown like his eyes, the color of deep delicious chocolate. But it was more the look in his eyes, the look of love, the pitiable stare burdened with desire for her. He was young, strong, virile and, like her, virginal. His intense yearning for her was his only vice, a vice she fully approved of, but encouraged with

---

* "Minas" is a variation of the French word "mine" which means ore; in this instance, copper ore, which the early inhabitants thought that the red clay indicated.

nothing more than a playful mixture of coy glances, modest blushes, and red-blooded kisses.

Evangéline also appreciated the look of envy in her girlfriends' eyes. In their envy, she felt a certain status that she tried hard not to flaunt. She made sure that she always smiled at her friends and didn't beam too brightly as she walked past them with Gabriel's hand in hers. Still, some of her girlfriends believed that her smile was, in fact, merely a show of appreciation for their jealousy, and they resented it. A few never forgave Evangéline for capturing the village prize, because each one of them had, at different times, seen Gabriel on horseback, riding towards her, and had felt both excited and sad; her knight in shining armor had come at last, but only smiled, waved, and galloped on by.

Between the covetous gaze in her friends' eyes, and the impassioned glaze in Gabriel's, Evangéline felt prouder each day. Love was, as everyone said, grand indeed.

Everyone in the village helped at harvest time. By September all of the barns were filled to capacity. And nothing happened. All seemed well. No news came from the new governor in Halifax. The Acadians went on with their lives as they always had, blissful and oblivious, cocooned in their language, their families, and their firm Catholic faith.

Chapter Three

The Replacement

September, 1754, Halifax, Nova Scotia

From his medical bag, the young army physician removed a jar of leeches, opened it, and placed one leech on each of Governor Hopson's temples. The leeches immediately bulged and grew fat gorging themselves on Hopson's blood.

"Shall I apply the ointments to your eyes now, Governor Hopson?" asked the young doctor. Hopson was getting the latest, most advanced treatment for the dreaded eye disease, opthalmia.[1]

"In a moment, doctor," said Hopson. "I'd like to have a few more words with my visitor first." Hopson, who after months of delay was returning to England on a year's medical leave of absence, turned in his chair to face the visitor, his replacement. The man who had been ordered to take over the governor's duties while Hopson was away, the new lieutenant-governor of Nova Scotia, was Charles Lawrence.[*]

With a wry smile, Lawrence looked at Hopson and tried to imagine this fine, respectable gentleman wrapped in the sweaty arms of a diseased prostitute. Hopson, with his boyish grin, his crinkly, smiling eyes, and his short pudgy build, looked absolutely asexual. As hard as Lawrence tried,

---

[*] Lawrence's family was related to the Montagus. George Mantagu Dunk, 2nd Earl of Halifax, was president of the Board of Trade. Family connections, then, probably played some role in Lawrence's appointment.

he couldn't imagine it, and yet such a sordid scene had undoubtedly and regrettably taken place earlier in Hopson's life because the most common cause of opthalmia, the sight-destroying type contracted by adults - the cause only whispered about - was gonorrhea.

Despite the unsavory gossip that his eye problem provoked, Hopson would be missed in Nova Scotia. One of the few English administrators who had behaved civilly to the Acadians, he was well liked because he was a contented man and because his contentment made him levelheaded and composed. He did not possess the heartless efficiency of some ambitious administrators. He had had greatness thrust upon him and was uncomfortable with it. In fact, he resented it as a boy resents being called in from play to do his lessons. Not that he was a childlike man but, lacking the mania necessary to dominate the lives of thousands, he saw the post of governor clearly, without vanity, and thus found it boring. The toughest part was in restraining the mania of the ambitious personnel around him. He regarded the post of governor, therefore, as a bit of a nuisance, an interruption in an otherwise undemanding career. He smiled a lot, and smiled at everybody so that the common people liked him while the higher-ups were confused by him. After all, no one in a position of grave responsibility was supposed to be outgoing, democratically friendly, and full of smiles.

And, as often happens with a change of top management in any organization, the pendulum swings and the departing manager is replaced by his exact opposite. Hopson's opposite was the visitor now standing before him. A man with few close friends, Charles Lawrence was a ferociously ambitious manipulator who tended to see enemies everywhere, and to detect behind every smile malicious intentions.

"I hope you don't mind, sir, that I took the liberty of bringing along my adjutant,* Mr. Stone. My memory fails me at times, and I thought Mr. Stone could record any detailed instructions you might give me. I'm not certain that I know all of the duties of a governor," said Lawrence.

Governor Hopson, though slightly suspicious, decided to let his suspicions pass. "Mr. Stone is welcome here, sir, if he is your guest," he said graciously. "The clever young doctor here has just given me the best diagnosis that modern medicine can provide on my eye disease; he tells me that I shall either have a full recovery of my sight, or else go completely blind when both of my eyeballs shrivel to the size of two green peas. I need no ghost come from his grave to give me such a wide-ranging diagnosis," said Hopson, smiling a good-natured smile. Hopson was not trying to embarrass

---

*   a general military assistant with secretarial duties

the young doctor but only trying unselfishly to make light of his serious medical situation for the ease of others. He was a kind man. His white hair made him look older than sixty, but it suited the man who was one of the most lenient, most understanding governors Nova Scotia ever had.

"Ghost, sir?" asked Lawrence, puzzled by the allusion.

"It's a line from *Hamlet*, Mr. Lawrence. I read Shakespeare. Reading gives me ideas, and a governor needs a great variety of ideas in order to govern properly," said Hopson, still smiling. "And, as you have mentioned, it is difficult sometimes to know exactly what the duties are of a governor in a new land. However, it's safe to say that the governor's first duty is simply to govern, in a humane way, those settlers who are within his jurisdiction."

"And what of those settlers who have no right to be within the boundaries of the governor's jurisdiction, sir?" asked Lawrence pointedly.

"Are you referring to the Germans we have down in Lunenburg, sir?" asked Hopson, knowing very well that the small number of Germans in Lunenburg were not the unwelcome settlers Lawrence had in mind.

"The Germans, yes, sir, and the Acadians, and any other group that may cause trouble by their presence here."

"Well, the Germans are settling in quite well and, as for the Acadians, I'm sure that you can appreciate how useful they are to us, and even necessary. They are a simple, domestic people."

"Not all of them. There are renegades among them who have assisted the Mi'kmaq in disturbing the peace here," said Lawrence.

"There are malcontents everywhere, sir, even in England. But my point is that it is impossible to live in Nova Scotia without the Acadian farmers," said Hopson. Lawrence looked down at the floor and said nothing. "I, of course, now have no authority to tell you what to do, but I sincerely hope that you will treat the Acadians in the same manner in which we treat the other subjects of His Majesty. We should take nothing from them by force, pay them the normal price for all their goods, and neither insult nor offend them. Our soldiers, as you know, can be very cruel to them."

"All those who take the complete, unqualified oath of allegiance to the English crown shall receive only the best treatment from me, sir. You may depend upon that," said Lawrence firmly.

"Aye, there's the rub, sir, for the Acadians have *not* taken the complete oath in the past forty years, and for that, we have no one to blame but ourselves. In the past forty years no Acadian has ever been seriously punished by us for *not* taking the oath, and to be honest, sir, they have not been a problem to the English government at all. Perhaps I should even say that they have done us more good than harm," said Hopson.

Only the scratching of Mr. Stone's feather pen on paper could be heard in the room. Lawrence made no reply and his silence indicated opposition to Hopson's defense of the Acadians. Hopson got the message, sighed, and said, "You may now apply your preparations, doctor." As though he were in a barber's chair waiting to be shaved, Hopson sat with his head tilted back ready to accept his treatment and his fate with patience and calm.

The doctor bathed Hopson's conjunctiva with a freshly prepared solution of silver vitellin. After a few minutes, he rinsed away the silver nitrate with a saline solution, inserted an unction of zinc and copper crystals under Hopson's eyelids, and covered them with warm gauze pads. To hold the pads in place, the doctor wrapped a bandage around the governor's head.

Lawrence, wide-eyed, looked on with great interest. He felt like a giddy mourner at a wake, studying the corpse, and knowing that he would soon be named the principal heir in a generous will.

It was, in retrospect, a scene of great irony. The only Englishman who, at that crucial historical moment, could clearly see the true value of the French Acadians in Nova Scotia, was now blindfolded.

Feeling a mixture of helplessness and foreboding, Hopson, nevertheless, stuck out his hand in Lawrence's direction and hoped for the best. "If all goes well for me, I shall see you a year from now, Mr. Lawrence. Thank you for coming to call," said Hopson.

Lawrence took Hopson's hand, shook it, and said diplomatically, "I also hope that you will see me one year from now and not a minute longer, sir. Godspeed, and may He grant you a full recovery."

Once outside in the cool Halifax street again, Mr. Stone handed Lawrence the notes he had jotted down. Lawrence glanced at them quickly and then said, "Some men in this world, Mr. Stone, are always shouting 'go!', and 'onward!', and 'full speed ahead!'. Other men are always whimpering 'stop!', 'wait!', and 'slow down!'. Our Mr. Hopson belongs to the second group." He held the two pages of notes in front of him, and slowly tore them to shreds. "I have no desire to preserve the whimperings of an administrator who lacks the courage to lead." Mr. Stone frowned but said nothing as the new lieutenant-governor threw his scribbled notes into the muddy gutter.

Chapter Four

Congratulating Judge Belcher

October 14, 1754

Charles Lawrence brushed his imposing six-foot-two frame past Richard Bellingham, the law student serving as the judge's secretary and, without knocking, marched into Judge Jonathan Belcher's office. "Good morning, sir. I just wanted to privately offer you my congratulations on your new appointment. A supreme court justice is just what this unruly province needs," Lawrence said, as he smiled a smile too broad to be merely congratulatory. The Lawrence smile was unreliable. Indeed, this time he was simply amused that Belcher was sitting in his office still dressed in his judicial scarlet robes an hour after his swearing-in.

"Thank you, sir," said Belcher as he put down the book he was reading and rose to shake Lawrence's outstretched hand.

"I see you are busying yourself with law books already," said Lawrence, picking up the book that Belcher had been reading. "Why, sir, this is a book of poetry!"

"You don't enjoy poetry, sir?"

"Yes, I enjoy poetry, but most of the time I can never make head nor tail of it. What is poetry good for anyway?" asked Lawrence.

"It's good for one's soul, sir," said Belcher with a smile. The poetry Belcher liked was the simple, sentimental sort, especially the simple, sentimental, religious sort.

"For 'one's soul,' you say?"

"Someone, an ancient Greek, I believe, once said that 'poetry contains messages for the soul'."

Lawrence shrugged and said, "I'm surprised you have time for your soul. I'm busy enough taking care of my body in this frozen part of the world. It's only October and already we have the icy winds of January."

"Indeed, sir. I had hoped to spend the second half of my life down in the colony of Georgia; alas, here I am," said Belcher.

"Alas, here we both are and I hope that we can make one another's stay here as painless as possible," said Lawrence.

"I am your servant, sir," said Belcher.

Lawrence looked Belcher in the eye and smiled. He made a perfunctory bow as if to ingratiate himself to an inferior and said softly, "I certainly hope that you are, Mr. Belcher. I certainly hope that you are. Good day to you," and he left the room as quickly as he had entered it.

Belcher gulped and shivered as though he had accidentally swallowed a hornet. Then he reached for the antidote, his book of poems, and read.

> Oh, that glorious life above us!
> Is it strange we long to be
> Sometimes freed from life's sad trials,
> God, and bliss, and Heaven to see?
>
> Yet, oh! yet be still, wild spirit!
> Long no more for things above!
> Live, and make thy 'lotted lifeway
> Heaven on earth, by deeds of love.[*]

"So beautiful!" he sighed. "If only I could express my thoughts as delicately as that!"

---

[*] Author unknown.

Chapter Five

The Incomplete Scroll

For the amusement of the Acadian children, Joe Joseph, the ten-year old Mi'kmaq boy, was again walking over broken, lead glass with his bare feet.

The school children were enjoying recess outside the one-room schoolhouse in the village. The little boys said, "One more time, Joe," while the girls said, "Don't, Joe, that's enough!" Joe walked again, back and forth, over the broken bottle as though he were walking on sand. Having gone shoeless since birth, except in winter, Joe had feet that were as hard as horn.

Joe Joseph was an odd name. When the Mi'kmaqs were baptized by the Jesuit missionaries, they were given Christian names. However, once the actual baptism rite had been performed and the sacred souvenir jewelry handed out, the Mi'kmaqs saw no point in remembering their new superfluous names. After all, they already had beautiful names. Do these Frenchmen also bait their fishhooks twice? they wondered. Young Joe could remember his last name, but quickly forgot his Christian one. The Acadian school children couldn't remember it either, so they quite naturally settled on Joe Joseph for him.

Joe stepped away from the broken glass, sat on the grass, and showed the bottoms of his feet to the children. No cuts, no blood. Amazing! "All right, Joe, here you are," and five children stepped forward to give Joe his promised reward, five delicious butter-soaked biscuits, their mothers had baked early that morning.

Pierre Melanson appeared from inside the improvised school-house, a large shed behind his house. "Time to come back in," he said. The children entered the shed that Pierre's father had worked in before his death. Pierre and Father Chauvreulx had equipped the building with an old stove so the smaller children would be warm as they were kept out of everyone's hair during the busy planting and harvesting times. There were tables and benches for the children to work at, and frilly curtains on the windows. The children were taught to read, write, and cipher during the months of spring, summer, and fall. In the cold winter months they were kept at home to learn the practical arts - mostly cooking and spinning for the girls, and leathercrafting and woodcrafting for the boys. Since Pierre couldn't perform physical labor because of a childhood accident that had left him lame, and since he was one of the few young people who could read and write, he was the village's main teacher. Father Chauvreulx was supposed to be both priest and pedagogue, but he was often too busy with weddings, sick-bed visits, last rites ceremonies, and burials to teach school.

Twelve years earlier, while Pierre's broken leg was mending, the more literate locals volunteered their time with him. Now he was returning the favor - teaching others - and he enjoyed it. In fact, he had become the village's resident intellectual. He read every book he could get his hands on. Whenever a ship arrived in the harbor, the other villagers were interested in the ship's trading cargo; Pierre was interested in the books on board. Ships often carried small libraries because, in those days, a ship captain's entire family usually traveled with him, and the children were educated at sea. Pierre could read a book faster than the crew could unload the ship's cargo, but he was not happy until he shared his new knowledge with others. He was most comfortable sharing it with small children because they didn't stare at his leg or snicker at his limp. Of course, he never shared his books with Father Chauvreulx who would have burned them immediately. Only religious books were tolerated by the Jesuits.

Pierre often had help in the classroom, too. Some of the older village girls would accompany their siblings to school and assist in tutoring them. Evangéline sometimes came to help Pierre in disciplining the little girls. She was there today as the children took their places and raved on about Joe Joseph's tough skin.

Just when the children had been quieted, Father Chauvreulx walked in. "Oh, oh," whispered Pierre to Evangéline, "another sermon for the children." Pierre groaned and said, "Welcome, Father! Children, say 'good morning' to Father Chauvreulx."

"Good morning, children," said Father. "I am just on my way to visit the sick in Rivière aux Canards.* But before I go, I want to show you something interesting. Look at this, my little ones," said Father Chauvreulx as he unrolled a large leather scroll and held it up.

The children stood and tried to see what was so interesting.

"Qu'est-ce que c'est?"* they whispered to one another.

Pierre and Evangéline stepped closer for a better look. They could smell the priest's familiar and unique odor, an odd combination of soap and dust, the static smell of chastity. His face and hands smelled of orange water, but his black cassock reeked of a dry staleness as though it had hung unused in an attic for years. Perhaps the clothes of all old bachelors smelled that way, clothes simply in need of a housewife's fastidious care. And yet this bachelor's odor was peculiar to Father Chauvreulx, like the mixed scent of spiritual solicitude and bodily neglect, of heavenly concern and earthly disregard, like the odor of a saint in a soiled human robe. "When I first came here, the Mi'kmaqs and I communicated with drawings. The drawings helped us to understand one another." The children were still straining to see. "This picture was painted on deerskin by an old Indian chief. I had asked him to draw a picture of all of the things in life that were important to him." Since the priest seemed to be so proud of the picture, a few of the children gasped politely.

"What is on it?" asked eight-year old Simon Aucoine. "I can't see!" Evangéline lifted the small freckle-faced boy above those who blocked his view. "Oh, I see animals," said Simon proudly.

"And what else?" asked the priest.

"And rocks and trees."

"Anything else?"

Another boy said, "The sun."

"That's right," said the priest. "What else?"

"The sky," said another child.

"That's right, the sky."

"And the earth," said another child. "And water and fish."

"And fire," said another. "Flames."

"Must have been a bad forest fire," said Simon, feeling sorry for the animals.

"Probably it was," said the priest. "So we can see that the important things in an Indian's life are the sun for warmth and light, the earth for

---

*   Now simply Canard.
*   What is it?

growing corn to eat, the fish and animals for meat, and the fire to cook the meat. But the most interesting thing to me, children, is what's missing from the picture." The children looked baffled.

Pierre shifted impatiently from one foot to the other. He felt a sermon coming on.

"Can you guess what is missing from this picture?" asked the priest. The little ones squinted hard, consulted each other in whispers, but came up blank. They waited dutifully for the answer. "Can anyone see a church in this picture?" No one could. "Can you see a cross or a crucifix anywhere in this picture?" Nowhere. "So, can you imagine how terrible it must have been to be living like an Indian for thousands of years *without* a church, and in a time when no one had ever heard of Jesus Christ, Our Savior? Can you imagine that?" Several children had to admit they couldn't.

Simon giggled at the priest's joke, but disagreed. "An Indian can't live for a thousand years, Father!"

Evangéline smiled, gently put her hand over Simon's mouth, and said, "Shhhh, Simon!"

Father Chauvreulx glanced at Pierre and asked, "One of *your* protégés?" Then the priest glared at little Simon and continued to glare while he hammered home his point. "Imagine a world without Jesus. Imagine a world without the gospels. Imagine a world without the saving grace of Christianity. Those poor people!

"And now, just think how fortunate we are to know the gospels, and to know Jesus Christ, and to have a beautiful church in which to worship and to thank God for His gifts." The priest held up the picture again for all to see. "Yes, my children, those days are gone now. Those days without Christ no longer exist, thank God. We have Christ in our hearts now, and we can neve go back to those primitive times. Why? Because we know that wherever in the world Christianity is introduced, it stays, and stays, and stays. Those pagan times that you see depicted here will never come back now that we have Christ in our daily lives. Those days are gone forever!'

As he rolled up his scroll, the priest smiled at the silent class, said goodbye, and went out the door flushed with accomplishment. Pierre whispered to Evangéline, "That man could find some religious meaning in a ploye." Evangéline smiled shyly, embarrassed to hear disrespect for her priest. "Come to think of it, there is something spiritual about a ploye," joked Pierre. "Now, children, back to work."

---

* a ploye is a traditional pancake-like staple served, in some Acadian homes, with every meal.

Evangéline squinted. "But you do believe what Father said about Christianity, don't you, Pierre?"

"You mean about Christianity being introduced and staying forever?"

"Yes."

"Oh, yes, I believe that. But, then again, once anything is introduced into our lives, it stays forever. He could have said the same thing about rum!"

"Pierre!" Evangéline gasped.

"But it's true. And he could have said the same thing about the English feelings of superiority!"

"Or anyone's!" she snapped, as she turned away to attend to the children.

Pierre's squinting gaze followed her.

Chapter Six

The Depth of Her Virtue

Gabriel's right hand was behind Evangéline's head while his left hand was resting on her ankle. They had just finished the lunch Evangéline had brought to the blacksmith shop where Gabriel worked with his father, Basil Lajeunesse. Gabriel and Evangéline had stepped around to the back of the shop where they would have some privacy. With lunch now out of the way, naturally it was kissing time again. The lovesick young lovers, whenever they found themselves alone were always kissing on a full stomach, except when they were alone and kissing on an empty one.

Gabriel's hand moved over Evangéline's left shin and up to her kneecap. He paused there pretending that his hand had reached its final destination and tried to read the braille of her tolerance. After another long kiss his fingers grew impatient and traveled farther. Evangéline's right hand gently covered Gabriel's. Gabriel waited. Nothing happened. No outright refusal. No reproach. His hand with hers on board began to move slowly upward. Suddenly he felt a piercing pain in the back of his travelling hand. Evangéline's fingernails were digging in. "Pain's not *that* bad," he thought and decided to continue his digital journey. Suddenly the pain was twice as bad. Evangéline was digging deeper. Now he was losing all concentration. He would simply have to give up. He couldn't win today. All he wanted now was to check his hand for blood. "We can't," whispered Evangéline.

"Why not?"

Evangéline smiled, looked around, and said, "Not here."

"Well, let's go, then."

"Go?"

"Somewhere else."

"Don't be silly. It's broad daylight," giggled Evangéline.

Gabriel sighed in resignation, shook the bread crumbs from his shirt, stood up, ran his hand over Evangéline's beautiful head of long brown hair, and went back to work grinning and kneading out the four purple indentations on the back of his throbbing hand. He was learning the hard way the depth of his sweetheart's virtue.

****

The autumn came, and all too soon it went, its vibrant colors drained, dried, and blown away in October's bluster and November's chill. Then the grays of December blended with January's whites, and together they subdued the great meadow to a colorless blank. In the iron coldness, even the pines and cedars appeared drained of their greenness. They stood on the hills looking lifeless and dark, like tapering, flat, serrated columns of coal, like primeval totems of dark foreboding. They looked even more forlorn when their sturdy branches sagged under the weight of heavy clumps of snow that threatened to bow them down forever.

From a distance, in the blue winter air, when the snow stuck to them only at wind-protected levels, the hills themselves looked like an elongated marble cake in unappetizing mottles of navy and white. And the apple tree by the house, stripped now of every leaf, its limbs grotesque in their nudity - gnarled, twisted, and spent in the bearing of fruit - resembled a large, black umbrella's skeleton mocked with a cold, white, inadequate covering.

Gabriel went to Evangéline's house every day "to help bring in the firewood," an excuse as transparent as the icicles that hung and shed silver droplets from the trellis over the entrance. No one minded, however, as long as some attempt at an excuse had been made. And after a few sticks of wood had been brought in and piled beside the hearth, Evangéline was content to sit and snuggle with Gabriel in front of the fireplace as her father napped - or pretended to nap - on the cot in the corner of the parlor. They snuggled and held each other tightly as the seasoned birch logs crackled and sometimes shot out an angry spark which they had to dodge and trample to a harmless powder on the floor.

Sometimes after a snowstorm when all the world was white and clean, they went for a walk and threw snow at one another until they were tired and plunked themselves down in a snow bank, laughing like five year-olds, and Gabriel kissed her chapped, reddened cheeks. He would kiss her until she complained that his nose was too cold. "Well, your nose is cold, too, and I don't mind."

"Yes, but mine is not running!" Then she would leap up and run away from him, shrieking with girlish laughter. Later, when they grew thirsty from their play, they'd pick up a handful of snow and eat it until their thirst was slaked, always a little surprised that it tasted like dusty, cold water which is, of course, the definition of snow. On Sunday afternoons, they warmed stones on the hearth, wrapped them in towels, and brought them along as heaters when they hitched up the huge workhorses and took their friends for a jangling sleigh ride. And they all laughed, gossiped, and sang until the early winter darkness sent them home.

They didn't know it then - no one knew it - but as the winter of 1754-55 drew irretrievably to a close, their days of playful innocence were almost over.

Chapter Seven

In a Storm Now

May, 1755

"Just because he's a cripple he thinks he can get away with murder," was the most common remark snickered behind Pierre Melanson's back. The remark was, in fact, justified because Pierre was the most outspoken young man in Grand Pré. The brash nineteen year-old schoolmaster liked nothing more than to shock his friends and neighbors with his outrageous comments on religion, sex, and politics. The villagers' diagnosis was that his childhood accident had made him bitter and that his bitterness, in turn, had spawned his rebelliousness. Oddly enough, Pierre was one of Gabriel's best friends, and Gabriel was anything but brash.

At the age of seven, Pierre was kicked in the leg by a horse. His new young pup had been barking at the heels of a roan mare. As the pup yapped, Pierre stepped behind the horse to remove the pup from harm's way when the horse kicked up its heels. The kick, directed at the dog, instead broke Pierre's left leg in two places. The break never mended properly and the growth of Pierre's left leg failed to keep pace with that of his right. As a result, his left leg was markedly shorter and caused him to limp. The limp now was slight thanks to the shoes made especially for him by the shoemaker, Monsieur Babin. On his right foot, Pierre wore a regular shoe, while on his left he wore a shoe with a two-inch sole and a three-inch heel. He was proud of his shoes since most villagers wore wooden sabots or clogs.

His limp, moreover, proved to be a romantic asset. It gave him a vulnerability and, as a result, young ladies were drawn to him. His impish grin, dark eyes, and head of shiny black curls increased his appeal which he cultivated and took complete advantage of. "Tell me, Gabriel," said Pierre as he walked into the blacksmith's shop, "will you be doing anything unusual on your wedding night?"

Gabriel began to laugh uncontrollably. Pierre, the village's pampered brat and rebel, was at it again, shocking people. "And will you be needing any assistance?"

Charles Le Blanc laughed, too. Charles, one of their young friends, was there in the blacksmith's shop working on one of his new inventions, a cushioned wheel. "Where do you ever get such disgusting ideas, Pierre?" asked Charles. Charles was a prude and not at all the bohemian one would expect a creative, inventive young man to be. However, as one *would* expect, he was a bundle of contradictions.

"Well, I've heard that girls enjoy … oh, a variety of … excitements. Elizabeth Anne does," he snickered, "but then again, she's an Indian girl."

"Have you done … a variety of … things … with Elizabeth Anne?" Gabriel asked.

"Every boy in the village has, except you, *Saint* Gabriel!" scoffed Pierre. "Even Charles has, haven't you, Charles?" Charles was laughing so hard he couldn't reply. All of the village boys leading sheltered Catholic lives relished Pierre's outrageous humor.

Then, Pierre suddenly stopped smiling and grew more serious. "Gabriel, I want you to come to our meeting tonight at my house. We've heard rumors that the English are going to seize all of our guns. Not only that, but they might take away our boats and canoes, too. I know you don't like politics, but this time I think you need to get involved."

"Oh, Pierre, we've been through all this before. People who are interested in government and politics are people who want to run things themselves. I don't want to run anything except my own shop someday and my own life with Evangéline," said Gabriel.

"But that's just it! You won't be able to run your life if the English are going to run it for you."

Gabriel sighed and smiled. After a pause he said, "It's just that we're very different, you and me. I like to sit in my comfortable house and look out the window at a storm. I don't ever want to be in one."

"You're in one now, my friend," said Pierre with a knowing look.

Gabriel was not as politically uninformed as Pierre thought. It was just that Gabriel didn't spend all of his spare time, as Pierre did, in complicated discussions about government and politics. In fact, Gabriel did have very definite political views, mostly anti-political ones. He regarded politicians and government officials the same way he regarded sea pirates and forest outlaws; yes, they do exist; yes, they do interfere at times with one's business; but no, one should never deliberately invite them, under any circumstances, into one's daily life. "You're trying to turn me into a kind of soldier. I'm simply not the soldier type, Pierre. I want to get married and raise a family and live here for the rest of my life with Evangéline. The way my father did, and his father before him."

"But what if things get worse? What if the English take away your freedom to work in your shop? Or begin telling you *how* to do your work in the shop?" Pierre stooped and picked up a horseshoe from the floor. "What if they tell you, for example, to shoe all horses the English way?" asked Pierre.

Gabriel laughed and said, "Well, I don't think my horse cares whether he is shoed the French way or the English way."

"You don't understand at all, do you?" asked Pierre, raising his voice. "Every part of our daily lives is tainted by the English. First they will take our guns, then our boats, then our religion, and then our language. Tell me, Gabriel, will you be teaching your own children the French or the English language?" Pierre, his face flushed with energy, was now fired up.

Because he could see that Pierre wasn't going to take 'no' for an answer, Gabriel sighed and gave in. "All right, my friend, I'll go to your meeting, but don't expect me to contribute anything. I'll just sit there and listen," said Gabriel, smiling.

"Thank you. This evening then, at my house, six-thirty. You, too, Charles." Now more relaxed and pleased with himself, Pierre left shouting. "Oh, Elizabeth Anne, where are you? I have something exciting for you!" Gabriel and Charles again doubled up in laughter.

Charles continued to wrap two-inch-wide strips of leather around the rim of a large wagon wheel. Then he covered the leather strips with a pliable strip of ash. Gabriel watched him and smiled. Charles, the eccentric genius, was always working on some new creation, or on a new version of an old idea that would make him rich some day. He was now working on a wheel that would make travel more comfortable. The older men in Grand Pré thought Charles was a young fool, but the village women were all in favor of any invention that would bring more comfort and some semblance of luxury to their plain way of life. "Are you really going to the meeting tonight?" asked Gabriel.

"Oh, yes, I always attend. Pierre will give me no peace if I don't," said Charles.

"Do Pierre's meetings ever accomplish anything?"

"No, but they keep Pierre happy. I don't think they do any harm," said Charles. "They *do* keep people informed, although it's hard at times to separate the information from the gossip."

"I have no interest in politics," sighed Gabriel.

"Me neither. I'm only interested in getting rich. If you're wealthy, you don't have to worry about politics or anything else. You can rise above it all and live in grand style. *Above it all*, that's what I want."

"And will this wheel make you a rich man?" asked Gabriel with a smile.

"Maybe. Maybe not. But each idea that I work at makes me a little smarter and some day, with luck, I'll make my fortune. Besides, you know, Gabriel, no matter what happens in politics, people will always need wheels, and the more comfortable the wheels, the more of them I'll sell. You'll see," said Charles, grinning. "You'll see."

Chapter Eight

The Young Hotheads

That evening, on the way to Pierre's house, Gabriel was again badgering his father for permission to marry Evangéline. (All of the men in the immediate neighborhood had been invited to the meeting.) "You're still too young to marry," said Basil.

"But others have married younger than us," protested Gabriel. It took great courage for Gabriel to protest his father's decision. In French households, a father's word was sacred, an unfortunate custom for sons because it has been said that a son's biggest misfortune is to have an extraordinary father. Therefore, having a whole village top-heavy with fatherly infallibles could constitute an oppressive environment indeed. Not that many young men wholeheartedly believed such a myth, but since they would be fathers themselves one day, they looked forward to their own dogmatic rule and hesitated to squander prematurely their own inheritance.

"You're just too young," repeated Basil.

"Why are we too young? I don't understand."

"Well, it's embarrassing to talk about it," said Basil nervously.

"You won't embarrass me. I promise," said Gabriel.

Basil was thinking more about his own embarrassment. Then he said, "Well, you wouldn't want to marry a girl who is not ... not ... uh ... not a complete woman, would you?"

"Evangéline's a complete woman. She's very mature for her age."

"Well, some girls her age have not fully grown … if you know what I mean."

"Evangéline looks fully grown to me. She's as tall as she's ever going to be," said Gabriel innocently.

"But is she strong? What about her back?"

"Her back?"

"Will she be able to carry water jugs, and milk pails, and firewood everyday without tiring?"

"She does all of that now, father."

"But will she be able to do all of that when she is with child?"

"She's perfect, father. You don't know how perfect she is! She's a perfect cook, and a perfect housekeeper, and a perfect—"

"Well, I can see that you've got the fever bad! There's no reasoning with you. It's too late for me to counsel you now." Then Basil softened and said, "Who knows? Maybe by autumn she will be ready. We'll see. We'll see. You cannot hurry the harvest, nor hasten the vintage. Patience, mon garçon, patience."

When they entered Pierre's house, the meeting was well under way. There were fifty men and one woman present. The woman was Berthe Commo, an elderly wife who went everywhere with her husband, Oliver, always sitting beside him, holding his skinny, wrinkled hand. Sometimes she sat with one of her long arms draped around his neck and shoulder. This positioning made observers smile because she was twice his size, and poor Oliver looked as though he were caught in a wrestler's stranglehold. But the joke was on them because Oliver loved every minute of it and wouldn't have dreamt of going anywhere or attending any meeting without his beloved Berthe. She would have followed him to the ends of the earth. She agreed with everything he said, boasted of everything he did, and laughed at all his jokes. Naturally, most of the other wives despised her. "We are servants enough to men as it is!" they whined. A few widows envied her. Behind their backs people called Berthe and Oliver 'the old honeymooners' because after forty-eight years of marriage, they were still as close as newlyweds, and every young couple in the village wanted to grow old together just like them. Berthe's whole attitude seemed to say, "I'm the luckiest woman in the world."

Her only fault - more of an annoyance - was that she rarely let her husband finish a sentence but she finished it for him. After spending almost five decades together, she had heard all of his stories, ideas, and theories, and she could spout them with only an introductory word or two from him. Most of the time her butting-in didn't bother Oliver. But whenever another man was present he became more aware of her tiresome interruptions, and then it embarrassed him to be cut off and completed by his wife as though he were somehow incomplete on his own. At such times, he would object, snap at her, and say that he could damn well finish his own sentences, thank you! Berthe then would look completely baffled by his uncalled-for remark and stare silently at him, trying to figure him out. She couldn't understand his sudden outbursts of male insecurity. After all, by finishing her husband's statements, she was merely showing her agreement with them, wasn't she? So, what was all the childish fuss about?

The older men were now trying to calm the young hotheads. Benedict said to Pierre and François Hébert, "But we French did that, too. When France took over part of Germany, the French made the Germans take an oath of allegiance. That's what all conquering people do."

"It makes me feel like a slave," said Pierre. "We've been here longer than these Englishmen! We were born here!"

"I tell you, it's nothing to worry about, Pierre," said Benedict calmly. "It's just a formality. Whenever we have a change of governor we take the oath again. So, we'll simply take the same one our fathers have been taking since 1713."

"But the rumor is that Governor Lawrence[1] wants us to take an *unconditional* oath. I, for one, will not do that because I will never fight against my own French people," said François Hébert firmly.

"Nor will I!" said Pierre.

"I won't either!" said Jacques Tibodot, one of the local bullies.

"Neither will I!" said André Dupuis, a close friend of Jacques's, but a more level-headed young man.

"I will run away and join Abbé Le Loutre's band before I will fight my own people!" shouted Jacques.

"Now, now," said Benedict, "we must not do anything as drastic as that. Father Chauvreulx has warned us about that renegade Le Loutre. Father Le Loutre is an outlaw now. He no longer does God's work."

After a short silence, another of Pierre's young friends, Jude Le Blanc, the son of René Le Blanc the notary, and a cousin of Charles, asked, "What about our guns? Are we going to hand over *all* of our guns to the English?"

"We can give them *some* of our guns. That will satisfy them. As long as we appear to be cooperating, we'll have no trouble with the

English," said Benedict. "We must not get the English upset. We'll take the *conditional* oath our fathers took and we'll hand over some of our guns. Then they'll go away and leave us in peace as they have done for the past forty years."

"But we need our guns for protection against the bears and wolves when we take our oxen into the woods to cut down trees," said Jacques.

"As I've said, we will hand over only some of our guns."

"And what will the Mi'kmaq do to us when they see us handing over guns to the English? They won't understand what is going on," added André. "They'll think we're joining forces against them."

"And what if the English demand more of us? Do we give in again?" asked François.

"What else can they ask of us?" asked Basil.

"Perhaps they'll take away our right to worship in our own churches," said Pierre. "Their ultimate goal is to turn us all into English-speaking Protestants like themselves!"

"Well, I hope it never comes to that," said Charles Le Blanc, the creative wheelwright. "But the most important thing is to survive; at least, some of us. We must do whatever it takes to keep ourselves alive."

"Does that mean you're willing to give up your religion and your language?" asked François, becoming more agitated.

"I want to live," said Charles. "I want to live a long, successful life, and I will do whatever possible to accomplish that goal!"

"I agree," said Michel Lanneau. "What good is our religion and our language if we're all dead? Why should we hold on to things that hold us back?"

Benedict laughed in disbelief. "Mon Dieu, what talk! Where will you be ten years from now without your religion and your language? These are the things that give us strength. Holding us back? These are the only things holding us *up!*" Benedict glared at Michel who then lowered his eyes. "I tell you that we're not all going to be dead at the hands of the English! Life will go on as usual, believe me. We must simply go through the motions. We'll take the traditional oath and we'll give them a few guns and they will go away happy. The English are fickle. They never stick to anything. Before they finish one plan, they come up with a new one, then off they go to some other corner of the world!"

Pierre sighed in resignation, as did François. The other boys began to relax with the calming words of Benedict. The old man, after all, probably knew best. Charles added to the mood of resignation by chuckling and saying, "Besides, the English from Boston will come here to sell us more guns. The English think more about money than they do about our oath, our language, or anything else." More relaxed now, the men smiled and nodded in agreement.

Gabriel and his father walked out the door and started for home. "By autumn, then?"

"What's that?" asked Basil.

"You said 'by autumn' I can marry Evangéline."

Basil sighed in mild frustration, his huge chest heaving, and Basil's huge chest heaving was a sight to behold. The biggest man in the village at six-foot-six, his chest as wide as a bale of hay, legs like cannons - twin minions, long, tapering, and powerful - hands like platters, and feet the size of two babies' cribs, he made an unforgettable impression. And although his face was homely with a long forehead, a nose as big as a fist, and a mouth with missing teeth, women were drawn to him like a magnet. He was so tall, strong and capable that, standing far below him and looking up, they felt like children again and secretly wished he'd pick them up, cradle them in his enormous protecting arms, and caress them with his huge, calloused hands.

He sighed again, good-naturedly. It was no use trying to reason with his son. He gave up. "Yes, yes, in the autumn you can have your wedding. Perhaps a wedding will do us all some good."

With both hands, Gabriel grabbed his father's right platter, and shook it vigorously. "Thank you, father! Thank you!" Gabriel was grinning from ear to ear. "That means we can start on our house."

"On what? Oh, no! I thought your badgering would stop for awhile. Now you're going to hound me about building your house!"

"That's right, father. You might as well give in. When can we begin to build?"

"I'll talk to the village men tomorrow and we'll choose a day."

"Thank you! Oh, thank you, father!" said Gabriel as he ran off.

"Where are you going now?"

"To tell Evangéline!" yelled Gabriel.

"Wait! Wait!"

"What is it, father?"

"She won't keep a fancy-style house, will she?"

"What do you mean by 'fancy-style'?"

"Some of the Quebec women now have carpets in every room of the house! What next? Where, I ask you, will a man be able to spit? I say that if a man cannot spit in his own house, he might as well remain a bachelor!"

"Don't worry, father! In our house, my father will be able to spit wherever he wants to!" said Gabriel as he raced off to see his bride-to-be.

Chapter Nine

The Recurring Suspicion

When Gabriel reached Evangéline's house, he informed her of his father's consent and then persuaded her to go for an evening stroll on the beach to watch the sunset. She still had chores to do but agreed because she could see how happy it would make him.

They walked along the shoreline holding hands and chattered on about the meeting. "Pierre is becoming such an agitator!" he said.

"What do you mean?"

"He's telling everyone that France is going to attack, that the English will take away our hunting guns, our right to go to church, our right to speak our own language, and that the Mi'kmaq are going to turn against us." He sighed and shook his head. Then he laughed. Pierre's fears, once they had been paraphrased so unsympathetically, now sounded a little unwarranted. "I think Pierre's an unhappy boy, and he wants everybody else to be unhappy, too."

"He does seem unhappy at times," said Evangéline. "Perhaps it all comes down to his leg. His accident. His lameness. He keeps it all locked up inside. I think he has a fence around himself, a fence that he hides behind so no one can get too close. Maybe if you could get him to talk some time about his accident he would be happier."

"He has already talked about it to me," said Gabriel. "So, I don't think that's his problem."

"When?"

"A couple of times."

"What did he say?"

"Oh, his leg doesn't bother him. He's over all that by now. He even jokes about it," said Gabriel.

"What did he say? Did he seem upset that you mentioned it?" asked Evangéline.

Gabriel smiled, remembering. "The fool just jumped around and said he was the best dancer in Acadia."

"And what about the other time?"

"Same thing. He laughed and challenged me to a race across the meadow."

"And he said nothing else?" asked Evangéline.

"Nothing. He just laughed."

"So, that's his fence, then."

"What?"

"Laughter. He jokes, and when nothing more is said, he's safe to go back into hiding again," said Evangéline sadly.

Gabriel looked at Evangéline in amazement. How could such a beauty also have such wisdom!

Suddenly, noises. Then, movement in the dimming light. A tangle of arms, brown and white. A curve of tanned hip, a flash of pale thigh. Small dusky circles within larger, softer ones. "A little privacy, please," said Pierre with a smirk. Naked as he was, Pierre was not at all embarrassed and nonchalantly rolled away from his companion to protest the interruption. His immodest partner was equally cool, making no attempt to cover herself. Gabriel and Evangéline recognized her as Elizabeth Anne, the dark-eyed, promiscuous Mi'kmaq girl.

Now more embarrassed than the unclad duo, Gabriel and Evangéline turned and scurried back the way they came.

A hundred yards down the beach they found themselves running when Evangéline stumbled and fell on the soft sand. Then she began to laugh. "What are you laughing about?" asked Gabriel, sinking to his knees beside her.

Evangéline couldn't stop laughing. "Why ..." She continued to laugh and couldn't finish her question. "Why ... are we—" Now she was lying on her back giggling hysterically, her white teeth gleaming in the faint light. Gabriel was enthralled. He lay down beside her and laughed along with her although he still didn't get the joke.

"What has struck you so funny?" asked Gabriel as he brushed some sand from her hair. It was wonderful to see her happy. He wanted to kiss her open mouth and steal some of her joy.

"They should be… (more laughter)… running… (more laughter)… not us. Ohhhhhhh!" she said dissolving into tears. Gabriel leaned over and kissed the salty tears of laughter from her cheeks. Then he kissed her on the mouth. For some reason, he was more passionate than he had ever been before. "I know what you're thinking," she whispered, "because I'm thinking about it, too. But we must wait, and when we are husband and wife, we'll come here in the night, you and I together, forever."

They rose and walked homeward. Evangéline suddenly wanted to reach home as fast as she could. She needed to be alone now. Resentment and jealousy were creeping in. After all, Gabriel's extra heat a few minutes earlier had not been all her doing. "I can find my own way home," she almost said, but she held her tongue. Gabriel, on the other hand, was perturbed as he thought of his friend, Pierre. It confused Gabriel that one minute his friend was preaching justice and honor and family pride, and the next minute he was frolicking on the beach - surely a mortal sin! - with a girl who almost certainly cared very little about the present political situation!

It was a night for contradictions. Disappointment was slowly filling the air, disappointment and the recurring suspicion that someone was always coming between them.

Chapter Ten

Two Hundred Hunters

June 6, 1755

Something puzzling was happening in the village. Pierre and the other young hotheads became suspicious. They didn't believe Captain Murray for one minute. Alexander Murray, the forty-year old English commander at Piziquid* fifteen miles away, had arrived with 150 men. Fifty of them had come from Halifax to join his company. "I don't believe they're on a harmless hunting expedition!" said Pierre to François Hébert.

"I don't either," said François. "Why don't they lodge themselves in our barns as they usually do?"

"And why are they lodging two of their soldiers in the houses that are the most crowded?" asked Pierre. "In Madame Doucet's house where there is only herself and her two nieces they have placed only one soldier for the night; and in Monsieur Gotro's house where there are five grown sons, they've placed two soldiers. To avoid overcrowding, it should be just the opposite."

"Our Indian friends have told us that there will be a frost tonight," Murray had told the villagers. "Your barns will be too cold for my men. But don't worry. In the morning we'll be on our way early. Thank you," he had said and smiled.

---

* Now Windsor, Nova Scotia

"I don't believe him," said Pierre. "There's something wrong here!" François wasn't sure. After all, Pierre was known to be a bitter, sensitive young man, resentful of the presence of any visiting Englishman.

As it turned out, Pierre was right; something suspicious was going on.

That night the villagers went to bed worried. In every home there was at least one English soldier - one unwelcome, inconvenient guest. By midnight, the households were quiet but many Acadians were not asleep. Suddenly all of the residents in all of the Grand Pré houses were simultaneously disturbed by their guests. "By order of Governor Lawrence, you are to hand over the remaining weapons you have in your possession. If you do not comply, you will be considered rebels and you will be executed!"

Monsieur Benedict's prediction now proved to be inaccurate. The Acadian pacification plan had *not* worked and the English were determined to confiscate every last weapon in Grand Pré.

Next morning, spread out on the grass by the church of St. Charles, were 2,300 guns.[1] The soldiers then marched to the shore and confiscated every boat and canoe owned by the residents. Now the Acadians were not only defenseless but, if they wanted one, they also had no means of escape.

Jacques Tibodot and André Dupuis stood watching as their guns were carried off. "We're going to have to run away, André, or else be murdered by these English swine!" said Jacques. "They mean to kill us all!"

"I'm afraid you're right, Jacques. I hate to leave home, but I don't see any other way. We'll leave tomorrow."

Chapter Eleven

The Murdering Priest

The man who was paying the Mi'kmaq Indians five pounds sterling* for each English scalp they delivered to him was saying mass. Under a leather lean-to in the woods, holding up a sacred communion host before a group of mesmerized Mi'kmaq and outlaw Acadians was the Jesuit priest, Abbé Jean-louis Le Loutre, rumored to be 'the murdering priest'.

"Ecce agnus dei, ecce qui tollit peccata mundi," intoned Le Loutre in a mellow monotone. "Domine non sum dignus ut intres sub tectum meum; sed tantum dic verbo, et sanabitur anima mea."

An ancient Mi'kmaw** sitting on the ground a few feet from Le Loutre watched in fascination. He eyed the priest's hands, the same hands that gratefully accepted English scalps still warm and dripping with blood. "Corpus domine nostri Jesu Christi custodiat animam tuam in vitam aeternam. Amen." Father Le Loutre stooped and placed a communion host on the tongue of the old Mi'kmaw. The old man did not lower his eyes in reverence but kept them wide open, searching the priest's face for the answer to the question on everyone's mind: was this priest a devil or a saint?

Since their own gods had apparently proved inferior by failing to protect them from invaders, the Mi'kmaq now sought spiritual help from the gods of their conquerors. This outlaw priest, however, was not making

---

*   In a later countermove, Lawrence offered 30 pounds for each male Indian scalp.
**   Mi'kmaw is the singular form.

their conversion easy. "Dominus vobiscum. Ite missa est," he said, blessing everyone with the sign of the cross, and the outdoor mass for the outlaws was over.

Now forty-five, Le Loutre was no longer the quiet, unassuming missionary he had been twenty years earlier when he was under the wing of his mentor, Abbé Maillard of Shubenacadie.*

Le Loutre had evolved over the years into the ultimate snob of snobs - the religious fanatic. A man of manic energy, headstrong and self-willed, he took his orders directly from God and not from his earthly superiors in Québec. Rationalizing the violence that was now a part of his new approach to spreading the gospel, he interpreted the movement of every branch waving in the wind as the beckoning of God's hand guiding him onward, and he took validation from the movement of the clouds whenever they were moving in his preferred direction. A Jesuit contemporary of his spoke of Le Loutre as, "One of God's regrets." However, he was acknowledged, even by his enemies, to be a charismatic leader. He was, in effect, Simon Zealotes, fully armed. His renegade subordinates referred to him as 'the general'. It was rumored that a former governor, Edward Cornwallis, had secretly offered Le Loutre a personal fortune to give up his subversive activities. Le Loutre refused. Not only did he refuse but, in one of his more manic moods, boldly sent Cornwallis a written declaration of war. Cornwallis promptly put a price on his head - one hundred pounds for his capture. Le Loutre's reward, if he wanted one, did not involve money. "Welcome," he said to André and Jacques who had arrived during mass. Some Mi'kmaq friends had led them to Le Loutre's camp about twenty miles from Beaubassin.** "That old Mi'kmaw I saw you staring at during mass is 140 years old. Well, that's what the Mi'kmaq say. I don't believe he's quite that old because he still likes to go moose hunting." [1] He shook hands with André and Jacques. "So, have you come here to join us?"

"Yes," said Jacques, "we want to help you fight the English."

"You are welcome. However, we must make sure that you are fit for the task. The work we do is not for the timid," said Le Loutre. "Many Acadian boys come to me, but few have the stomachs to remain. Have you ever killed a man?"

"No, Father," said André, slightly ashamed for having such a clean record.

---

*   About thirty-five miles northwest of Halifax.
**   The Beaubassin-Beausejour district, by the Missaquash River, is the Amherst area of Nova Scotia.

Le Loutre looked at Jacques. "No, Father," said Jacques, "but I know that, if I have to, I can easily kill an Englishman."

Sensing more weakness in André, Le Loutre looked into his eyes and asked, "And you? Can you, if you have to, kill an Englishman?"

"To be honest, Father," said André, "I'm not sure."

"Then why did you come here to me?" asked Le Loutre.

"I just had to get away from Grand Pré, Father. The English took away all of our guns, our boats, and canoes. Life there is getting worse every day," said André. "I wanted to come along with Jacques, and I thought perhaps I could help you in some other way… other than killing."

"I see," said Le Loutre. He walked over to his horse, opened his saddle bag, and placed his chalice and paten inside. He removed his stole, kissed it and placed it, too, in the bag. Then he unbuttoned his long black cassock and stepped out of it revealing a homemade, woolen long-sleeve sweater, a pair of buckskin breeches, and brown colorfully beaded Mi'kmaq moccasins. André caught a whiff of him and it was not the familiar priestly odor of soap and dust. This man reeked of horse hair, animal perspiration, spruce balsam, campfire smoke, and the sour scent of dried-up rainwater on wool and leather. His was not the aroma of security, but of risk. There was dust on Le Loutre's breeches, but it was not the dust that slowly sifts and settles down upon the stock-still, but the fresh dust of the open road. His church was the wide outdoors, the vast, untamed Nova Scotia wilderness, and among his parishioners were the wind and the rain, the sun, the clouds, the sky, the stars, and the earth itself. He turned to André and said, "I know what you are thinking. I had the same thoughts myself years ago. You are wondering how you can kill Englishmen and still be a good Catholic boy. It's a good question. In simple terms, it's an eye for an eye; if an Englishman bites you, bite him back."* Le Loutre looked over at Jacques who was smiling and nodding his head. "And yet, it's not quite that simple," he continued. "The gospel urges us to be gentle lambs of God. But the problem is that we cannot all be lambs of God. Some of us must be shepherds who protect God's flock. And in protecting God's flock, sometimes it's necessary to kill predators who prey upon the flock. The English lion has two heads; the head of a predator, and the head of a heretic. We have no choice. Predators, naturally, must be killed, and heretics, who are agents of the devil, must be killed, too. We have no choice. Do you understand me?"

---

* The motto of Morlaix, Le Loutre's birthplace in France, was, "If the English bite you, bite them back!"

"No choice? I don't understand that part, Father," said André.

"Let me make it clearer, then. You know that Christ died on the cross for our sins, did He not?"

"Yes."

"Well, the sins He truly died for are the ones we can't help committing. The others we'll have to pay for, the ones committed by our vices and our stubborn wills. You see, sometimes we are placed in terrible situations where there is no sinless way out for us. We have no choice, or else we have two choices and both of them are bad. We are in one of those terrible situations now. Do you understand?"

André looked at Jacques who seemed convinced. Then he asked, "But, the fifth commandment? If we kill, Father, will God forgive us?"

"God's house has many rooms. He has a room for his humble lambs, and he has a special room for his shepherd-warriors. Yes, my son, there is a place in heaven, a very high place, for God's warrior-saints. And here, at this time, and in this wilderness, we must make room for God's kingdom on earth."

The two new recruits nodded and the priest flashed a broad grin. "We're willing to try!" said Jacques.

"God bless you!" said Le Loutre. "Now. We are going to Beaubassin today on a mission. Are you willing to come along?"

"Oh, yes, Father, we're ready," said Jacques anxious for a fight.

"Good," said Le Loutre, "but first you will need some scalping lessons. Oh, Vatel! Come here!"

A huge Acadian with badly healed scars on both cheeks, and a dirty black beret covering only half his head and one ear, shouted, "Here I am, Abbé."

"Vatel, take these boys and give them a few lessons in removing scalps. They are riding with us today," said Le Loutre grinning and chuckling as he walked away.

****

"First, you take the whole scalp in one hand," said Vatel, "while your other hand holds the knife. Your knife must be kept sharp at all times. Always carry a stone in your pocket as a sharpener." A young brown rabbit very much alive, was wriggling, held up by its long ears, in Vatel's left hand. André began to squirm. Jacques snickered, hoping he would soon have the opportunity to practice this new skill. "Then you start at the back of the head." Vatel's knife moved slowly to the back of the young rabbit's skull. Vatel always enjoyed seeing the faces of the new recruits when he sliced open a rabbit's head.

"Aren't you going to kill it first?" asked André.

"No," said Vatel, "because we have to make the situation as real as we can."

"Real? What do you mean?" asked André.

Vatel snorted, "Because sometimes the Englishman is still kicking, too!" Then he laughed so hard he dropped his knife. He stooped to pick it up and looked at the two boys. Jacques was smiling and André was growing pale. To ease André's queasiness Vatel decided it would be best to speed up the lesson. He moved the rabbit from his left hand to his right, holding it by its kicking back legs. Then he walked calmly over to the trunk of a nearby pine tree, and with one hard swing, bashed the rabbit's head against it. The rabbit hung limply in his hand. He then returned to the boys and, working from the back of the head to the front, quickly sliced off the rabbit's scalp. In fifteen seconds the job was done and Vatel held up the tiny bleeding scalp for all to see. "Easy, eh?" He grinned. "But I warn you! You may not always find an Englishman light enough to swing against a tree!"

****

It was Sunday morning. As usual, Father Le Loutre's regular parishioners (not the members of his renegade band) were nervous. He was back from another of his raids on the English. Perhaps he felt guilty with fresh blood on his hands. Whatever the cause, one thing was clear - Pastor Le Loutre was in another frightful rage. "I returned to my parish here yesterday. Something I saw upset me. I had not expected to see such a sight. I could not believe my eyes, so I took a closer look. And, yes, it was true. My eyes had not deceived me. I saw some of my own parishioners, some of my Acadian brethren, some of my fellow Frenchmen lending a helping hand to our enemies, the English!" Father Le Loutre paused to let his words take effect. A few parishioners began to fidget. "Yes, my friends, it is true. Acadians were *helping* the English. And do you know what help they were giving our English enemies? Do you know? They were helping our enemies build a stockade, a stockade across the Missaquash, a stockade to drive *us* from this area, a stockade built to destroy *us*! My friends, this madness must stop immediately! What will you be doing next? Helping the English load the guns they will use to shoot us?"

The men who had helped the English were sitting there bristling, but dared not speak. They wanted to tell their priest that they had been given no choice by the English upon pain of death. "Now this is what you must do, and do it quickly. The Bishop of Québec has promised to send us supplies if we move to Fort Beauséjour. We will not need supplies from your farms. We must unite! We cannot defeat the English if we are scattered over ten miles, living selfishly, each on his own little patch of ground. It is time to become soldiers. It is not time to be farmers, and it is certainly not time to be farmers who assist the enemy. You must leave your homes and move to the Fort Beauséjour area. You will be safe there and together we will have a chance to fight off any attack by the heretic English!"

Again the men didn't dare speak, although they sincerely doubted they would get support from Québec or anywhere else. They also wanted to ask what would happen to them if they were to fortify Beauséjour and yet lose the fight with the English. But sitting in their church on Sunday morning, hearing the thunder in Father Le Loutre's voice, the men lowered their eyes not daring even to look sideways at each other. "I shudder to think of what will happen to you and to your houses if my Indian friends discover that you have been friendly with the English. I shudder to think of it! The Mi'kmaq are my friends, but there are times when even I cannot control them. Be warned! You must all move to Beauséjour because this is the last mass that will be said in this church. No more sacraments will be administered from this parish. I repeat: no more sacraments will be administered from this church. Therefore, if you choose to remain here, you will be risking not only your lives but your immortal souls! Starting tomorrow you must help one another move. And may God have mercy upon us all." Father Le Loutre made the sign of the cross thereby ending his Sunday sermon.

After mass, the parishioners filed out of church, mounted their horses and wagons, and headed back to their individual farms. They couldn't risk staying and having a discussion among themselves with Father Le Loutre still around. Besides they already knew what to do; that is, they knew what *not* to do. They had been threatened before by Le Loutre, by the English, by the French authorities in Québec, by the Indians, - by everybody. One more threat wouldn't hurt them. They drove off in all different directions waving goodbye to everyone, and by the time they reached home, Father

Le Loutre's Sunday sermon was like a dreary overcast sky that, over a ten-mile radius, had completely cleared in the bright morning air.

****

Three days later, Jacques and André were sitting by an open fire in Le Loutre's encampment. The bandit band to which they now belonged was positioned along the English courier route between Halifax and Piziquid. They were hoping to intercept another important communication between English commanders.

It was the quiet time between campaigns, that slow dead time when those with consciences looked back shuddering with guilt, while those without them looked forward sharpening their knives. And some others, who looked neither ahead nor behind, slept the day away, or drugged themselves happy with brandy; while a few others, like Vatel, spent long hours in self-hypnosis staring at a spider's web in progress, on their elbows gazing at the deliberate design and the businesslike construction of a place of future horror, a soft delicate place of poisonous execution and leisurely devoured prey. Then, feeling absolved by nature's precedent, these few rolled over, smugly looked to Heaven, and silently renewed their vow of violence.

Suddenly, the sound of slapping came from inside the birch bark wigwam. The two boys looked at each other, searchingly. Slap! Slap! Vatel stood nearby chuckling to himself. Slap! Slap! Slap! "What's going on in there, Vatel?" whispered Jacques.

"It's contrition time," snickered Vatel.

"Contrition time?" asked André.

Slap! Slap! Slap!

"Yes, one of the young Mi'kmaq girls is making her act of contrition." Vatel looked towards the wigwam with a cynical grin.

Slap! Slap! Slap!

"I don't understand," said André.

Vatel leaned closer and said confidentially, "Last night some young braves gave a few drinks of whiskey to a pretty young Mi'kmaq girl. She got drunk and started running around the camp. Without any clothes on! You missed a good show! Abbé Le Loutre heard the ruckus and came outside and saw her. He's punishing her now," said Vatel.

Jacques and André stared in disbelief.

Slap! Slap! Slap!

"Does he do this often?" asked André.

"Not often. But you don't have to worry," grinned Vatel. "He doesn't do this to everybody, just girls. And only young pretty girls."

The wigwam flap opened and a plump, dark-skinned young Mi'kmaq girl emerged. She was about sixteen and one of her front teeth was only half there. Vatel had said she was pretty. Mon Seigneur, thought André, not only have Vatel's morals deteriorated in the wilderness! The girl was straightening her deerskin dress when she noticed André studying her. André was always studying people. He studied everybody, looking for guidance and reassurance, sometimes in the most unlikely faces. The young girl looked embarrassed, bashful, defiant, mischievous, and seductive all at the same time. Then she turned and saw the lust in Vatel's grin. Apparently flattered, she giggled, flashed a childlike grin with her broken tooth, and then scurried down the path where three of her girlfriends were waiting for her. She stopped and said a few words to them. All four Indian girls looked back at the boys, and then with loud shrieks of laughter, went running off through the woods. "So what do you think of contrition time now, boys?" asked Vatel.

Jacques grinned. "I don't know what to make of it. But I'd like to help sometime!"

Vatel looked at André. "And what about you?"

"I'm not sure. And I'm a little shocked. It just makes me wonder."

"It makes me wonder, too," said Vatel, "and I always end up wondering the same thing. Tell me, though, what is it that you wonder about, my friend?"

André paused. "Well, I wonder what Father Le Loutre's real intentions are … I mean if she's young … and—"

"And pretty?"

"Well—" Then, looking again for guidance, he asked Vatel, "And what is it that you wonder about?"

Vatel put his hand to his chin, rubbed it, and said in a mock-solemn tone, "I always wonder if he sometimes has regrets."

"Regrets? Father Le Loutre?"

"Yes. When he's spanking her bottom, does he … perhaps … regret not getting married?"

André smiled and then felt guilty for encouraging Vatel's crude jokes.

Nothing was more attractive to young Catholic boys than the brash attitude of a cynical rebel like Vatel who was fast becoming Jacques's idol. That worried André. He also began to wonder what Vatel's personal motive was in all this rebellion. After all, Vatel was once a good Catholic boy, and now he was a murdering savage. Did Vatel believe in anything? Did he sincerely believe in Le Loutre's cause? Did Vatel hope to go to that special room in Heaven reserved for God's warriors? André strongly doubted whether Vatel believed in anything anymore, and he wondered where Vatel would be thirty years from now. Would he be quietly meditating in a monastery somewhere, tonsured and repentant? Or would he be locked away guilt-sick in some madhouse, his cynical laughter continual and louder? André understood that Vatel's cynicism was a method of survival; yet he sensed that such a method was irreversible and that he, therefore, should not adopt it.

For André, it was becoming clear that, in this wilderness, surrounded by savages - native-brown and imported-white - his biggest daily temptation was the easy, enjoyable, slippery slide into cynicism and its negative suspicion of all human motives. His way out of this wilderness in a few years would depend on the resilience of his trailing thread of innocence and good faith, a thread he feared was getting thinner with each passing day.

The wigwam flap opened again and Father Le Loutre came out kissing the silver cross he wore on a long chain around his neck. "Are we all ready?" he asked casually, as though nothing of importance had just taken place inside.

"Ready!" said Vatel. Jacques and André said nothing. They stood staring at the slapping priest. Jacques smiled at the priest's shameless confidence. André, confused, was studying again.

"Good!" said Le Loutre. "Let's go to Beauséjour and see how many of our friends have moved into the fort." No one budged. The regulars knew the routine. Father Le Loutre mounted his horse, then gave the signal, and the motley band of Mi'kmaq and rebel Acadians rode off to visit Father Le Loutre's neutral, apolitical, happy-go-lucky parishioners.

Hours later they arrived and Le Loutre made a quick tour of his parish. *No one had moved into the fort.* He was beside himself. Almost breathless with fury he fumed, "All right, you know what to do. Remember," he said to his anxious band, "do not harm any Acadians. No one must get hurt. Burn their houses and their barns, but do not harm the people. We need them to fight the English." The well-trained band did not stir. Le Loutre had not yet given the signal. "One more thing," he said, "do not harm my church. I repeat: do not burn my church!" Then he removed the silver cross from his neck and pointed it in the direction of Beauséjour. With that signal, the Indians moved out first, and the rebel Acadians followed. All members of the band, except Jacques and André, howled as they sped towards the homes of the stubbornly settled residents.

Within a few hours, all 150 houses and barns in the Beaubassin area were in flames. The scene was total devastation. Men, women, and children ran screaming in the direction of Fort Beauséjour. To have witnessed one arsonist or pyromaniac in the act would have been hard to accept; but to have seen a whole troop of them! And led by a priest!

One spectacle was particularly disturbing to André and Jacques, and even to some of the other less-hardened renegades. Father Le Loutre walked into his own church and came out with the sacred objects - the monstrance, chalice, paten, altar crucifix, censer, his vestments, and beret. He placed them on the ground a hundred yards away. Then he walked back to the church, and said to a young Mi'kmaq, "Give me that!" as he took a burning torch from his hand, and proceeded to set fire to his own parish's place of worship. Then, businesslike, he packed the sacred objects into two saddle bags, mounted his horse, and shouted to his crew, "Thank you. Now we have Beauséjour fortified the hard way," and he rode off quickly towards the fort.

Chapter Twelve

The Hieroglyphics on the Wall

Father Le Loutre wheezed heavily again. Vatel, Jacques, and André sat outside the priest's wigwam in the Mi'kmaq camp and listened to him wheeze, cough, and struggle for air. "He always gets this way after a raid," said Vatel. "He'll go to visit Abbé Maillard now."

"Who is Abbé Maillard?" asked André.

"Abbé Maillard is his old pastor. At Shubenacadie. Priests have to go to confession too, you know. Yes, he will go to Abbé Maillard. Probably today by the sound of him," said Vatel. Le Loutre wheezed, gasped, and sputtered again. He didn't understand his asthma. He only knew that a visit with his old mentor always soothed him.

Vatel's prediction was accurate. That evening Le Loutre was back with Father Maillard in his first Nova Scotia parish, a setting that, for all its seeming familiarity, was now a world apart. But the restful calm in Maillard's demeanor was again working its magic, and Le Loutre was already breathing easier.

Father Maillard's unruffled air was like balm on Le Loutre's troubled spirit. In some ways, Maillard had a lot in common with Peregrine Hopson, the sympathetic governor replaced by Lawrence. Both men had calm, tolerant, and unselfish dispositions; both hated pettiness, and carefully avoided involvement in the daily squabbles of life; both encouraged others to share their long-range view. Hopson governed all, not caring whether they were legal or illegal immigrants because he needed to populate a wilderness; Maillard administered sacraments to all, not caring whether they were Indian, French, or English because he needed to populate heaven. Both men thought in general, not specific, terms. To them, people mattered collectively; individuals mattered hardly at all. Maillard borrowed this specks-in-the-universe viewpoint from Saint Augustine; Hopson came by it naturally because it harmonized with his non-confrontational governing style.

"Have you been neglecting your spiritual duties again, Jean-louis?" asked Father Maillard. Le Loutre did not answer. "Is there blood on your hands again?"

"Not blood. Only ashes this time."

"What kind of ashes?"

"The ashes of my own church. My church at Beaubassin."

"Oh, no, Jean-louis! Oh, no! What happened?" asked Maillard.

"It was a necessary evil. I had to unite those stubborn people and fortify Fort Beauséjour!"

"You set fire to your own church?"

"I had to do it!"

"If you feel you *had* to do it, then why are you feeling so bad?"

"Because my heart does not always understand my logic," said Le Loutre with a weak smile. "Oh, Father, I get so sick of being a Catholic pioneer! Sometimes I ache to be deeply rooted in an ancient parish in an ancient city where all the paths are paved and worn."

"Now, now, you have carefully *avoided* paved and worn paths all your life, Jean-louis. You were a rebel even in your seminary days."

"But I'm so tired, so tired. I need to rest."

"You are welcome to rest here. Stay as long as you like. Stay until God puts out some of the fire in your spirit."

"Thank you, Father. Now tell me about yourself. How have you been surviving on your own here with the Mi'kmaq?"

Father Maillard smiled and said, "As you can see, I'm still alive. You need a trinity to survive in this place: patience, patience, and patience." Le Loutre laughed. It felt good to laugh. "It's patience that one needs to learn a new language."

"You are still learning Mi'kmaq?"

Maillard walked over to a table by the window and returned with a manuscript. "Look," he said, beaming with pride. "I'm trying to write their language. It's all very interesting. See these? These are the symbols that the Mi'kmaq use to represent words and ideas," said Maillard pointing at a page. "It's slow work, and tedious at times. But before too long, I'll have an entire Mi'kmaq dictionary." [1]

Le Loutre looked at the page, fascinated - not by the Mi'kmaq language on the page - but by the diligence it took to transcribe it there. "Before too long? How long?"

"Oh, soon. I'd say nine or ten years perhaps."

Le Loutre gasped. "Nine or ten more years!"

Sensing some interest in Le Loutre's surprise, Maillard said, "You could stay here and help me with this important work. With your help, it could be done in five years, maybe four. If we are to win the souls of the Mi'kmaq, we will first have to win their hearts. And the way to their hearts is through their language. Our interest in their language tells them that we are committed to them, don't you see? And, of course," he laughed, "it's always good to know what is being said behind our backs."

"Yes, that would be helpful to me with my merry band as well," said Le Loutre.

The two priests chatted amiably for the rest of the evening. By morning, Le Loutre was breathing easier. He stayed for three more days, greatly enjoying his mentor's hospitality.

****

On the evening of the fourth day, Le Loutre became agitated. Something Father Maillard had said upset him. "You can't be serious!" Le Loutre spouted.

"We must have a long-term plan to convert not only the Indians, but the English as well. That is our job here, Jean-louis, and it can't be accomplished overnight."

"You've changed, Pierre," said Le Loutre. "Five years ago you would never have said such things. You seem to have forgotten that the English are our enemies. They are heretics! They will never be converted to Catholicism! They are lost souls!"

"Of course, they are lost souls! That's why we must work with them to win them over! We can't win over people by shooting them and scalping them! The big goals in life are accomplished slowly and *undramatically*. They take time. Flashy little revolutions never last. It's what we accomplish between revolutions that counts."

"So this is what you mean by the long-term view: comply with the English demands? Take the unconditional oath? Kiss their boots? Has it never occurred to you that, by complying over the next fifty years, the Acadians and the Mi'kmaq might all become English Protestants instead?"

"God will never let that happen, Jean-louis."

"Nor will I let that happen. I think that you've been in one place too long! You've forgotten your original purpose in coming to Nova Scotia!" said Le Loutre, as he rose to leave.

"It is you who have strayed from God's work, Jean-louis." Maillard walked over to the table and returned with a letter. "This is for you. It arrived two days ago. It's a letter from our bishop in Québec. I hesitated to give it to you because I know it will upset you."

Le Loutre opened the letter and silently read.

> "You have at last, my dear sir, got into the very trouble which I foresaw, and which I predicted long ago. I reminded you, a long time ago, that a priest ought not to meddle with temporal affairs, and that if he did so, he would always create enemies and his people to be discontented. Is it right for you to refuse the sacraments, and to threaten your parishioners that they shall be deprived of the services of a priest?"

Le Loutre stopped reading. There was more to the letter but he didn't finish it. He didn't have to. It was the usual reprimand from a high church official. All high officials said the same things: 'don't cause trouble; do what you are told; stay in line; don't speak out on your own; stick to the beaten authorized path.'

"I must go now. I will not be seeing you again, Pierre. But I thank you. And the bishop. You have both helped me to see how much more pioneering work there is for me to do." As Le Loutre turned and walked past the table, he laid the bishop's letter on an open page of Mi'kmaq hieroglyphics. To him, one page was now as unintelligible as the other.

Maillard exploded. "Can't you see," he said holding up his Mi'kmaq manuscript, "that this book will do more to civilize and stabilize this province than all your rebellious pioneering will ever do? Can't you understand that?"

Le Loutre shot back, his voice rising in angry crescendo, "Understand? Words? Words on a page? Mi'kmaq hieroglyphics on a page? Do you really believe that a *dictionary* will stop Governor Charles Lawrence? You can't believe that!" He paused to catch his breath. The terrible wheezing began again. "No, my friend. It's you who do not understand. You poor man! You don't even understand that there's a war going on out there! A great war against the English! And we don't have that much time left!"

Gasping and panting, Le Loutre stormed out the door. He never saw his mentor again.

Chapter Thirteen

Remembering Her Face

It was Saturday evening and that meant a visit from Gabriel and his father, Basil. Basil and Benedict were the best of friends and they faithfully played draughts* and drank ale together every Saturday night in the flickering light of the wide-mouthed hearth. Joking with one another, mocking each other's moves, and shouting loudly when a victory was at hand, they behaved like brothers - better friends than some brothers - and Saturday night was sacred to them both.

Gabriel sat with Evangéline in the window's embrasure, and whispered his pressuring words to her. The moon illuminated a silver pathway on the sea, a dazzling hypnotic spectacle, one minute like a series of long thin diamonds lying flat on the soft black sea, the next like the flashes of gleam in an advancing feline's eyes. The young lovers held hands and stared into each other's eyes. Gabriel fell silent once he saw that his pleas had again fallen on cute, but consistently deaf ears. Anyway, it was enough for them to be together. They were sometimes so quiet, in fact, that their fathers forgot they were in the same room.

About nine o'clock Gabriel and his father rose to leave. "Father will be sad now," whispered Evangéline to Gabriel. "For a while the ale makes him happy; then he starts to remember maman."

"Yes, I know, but he'll be strong again tomorrow," said Gabriel, and he gave Evangéline a brief good night kiss.

---

*   checkers

After Basil and Gabriel had gone, Evangéline wiped the table and cleaned the ale glasses. "It's odd, but I have a hard time remembering your mother's face," said Benedict.

"What do you mean, father? It's only been five years since maman passed away."

"I try and I try, but I just can't picture her face anymore," said Benedict, looking at his daughter for some explanation.

Evangéline, though mature for her years, had a hard time understanding her father's remark. "You can't remember maman? I don't understand."

Benedict struggled to explain himself. "You will be married soon, and Gabriel will love you as much as I loved your mother. He will spend long hours gazing at you." Evangéline lowered her eyes. "He will study your face. He'll study every inch of your healthy young body just as I did your mother's. He'll feel your skin a thousand times so that when you are apart he will be able to close his eyes and feel you there beside him. He will try to impress the color of your eyes upon his memory. Like an artist he'll try to remember the exact shade of red in your cheeks." Benedict reached over and touched his daughter's face. He shook his head. "For thirty-two years I stored up pictures of your mother, and now I can't clearly remember one of her smiles. I can't even remember one of her frowns."

"Oh, father, just remember that she's now looking down on you from Heaven. She has not forgotten you." Evangéline squeezed her father's hand and smiled at him. "Come, now. It's time for you to rest. I'll help you to your bed."

"At night, I always have such unhappy thoughts."

"Unhappy? But you were not unhappy with maman."

"My mind must be playing tricks on me these days because when I try to remember … holding her in my arms … it's very strange, but I see her turning away from me."

"Maman never turned away from you. She always loved to have your arms around her. She told me so."

"Near the end, when she couldn't move her right arm and her right leg, she didn't want me to bathe her in the big wooden tub. In my mind, I see her turning away her shoulder from me."

"Your mind is playing tricks on you, father. Perhaps you don't know this, but many times I wanted to bathe maman when you were weary coming in from the fields. Maman would always whisper to me, 'Your father will do it.'"

"No, I did not know that, but I'm glad to hear it now. Oh, I wish she were here now," said Benedict. "I wouldn't even mind being scolded for drinking too much ale." Then he grinned and said, "She always had *such* a good time scolding me."

"To bed now, father. It's late. Oh, I almost forgot! I saw the widow, Madame Boudro, today. She wants to cook supper for you some evening soon."

"No! Her thighs are too big!"

"Now, father, she only wants to be friends with you. You don't have to marry her."

"Her thighs are too big!" Madame Boudro, an elderly widow who carried around two hundred pounds and a flagrant fervor for matrimony was, for Benedict, entirely out of the question.

Worn out from his day's work in the fields and groggy with nut-brown ale, Monsieur Bellefontaine headed for his bed. Evangéline covered him with a woolen blanket. "I think that raccoon stole one of my new boots last night."

"Which raccoon?" asked Evangéline, smiling. "Are you joking?"

"A raccoon has been prowling outside our house and I think he stole one of the new boots that Monsieur Babin made for me. Because they were wet and dirty I left them to dry out on the step last night." Evangéline laughed. "It's not funny. They were *new* boots!" Benedict thought it over for a minute and then he laughed, too.

Within minutes, he was snoring loudly. Evangéline went to her room and sat on a wicker chair by the window. She thought of Gabriel and frowned slightly. Thoughts of Gabriel usually made her smile, but tonight was different. A sad thought ran through her mind, the sad thought that someday she might suffer the same fate as her mother. "Will Gabriel forget me, too, when I'm only a few years out of his sight?" She looked out the window into the darkness. "Oh, I'd better get to sleep," she said. "I'm my father's daughter all right! When I'm tired, I also have unhappy thoughts." She stood up and began to undress. The night air was not cold, but the thought of men's short memories made her shiver as she stepped out of her long dress and let it fall in a heap on the moonlit floor. Crawling between the covers, she yawned. Benedict slept quietly now. She sighed and lay listening to the night. Peace came slowly drifting up to her from the solemn stillness of the great meadow, that tranquilizing expanse of misplaced prairie that stretched on, and on, and on.

Chapter Fourteen

Bad News From Beauséjour

At first, it appeared to be an ordinary Sunday in church like all other Sundays. The parishioners in the Grand Pré church of St. Charles des Mines were sitting where, without variation, they always sat. Some of the women, and a few of the men, scanned the congregation to see if anyone were sporting a new chemise, frock, or bonnet. Héloise Richard, ever mindful of public opinion, removed a speck of lint from the back of her cousin's dress in front of her. Hardly a spiritual woman, Heloise's complete faith, body and soul, lay in the importance of keeping up appearances, a faith that was, unfortunately for the parish, more communicable than mere Christianity.

Then Father Chauvreulx, from his pulpit, related the bad news. "Fort Beauséjour was taken* by the English a few days ago, on June 15." The parishioners gasped and whispered their shock. "Yes, my children, it's true. Beauséjour has fallen." He paused and waited for the congregation to settle down.

Pierre Melanson, sitting near the back, said to no one in particular, "Now here comes a sermon on the patience of Job."

"But the worst news of all, my friends, is that two of our former parishioners were killed in that terrible attack on the fort. It is my sad duty to inform you that Jacques Tibodot and André Dupuis are both

---

* Beausejour was captured by the British under Colonel Robert Monckton and renamed Fort Cumberland.

dead. Jacques died from a wound to the head; André was shot through the heart." Loud sobs issued now from the younger listeners, the friends of the boys. Pierre could not believe his ears. "They had been inside the fort with Abbé Le Loutre who managed to escape, it is rumored, through a secret underground passageway. We believe that Abbé Le Loutre has fled to Québec.

"And now, my children, you may be asking yourselves 'why has God forsaken us?' And to your question I would answer that it is sometimes hard for us to understand the will of God. And I would remind you that it is not for us to question the will of God. He works His wonders in mysterious ways." Pierre went pale and squirmed in his seat. Jacques and André dead! "And I would also say to you that God has already provided answers for us. He has given us the answer we now need in the Bible story of Job."

Pierre snorted in disgust, rose from his bench, and limped outside for fresh air.

"Job, you will remember, suffered terrible afflictions and he endured them with great patience because he had faith in God. Why has God forsaken us, you ask? Could it be that *we* have lost faith in Him? Could it be that we have lost faith in Him and have taken the law into our own hands and are now being punished for our own willfulness?

"I tell you, my children, that we must have faith. We must! We must! Without faith we cannot go on living. Faith is our spiritual meat and drink. If we lose faith, we make ourselves sick spiritually and physically. It is not healthy to lose faith.

"Some of you have been feeling sick lately. And *why* are you sick, my children? I tell you that it is despair that makes you sick. We get sick when we lose faith in God's guiding hand.

"I know that these are troubling times, but we must have faith that things will work out for the best in the end. Believe me, my children, God is watching over us. Go in peace now, and remember Job. Be patient and trust in God's guiding hand." To the parishioners' dismay, he didn't let them go in peace, but rambled on for another half hour on his single theme of patience, stretching his parishioners' patience to its absolute limit. With poor Job hammered redundantly to death, the priest finally said, "In the name of the Father, the Son, and the Holy Spirit. Amen," thus concluding his homily.

Twenty minutes later mass ended and the congregation stood around the churchyard discussing the crushing loss of Jacques and André. Pierre, standing in the shade of the church steps, gnawed on a fingernail. He felt resentful eyes upon him. After all, it was partly his fault that Jacques and André had run away to join Le Loutre. With his subversive talk, Pierre had influenced almost every young man in the village. He felt especially guilty with the look Gabriel had given him in church. Perhaps it had been an innocuous glance, but Pierre interpreted it as an accusation. The younger men gathered together, Gabriel, Michel Lanneau, Charles and Jude Le Blanc. Pierre spoke first to Gabriel. "Well, why don't you say it!"

"Say what?" asked Gabriel.

"That you think it's all my fault!"

"I wasn't thinking of you at all," said Gabriel. "I was thinking of Jacques and André."

"I don't believe that. You're thinking that I'm to blame for their deaths!" snarled Pierre.

"Not everything that happens in this world has to have some connection to you, Pierre," said Gabriel. It annoyed Gabriel that Pierre's egotism couldn't take a day off, not even for mourning.

"At least they died *doing* something!" shouted Pierre. "It's always better to do something than to do nothing!"

Gabriel, angry now, wanted to shout back, but when he looked into Pierre's eyes, he could see that they were brimming with regret. His friend was in agony and Gabriel, not wanting him to feel any worse, walked over to Pierre and put his arms around him. Pierre made a feeble attempt to pull away, but Gabriel's powerful arms held his crippled friend tightly until Pierre sobbed convulsively and buried his face in Gabriel's shoulder. The arms of the other boys surrounded Gabriel and Pierre, and together they all wept openly for their two fallen comrades.

Chapter Fifteen

Signing the Petition

July 1, 1755

Pierre Melanson's house was packed with villagers. Because the small house couldn't hold them all, Pierre had opened the two doors and all of the first-floor windows to allow those outside to hear the speakers at the meeting. For some, this careless lack of space showed Pierre's typical lack of respect. One's place at a meeting, after all, was as important as one's place in church. "He could have held the meeting somewhere else. At a bigger house," they whispered, "but then, of course, Pierre and his home wouldn't have all the glory!" Thus, feeling slighted and peeved, and yet knowing there was a petition to sign, they wanted to sign it blindly and go home. Others, more worried about possible legal repercussions, wanted to know exactly what it was they were being asked to affix their names to. Berthe Commo stood by the fireplace, arm in arm with her Oliver. Pierre spoke to the old honeymooners. "I'm happy to see you here. Thank you for coming."

"We wouldn't have missed your meeting, Pierre," said Berthe.

"No," said Oliver. We wanted to come here and—"

"… sign your petition," finished Berthe.

"Thank you, both," said Pierre. Then he stood up on a nearby kitchen chair and addressed the villagers. "As you know, we have already sent a petition to Governor Lawrence respectfully asking to have our guns and our boats returned to us. In the petition we said that we need our boats for fishing, and our guns to protect our cattle from wild beasts. We also said that we were all willing to take the oath of allegiance that our fathers and grandfathers took." Pierre paused to clear his throat. "Now Governor Lawrence wants to see our village delegates in Halifax on July 3. We have a copy of that petition here for you to sign. We want Governor Lawrence to know that our delegates have our support. Our fifteen Grand Pré delegates will be joined by representatives from Piziquid, Annapolis Royal, and all the other communities with Acadian citizens." Some of the listeners began to cheer. "That's right, over one hundred delegates will stand up to Governor Lawrence!" Louder cheers broke out. "So, before you leave, make sure that you sign your name or make your mark on this petition. Thank you."

Pierre smiled as he stepped down and, when he mingled with the crowd, he received a dozen hearty pats on the back. When he reached Gabriel and Basil, Pierre asked, "Have you signed yet?"

"Are you sure that no harm will come from this petition, Pierre? We're not making things worse for ourselves, are we?" asked Gabriel, who was thinking of Jacques and André's fate.

"Of course not. What harm is there in making a request? All the English can do is say 'no'," answered Pierre.

"But are you absolutely certain of this?" asked Basil. "The English can be cruel, you know."

"Why should they be cruel to farmers who are now unarmed?" asked Pierre. "Are you suggesting that we should do *nothing*?"

"No, but we *are* suggesting that we should be careful not to make matters worse for ourselves. After all, some of us are not politically minded. We just want to go on with our lives," said Gabriel.

Pierre shouted, "But that's exactly what I've been trying to tell you! We can't go on with our lives! The damned English won't let us! Can't you get that through your head? We can't do anything as long as we are in chains!" Pierre was yelling now for all to hear because not only Gabriel needed his instruction. "We live on land that is not ours. We raise crops that can be taken away from us at any minute. We practice our religion only because the English have given us temporary permission to do so, permission that can be withdrawn at any time. Nothing we have is truly ours. The English spoil everything they see. They foul everything they touch, and they touch every part of our daily lives." Pierre paused to catch his breath. Then he looked at Gabriel and said, "Even slaves need to hold on to some of their dignity!"

"Pierre, those words 'slave' and 'dignity' don't mean anything to me. They're only words you use to get people fired up. But the words 'peace' and 'love' and 'family' mean more to me. All I want is to live in peace and to raise a family here where my father lived and raised his family," said Gabriel.

"What will it take to make you understand, Gabriel? Will some Englishman have to come and put his foul hands on Evangéline before you wake up?"

"The Englishman who does that will not live to see another sunrise," said Gabriel. "And neither will anyone else who makes it possible for an Englishman to do so. So, I'll ask you again, Pierre: can you guarantee that this petition will not make matters worse for us here?"

"Slaves have no guarantees for anything, except more slavery, " said Pierre.

"Come, then, Father. Don't sign any paper that may only cause more trouble," said Gabriel.

Basil looked at his son but didn't move. "You go," he said. "I'm staying with the others."

Gabriel pushed his way through the crowd and hurried home.

Chapter Sixteen

We Most Definitely Refuse

July 3, 1755, Halifax, Nova Scotia

The tapping distracted Paul Richard, the father of the twins. As one of the Grand Pré delegates he was standing in the Halifax council chamber reading aloud the petition signed by 203 residents. The tapping grew louder and Paul raised his eyes from the page. Charles Lawrence sat at the center of a long table drumming his fingers impatiently. He was not looking at Paul, but at some of the other delegates. His eyes moved up and down incredulously over each clean, well-dressed delegate. He had expected the Acadian delegation to consist of a scruffy bunch of ragamuffins wearing dung-covered clogs, and it upset him that he was wrong. He was also beginning to wonder whether he might have underestimated their intelligence and their determination as well. His face reddened, and the pulse in his temple throbbed visibly as he listened to Paul's words. "Permit us, if you please, sir, to make known the annoying circumstances in which we are placed, to the prejudice of tranquillity we ought to enjoy." Lawrence's fingers tapped louder. "And we have not violated our oath but have kept it faithfully in spite of the dreadful threats of another power." Lawrence could not believe he was hearing such insolence. "Moreover, the arms that have been taken away from us are but a feeble guarantee of our fidelity. It is not the gun which an inhabitant possesses that will induce him to revolt, nor the privation of the same gun that will make him more faithful; but his conscience alone must induce him to maintain his oath."

How intolerable the French are! thought Lawrence. Exasperating! They compliment themselves on being honest when they are simply being tactless, and on being direct when they're merely being blunt and inelegant! 'Maladroit' is the only word for them. A faint smile crossed his face. Yes, the 'Acadian Maladroits' is what we should call them. 'Maladroit' is a French word, too, isn't it? I should use it on them now - to their faces! Probably wouldn't understand it, though. Don't want to speak English and don't fully understand their own French. Intolerable!

Unwilling to listen further, he interrupted Paul, "That's quite enough, thank you! Well, gentlemen," he said, addressing his council members, "have you heard enough insults for one day? Apparently *we* are responsible for *their* 'annoying circumstances' and for disturbing *their* 'tranquillity'." A few councilmen laughed. "And we have been accused of making 'dreadful threats' and of exacting 'feeble guarantees' from these law-abiding martyrs. I have been called many names, gentlemen, but 'feeble' is not one of them."

As more obsequious laughter came from the councilmen, the delegates stood fidgeting. What had they said that was so wrong? They had taken such care in composing their memorial. "And, gentlemen, I will not even mention the Sunday sermon we have just been delivered on the necessity of following one's own private conscience."

Lawrence then turned to confront Paul and gave him his most fulgurant glare. Paul, however, hadn't fully grasped Lawrence's irony and, therefore, stood his ground, seemingly undisturbed. He looked back at Lawrence with a businesslike expression. Lawrence fumed, "I tell you, sir, the selfishness and arrogance you are showing here today is appalling. You have the unmitigated gall to stand there and tell me that you and your people have been treated *unfairly*! On the contrary! You have always been treated with the utmost lenience and tenderness and you have enjoyed more privileges than our own English subjects here in Nova Scotia! You have been permitted the free exercise of your religion and the full liberty to consult your priests! Furthermore, you have not only been permitted to engage in trade and the fishing industry but you have been protected in doing so *by the British government!* And, as if that is not enough, you have been permitted to possess your lands - the best soil in the province - even though you have not complied with the terms on which those lands were granted by taking the oath of allegiance to the Crown! So, would you be kind as to produce one instance in which any privilege was denied to you, or one instance of any hardship that was imposed upon you by the government?"

Paul turned to his friends and spoke to them in French. Lawrence's angry tone intimidated them and they decided not to make him any angrier. Paul said, "No, monsieur, we cannot."

"I thought so! And for our lenience and kindness towards you, what, may I ask, have you given us in return? I shall tell you. In return, you have shown nothing but a constant disposition to assist His Majesty's enemies and to distress his subjects! You have furnished the enemy with provisions and ammunition, and yet you have refused to supply the government with provisions. And when you did supply the government with provisions, you demanded three times the price for which they were sold at other markets! In return for our kindness, did it ever occur to you that you might *freely* offer some service to His Majesty's government? Can you now, in fact, mention one single instance in which you *freely* offered some service to the government?"

Paul again turned to his friends, and they all began to talk at once. "What does he mean?" "Why is he so angry?" "Who does he mean? Does he mean you personally?" "What kind of 'service'?"

Lawrence turned to the councilors and said, "Gentlemen, the idea of 'service' seems to escape them completely."

Paul faced Lawrence again and said, "I am no lawyer and cannot answer these heavy questions. But, monsieur, I beg you, we must have our boats returned to us for our fishing business. We have no means to carry our fish from port to port. And our guns, monsieur. We ask for our hunting guns only to protect ourselves from the wild animals in the woods!"

Lawrence clenched his fists and struggled to remain calm. "May I remind you that we have a law in this province stating that any person caught carrying provisions from port to port must forfeit his boat and pay a heavy penalty?"

Paul's jaw dropped and he said, "I didn't know of such a law."

"Perhaps not, because it has never been enforced *out of the kindness of the British government*! You are probably equally ignorant, then, of the law which forbids Roman Catholics to possess arms, and which imposes penalties if guns are found in their houses."

"I was not aware of that law either," said Paul.

"Naturally. You were not aware of it because the British government has been lenient enough not to impose it upon you and your ungrateful friends," sneered Lawrence.

Paul's back stiffened and he replied, "If the British government chose not to enforce those laws, then it must have been for some advantage to the British government!"

"Now you listen to me! I will hear no more insolence, and no more requests, propositions, or explanations from you or any of your rebel friends. You seem to think yourselves independent of *any* government; and you wish to treat with the King as if you were so. It is only out of pity for your … inexperience that we condescend to reason with you; otherwise the question would not be reasoning, but commanding and being obeyed. And so I ask you plainly and reasonably now, will you or will you not swear to the king of England that you will take up arms against the king of France, his enemy?"

Paul turned and whispered in French to each of the fifteen Grand Pré delegates. A minute later, he and the other delegates faced Lawrence, and in one clear, united voice they said, "We most definitely refuse!"

"In that case, you leave me no choice. Sergeant, escort these men to the prison on George's Island," said Lawrence. He looked at Paul and the other Acadians and said, "I could send you home, but I would only have to arrest you again in a few months." The Acadian delegates, more confused than frightened, were led away. Then Lawrence turned to his councilmen and said, "Now, gentlemen, only 6,985 more of these traitors to go."

With their petition ignored, the delegates were marched off to prison. Their arguments had failed, failed because they were naively contingent on presenting a moral argument of fairness to an imperialist regime not open to moral persuasion, and naturally not open to persuasion, moral or otherwise, by their arch-rival, the French-speaking, Acadian, Roman Catholics.

The imprisoned delegates were not, of course, given the local newspaper to read. But had they seen, in the *Halifax Gazette* of July 10, the notice of Vice-Admiral Edward Boscawen's arrival in Halifax, they might have been alarmed even though his visit there was a coincidental one. His small fleet had been patrolling the waters farther north, trying to prevent the French fleet from supplying arms and provisions to Louisbourg, when many of his seamen came down with typhoid fever. Because Halifax had more medical help available, he brought the fleet there. He was, therefore, in Halifax where Charles Lawrence could make use of him, but he was there - according to the newspaper - by accident.

Thus, in another ironic twist of fate, illness played a crucial part in the future of the Acadians. An eye illness had sent the good Governor Hopson packing, and typhoid fever now brought the formidable English naval hero, Edward Boscawen, to Lawrence's doorstep.

Chapter Seventeen

Belligerent Neutrals

July 15, 1755

Jonathan Belcher, Chief Justice of the Nova Scotia court, walked into Governor Lawrence's office. Lawrence had sent for him, and he dutifully came. "Ah!" said Lawrence. "So good of you to come. Please excuse the disorder of my office. I have been too busy to keep it tidy."

Judge Belcher looked around the immaculate office and saw nothing out of place. Lawrence's oak desk was especially neat with only an ink bottle, a feather pen, and a blank sheet of parchment on it. It occurred to Belcher that this desk with its highly polished surface couldn't possibly be a working desk, just a handsome piece of furniture arranged to impress visitors, a desk merely for show. The *real* orders of the day always remained in Lawrence's head.

Lawrence picked up a pile of legal documents from the seat of the chair behind his desk. He held up the stack at eye-level for a moment, and then let it fall with a thud on his desk. Lawrence said nothing, but only stared dramatically at Belcher and waited for some reaction.

Judge Belcher smiled faintly and asked, "And what do we have here, sir?"

"Lawsuits! We have lawsuits here. Dozens and dozens of lawsuits for you and me to waste our time on." Belcher stared directly at Lawrence, and this time said nothing. Lawrence then said, "Lawsuits, sir, that our ridiculous Acadian residents have filed against *one another*!"

"Against one another? Concerning what, if you please, sir?"

"All petty suits[1] over farm boundary lines in the village of Grand Pré. The peaceful, law-abiding citizens of Grand Pré are taking one another to court over a few vegetable patches!" Lawrence was practically shouting now.

In an attempt to calm Lawrence, Belcher tried to make light of the situation. "Well, perhaps these suits will work to our advantage. Perhaps the residents will come to blows and kill one another off in their own gardens." When Lawrence didn't smile, Belcher continued in a more serious tone. "I don't understand, sir. Aside from the time they will take up in court, why are these petty disputes of any great concern to us?"

"They are of great concern to us, sir, because these bloody Acadians do not *own* any of the land mentioned in these lawsuits! The land they are fighting over is not *their* land, it is *English* land! It's *our* land, and they have the audacity to ask *our* English courts to decide which group of Acadian thieves we will award it to!"

Judge Belcher, the lawyer rising within him, then said, "You are right, of course, in that these lawsuits may have no legitimate foundation whatsoever. However, it's a complicated matter because we have been permitting the Acadians to own and sell land here since 1713." Belcher paused. He saw anger growing in Lawrence's face, his cheeks a hectic red. "Still, I fail to see why we should upset ourselves over such frivolous litigation."

"You don't seem to understand. These Grand Pré peasants are making complete fools of us all! They file lawsuits over land that doesn't belong to them; they refuse to take the oath of allegiance to the English crown, and yet they demand English protection against *their* enemies. And do you know what, sir? We give it to them! Not only do they refuse to become good Protestant citizens of English territory, but they *insist* upon retaining the freedom to practice their own lunatic Catholic superstitions on our Anglican soil! And do you know what, sir? We let them! They swear they have no military ambitions, and yet every Acadian home had at least two guns which they refused to hand over to their English governors! Just who, may I ask, sir, is running this country, we English, or these belligerent neutrals?"

"I am beginning to see your point, sir," said Belcher, now wanting to end the conversation and leave the room as soon as possible.

"Mister Belcher, I am surrounded by incompetents and I am astounded by the small number of Englishmen who do their duty in this God-forsaken province."

Belcher ventured, "I believe everyone in his majesty's service wants to serve his king, but not everyone knows exactly how best to serve, sir."

"Is that what you believe? Are you aware that not one Nova Scotia governor in the last forty years did his job with regard to these goddamn Acadians?"

"But Governor Hopson—"

"Governor Hopson was a spineless fool terrified of any sort of confrontation!" Lawrence then smirked, and sniffed, "Besides, any governor who spends his administration kissing the backsides of French farmers is bound to arouse only the liveliest sort of speculation."

"And Governor Cornwallis?"

"When the Acadians refused to take the oath of allegiance to England, the oath that he demanded they take, do you know what Governor Cornwallis did?"

"No, sir."

"He turned away and built Halifax!"

"And before him, I believe it was Mascarene and Philipps?"

"Philipps, the weakest of all. It was he who set the bad example that all of his successors followed. Governor Philipps allowed the Acadians to take half of an oath! Now I ask you, as a man of the law, of what real value is half of an oath?"

"Of no value, sir, as you know." After a slight pause Belcher tried again to pacify Lawrence by saying, "But, of course, as you have certainly noticed, doing one's duty in this part of the world is not easy. And Englishmen do not, as a rule, escape the scrutiny of their London employers and immigrate to Nova Scotia for the purpose of working harder."

"Geography is irrelevant. Englishmen are duty-bound to do their jobs wherever in the world they are sent by His Majesty."

The Chief Justice of Nova Scotia sighed resignedly and said, "Well, sir, in what way may I be of service to you and to His Majesty? I shall be happy to assist you in any way I can."

"I need a piece of paper."

"A piece of paper. I see. And is there anything to be written on that piece of paper, sir?"

"I need written permission from the chief justice to deport all of our perfidious Acadians from the province of Nova Scotia!"

"But I am not certain, sir, that I—"

"I have just received this letter from London, sir. One part of the letter pertains to you, and I quote,

> 'The deportation is a question, however, which we will not take upon ourselves absolutely to determine, but wish that you would consult the chief justice upon this point and take his opinion, which may serve as a foundation for any future measure it may be thought advisable to pursue.'

Therefore, we have consulted, and all I need from you now is to know when I shall receive your piece of paper."

"You shall have it in your hands in the morning. However, sir, as a lawyer, I must advise you that my signature on that piece of paper is not quite enough."

"And why not? You are the supreme court justice here."

"Yes, sir, I am, but despite that letter, I do not single-handedly make the laws of this province."

"I thought your job was precisely that."

"I must act upon orders of our council."

"Our council members are a pack of scoundrels. They are no better than the merchants in this town who are a parcel of villains and bankrupts. What do any of those people know about running a province in the wilderness?" Lawrence was red-faced, his blood pressure rising. He glared at Belcher. "Well, you are the legal advisor here, tell me: how can I legally rid the province of this Acadian blight?"

Judge Belcher hesitated. He knew what to tell Lawrence; he was just afraid that his legal advice would provide the decisive ammunition Lawrence needed to carry out his reckless plan. But right now Lawrence, his face the color of brick, was again glaring at him and waiting for an answer. Belcher could see a pulse popping in and out of Lawrence's left temple. "Well, sir, the oath is all that you need."

"The oath? What do you mean? That useless tool has been around for over forty years! It amounts to nothing more than a threat, a ridiculous, impotent threat on our part. I use it as a threat myself, and it's an embarrassment because I know it has no real authority."

"It has been an embarrassment, sir, but it does carry *real* authority. It's a perfectly legal tool that has never been *fully* exploited."

"I don't follow, sir."

"The law of the oath, sir, which has never been fully enforced, states that anyone who does not take the complete *unqualified* oath of allegiance to the English crown is not, in the eyes of the law, an English citizen. And if one is not a legal English citizen, then one does not have any legal right to be here on English soil. And no right certainly to be selling and buying English land."

A look of quiet calm crossed Lawrence's face. It was as though he had just heard a lovely new piece of music. The pulse in his temple slowed. "The solution has been right under our noses all along. Belcher, you're a legal genius. This way, we can demand, once again, that the Acadians take the complete oath - which we know they will never do - and then we can deport them without anyone's specific permission. Thank you, sir. Thank you very much, indeed. I shall see that you are properly rewarded for this expert advice."

"No need to reward me, sir. Legal counseling is my duty."

"Nevertheless, you shall be rewarded for this."

"Thank you, sir. And now if there's nothing else—"

"I think I have all that I need now. Good day to you."

Judge Belcher made a slight bow, turned, and walked towards the door.

"Oh, just one thing, Judge Belcher. When did you say I may have that piece of paper with your signature on it?" Lawrence was staring again as though at a thief slipping away.

Belcher replied, "Will tomorrow morning be soon enough, sir?"

"Thank you, Belcher. I am happy to see that you are a man unafraid to do his duty here. Good day." Belcher opened the door and exited the governor's office, his head and shoulders lower than they had been when he entered.

Once Belcher had gone, Lawrence sat at his desk smiling broadly. A few seconds later the smile dissolved into a worried look. "And now," he said to himself, "all I need is another man, a man with a small army." He thought for a minute and then said, "And I know that my old friend, Governor Shirley of Massachusetts, will be my man." Lawrence sat back in his chair, sighed, and allowed the former smile of glee to return to his puffy, pink face. "By God, I almost forgot! Shirley's men, and Colonel Monckton are still holding Fort Beauséjour! All that I need is for them to remain there!" He clapped his hands in applause. "Now, let me see, what's the fastest way to get a message to Beauséjour?" He continued to smile but abruptly rose and entered the anteroom. "Sergeant, send messages immediately to all the members of the council to meet with me at seven o'clock this evening at the governor's house."

"Yes, sir. Very good, sir," replied the sergeant.

"Oh, and also send invitations to Vice-Admiral Boscawen and to Rear-Admiral Mostyn.[2] Their presence always carries some official weight," said Lawrence smiling.

"Weight, sir?" said the sergeant, bewildered.

Lawrence looked at the sergeant, laughed heartily, and without replying, strode out the door and into the muddy Halifax street whistling a happy tune. He whistled as he thought about the meeting. Knowing that the London court of public opinion would frown upon the sudden and full enforcement of a dusty, forty-year old law, Lawrence would have his unsuspecting council do the dusting for him. Almost giddy with thoughts of it, he walked on, whistling louder.

****

Chief Justice Belcher went directly to his own office to prepare the letter of permission Lawrence had demanded. When he entered his office, his secretary, the young law student, Richard Bellingham, asked, "And in what mood was Mr. Lawrence today, sir?"

"A very busy mood, Richard. Busy and angry."

"And could you detect the cause of his anger, sir?"

"I believe that Mr. Lawrence must have had at some earlier time in his life an unrequited passion for a pretty French girl."

"If you don't mind my saying so, sir, I find it difficult to imagine Governor Lawrence with *any* girl, French or otherwise." After a pause, Richard continued. "And will there be any correspondence as a result of your meeting, sir?"

"Yes, Bellingham, we must prepare a letter, a letter giving Governor Lawrence just cause to deport seven thousand Acadians to other shores."

"But," said the intelligent law student, "without England's written permission such a letter will have no legal power, will it, sir?"

"And that, Bellingham, is exactly why we should not hesitate to provide it. My letter will not be worth the paper it's written on."

"As you say, sir. Are you ready to dictate the letter now, sir?"

Despite his cavalier bluster with Bellingham, Belcher was not ready to give Lawrence the note of permission he wanted. "Not just yet."

"And perhaps when I deliver the document to Governor Lawrence I should bring along for him a pretty French girl?"

"If I were you, Bellingham, I would deliver the letter and then get as far away from Governor Lawrence as ever I possibly could."

****

At seven that evening, all those summoned by Lawrence had assembled in the governor's conference room. Chief Justice Belcher sat alone in a corner reading a book of poetry. John Rous, the chief naval officer in Nova Scotia stood by the window talking quietly to the visiting admirals, Boscawen and Mostyn. (Rous was one of the few admirers of Charles Lawrence. He had witnessed firsthand Lawrence's military skill in routing a group of Le Loutre's Mi'kmaqs near the Missaquash River five years earlier.) Benjamin Green, a Halifax merchant and Harvard graduate, stood by the fireplace whispering to John Collier and William Cotterell. Neither Collier, a retired army officer, nor Cotterell was a personal friend of Lawrence's, although Cotterell, as provincial secretary, owed him his professional loyalty. Green whispered, "There's trouble brewing in the town. The merchants and townspeople are upset about the tactics of our Mr. Lawrence."

"What are they saying about him?" asked Collier.

"They don't like his dictatorial rule of Nova Scotia. They want an elected assembly."

"Elected assemblies are a farce!" hissed Collier. "How can a town full of imbeciles govern itself? All we need is a more humane governor. A humane governor is better by far than any idiotic elected assembly."

"I agree with you on that point, sir. But what else is being said about Lawrence?" asked William Cotterell, as he cast a nervous, sidelong glance in the direction of the admirals.

Green continued to whisper. "The local merchants, Joshua Mauger and Ephraim Cook, say that no settlers will come here from New England unless there *is* an elected assembly. And no one from New England will come here if the economy is a shambles. That's why we must continue to allow the Acadians to farm this province. We need them!" Green looked nervously towards the door. "Furthermore, there are rumors that Lawrence is lining his own pockets a bit thickly. Everyone expects a little government graft, but the word is that he profited too greatly from the capture of Fort Beauséjour," whispered Green.

"How did he do so? In what way?" whispered Mr. Collier.

Benjamin Green replied, "Over ten thousand pounds of beef, pork, molasses, and rum were taken at Beauséjour and no one knows what became of them. Some say Lawrence sold them privately to Mr. Saul."

Cotterell fumed, "Why, that's an outrageous accusation! I don't believe a word of it!"

"Well, you are the provincial secretary, sir. Do you have any record of those goods or of the sale of those goods?" asked Green.

"Preposterous!" exclaimed Cotterell, blushing. "These matters are military matters and are not for the public record!"

"Very little these days is for the public record," sniffed Green. "It is also well known that Lawrence does not advertise the government contracts. He simply hands them out quietly to his confederates," said Green.

Cotterell objected. "Another lie, sir. Only last week a government contract was advertised locally. Besides, what is so wrong about giving the contracts to the most capable people at the fairest price to the government? That's exactly what a good administrator should do!"

"The most capable people? Or the most capable people that Lawrence knows personally? The advertised contract to which you refer was the first of its kind this year, sir. And what about the money from the fines he levies? Where is all of that money?" asked Green.

"What fines are you referring to, sir?" asked Collier.

Benjamin Green looked towards the door because he had heard footsteps approaching. Then he whispered, "Our Mr. Lawrence levies fines upon ship captains who provide transportation to anyone who has not obtained a license to leave Halifax. Not only that but he demands the townspeople also have a license to travel more than three miles from town and the license money paid to him personally. Dozens of ships' captains, and hundreds of townspeople have paid for these special licenses, but no one except Lawrence has ever seen the money."

"Shhhh!" said Collier, as he spotted Governor Lawrence entering the room.

"Good evening, sirs. I was unavoidably detained," said Lawrence with frosty courtesy. No excuse for his lateness followed. Lawrence rarely apologized, and he never gave excuses to inferiors. His personality was abrasive and those who came in contact with him came away with a little less skin. When he entered a room, the air suddenly seemed less breathable. Exuding a kind of repugnant potency or negative charisma, he had the ability within minutes to annoy complete strangers. There was something sarcastic in the way he said 'good morning', and something sinister in the way he whispered 'good night'. Few liked him; everyone feared him. He knew the intimidating value of a well-placed sneer and a timely scoff. He was such a master of the callous shrug that he could send chills up the spine of the most hardened petitioner. He was that most dangerous kind of man, the man with a single purpose, a purpose for which he was now aligning all of his focus. Many were already beginning to feel the pinch, if not the crush, of this human juggernaut. The God-fearing Acadians, now concerned only with the success of their harvest, were about to hear the first rumblings of Lawrence's mighty wheels, the new Lord of the world - the Lord of the New World - moving inexorably in their direction. "Mr. Cotterell, are you prepared to record the minutes?"

"Yes, sir," said Cotterell, who was not fully prepared, but no one wanted to say 'no' to Charles Lawrence.

"We were under the impression that this was to be an *informal* meeting," said Benjamin Green with a sociable air.

"It is. It is, Mr. Green, and I assure you that Mr. Cotterell will record only those things that we all agree upon unanimously."

"Very well, sir," replied Green, satisfied.

"I wish to discuss the Acadian problem with you once again, gentlemen. As you know, I have written to His Majesty requesting permission to deport them if I am unsuccessful in bringing them to a compliance with our laws."

Mr. Green interrupted, "But, sir, how may we help you in this matter? You are aware that we, the council members, have also written to His Majesty on the Acadian question. We cannot at this time form a proper judgment until we have His Majesty's directions upon it."

Lawrence looked disappointed and said, "But that could take months. Perhaps years!"

"I'm afraid our hands are tied, sir," said Collier in a quiet voice.

"Well, then, I suppose we'll just have to wait, won't we, gentlemen," said Lawrence affecting a defeated tone. "But we all agree upon the question of the oath of allegiance, do we not?"

Benjamin Green inhaled, bracing himself for Lawrence's next disappointment, and then said boldly, "The oath, sir, is also a question which we will not take upon ourselves absolutely to determine; but we could wish that you would consult with the chief justice, Mr. Belcher, upon this point and take his opinion with regard to the inhabitants in general." (The council members apparently had seen a copy of the same letter from London.)

Lawrence could not stifle a faint smile on hearing this good news. "As a matter of fact," said Lawrence, "I have spoken to Mr. Belcher on this matter and he has not been of much help to me either." Lawrence grinned and looked around the conference table at each member of the council. They smiled in return, happy that Lawrence, for a change, was acting like a humble loser. Belcher stirred in his seat, unsmiling, and felt a mixture of disgust and admiration for the wily Mr. Lawrence. "You see," Lawrence continued, "I was not able to get Mr. Belcher to help me to break the law either," and he laughed loudly at his own joke. Grateful for the tension-breaker, everyone except Green and Belcher laughed along with Lawrence. "We wouldn't want to be accused of breaking the law, of course. We must uphold the laws that are already in place." Lawrence paused a minute and looked out the window. Then he continued, "I suppose all I can hope to secure from this meeting is everyone's agreement to uphold the present law pertaining to the oath of allegiance. I am sure you gentlemen realize that a law is simply worthless unless it is properly enforced. Many of our laws are like old, unused tools rusting in the shed." Smiles vanished while all ears were suddenly lawyers' ears, carefully attentive to every word uttered by Lawrence. "The present law states, gentlemen, that anyone who refuses to take the oath of allegiance completely deprives himself of his legal right to possess his lands." Lawrence looked at each councilman and spoke softly, "The law states that those who refuse to take the oath are simply not citizens of this province, and non-citizens have no legal rights in this province. Isn't that correct, Chief Justice Belcher?" asked Lawrence relishing every word of his coup.

"That is correct, sir," said Belcher without looking up. "The law states that 'persons are declared recusants if they refuse to take the oath at the sessions, and one can never after such refusal be permitted to take it'."

"Now, we all do agree with the law, do we not gentlemen?" said Lawrence. It was checkmate and everyone at the table knew it. "All those in favor of upholding and enforcing the present law?" As he saw all hands raised, Lawrence gloated. Then he said, "Mr. Cotterell, please record that we are unanimous on the matter of the oath.[3] And thank you, gentlemen, for your time this evening." With a smile that looked more like a scowl, Lawrence looked around the table at his councilors as though he were looking at a group of hopeless competitors. Then with an about-face he added, shamelessly flattering them, "The future of the world is now in English hands, and the history books will certainly include your names."

Unimpressed, Benjamin Green rose in disgust and hurried out the door. He was quickly followed by Collier and Cotterell. Once outside in the hallway, Green whispered to Cotterell, "So, perhaps that old Acadian suspicion was justified after all."

"What Acadian suspicion?"

"For the past two years, the Acadians have been saying that Governor Hopson was not seriously ill."

"Hopson not ill? But he was going blind!"

"The Acadians didn't believe that story. They believed that Hopson was removed to make way for a more ruthless man - Lawrence!"

"Preposterous! Absolutely preposterous!" hissed Cotterell, and he hurried out the door ahead of Green.

Back inside the meeting room, the two admirals, whether or not they agreed with Mr. Lawrence's slippery boardroom tactics, both came forward to shake the hand of a man who cleverly knew how to outmaneuver other men.

But in a mood of spiritual paralysis, Judge Belcher remained in his seat trying to predict the future repercussions of the meeting he had just attended. It amazed him that he had just been present at one of the most important meetings ever held in the province of Nova Scotia, and that it had been such a bland affair. He sat thinking how odd it is that we are always waiting for the great transforming experiences in our lives; but when they present themselves, they always arrive so quietly, and are over so quickly. When the Roman Empire fell, he wondered, did it also fall so soundlessly?

"Mr. Belcher," said Lawrence, to the only man still in the room, "I hope that you, too, will not desert me. Please stay and have a glass of wine with me. I know it's probably an unhealthy habit, but I *do* love to drink. And perhaps you can tell me what was said here tonight that moved you to such reverie." Lawrence smiled at his use of a poetic word on a man who loved poetry. Belcher didn't move. That fateful letter he had to write was stuck in his craw. He looked Lawrence in the eye, considered challenging him, and then thought better of it. He knew how unwise it is to challenge an unstable man who is in a position of power.

"I would love a glass or two, sir, but I have visitors at home that I must entertain. If you will kindly excuse me." Before he could finish his sentence, Lawrence had filled two large glasses with Madeira.

"Visitors?" asked Lawrence, as he handed Belcher a glass.

"A lady friend of mine is up from Boston."

Lawrence pretended to look surprised although he knew all about the arrival that morning of Belcher's friend. Lawrence had information on every ship and every visitor that entered Halifax.

"I should think at your age that you would take a greater interest in her chaperone," said Lawrence, chuckling. When Belcher didn't laugh, Lawrence said, "I meant that only as a little joke."

"I understand that, sir. It's just that your little joke is too true to be funny. I am, after all, old enough to be her father. But the time has come for me, at last, to make the big bold decision to marry."

"Indeed, sir, it is a time for big, bold decisions, decisions that have been far too long in the making." Lawrence paused to let his loaded remark sink in.

Apparently it wasn't loaded enough because it didn't sink in far, and Belcher blurted, "Besides, the chaperone is my mother."

Lawrence laughed heartily. "Well, that makes my little joke even more amusing, don't you agree?"

"Indeed it does, sir," said Belcher, without even the hint of a smile. Lawrence, a bit chagrined that his joke went unappreciated, frowned. But had Lawrence known him better, he would have understood that Belcher rarely laughed heartily at anything. Moreover, his perpetual seriousness was often taken for aloofness, even snobbishness. The fact was that Belcher simply had very little sense of humor. Then again, he might have been slightly snobbish, but he was not half as snobbish as he looked. It was the way he reared his head back and looked down his nose like a startled horse whenever, in conversation, he was struggling to absorb information. Strangers and enemies thought his nose in the air made him look like an aristocrat trying to breathe some higher air, or like some superior being trying to keep himself from drowning in a sea of mediocrity. But his head-tossing was, more tellingly, the mannerism of one whose ambitious reach far exceeded his mental grasp.

Lawrence changed the subject and said, "But tell me, sir, why you were so deep in thought throughout all of the meeting tonight." Belcher stared down into his glass, but didn't answer. "Come, come, sir, speak your mind. You are in the presence of an ever-grateful friend, remember?"

Belcher gulped some wine, and began cautiously. "It is probably just my present frame of mind."

"Present frame of mind?"

"Well, sir, my present thoughts are now on marriage and on starting a family of my own."

"That's admirable, sir. I, as you know, am a single man devoting all of my energies to the service of my country." Lawrence had a way of insulting a man without even trying. However, it was true that he was unmarried and unattached. Lawrence's lust was not for women, but for dominion.

Belcher took another drink. "Well, sir, hundreds, perhaps thousands of Acadian families will be uprooted if we pursue the policy of deportation, and I'm just wondering if—"

"If what, sir?" asked Lawrence, two Madeira roses blooming in his cheeks.

Fortified by the drink, Belcher grew more courageous. "Well, sir, I wish to know why four previous governors have all tolerated the presence of the Acadians - in fact, most of them were thankful to have them farming Nova Scotia—" Belcher paused. He looked Lawrence straight in the eye, but with a trembling voice, asked, "Why, sir? Why now? Why you, sir? Indeed, why me?"

Lawrence's first impulse was to bury his fist in Belcher's self-righteous mouth. But seeing how filled with emotion the chief justice was, Lawrence turned away and walked over to the window. He looked out into the street. The rain poured down again, that driving, slanting, irritating Atlantic-coast rain, that persistent drizzle that comes at you as though it wants to get not only *on* your skin, but *under* it. Without turning, he spoke in a surprisingly confessional tone. "It seems to be my misfortune in life that whenever I reach out for something, it somehow manages to slip away. Or worse, someone removes it from my grasp. And in the past, whenever I reached out for someone, she also somehow slipped away." Lawrence sighed. Belcher was spellbound. "And, ironically, the few times in my life that I have succeeded in holding on to something, I've felt as guilty as a thief. Therefore, it seems that with me, win or lose, personal misery is always the end result." Another pause. "So, you see, it really doesn't matter to me. For me, the outcome of *all* my actions is misery. As a result, I no longer dwell upon successes and failures. I simply act and then move on." Then, turning from the window, and walking towards Belcher with cheeks ablaze and gritting his teeth, Lawrence said in a low, deliberate voice, "But of this be sure: this land will *all* be English land. Its care has been entrusted to me. It is my duty to keep this land English and, by God, *I* shall do *my* duty! At this moment, Nova Scotia is in my hands and I'll be damned if I ever let it slip away from me! And if my actions cause suffering to some, so be it! I shall entirely welcome fellow sufferers to join me in my inevitable misery." Lawrence's eyes were wet with venom. "Another drink, sir?"

"Thank you, no. I've had enough," said Belcher softly, and he laid his empty glass on the conference table.

As though about to scold a naughty child, Lawrence seized Belcher's arm. Belcher reared his head back and tried to pull away, but the big soldier's firm hand on his forearm restrained him. Pulling Belcher closer to him, he breathed warm air in his face. The humid intimacy repulsed Belcher, and yet ... there was something ... what was it? Something. He didn't know. He had never been this close to a man before. Was this what a fatherly squeeze felt like? His father, the cold New England governor, had never embraced him, had never kissed him, his own son. His father, a gruff, undemonstrative man, communicated only goals to him. But, no. It was not his father's hand. Would that it were! Not his father's. More like a doctor's hand, part of the bedside manner of that doctor who had helped cure his measles when he was twelve. The doctor had been a comfort, but in this case, there was a disturbing element present, too. Lawrence's hand felt more like that of a surgeon, a surgeon about to operate. But which part of him was Surgeon Lawrence now preparing to amputate, or to extract? His heart? His soul? His integrity? "Try to look at it this way, Belcher," said Lawrence in an uncharacteristic, pleading way. "By ridding the province of these troublesome, superstitious people we will merit the everlasting gratitude of England. Think of it! Once the Acadians are gone from here, their departure will be simply an established fact of life, and no one will then be able to argue with our success. It will be ... ah, how do the French say it? ... a 'fait accompli'? There, you see, I am not at all prejudiced. I am speaking the French language," snickered Lawrence and he slapped Belcher on the shoulder, laughing heartily.

Belcher, conceding, closed his eyes. He hardly felt the scalpel. One quick incision and - snip - his integrity was gone. Snip! Gone, just like that!

Now the only question was - would anyone notice? Would there be visible surgical scars? Would he still look like the same man? Surely no one in this frozen northland kept an integrity watch! Besides, there was no one here that mattered much, was there?

One thing, however, was crystal clear: his father would be pleased. Now his son, the judge, was Governor Lawrence's right-hand man and would be a new link - snap! - in the North American chain of power. A son he could finally be proud of. Just like that! Snip! Snap!

Belcher looked at the floor and nodded his head in resignation. He had raised his last objection. Lawrence loosened his grip. Belcher turned and, like a sleepwalker, moved towards the door. Lawrence watched him with disdain and gulped the last of his drink. When he laid his empty glass on the table, he saw Belcher's book of poetry. He held it up and said, "Mister Belcher, you are forgetting your book!" Belcher turned, looked at Lawrence, stared at the book as though it were a mysterious foreign object, said nothing, and walked slowly out the door.

As soon as Belcher had exited, Lawrence opened the book and leafed through a few pages. He stopped at a page randomly, read for a minute, looked interested, then as if to scold himself, slammed the book shut and threw the messages for the soul into the cold fireplace.

When Jonathan arrived home, his mother, Mary Belcher, was waiting for him in the sitting room. "There you are!" she squeaked. A tall, thin Bostonian in her seventies, Mary had an annoying voice, the kind of high-pitched, whining voice that a neglected child sometimes develops in order to get attention. Even when she made a flat statement about the weather, it sounded like an irritating complaint. Perhaps living with her bullying husband for forty-seven years had had something to do with it. This grating tone of voice, unfortunately, prevented her from getting the attention she properly deserved as a quick-witted conversationalist. She was also a dutiful wife, and a practical, down-to-earth woman who adored her son. "Where's Miss Allen?" asked Jonathan.

"It's Abigail, Jonathan, dear. You need not refer to your bride-to-be anymore as 'Miss Allen'."

"I am not quite certain, mother, that she wants to be my bride."

"Well, my dear, she's here, isn't she? Why else do you think she has come to Halifax?"

"To negotiate a marriage contract, I presume."

"'Negotiate'? What a terrible, unromantic word!"

"I am not a romantic man, mother. I am a lawyer."

"Not tonight. Tonight you are a romantic suitor and don't you dare use that word 'negotiate' again!" she said with a smirk.

"And what word should I use, mother? Love? If I tell Miss Allen … Abigail … that I love her, she wouldn't believe me anyway. After all, I hardly know her."

"You know her as well as any man knows his wife before the wedding. And, no, you should not tell her you love her, but you could be honest and tell her that you need her."

Mary Belcher spoke bluntly. Old age had liberated her. In her long life she had played many roles – obedient daughter, responsible daughter; obedient wife, responsible wife. Lately she had cast aside those roles and began to play herself. Finally free, she spoke her mind. A liberated looseness now prevailed, a looseness she had achieved over the years by rolling with the punches and the low blows of outrageous fortune. She now rolled merrily along even when there were no punches in sight; relaxed, unrestrained, at times almost giddy with freedom. She felt especially free when she communicated thoughts and feelings to her son in a way she never could with her husband.

"Speaking of honesty, you told me that Abigail was twenty-four. I have recently been informed that she is twenty-eight."

"It doesn't matter. She's still a virgin."

"That's hearsay evidence, mother."

"Please stop talking like a lawyer for five minutes, Jonathan. You know perfectly well that she's a highly respectable girl. Besides, you're forty-six years old and that does not put you in a great bargaining position."

"Aha! Bargaining position! So, we are negotiating after all!"

Mary Belcher laughed. She was enjoying this banter with her son.

Jonathan enjoyed it, too. With his mother, as with no one else, he could completely relax because he knew that, in her loving eyes, he could do no wrong.

However, what she said about her son was true. He certainly was past any prime he might have earlier enjoyed, and was no great romantic catch even for a twenty-eight year old, lonely, eager-to-be-attached woman.

Like Lawrence, he was over six feet tall, but was paunchy and had a large double chin; or more correctly, his second chin was double the size of his first. His high forehead was believed by some to indicate intelligence, but actually it was just difficult to know where his forehead ended and his bald head began; and, Lawrence's insincere flattery aside, no one who knew Belcher well ever testified to his intelligence. As many unintelligent people do to acquire tone, he acted reserved, spoke little, seldom smiled, and in ticklish situations, always stood on his dignity even though, in some instances, he didn't have a leg to stand on. And whenever he felt challenged by inferiors, he demanded respect although he hadn't yet earned any on his own. It was the how-dare-you-accuse-me tactic of the man caught red-handed. His eyes bulged like those of a sufferer with a thyroid enlargement while his nose and mouth were disproportionately small giving him a naturally peevish look as if he were thinking, "I was meant for better places than this!" which he was not really thinking. Much of the time, he wasn't thinking at all. When he was, his thoughts usually settled on good food and fine wine. One final striking feature of his appearance was his small, pale-pink hands, a clear indication that he was not a man of the soil. "Abigail will be good for you, Jonathan. She will be a social asset to you here in Halifax because she loves to entertain. You will soon be the next governor of Nova Scotia and, believe me, as governor, you will need a hostess more often than you will need a lover. Your father was governor of both Massachusetts and New Jersey, so I speak from experience. Abigail Allen is the right girl for you."

"And what will father say? Will he be disappointed? His plan was always to have me marry a rich English girl?"

"I'm afraid there aren't as many available, rich English girls as there used to be. And at your age, why should you worry about your father's wishes?"

"I don't exactly worry, but it is only prudent not to invite his everlasting disapproval," said Jonathan.

"Ever since your father reached middle age, he has been in a mood of everlasting disapproval. I shall take care of your father for you." She paused and looked at her aging boy and smiled. "Are you ready? Shall I fetch Abigail now?"

"Now? Can't it wait until tomorrow? It's late and I've been drinking Madeira with Governor Lawrence."

"That's good. If Abigail is going to marry a government man, she should get accustomed to the smell of alcohol early. I'll fetch her. And remember my advice: if a woman doesn't feel *loved*, she'll settle for feeling *needed*."

Five minutes later, a plain but perky, five-foot, ninety-six pound, stereotypical dark-hair-in-a-bun spinster entered the sitting room, walked straight up to Judge Belcher, stuck out her tiny hand, curtsied, and stated in a strong, clear voice, "I understand it's time now for us to negotiate, sir."

The judge smiled in spite of himself. Abigail's use of the word 'negotiate' won him over completely. Even if she had been coached by his mother to use the word, that only proved that she was tractable, like a good horse. And if she had used the word completely on her own, she was obviously brilliant because, with identical vocabulary, she spoke *his* language. Therefore, she was either the right girl for him, or she was the right diplomat for him. Either way, she would do nicely. Jonathan relaxed and said, "I understand that you enjoy playing hostess."

"I do, sir. And I understand that you enjoy playing the bass viol and the flute. I find that house guests always enjoy a little music."

Jonathan smiled again. He had not smiled this much in years. "Well, I am in great need of a hostess." He paused. Abigail frowned. "And what is it that you need or hope to gain from our ... arrangement?"

"I would like to have children," said Abigail. "I love children."

"I shall do my part." He paused again. "And what else will you be requiring?"

"Honesty."

"Honesty?" he asked.

"If you ever grow tired of my company, I would like to be the first to know."

They stood for a moment in silence and stared into one another's eyes, he into her small, dark ones, she into his large, bulging ones. She was a full foot shorter and 110 pounds lighter, but she was all the woman he would need. "It's settled, then," he said quietly.

"Not yet," she said, smiling.

"What else must be done?"

"You have not yet asked me."

"Oh, that. Yes, well. Let me see. How shall I put this? Well, Miss ... Abigail, please take some time to consider the terms of our negotiations here tonight, and when we meet again in a few months I hope that you will agree at that time to my proposal of marriage."

"In a few months?" asked Abigail. "I had thought to remain here for a few weeks so we could get to know one another better."

"I'm afraid that that's impossible. You must return to Boston right away. Halifax will not be a safe place in the next few months. I am not at liberty to say much more at this time except to add that we may have some trouble here with the French inhabitants."

"I see. Well, should I leave tomorrow?"

"That would be best. There may be violence, and I would not want you caught in the crossfire. Nova Scotia is now a dangerous place."

"Well, I shall return to Boston, then." She smiled faintly and turned to go. When she reached the door, she regained her courage and asked, "Am I to assume that I am now *under contract*, sir?"

Jonathan grinned from ear to ear. He was positively beaming. "Most assuredly, you are, my dear. Most, most assuredly!"

Abigail, her hopes now restored, grinned back at him, and hurried out the door. "What a woman!" he said, as he watched her go. "What an absolutely splendid little woman!"

The next morning, Belcher's secretary, Richard Bellingham, delivered Belcher's 'piece of paper' to Lawrence. The document stated that the presence of the Acadians of Nova Scotia could no longer be tolerated since tolerating them would:

"1. - be contrary to the letter and spirit of the instructions of his majesty to Governor Cornwallis (in 1749);

"2. - render void and sterile the results of the expedition of Fort Beauséjour;

"3. - hamper the progress of establishment of English settlers and prevent realization of projects that Great Britain envisaged when it spent considerable sums in the province."

As soon as Bellingham left with the letter, Belcher felt ill. He tried to convince himself that last night's mixture of a late supper and too much Madeira was at fault. But he knew better: post-operative nausea and the unsettling interaction of politics and poetry still in his system. Dizzy from compliance, he felt bizarrely compromised, like the man who had campaigned against capitalism until his rich uncle died and left him the company.

But it was too late now, wasn't it? His system would have to adjust to his new condition. From now on, he would have to eat and drink politics, and purge himself of poetry, the less powerful element in the nauseating mixture.

Though poetry hath charms and may possibly improve the character of some people, in Belcher's case, it acted only like a mild drug, chemically producing in him sentiments which prompted him either to laugh, to cry, or to pray. But its chemical power proved too weak to convert his sentiments to backbone. As many drugs do, it promised more than it could deliver. The fine art of poetry elevated Belcher to finer feelings, but not to finer actions.

Well, he could atone later, couldn't he? He was sure to be handsomely rewarded and could use his fortune to accomplish some future good, some grand act of charity. Yes - snip! - that was all – snap! - that he could hope for. Some future goodness.

Snip! Snap!

Chapter Eighteen

If That Be the Case

July 19, 1755

How eerie! thought Charles Morris, the provincial surveyor. The silence in the governor's office was beginning to get on his nerves. Governor Lawrence stood quietly looking out the window. Vice-Admiral Boscawen sat grinding his teeth, clenching his fists, and staring at the floor, while Rear-Admiral Mostyn, his right eye blinking furiously, sat studying a bare space of wall. Morris squirmed in his chair, uneasy in a room with so much military muscle un-flexed - the three most powerful men in Halifax brooding like three wounded lions. Morris hardly dared to breathe. He was not exactly a timid man, but was only twenty-four years old at this time and anxious to perform well in his new high-paying job. As in a hospital ward thick with the odor of festering wounds, the room's air was heavy and nauseating. Boscawen "continued mute for some time, when on a sudden he started up, and with great emotion said, 'If that be the case, I then know what I have to do'." [1]

"I do not believe it," said Lawrence softly. "I simply do not believe it."

"Neither do I, but I'm afraid it's all too true," said Boscawen cocking his head to one side.

The unbelievable and shocking information that the three lions were finding so indigestible was the recent news of the death of their friend, Edward Braddock. General Braddock, the commander-in-chief of all

British forces in North America, was dead. Not only was he dead, but he was humiliatingly dead, he and five hundred of his men. They had been routed by a handful of Indians and Frenchmen near Fort Duquesne.[*] Adding insult to injury were confirmed reports that the Indians had been seen returning from the skirmish "clothed with the English regimentals." The loss was "a frightful embarrassment," an embarrassment because the enemy had lost only twenty-five, and frightful because if it could happen there, it could more easily happen here in Nova Scotia where the English were surrounded by Acadians and Mi'kmaqs every day.

"Shocking!" said Mostyn. "Absolutely shocking!"

"And ambushed, too!" said Lawrence shaking his head in disgust.

"Even as he was engaged in an orderly retreat!" said Boscawen.

"The same treatment they gave to brave Captain Howe[**] five years ago near Beauséjour. Murdered him in cold blood!" snarled Lawrence.

"And Howe had gone to all that trouble to learn the French language in order to communicate better with the wretched French," said Boscawen. "I advised him he was wasting his time."

"And Mi'kmaq, too," said Lawrence. "He even studied the Mi'kmaq language."

"And that's the gratitude he received! Savages! Absolute savages!" said Mostyn.

"It certainly was not a fair fight!" said Boscawen.

"And yet these Acadian vermin here expect - even demand - fair treatment from us every day," said Lawrence.

"Savages!" repeated Mostyn. "Filthy bush fighters with no sense of fair play!"

Morris sat like a stone. If he moved an inch, he might brush up against one of the thorns in the three, gigantic, festering paws. He looked down at his lap and re-read the first page of his report. Hearing the rustling of pages, Lawrence turned and said, "Well, Mr. Morris, what do you have for us?"

"The report you asked for, sir." Morris swung into officious action handing out copies of his report to each lion. "It's all here, sir, the numbers you wanted - the number of ships needed, the number of deportees per

---

[*]   Now Pittsburgh, Pennsylvania.
[**]   The admirable English Captain Edward Howe spoke French fluently and was very popular with the Acadians until Le Loutre's renegade band senselessly ambushed and killed him by the Missaquash River near Amherst, N. S. in 1750. Hence, Le Loutre's renegades unwittingly murdered a sympathetic Francophile.

ship, the amount of food necessary, the minimum armed escort, and so forth. It's all here, sir."

"Very efficient work, Mr. Morris," said Lawrence.

"Thank you, sir," said Morris.

"Is there anything else we should know?" asked Lawrence.

"Just some recommendations to avoid panic, sir."

"Ah, yes, and what are your recommendations in that regard?"

"We, of course, at all costs, want to avoid any sort of last-minute panic. It may be wise to spread a prophylactic rumor among the Acadians that they are merely being shipped to another French area of Canada," said Morris.

"Good idea!" said Lawrence. "Very good, Morris. Anything else?"

"The critical component of the rumor, sir, is that the Acadians must be made to feel that they are *all* being transported to the *same* French area," said Morris.

"Very wise, indeed," said Lawrence. "Anything more to add?"

"No, sir. The report, I think, will answer any other questions you may have," said Morris.

"It sounds to me as if you have a good man in your service here, Mr. Lawrence," said Mostyn, patronizingly.

"A good man, indeed," agreed Boscawen.

"Thank you, Mr. Morris. Splendid job!" said Lawrence.

When Morris had closed the door behind him, Lawrence said, "Well, gentlemen, please look over this report at your leisure. Let me know what you think of it. We shall have to meet several times in the next month. The work we are about to do has suddenly taken on an even greater urgency because now we must make absolutely certain that Eddie Braddock and Captain Howe did not die in vain."

****

Quite unexpectedly, the triumvirate met again the next morning. Lawrence and his adjutant, Mr. Stone, had walked down to the dock to request a launch to George's Island, the site of the prison. When they arrived at the dock, Rear-Admiral Mostyn was just about to leave in a launch for the island (a tiny drumlin just a short swim's length from the Halifax shore), so Lawrence and Stone joined him. Having recently gained so much weight that he looked like a balloon in uniform, the corpulent Mostyn had to be helped into the launch. His naval jacket's shiny brass buttons with the embossed English lion's head were ready to pop, to be sliced off by their own finely stitched buttonholes - heads about to roll. This noticeably nervous, fidgety man who exhibited a creative streak in the amazing variety of tics, twitches, and twinges he had developed over the years, was slowly but surely eating himself to death.

Just as they pushed off, they heard a loud roar of laughter from half a dozen sailors on an English trading vessel just arriving in the harbor. Mostyn cringed. Any kind of male laughter near him made him cringe these days. He took a deep breath and tried to calm himself. Perhaps the laughter had nothing to do with him this time. But suddenly, one of the brazen tars shouted, "All's well, Mr. Mostyn, sir! There's no Frenchman in the way!" And with that, the six catcallers laughed hysterically. Mostyn knew then that he had been recognized and that the sailors were indeed laughing at him. Humiliated beyond words, he sat in the launch with his head down, his bloated hands trembling with anxiety and indignation and, despite his authority, made no attempt to lash back. He secretly wished that a gaping hole would appear in the bottom of the boat large enough for him to slide into and disappear. His breathing quickened. Trapped he was, trapped once again even though he had traveled - *escaped*, he thought - five thousand miles across the ocean. It will not go away, he thought. No, it simply will not go away.

Seeing Mostyn in such misery, Lawrence thought of rowing to the ship, boarding it, and reprimanding the ruffians. But then he changed his mind.

What would not go away for Savage Mostyn was the scandal of ten years earlier, his court martial on the charge of cowardice. On December 29, 1744 the ship he commanded, the *Hampton Court*, and three other vessels were separated from the English fleet in a heavy fog. A week later, the *Hampton Court* and one of the other separated ships, the *Dreadnought*, came upon two French ships, the *Neptune* and the *Fleuron*. However, thinking that the French vessels were merchants and not warships, the captain of the *Dreadnought* allowed his ship to drift off in another direction. It was, therefore, two against one, and although there was an unwritten English naval rule about never running from a battle no matter how outnumbered, Mostyn chose to run. He refused to attack and the two Frenchmen sailed safely into Brest. His excuse later was that the waves were so high at the time that his lower-deck guns were under water.

Now, here he was ten years later still being ridiculed by common English sailors - hunted down, it seemed - even though he had been acquitted of the cowardice charge. The military court had decided that Mostyn "had done his duty as an experienced good officer, and as a man of courage and conduct." He was not, however, now being ridiculed because he had been *charged* with cowardice; nor was it because he had been let off the hook. Rather it was because the whole court martial itself had been a farce from start to finish.

In the first place, it had been publicized that Mostyn himself had requested the naval court martial in order to clear his name. What was not publicized was the fact that his uncle, Daniel Finch, his mother's brother, was First Lord of the Admiralty.* (Most people did know, however, that Mostyn's father had been a Member of Parliament.) And just for good measure, there was no prosecutor and no cross-examination. He couldn't lose. In fact, the only negative criticism he received at his court martial was that he was a pampered aristocrat with very little practical sailing experience. Even that was not true. He had been in the navy for the previous twenty years.

Mostyn suddenly felt hungry. His stomach growled even though he had finished breakfast just an hour earlier. He felt a great need to eat a few Frenchmen. He ate a few everyday now. Whenever he thought of those two goddam French ships sailing safely into Brest, a hunger grew inside him. To squelch it, he ate, and ate, and ate. And then the hunger went away. For a while. But later, while quietly reading, or while attempting to drown himself in ale and hearing raucous laughter behind him, or when catching, out of the corner of his eye, someone - even a perfect stranger - staring at him, the hunger in him rose again. Some days, he ate the *Neptune*. Others, the *Fleuron - the (Carved) Jewel,* the jewel in the French navy's crown, the jewel he allowed to sail away.

On a few special days, he ate both ships with all French hands on board. *That* was most satisfying! Every last one of them! Jewels and all!

Knowing all this, Charles Lawrence quietly sat in the launch and refrained from reprimanding the jeering sailors. He wanted the rear-admiral's humiliation to continue. It could only fuel Mostyn's hatred of the French and make it flare and explode. After all, the French were to blame for the loss of his reputation, weren't they? Mostyn's hatred would be a useful tool in the months ahead.

What a stroke of luck this taunt was, thought Lawrence. Mostyn surely wants to get even!

---

* Finch had just gone out of office as First Lord, but was eligible for re-appointment.

Mostyn sat in the launch with his head bowed in disgrace and despair. Where can I go? he thought. Where can I hide? How far do I have to run? How far? How far?

When they arrived on the island, Vice-Admiral Boscawen greeted them. When they saw each other, the three lions laughed at the coincidental similarity in their thinking that morning. To avenge Braddock's death, each wanted to get his hands on an Indian or a Frenchman as quickly as possible, and each had remembered that the prison on George's Island[2] held fifteen French-speaking Acadians. This trick of thought that had simultaneously brought them all to the island relaxed the three, and made them almost jovial. Boscawen grinned, tilting his head to one side. (His nickname was 'Wry-Necked Dick' for his odd habit of cocking his head to one side. He *should* have looked rather handsome, but his tilting head, his ice-blue eyes, and his light blond hair combined to give him more of a sly, cunning look. He looked especially sly when he flashed a tilted smile.) Fortunately, their relaxed joviality saved the life of at least one unsuspecting Acadian that morning. "Bring the prisoners out, sergeant!" shouted Lawrence to the prison guard.

"At least we can spit on a few of them," muttered Mostyn.

The Grand Pré delegates emerged from the dungeon squinting in the bright July sunshine. The humid morning air prompted some of the prisoners to take off their shirts. "They say they are ready now to take the oath, sir," said the sergeant.

"They are, are they?" asked Lawrence.

"That's what they say, sir," said the sergeant.

"Well, I am quite sure that their willingness does not proceed from an honest intention. They merely want to save their necks. Is the interpreter here?" asked Lawrence.

"Here, sir," said an English officer, as he stepped forward.

"Ask these scoundrels if they wish to take the oath now."

"Yes, sir." The interpreter spoke in French to the prisoners. They replied that they were still hesitant to take the oath, "Because we do not yet know in what manner the English will use us," said Paul Richard, the father of the twins.

"What impertinence!" declared Lawrence. "Has the world ever seen such ingratitude!" Lawrence walked in front of each prisoner and looked into his face. "I thought that a few weeks in this dreadful hole would have softened them up. But I see that they're as impudent as ever."

"Let me deal with them!" said Boscawen, losing his composure. Lawrence's words, and the thoughts of their dead friend, Braddock, were inciting Boscawen to violence. He slid his sword from its sheathe and raised it above the head of Paul Richard. Paul stepped back and said, "Perhaps you are forgetting, sir, that we are Neutrals."

"Frappez-moi, monsieur, si vous osez!"* Joseph Doiron, the oldest delegate from Grand Pré, stepped forward from the back of the line and brazenly faced the admiral. "Avancez! Je serai le premier martyr entre nous. Vous pouvez tuer mon corps, mais vous ne pouvez pas tuer mon âme!"**

Boscawen, furious, wanted to decapitate the old man but Lawrence stayed his hand. "Wait, sir. They know something! They know something!"

"Know something?" shouted Boscawen. "What could these blackguards possibly know?"

"They are far too confident. They have some new knowledge, some new information. A French fleet must be coming this way, or some French infantry coming here from Louisbourg. They know something! Otherwise, what could account for such arrogance from condemned men?" asked Lawrence. Then he turned to Paul Richard and said, "You may try to hide behind that label 'Neutrals', but with another war brewing between England and France, you will be something worse than neutral, sir. You will be irrelevant!"

Boscawen bristled. Rendered impotent by Lawrence's caution, he tilted his head, shuddered with outrage, and sheathed his sword.

"But, in time of war, neutrality must be respected," said Paul.

"Not while I'm in charge here!" roared Lawrence. "That old game won't work with me! I know the game that Neutrals play. They want to stand aside in safety, and when the war is over, they expect to enjoy the same benefits as the victors although they themselves have taken no risks whatsoever. No, sir, I tell you, not while I'm in charge here! Not while I'm in charge!" Lawrence then stepped to one side and shouted, "Take the prisoners back to their cells!"

The prisoners turned and started back towards the dungeon. Old Joseph Doiron didn't move. He was still glaring at Admiral Boscawen who was glaring back at him. Mostyn stood to one side, looking on. The old Frenchman's disrespect made his blood boil. Not having worn his sword on this hot morning, he instead approached Monsieur Doiron and, with

---

* "Strike me, sir, if you dare!"
** "Go ahead! I shall be the first martyr among us! You can kill my body, but you can't kill my soul!"

his left eye furiously twitching, spat in the old man's face. Then he turned and strode quickly back to the launch. Old Doiron wiped the spit from his face with his sleeve, grinned victoriously, turned away, and swaggered off to catch up with his friends.

Chapter Nineteen

No Priest, No Wedding

August 4, 1755

"Hurry, Evangéline, hurry! We have to help Father Chauvreulx! He's going to be arrested!" shouted Cécile.

Evangéline, startled, left her spinning wheel to see what the twins were excited about this time. "We have to go to the church right now to help Father Chauvreulx!"

"Why? What is going on? Why would anyone arrest a priest? *Who* is arresting him?"

"It's true! Father Chauvreulx told us! He said that Father Le Maire at Rivière aux Canards will also be arrested!" said Céleste, breathlessly.

"And Father Dauphin at Piziquid!" said Cécile.

"It's Daudin, Cécile!" scolded Céleste.

"But that is crazy!" said Evangéline. "Why are they arresting priests?"

"I don't know. But Father Chauvreulx said he needs the help of at least three young people, so we came to get you," said Cécile. "Hurry! He's waiting at the church for us now!"

The three girls ran as fast as they could to St. Charles des Mines. When they arrived, the twins curtsied in flawless synchronization, and Evangéline followed suit a full second later. Looking up, they saw a forty-nine year-old Jesuit in a complete panic. "It's so unnecessary, so unnecessary!" he sputtered. "All of this did not have to happen, you know. So unnecessary!"

"Yes, Father," was all the girls could say.

"Not at all necessary. Those delegates could have taken the oath, you know, and none of this would be happening now. Stubborn men! They think they know more than their priests! It's pride, you know. The greatest sin! Now look at the mess we're in."

"Yes, Father," said the girls.

"It's only a political oath, not a religious oath. A political oath is not a *real* oath, not a *sacred* oath. It's only a temporal one. Political oaths are not eternal; they change with every change of governor. Poor Governor Hopson lasted only a year and a half. So unnecessary!" Father Chauvreulx raved on while the three girls nodded their agreement with every word he uttered. He removed the cover of the mass ciborium and turned to the girls. "Here, now, open your mouths and receive the body of Christ. These communion hosts were left over from this morning's mass, and they must be consumed by Catholics before the heretics arrive to take me away." Evangéline opened her mouth and piously closed her eyes. "Corpus domine nostri Jesu Christi." The communion ritual had to be repeated six times for each girl. "Thank you, my children," said Father Chauvreulx. "Now, go in peace. God will surely protect you from all harm today. You have been honored many times by the body of Christ. Go now, and God bless you."

"Will they arrest you today, Father?" asked Evangéline. "Maybe you should let the Mi'kmaq hide you."

"No, my child. I will not run and hide like a guilty fugitive. I have done nothing wrong. Besides, in a way, I hope it will be today. Today is the Feast Day of St. Dominique, a holy man who spent years fighting Albigensian heretics in France. I'm beginning to feel that, on this day, I am in good company."

"Is there anything else we can do for you, Father?" asked Evangéline.

"You have already helped me a great deal. Merci beaucoup, beaucoup."

"Where will they take you, Father? Will they harm you?" asked Evangéline.

"I don't know where they will take me. To Québec, to France, I don't know. But I don't believe the English will harm me. Their policy now is to discourage and to inconvenience." Evangéline looked at the priest with tears in her eyes. "Now don't cry, my child. I'll be fine. Everything will be all right. Just pray for me."

"But our wedding, Father! Gabriel and I are getting married a month from now and there'll be no priest here to perform our wedding ceremony."

"Oh, dear, I forgot about that. Yes, well, I can only promise that I shall try my best to be back here as soon as possible. Just pray, Evangéline. Pray hard, my child. Pray very hard."

Evangéline left the church. Outside, the twins stood waiting for her. "Don't you feel holier than you ever have before in your life?" asked Cécile. "I know I do. My stomach is full of God."

"Mine, too," said Céleste.

A short time later, Céleste and Cécile again knocked frantically on Evangéline's door. "Come in," said Evangéline to the breathless twins. "What's the matter now?"

"They've done it! They've taken Father Chauvreulx away![1] About an hour ago, four English soldiers arrested him!"

"Where are they taking him?" asked Evangéline.

"Everyone says that he is being taken to Halifax, and that he and Father Daudin of Piziquid, and Father Le Maire of Rivière aux Canards will all be shipped off to France," said Céleste. "All of our priests are going back to France."

"To France? But why not to Québec or to Louisbourg?" asked Evangéline.

"We don't know," said Cécile. "Oh, Evangéline, what will we do now? We have no one to say mass for us!"

"And on Sunday, we'll miss communion for the first time since we made our first communion five years ago," said Céleste.

"Oh, by the way, here is a gift for you from Father Chauvreulx. It's a new rosary. Look, he gave one to each of us for helping him with the extra communion hosts," said Cécile. She handed Evangéline a new rosary with white beads that shone like mother-of-pearl.

"Merci," said Evangéline, touched by the generous gift . "Poor Father Chauvreulx! Such a kind man! He was thinking of others even as he was being arrested."

"Mine has green beads," said Cécile proudly.

"And mine has black beads," said Céleste.

Evangéline thought she detected a note of disappointment in Céleste's voice. "Perhaps you'd rather have the white beads," said Evangéline holding out her white rosary.

"Oh, no," said Céleste, "black is the color of a nun's rosary. I wouldn't trade mine for the world!"

The three girls looked at one another silently. They were happy with their gifts, but fear of the future overshadowed their joy. Céleste broke down in tears. Evangéline said, "Perhaps we should say some prayers for Father Chauvreulx on our new rosaries. Let's pray that he'll be returned to us soon."

"Yes, let's pray," said Cécile, "and for the other priests, too."

"We'll pray for all of the priests and for everyone in our village," said Evangéline. "We'll pray that God will keep us all safe."

"And let's pray that they won't arrest us, too," added Cécile.

Chapter Twenty

Enter Colonel John Winslow

August 19, 1755

High on the south ridge above the village, two Mi'kmaq sentinels, with enchanted alarm, saw them first. Five large English[1] vessels were sailing, one behind the other, into Minas Basin. In the full wind, their sails bulged like great white stomachs straining towards the dinner table.

Half an hour later, others noticed. Cécile's mouth dropped open. "Look!" she gasped and pointed towards the shore. Céleste's eyes widened. Strangers were marching towards their village. Soldiers! More soldiers! The twins had never seen so many uniforms. They considered running off to inform others, but not wanting to miss a thing, they just stood there speechless as Colonel John Winslow's army of 313 men marched up from the shore and into the peaceful village of Grand Pré.

Upon arrival, Winslow found a translator and immediately issued orders to the villagers. "I bring orders to you from Governor Lawrence. I shall inform you of those orders in the days ahead. In the meantime, I shall use the priest's house for my personal lodging, and the church as my command post."

A wave of shocked silence swept over the residents. They could not express a protest in English, nor could they in French since they knew of no precedent, in any language, for such blasphemy. "Because your parish priest, who was arrested two weeks ago is not here to do so, some of you must remove the religious objects from the church immediately." The twins, volunteering for the sacred task, took a step forward. Their mother, Héloise, seized their collars and pulled her daughters back. "During our stay here, my men and I will also need food supplies for which you will be paid. We are not here to interrupt your harvesting. Please continue to reap your crops."

Héloise Richard stood holding the hands of her twins. She looked the soldiers up and down. Then she mumbled, "Alors, nous serons gardés par des souillons! Ils ne sont même pas en grande tenue!"*

Within three days a picket fence was erected around the church grounds, and the soldiers were billeted in over a hundred white military tents.

Colonel John Winslow, a short, stout man, had been recommended for the "unpleasant" task by Governor Shirley of Massachusetts, Lawrence's friend. Shirley did not want the business at Grand Pré to turn into a complicated mess, and John Winslow was a man who believed in keeping things simple. A stolid man, he dealt with only one thing at a time, and seldom took any initiative on his own. Thinking of alternatives only caused confusion. When he was given an order, he obeyed it; when he was given a job, he did it. Simple. No good could be accomplished by looking at all sides of a question. There were only two sides; the wrong way and the army's way. Besides, even if he were to consider all aspects of a situation, he would just end up realizing that his own position was, after all, the best one possible. So, why bother? The perfect soldier.

Winslow was a member of the Massachusetts establishment, as limited as it was at that time. His father was the Honorable Isaac Winslow of Marshfield. His great grandfather, Edward, had come over on the Mayflower, and had been a governor of Plymouth Colony. Like most military men, Colonel John relished nothing more than the offer of a key post, and not only had he accepted the job of occupying Grand Pré, he had applied for it. His application read:

---

* "So, we are to be guarded by a bunch of slobs! They are not even dressed in full uniform!" It was true. Winslow's soldiers had been issued only the blue tunics of army uniforms. Their breeches were buckskin.

"I come from one of the oldest and
most respected families. No one can raise
an army faster than I can for this mighty and noble task."

He got the job. He and his men were now firmly entrenched in Grand Pré, and not one of the Acadians clearly understood why.

Chapter Twenty-one

The Leopard

August 20, 1755

The five-inch night crawler wriggled in panic, behaving the way all night crawlers do when they are about to be impaled. Evangéline tried harder. Finally, the dull barb of her fishhook penetrated the squirming worm's epithelium, and slimy plasma oozed out on her fingertips. She yawned, nonchalantly wiped the slime on the side of the fishing basket, and dropped the fishhook over the side of Gabriel's makeshift raft. Observing her, as he always did, Gabriel said, "You're a brave girl."

"Brave? Why?"

"Lots of other girls wouldn't do that."

"Do what?"

"Handle night crawlers."

"Oh, I'm not brave. My father taught me when I was little. I've done it all my life."

Gabriel smiled, "Quel beau trésor!"*

It was true that she had been taught many useful tasks. She knew how to sew, spin, weave, and embroider. She could harness the horses, shear the sheep, and herd the cows to pasture. Without blinking an eye, she could chop off a chicken's head and prepare a fricassee. In a pinch,

---

* "What a beautiful treasure (you are)!"

she could slaughter a pig and cure its pork. Moreover, like all the other girls, she had been taught, by Monsieur Beliveau* to cultivate a healthy orchard. Best of all, she could churn butter, prepare curds and cheese, bake bread, make ployes, press cider, and brew nut-brown ale. Quel beau trésor, certainment!

It was Saturday and, though they were fishing their usual bountiful spot, after two hours they hadn't caught a single fish. "It's those ships!" said Gabriel. "They've scared away all the fish!" Evangéline looked up and saw Winslow's fleet, aligned in a radiating arc, in the Minas Basin. The tall ships rocked and creaked with each heave and sigh of the sea.

Refusing to give up, they fished for another half hour and didn't notice when their homemade raft drifted into the shadow of one of the fleet. "Hey! You there! Shove off!" yelled a scruffy, bearded sailor from the vessel's stern. "No one's allowed out here! Shove off, I say!"

Startled, and without understanding the sailor's English, Gabriel seized a pole and quickly steered the raft away from the shadow of the schooner. As he paddled away with the sun in his eyes, he squinted at the stern of the ship. Its name had been burnt with a hot poker into a simple square of wood.

"L_E_O_P_A_R_D," Evangéline spelled out. "Hmmmm," she said, "It's the name of an animal."

"A wild animal!"

"Yes, a wild animal," she said. "An animal so fast, they say, it can run like the wind."

---

* A variety of apple, the Beliveau, was later named for him.

Chapter Twenty-two

Impasse At the Aboiteau

"Ni trop près, ni trop loin."[*]
Late August, 1755

In a rare display of curiosity, Colonel Winslow told his interpreter, Monsieur Landry, that he wanted to watch the dyke repair work going on a mile up the coast from Grand Pré village. Captains Osgood and Adams also were to go along as security for Winslow.

When they arrived at the site, Winslow was surprised to see Benedict Bellefontaine laboring alongside men half his age. Winslow grinned at Benedict's vigor. He and Benedict were the same age, and Winslow knew he could never put in a long day of physical labor. "Tell him he's too old for such work," said Winslow to his interpreter.

Monsieur Landry translated and Benedict laughed and said, "This is what keeps me young, monsieur."

"How does a dyke like this work, sir?" asked Winslow.

Benedict smiled, happy to explain. "If it were not for our aboiteaux, monsieur, all of this fertile land would be under sea water. We build each one on a creek. This sluice allows the heavy rains to drain off into the ocean at low tide, and the gate here closes when the tide comes in and pushes against it."

---

[*] "Neither too near, nor too far" was the motto of the Saint-Castin family. It could have been the motto for all of the Acadians, a French-speaking people who were no longer tied to France, a people in the middle, caught between. (Jean Daigle)

"I see," said Winslow. "Quite ingenious!"

"Some of these aboiteaux have been here for over a hundred years. Our ancestors built them. They came from La Rochelle," boasted Benedict.

"And who taught your ancestors to build dykes?"

"They learned from the Dutch, monsieur, or so I've been told," replied Benedict.

"And who instructed the Dutch?" asked Winslow.

"I don't know, monsieur."

"It was *English* engineers who taught the Dutch. You didn't know that, did you?" said Winslow.

John Winslow's personality was a lot like Charles Lawrence's, but more aseptic, and only slightly less spiteful. Like Lawrence, he behaved as though every situation in life were a competition, and he played to win. He also had the uncanny ability to assess his chances. If he thought he couldn't win, he didn't play. He, therefore, avoided any doubtful contest, broke off any relationship he could not dominate, and failed to show up at any meeting that promised formidable opposition to his ideas. When he did attend, he would stoop to any level to win the argument. He shamelessly distorted statistics, magnified irrelevancies, mocked and minimized opposing testimony, and never failed to include a few demoralizing ad hominems, smiling all the while. His opponent, at this point sensing defeat, would lower his head, back off, and whisper to an ally something like, "Well, he won't be in this job forever"; or, "Someday he'll insult the wrong man and that will be the end of him!" And, like Lawrence, he was a masterful intimidator who could easily make a beautiful woman feel unattractive, and a millionaire feel financially insecure.

Benedict frowned and scratched his head. A minute earlier he had thought Winslow seemed friendly. Now he was not so sure. Was Winslow telling the truth about English engineers, or was he insulting Benedict's intelligence? However, to avoid a serious confrontation, Benedict said diplomatically, "Well, together then, the Dutch and the English help us to keep away our only enemy, Mother Nature. Only the tides and the early frosts are our true enemies."

"And are we English not your natural enemies, too?"

"We only want to keep you, like the sea tide, off our farmland. We only want to be left alone to farm and to live in peace, monsieur. That is all we ask. That is all we pray for, daily."

Benedict looked so sincere that Winslow softened. "Well, sir, you have 'naturally' occupied very strategic ground. You block our way to the west where the fur trade is, and you block our way to the east where the world's greatest fishing grounds are."

"But we are neither fur traders nor full-time fishermen, monsieur."

"Perhaps it's true that you and your neighbors have no political or military ambitions. Still, you may provide the foundation which other more ambitious Frenchmen may build upon."

"We are not a foundation for anyone but ourselves, Monsieur. We're mere farmers, nothing else."

"Perhaps that is true. Nevertheless, you do occupy very strategic ground," said Winslow.

"With all due respect, sir, because our French governors have been just as harsh as our English ones, our only strategy is to stay equally far away from both."

"Perhaps, then, we should leave it at that. It is all Mother Nature's fault that we are enemies. Let's just blame it all on Mother Nature and geography."

This conclusion to lay the blame elsewhere, specious though it was, went unchallenged. Benedict simply nodded his head. The conclusion was incorrect and not at all logical, but then, the world was no longer a logical place. Benedict, solid and stable, did not panic easily. However, the recent disappearance of logic in Nova Scotia disturbed him. A mad syllogism now seemed to have control of his orderly world, a syllogism with a fallacious major premise, an invalid minor one, and an absurd conclusion: *something terrible will happen soon in Grand Pré; this terrible something will undoubtedly happen to you and to your neighbors; therefore, this terrible something will all be the fault of geography.*

Winslow looked at Benedict, cleared his throat, and quietly said, "Good day to you." Then he turned and walked towards his waiting horse.

Shaking off his disturbing thoughts, Benedict asked, "Before you go, monsieur, may I ask why your ships' guns are always pointed towards our village?"

"In the next few days, I shall be transferring some of my troops to other areas of the province. The ships are merely positioned for easy loading. There is no need for you to worry."

"I pray each day that your great King George will not molest a land that is strong only in its weakness," said Benedict.

"Prayer may be helpful to you, but if I were you, I would spend some more time re-thinking my position on taking the unconditional oath. You and your neighbors may be given one last chance to take it. You have a certain amount of influence in the community, and you could save your people a lot of hardship by persuading them to swear the full oath of allegiance," said Winslow.

Benedict smiled, lowered his head, and shook it as though he were hearing some tired old refrain. "Your Governor Lawrence thinks that an oath guarantees him one hundred percent allegiance. But I never get one hundred percent loyalty even from my paid farm workers, and many of them are my friends," said Benedict. Then he said more seriously, "Besides, Monsieur, men cannot work when they are always on their knees to someone." He paused for a reaction. Winslow was now glowering at him impatiently. "We all have to learn to move about with a small amount of uncertainty in our lives, monsieur."

"I'm afraid Governor Lawrence will not accept that argument," Winslow said, as he walked back to Benedict and spoke only inches from his face, "The complete oath is your only hope."

"Then, if you don't kill us, the Mi'kmaq will," said Benedict.

Winslow looked confused. "I thought the Mi'kmaq were your friends."

"Sometimes they are, monsieur. But the last time we took an oath of allegiance, the Indians raided our village and burned our homes."

"The Indians are savages. No one understands why they do the things they do."

"Not exactly, monsieur. When they see us signing pacts with the English, they believe that all of the white men are joining forces against them. The Mi' kmaq are intelligent people."

"But that's the fault of your own Jesuit priests. They control the minds of the Mi'kmaq, and the minds of your people," said Winslow.

"We wish to be controlled by no one, monsieur. We want only to be neutral, and to live in peace. To live only in peace."

Winslow raised his voice. "And were your people *neutral* at Fort Beauséjour two months ago? Do you remember that? Over three hundred so-called neutral Acadians tried to fight off our troops there! Do you call that 'neutral'?"

"They were given no choice, sir. They were ordered to fight, and if they had refused, they would have been shot." Benedict paused and looked at Colonel Winslow. "Please try to understand, monsieur. It seems to be our fate that we have enemies who don't even know who we are. We are Acadians. Acadians, sir. We speak the French language, but we are Acadians more than we are Normans, or Basques, or Bretons. We are no more in love with France than you are." Winslow felt that he was being lectured, but he was more puzzled than irritated. "And we are Christians, above all. If we show loyalty to France, you despise us. If we show loyalty to you, both the French and the Mi'kmaq call us traitors. We risk our lives every day that we supply your soldiers with food and drink. We risk our lives every time we help you repair your fortifications; and we risk our lives if we don't. To keep ourselves alive then, we must be loyal to everyone and to no one in particular. And all we wish is to be left alone. We have no wish to rule the world, sir. We are ambitious only for peace."

The two adversaries stood face to face and looked into each other's eyes. Each understood, more fully now, that the other's position was immovable. After a long pause, Winslow quietly said, "Well then, sir, there is nothing more to be said." He turned away and mounted his horse.

Benedict shouted after him, "You belong to a brave and generous nation and—" But Winslow, without looking back, rode off in the direction of his quarters.

Chapter Twenty-three

A Loving Ritual

A barn-and-house-raising* is a joyous event. It begins as a communal act of love and it ends with a communal act of intoxication.[1] The workers arrive in the early morning in a good mood and, although they work like oxen all day, go home in the evening in an even better mood. It's one of those special days of the year when something constructive is accomplished and the men are expected to get pleasantly drunk, all for a good cause.

The men are also expected to take advantage of the opportunity to make risqué remarks, especially when they are hammering away, for example, in the bedroom area of the engaged couple's house. One bawdy remark leads to another. A scandalous double-entendre is followed by an atrociously lewd pun, and on and on it goes all day long. Today the barn and house were for Evangéline and Gabriel.

Evangéline was nervous. The tawny cream foam spilled over the rims of the amber ale glasses and onto the pewter tray as she gingerly tiptoed her way to the construction site. She was happy when the delicious odor of fresh pine sawdust replaced the musky aroma of ale in her pretty nose. Other village ladies, also mindful of the venerable nectar, carefully approached from all directions. Their trays carried a darker ale rich in the color - and almost the density - of russet potatoes. Fat tender chunks of ham, and large

---

* Acadian log homes and barns were built with the logs set vertically. The horizontal log cabin design did not appear until the Swedes came to Canada and introduced it.

loaves of bread like giant toadstools with beige stems and bronze tops still steaming from the oven completed the moving still life.

Unable to resist the temptation to be first, 'Tit N'Ours, the village joker, jiggled in an upstairs window-hole and shouted, "Look, Evangéline, I'm dancing in your bedroom!" Evangéline blushed. 'Tit N'Ours (Little Bear) loved to joke and tease. 'Tit N'Ours was a nickname he had received as a baby. Apparently when he had scampered across the floor on all fours he looked exactly like a chubby little pink bear.

He was now a very large pink bear whose funniest jokes were, unfortunately, always at somebody else's expense. But since he picked on everyone equally, no one took offense for long. His real name was Joseph Blanchard.

"That'll be enough of that," said one of the older men to 'Tit N'Ours.

It was also part of the barn-raising ritual that the older men, at appropriate moments, should appear shocked at the vulgarity of the younger ones. "Don't pay any attention to him, Evangéline," said another of the elders.

Gabriel blushed also. He put down his hammer and went to greet his sweetheart. Evangéline wanted to, but didn't dare kiss him for fear of prompting another embarrassing comment. She took his hand and led him under a nearby tree where he could eat the lunch she had prepared for him. The other women, too, some quiet, some laughing, led their men away to shady spots where they could describe for them, in vivid detail, their eventful morning spent in minding the children and feeding the chickens. Some prankster suddenly whistled appreciation for the female form and everybody laughed. The sun shone warmly, and it was peaceful now that the hammers and handsaws were idle. The only sounds were the caws of black crows high in the pines and the cries of gray-and-white seagulls as they swooped and soared, complaining all the while, above the copper-colored shore.

The only two men still standing were Benedict and Basil, the fathers of the betrothed. The two fathers, acting as supervisors, (also part of the ritual), were going through the motions of critically inspecting the new buildings. Had either one detected a carpenter's error, he would not for all the world have pointed it out to anyone. Yet even the two fathers couldn't resist the masculine temptations of this day, and Benedict made the lovers blush again when he announced, "We shall all be glad when this house rings with the laughter of our grandchildren."

"And this is a day," Basil added, "we should all be thankful for because it brings our whole community together. And in such uncertain times as these, we need to spend more time together."

"Please, no speeches today!" shouted 'Tit N'Ours. Everyone laughed, and Basil, naturally reticent, blushed and was now sorry he had tried to say anything.

In the middle of his meal, Gabriel wanted a kiss. He looked cautiously around. The others seemed preoccupied. He took his napkin, leaned towards Evangéline and pretended to wipe away a crumb from her mouth. She smiled and looked at him with adoring eyes. She felt the napkin touch her lower lip. When his lips were about to take the napkin's place, she whispered, "Not too blue now, my love. My father's here."

After he had kissed her, Gabriel looked serious. "Evangéline?"

"Yes, my love?"

"There's something that I need to ask you."

"What is it, Gabriel?" she asked.

Gabriel looked around to see if anyone else might hear him. "Well, … it's … just that I want to be a good husband."

"I'm sure you will be a wonderful husband," said Evangéline.

"And I want to be a … a … good lover, too." Evangéline blushed and lowered her eyes.

There was a long pause as Gabriel gathered his thoughts. "Well, Pierre says that—"

"Oh, has Pierre been giving you lessons in politics *and* in love?" Then she whispered, "I'm sure you won't need advice from any of your friends."

"I need … to … be certain, that's all," said Gabriel.

"Well, what is it, then?"

Gabriel took a deep breath. Too self-conscious to look at her when he spoke, he lowered his eyes and said, "Pierre says that … that … Elizabeth Anne likes … a variety of … excitements … and I don't know what that means … exactly."

Evangéline smiled, put her hand under her lover's chin and lifted it. "Some of your friends have taken advantage of poor Elizabeth Anne. Everybody knows that." Then she looked straight into Gabriel's dark brown eyes and whispered, "When we are alone together, absolutely alone, that will be excitement enough for me."

Gabriel gulped. "Well, Pierre says that girls like surprises. He says they like to be shocked, too."

"Surprised, yes. But shocked, no, no, no."

"But I'm not very good at surprises," he said. "You are my surprise. You surprise me everyday. The way the sun shines on your hair. How the light inside you brightens your eyes."

"Oh, Gabriel, what a beautiful thing to say!"

"Are you surprised?"

"Shocked!"

As if to rebuke the lovers for their secular concerns, the Angelus rang from the steeple of St. Charles. Everyone stopped eating lunch, knelt automatically, and said the noontime prayer. "Behold the handmaid of the Lord./ Be it done unto me according to thy word./ And the Word was made flesh./ And dwelt among us."

The warm sun continued to shine, the men went back to work, the women returned home to their children, and the rest of the glorious barn-and-house-raising day proceeded just as it should have according to the unwritten, but indispensable ritual. By day's end, the grinning, exhausted workmen were safely home and appropriately scolded for "overdoing it", and by week's end the new barn would be filled with hay, and the house stocked with food enough to last a year.

Later that evening, Evangéline was about to say good night to her father. She ran her hand over the linen and woolen stuffs she had made for her new home. "Mon père?" she said.

"What is it, my dear?"

"Will Gabriel and I ever get to live in our new house? Will Governor Lawrence spoil everything for us?"

"He will bring no harm upon your house!" Benedict clenched his fist. "*He will bring no harm—*"

"Don't upset yourself, father."

"We built your house and barn because we must keep moving forward. We can't give in to doubts and fears about our future, about the dangers that may lie ahead for us. Forward. We must move forward. We must! We must! Just stay close to Gabriel from now on. Stay close to me, too. Whatever happens, we must all stay together."

"Oui, mon père. Bonsoir, mon père."

Chapter Twenty-four

A Tentative Date

The wedding day was set, almost in defiance, defiance against the rearing of pessimism's ugly head. Saturday, September 6, was a tentative date, of course, since no wedding could take place without a priest to officiate, and the priests had all been arrested. But it was important for their lives to go on, less with defiance than with hope. The residents of Grand Pré could not allow their spirits to be dampened daily by the presence of Colonel Winslow's army, and went about their business as normally as they could. It was not easy, however, because the sight each morning of those hateful white army tents, like large white galls of mites blotting the great meadow, renewed the pain that had temporarily been remedied by sleep. They felt an even deeper stab of pain at the sight of English army uniforms moving in and out of their sacred building, the church of St. Charles des Mines. Yet, as difficult as that blasphemy was to absorb, the village elders, Benedict among them, assured everyone that the church could easily be re-consecrated once the barbarians had left Grand Pré and marched off to harass other Acadians in other areas of the province. All would yet be well, they firmly believed, despite the overwhelming evidence to the contrary.

Evangéline kept herself busy preparing her new house for occupancy. Every day she furnished it with some new piece of handiwork - a blanket, a towel, or an apron. On the mantle above the hearth, she arranged some pewter plates and candlesticks that had belonged to her mother. Her father had given her the large wooden linen chest and one of their cozy black bearskins to drape festively over it. He also had filled the chest with fragrant cedar boughs. So far, though, the only actual furniture was a kitchen table and two chairs. And although the fresh smell of the squared-log walls and the birch-bark insulation betrayed its recent construction, the place was beginning to feel like home.

After working all day in the blacksmith shop, Gabriel brought to their new habitat tools, barrels, harnesses, and several layers of tanned leather from which he would later make shoes, saddlebags, and some haversacks to be used either as feedbags for their horses, or as apple carriers at apple-picking time.

Together, in their new house, the lovers worked side by side every evening, planning, praying, anticipating, and dreaming of their wedding day. But each night at nine, the sound of the cursed curfew, their dreaded and infuriating bête noire, sent them scurrying home to their parents like humiliated dependents. With the English occupation lingering like a poisonous, suffocating mist, life in the village became more and more unendurable. Gabriel, though he hated to admit it, began to believe that Pierre was right after all: the English befouled *every* aspect of their daily lives.

Chapter Twenty-five

They Have Befouled Our House

September 4, 1755

All summer long, a sickness slowly spread itself through the village, a sickness ignored in conversation as if talk of it might hasten and intensify its impact. The symptoms of this insidious malady included a gradual debilitation, a general loss of appetite, restlessness, and a rising fever accompanied by disorientation and mental confusion, especially among the elderly; nausea that could be relieved only by a series of unlikely reassurances; and worst of all, palpitations, irregular beats in a thousand hearts whose normal rhythm had been disturbed by anxiety over an uncertain future. Unspoken fears were the pathogens. Dread was metastasizing. More than ever, it was a time for fervent prayer, with prayer providing the only medication that seemed practical and that held any hope for a permanent cure. But even their prayers were weakened by the local contagion as they rose listlessly heavenward, secularized outside the walls of St. Charles des Mines, the dispossessed sanctuary blighted now by the boots of the malignant military invader.

Despite the poor morale of the villagers, it was another lovely autumn day in Acadia. The air was warm when the sun shone, and slightly cool when passing clouds blocked the sun's rays. The hills to the south were splotched with the reds and yellows of the already frostbitten oak, alder, birch, and maple leaves. But because the summer had been a dry one, the colors of the leaves were subdued and muted, missing the moisture that would have made them blaze. This autumn, there was only rust on the iron hills, and the pale birch leaves were so bleached and leeched of their yellow that you could easily see the paper in their future.

The villagers, gathering once again at Pierre's house, tried hard to rise above their misery, and tried not to mind that summer was, once again, turning its back on them and moving south.

Benedict stood to speak. "Tomorrow, in the church, Colonel Winslow will ask the men and boys to take the *unconditional* oath of allegiance. That, we think, is the main purpose of the meeting. We will, of course, refuse to take that oath. We *will agree* to take the *conditional* oath that our fathers took. And we believe that, if we all stand firm on this, we will prevail in this battle of wills."

"With all due respect, sir, what if we do *not* prevail in this?" urged Pierre.

Basil spoke up. "We don't know what will happen. We have made inquiries every day, but we've gathered no useful information. We've begged Colonel Winslow, his officers, and the ship captains and their crews to tell us what is going on. No one talks. They've all been sworn to secrecy."

"Someone said that we were all being sent to Louisbourg," said Pierre.

"That's a possibility," said Benedict.

Oliver Commo said, "I heard that they are sending us—"

"… to Québec," finished Berthe. Oliver glared angrily at her. She looked confused for a minute and then lowered her eyes.

"I heard it was to Isle Saint Jean,"* said Paul Richard who had just returned with the other delegates from the prison on George's Island. Lawrence had released them after all. Only Paul and one other delegate were well enough to attend this meeting. Both men had lost weight and had dark circles under their eyes. The other delegates were home in bed too weak to walk. Since July 5 they had been fed only water, a slice of bread, and one ounce of meat per day.

"That's also a possibility," said Basil. "But the truth is that we just don't know what the English will do with us."

"They're always saying one thing and doing another. They said they wouldn't release us from prison, and yet here we are," said Paul.

---

* Isle Saint Jean is now Prince Edward Island.

"Well, no matter where they send us," said old Oliver, "with the help of the Mi'kmaq, we can always find—"

"… our way back home," concluded Berthe.

Everyone cheered on that hopeful note, except Oliver. "Oh, what's the use!" he mumbled.

"That's right," said big Jean Arsenault, "and when we return, the English will have packed up and left." More cheers. The crowd relaxed. Maybe things were not so bad after all. Québec was five hundred miles away, but Louisbourg was only half that distance.

Benedict, however, was getting annoyed. "I tell you, we will not be going anywhere! The English are all bluff! When they see that we are firm in our refusal, they will sigh, scratch their heads, hold meetings about us until they are sick of going to meetings, curse us, and then move on to some other project. A year from now they'll be involved in some new conquest, and they won't even remember why Colonel Winslow came here to Grand Pré in the first place! If there's another undiscovered corner of the world to get to first, the English will be racing to it!"

Pierre could not stay quiet any longer. This was not a time to show respect for one's elders, but a time for clear thinking. "You do not believe we are to be shipped away from here, Monsieur Benedict?" he asked.

"No, I do not!" said Benedict.

"Then what are all of those damn ships doing in our harbor?" asked Pierre, raising his voice to the old man.

"Do you believe that the English are planning to send us away so that they can proceed to starve themselves to death?" shouted Benedict.

"What do you mean?" asked Pierre.

"We are the farmers of Nova Scotia! We are the only successful food producers in Nova Scotia! Without us this province couldn't survive! The English couldn't survive by themselves! We grow wheat for their bread! We fatten pigs and cattle for their meat! Do you believe that the English are *complete* fools?" No one dared to speak. Pierre looked at the floor. Benedict continued. "Remember that we are Neutrals. We are French, but we are French Neutrals. We will fight for no one! For no one! The English should know that by now."

Pierre could see that the old patriarch was upset, but he couldn't hold his tongue. "The English should know many things about us, but they don't listen. Englishmen have no ears, only fists! And what will happen, Monsieur Benedict, if the English do not respect our neutrality? What's the good of being neutral if our neutrality is not respected?"

"But the English have respected our neutrality for the past forty years!" roared Benedict.

"But why should the English believe we are neutral when we still have villagers who continue to trade with France?" asked Pierre.

A hush fell over the crowd. "I suppose you are referring to me," said Felix Laurent, a wealthy trader, blushing. "I do trade with France, but I also trade with the English at Halifax, and I trade with the Americans at Boston. I am a trader. That's how I earn my living, and I trade with everybody I can. I always have."

"You see," said Benedict to Pierre, "that's what I mean. Felix is neutral just as we all are. We favor no one in particular."

Pierre gave up. Trying to get a new idea across to an elderly Frenchman was like trying to teach a cat to swim. Then Paul Richard said, "Just remember tomorrow that all of the men and boys must refuse the oath. No exceptions! We can only be strong if we are united." Not a sound came from anyone. For a minute there was only a communal sense of dread.

To discourage any other opposition and to fend off further gloom, Benedict announced, "Don't forget the wedding on Saturday. And after the wedding, the big feast to which you're all invited." That announcement brought the loudest response of the meeting. "And tonight, Gabriel and Evangéline will make it official at my house. Our notary, René Le Blanc, will be there to put their names in his record book, and you are all invited to be witnesses." One last great cheer went up and the crowd moved towards the exits. About half of the crowd strolled home while the other half accompanied Benedict, Basil, and Gabriel to Benedict's house for the signing of the contract.

When she saw them coming, Evangéline quickly lit the brazen lamp on the table, and filled the big pewter tankard until it overflowed with powerful, home-brewed, nut-brown ale.

The notary entered and went straight to work. From his pocket he drew his papers and inkhorn and, with a steady hand, recorded the date, the names and ages of the parties, and the dowry in terms of sheep and cattle. Then he set the great seal of the law, like a sun, in the margin and, with that, the legal part of the nuptial contract became official. "Let's all pray that we can see you *properly* married in church on Saturday," he said to the beaming young couple.

Benedict, feeling generous, threw on the table three times the old man's fee in silver pieces. The notary then rose, lifted the tankard of ale to his lips, drank to the happy couple's welfare, and departed. "Now," shouted Benedict, "where's Michel, our fiddler?"

"Here I am," said the local musician holding up the fiddle that he took with him everywhere just in case a party erupted.

"Play us a cheerful tune, Michel, while we all toast Gabriel and my beautiful daughter, Evangéline," said Benedict.

Michel played a cheerful tune, and another, and another. The ale flowed freely, the talk grew louder, the cheeks turned crimson, and for a few brief hours, the villagers laughed, sang all the old songs, and forgot their troubles.

Suddenly, the door flew open and in burst Madame Boudro, the large lady with the crush on Benedict. "Monsieur Benedict! Monsieur Benedict," she cried, "I've found your boot! I've found your boot!"

"Where did you find it?" asked Benedict, smiling.

"By the side of my house. Your raccoon must have dragged it there," she answered, grinning with pride.

"Are you sure you found it beside your house and not under your bed?" roared Tit N'ours, unable to resist the opportunity for a joke. Everyone laughed, but Madame Boudro blushed. She had expected only praise and gratitude for returning the boot, not ridicule. Looking for more laughs, 'Tit N'ours continued, "You know, Benedict, you will be the talk of the town if that raccoon returns tomorrow with your underwear!" The guffaws were so loud this time that Madame Boudro wanted to slap 'Tit N'ours right across his insolent face.

But Benedict took her hand and said, "Merci, madame, merci beaucoup, beaucoup." This tenderness immediately erased the ridicule and brought a wide smile to the widow's fleshy face. "Come and have something to eat with us," he said, guiding her towards the table. Now, as far as Madame Boudro was concerned, 'Tit N'Ours no longer existed as she marched with Benedict to the table, and she didn't let go of his hand until she reached a large pewter plate piled high with mouth-watering apple tarts.

At nine, the curfew sounded, the merriment ceased, and the crowd, like obedient children, headed home. Gabriel kissed Evangéline and also left.

Benedict was so exhausted that he felt sick. In trying to relieve the anxiety of others, he had absorbed it all himself; in trying to reassure others, he had become doubtful; in trying to calm others' fears, he had become fearful. He felt like a dyke about to give way. As he climbed the stairs to go to bed, a tightening gripped his chest and his usual shortness of breath was worse than ever. He had done too much in one day and was now paying for it.

A few minutes later, lamp in hand, Evangéline climbed the oaken stairs. She opened the door to her chamber - Spartan in its simplicity - extinguished the lamp, and stood in the window bathed with moonlight.

Thinking of Gabriel and of her love for him, she looked down and saw something moving beneath the oak tree near the house. The figure left the shadow of the tree and stepped out into the moonlight. It was Gabriel! He waved to her. She left the window and listened at her door. In the next room, Benedict was already snoring. Down the stairway she stole and, in a minute, was warm inside her lover's arms.

They had to be careful as it was well past curfew, a dangerous time. No one had as yet been shot after curfew, but it was not uncommon for shots to be heard late at night, gunfire intended to discourage subversive attitudes and clandestine meetings.

Hurrying along to their new house - now their usual meeting place - they looked down towards the harbor and saw in the distance the yellow lights of the ships' lanterns on bow and stern, blinking at them like a sinuous menace with ten luminous eyes. On reaching the side door of their house, they entered, and then looked out the window. No one was in sight. They were safe.

Gabriel, in the darkness, took Evangéline's hand and led her to a corner of the room near the fireplace. With straw from the barn, he had made a crude bed that afternoon. He now placed a woolen blanket over the straw, sat on it, and pulled Evangéline down to him. "What was that?" asked Evangéline.

"What was what?"

"That noise!"

"What noise? I didn't hear anything," said Gabriel. They listened intently but heard nothing.

Then he kissed her passionately and she responded with equal intensity. He kissed her hands, her lips, her neck, and she made deep sighs and sweet moans.

Gabriel was a furnace! And warming herself by the fire she had started, she almost surrendered completely to love, but regained control and whispered, "Just two more days, my love. Just two more days."

"Oh, why do we have to wait? I can't sleep at night thinking about you," Gabriel complained.

"Just two more days. Then we'll be together for the rest of our lives," said Evangéline, as she kissed his forehead.

"But I don't see the point in waiting. I love you now, and you love me now."

"A girl has to be pure for her husband."

"Why is that so important?"

"It's more important for you than for me," said Evangéline.

Gabriel looked baffled. He heaved a heavy sigh. There again was that senseless, harebrained female logic. "I don't understand what you mean. More important for me?"

"Yes, it's much more important for you because on your wedding night you must feel completely certain that I am pure, and that I have been impure with *no one, not even with you*. That will be my wedding gift to you."

"But if you're going to be impure with me later, then—"

"But later you will think 'if she was impure with me, then perhaps she was also impure with other boys'," said Evangéline.

"Ohhhh! It's so confusing!" sighed Gabriel.

Evangéline smiled and said, "Just two more days."

"Two more days!" said Gabriel. "It could be two more months, or two more years! We still have the English here, and we have no priest to marry us!"

"My father says that after the meeting tomorrow, the English will leave and our priest will be allowed to return to us. My father understands these things better than we do, Gabriel."

Although Gabriel had great respect for Evangéline's father, he was about to continue his protest when she touched his hand and said, "I already know the strength and the love in your arms. Now let me *hear* the strength of your love. Rest your arms awhile and whisper sweet words in my ear. Tell me *why* you love me and what it is that your heart sees in me."

"I don't know if I can clearly say what is in my heart. I am still drunk on the moisture of your lips."

"That's a lovely start," she cooed.

"Promise you won't laugh if I gush and overflow. It's because my heart cannot hold back my tongue. Forgive me if I overdo it, but it's impossible to speak calmly of the joy you bring to me. There is fresh delight each day in the pleasure of your company."

Her wide-open eyes said, "Tell me more," but she held her tongue for fear of interrupting his flow and the spell.

"When evening comes, you quench my thirst, but in the morning, I am thirsty once again."

"Oh, Gabriel!"

"You are like the clean rain that washes the red dust of Minas from the apple leaves. And when the rain is over, you are the bright returning sun. You are my garden and my harvest feast. I make to you this promise: I will love no one but you until the day I die."

Confirmed now in her love, she whispered, "Oh, Gabriel, you are! You are! You are my own true love!"

He lowered his head as though he suddenly felt guilty. "But I have a confession to make. Those words are not mine. As you once told me, I'm not very original."

"Not your own words?"

"I learned them from my father. I've heard him say those words so often to my mother that I know them all by heart. Those are words my father learned from the Bible."

She hesitated a moment and then said, "Then you honor me as your father honored your mother. And I promise you that I will love you, too, until the day I die."

"I hope that—" He paused. Something had touched his hair.

"What is it?"

He felt the top of his head. "Sawdust," he muttered.

"What?"

"Sawdust," he repeated. He ran his hand over his hair and then looked up. Sawdust was snowing down on them. They squinted to see more clearly in the darkness. Then they heard malicious giggling and snickering. When their eyes adjusted to the poor light, they saw uniforms, the uniforms of two English soldiers who were sitting on the open rafters above them. Gabriel clutched Evangéline's hand and they fled racing out the door. The English soldiers laughed hysterically as the humiliated lovers ran leaping over the high grass like frightened deer and didn't stop until they reached Evangéline's house.

Beneath the trellis, Evangéline caught her breath, but Gabriel was still panting with outrage. "Pierre was right!" he hissed. "Pierre was right!"

"Why? What do you mean?"

"Pierre was right! The English … they spoil … they foul … they poison every part of our lives! They soil everything! Now they have befouled our house!"

"Shhhh! Gabriel, you'll wake my father. Shhhh!"

"I understand now. Pierre was right. They are poison! They've poisoned our new home! I hate them! I hate them! I hate them!"

"Shhhh! Calm yourself, mon amour, calm yourself!"

"Pierre was right! We should have killed every Englishman that set foot in Grand Pré!"

"That's enough, Gabriel! Please don't say any more!" said Evangéline firmly.

"I *hate* the English and from now on I'll kill every one I can get my hands on!"

Evangéline startled Gabriel when she covered his mouth with her hand. "Listen to you! Now you sound just like the rest of them. Hate, hate, hate is all I hear!" Her eyes glistened in the moonlight. "Hate is all around us! Governor Lawrence is full of hate! Colonel Winslow is full of hate! The English soldiers are full of hate! Abbé Le Loutre is full of hate! And now Pierre has filled you with hate! What's happening to you, Gabriel? What's to become of us if you join in the hatred?"

Gabriel, still in shock from her angry outburst, was now more confused than ever. And just when he was getting things straight!

"You must not hate, Gabriel. Hatred does no good to anyone. It's like a poison that spreads. Don't let it spread itself on you. I need you!"

Gabriel unclenched his fists. He looked into his open palms that were still shaking. "But as long as the English are here, these hands will never truly own the things they touch. Pierre was right!"

Evangéline placed Gabriel's arms around her. "Hold me," she whispered. "Touch me. I'm truly yours. I am yours forever. No one can soil our love but ourselves if we give in to hatred. Just love, Gabriel, don't hate. And love me, and never, never stop loving me."

They held one another in the autumn night. A damp, chilly breeze blew her hair in his face. Shivering and not wanting to part, she whispered, "Come inside. It's too dangerous for you to go home now." Opening the door, she led him inside. Red embers still glowed in the fireplace. Gabriel placed two more logs on the fire. Upstairs, Benedict was snoring. She took a woolen blanket and placed it on the floor in front of the fire. Sitting down, and pulling Gabriel down beside her, she gazed into his sad, troubled eyes and said, "Now just hold me, Gabriel. Just hold me all night long."

Chapter Twenty-six

His Majesty's Instructions

September 5, 1755

Copies of the public notice - drafted by Winslow and Murray three days earlier at Piziquid - had been posted all over the village.

'To the inhabitants of the District of Grand Pré, Mines, river Canard (sic) and places adjacent, to the elderly, the young Men and boys of ten years of age. 'Whereas, His Excellency the Governor, has instructed us of his late resolution respecting the matter proposed to the inhabitants, and has ordered us to communicate the same in person, His Excellency being desirous that each of them should be satisfied with His Majesty's intentions, which he has also ordered us to communicate to you, as they have been given to him. 'We, therefore, order strictly by the present, all of the inhabitants of the above named District as well as all the other Districts, both old and young men, as well as the lads ten years of age, to attend at the church of Grand Pré, on Friday, the 5th instant, at three o'clock in the afternoon, that we may impart to them what we are ordered to communicate to them; declaring that no excuse will be admitted on any pretense whatsoever on pain of forfeiting goods and chattels, in default of real estate. Given at Grand Pré, 2ⁿᵈ of September 1755.

Signed: John Winslow.'

This important Friday morning was so quiet in Grand Pré that Winslow couldn't believe it. He wrote in his journal, "Very quiet morning and the inhabitants very busy about their harvest."

He had not expected an open revolt but, at least, an orderly march of protest. But nothing happened; he got neither, just another morning and its ordinariness made him shudder.

Around noon the farmers left their fields, went home, and ate lunch. Not wanting to go dirty into the sacred church they hadn't been permitted to enter for the last two weeks, they scrubbed themselves twice. Some of the more religious men couldn't wait and hurried to get there early.

At two-thirty most of the men and boys had arrived and were milling about the churchyard chatting in normal tones. No one panicked. No women came, not even Berthe Commo. They were all at home cooking and baking. After all, there was a wedding the next day. Besides, unless a major earthquake hit Grand Pré, supper would have to be on Acadian tables at five o'clock sharp.

"Why are there so many soldiers here just for a meeting? There must be four hundred of them!" said Pierre.

"I don't know," answered Benedict. "It's strange!"

"How long does it take a priest to re-consecrate a church?" asked Gabriel.

"Why do you ask?"

"Well, if they let Father Chauvreulx return tomorrow, the first thing he will have to do is re-consecrate the church. Then he can marry us," said Gabriel.

"I don't know how long it takes," said Benedict distractedly as he looked up at the church steeple where he saw a British flag wafting in the afternoon air. "But I'm sure he'll consent to marry you anyway," Slowly the men climbed the church steps, talking of the harvest and of the reaping left to be done.

Once inside, they balked at the absence of the sacred objects, forgetting that they had removed them weeks earlier. Particularly disturbing were the walls between the stained-glass windows being used as bulletin boards for military matters. The altar was covered with long strips of dust-coated cloth. In the middle of the church stood a long pine table surrounded by soldiers.

At three o'clock, everyone went silent as Colonel John Winslow emerged from the presbytery. He walked to the pine table. Suddenly, sickening sounds were heard - the sounds of doors closing, bolts sliding, and keys jangling and turning in locks.

A man named Isaac Deschamps, a merchant of Swiss descent now living in nearby Piziquid, moved next to Winslow to translate as Winslow spoke.

'The duty I am now upon, though necessary, is very disagreeable to my natural make and temper, as I know it must be grievous to you, who are of the same species. But it is not my business to animadvert on the orders I have received, but to obey them.

'Therefore, without hesitation, I shall deliver to you His Majesty's instructions and commands, which are, that your lands and tenements and cattle and livestock of all kinds are forfeited to the crown, with all your other effects, except money and household goods, and that you yourselves are to be removed from this province.

'The peremptory orders of His Majesty are, that all the French inhabitants of these districts be removed, and, through His Majesty's goodness, I am directed to allow you your money and as many of your household goods as you can take without overloading the vessels you go in. I shall do everything in my power that all the goods be secured to you, and that you are not molested in carrying them away, and that whole families shall go in the same vessel; so that this removal, which I am sensible must give you a great deal of trouble, may be made as easy as His Majesty's service will admit; and I hope that in whatever part of the world your lot may fall, you may be faithful subjects, and a peaceable happy people.'

A shocked silence, and then a whispering. "Is it true?" "Did he really say that?" "Did he say *all* of us?" "What did he say about our money?" Voices grew angry. The soldiers at the doors pointed their rifles at the angriest. François Hébert clenched both fists and raised them in defiance. Someone near the back of the church vomited.

What was all of this? What was happening? Was this all a part of the big English bluff Benedict had talked about? And if not a bluff, how could the high and mighty English behave so treacherously low? Benedict held his hand over his heart.

Gabriel stared at the altar, covered and fouled with dirty cloth. "They foul everything," he mumbled to himself.

The irony of their impious arrest in their sacred church sickened Pierre. "Ils se sont même servi de notre église comme un attrait! Je vous ai dit que les Anglais ne sont que des cochons!"*

A few men prayed aloud; others wept even louder.

"What about our wives and our children?" Paul Richard shouted at the interpreter, Deschamps. "Who will tell them?"

Isaac Deschamps turned towards the pine table. Colonel Winslow was no longer there. Then Deschamps turned towards the door of the presbytery and saw only Winslow's back retreating as the door closed quietly but firmly on the long-overdue and futile voices of dissent.

---

* "They even used our own church against us! I told you that the English are nothing but pigs!"

Chapter Twenty-seven

Gaps To Be Filled

September 7, 1755

Through an opening in the picket fence, Gabriel slipped his hand. Evangéline pressed it to her mouth and kissed it. Gabriel's mouth twitched in anger. He loathed the English now.

The purpose of the fence that surrounded the church property was now apparent. The fence had been erected two weeks earlier and the Acadians had assumed its construction was intended to keep them out, not in. Fortunately, it had been hastily built and the builders left small gaps here and there. Since there was a limited number of them, these gaps, unfortunately, caused some contention among the prisoners. When the guards released the men from the confines of the church for their daily walk within the fenced area, the freed prisoners raced to the openings pushing and shoving one another until they almost came to blows. At first, the women, on the other side of the fence, had competed in the same manner; however, they had soon learned to wait and see which men appeared at the openings, and then the matching wives and girlfriends took their lucky places. Today, Evangéline was one of the fortunate ones.

To calm him, she joked, "I told you that Pierre was hiding behind a fence."

Gabriel laughed in spite of himself. "But you didn't say all of us."

She suddenly turned to her left because she had heard loud sobs. The old honeymooners, Berthe and Oliver, were both crying at the next gap in the fence. "I promise I won't do that anymore," Berthe sniffed.

"Shhhh! It doesn't matter, now," replied Oliver. "It doesn't matter now. Shhhh!"

"Evangéline," said Gabriel, "your father's here beside me, and he wants to talk to you." Gabriel released Evangéline's hand as Benedict appeared in the opening.

"Oh, father, how are you? Are you well? Our house is empty without you." She held her father's trembling hand.

"And I miss you, too," said Madame Boudro, the widow, who had been hovering nearby. She sat beside Evangéline and put her hand on Benedict's wrist.

"Bonjour, Madame Boudro. I'm fine," said Benedict. "Don't worry about me. The English will soon tire of this game and let us go home. They want to show us which rooster rules the barnyard, that's all. Governor Lawrence is just a little more stubborn than the previous governors."

"Oh, father, do you think it will be soon?" asked Evangéline.

"They can't keep up this nonsense much longer, my dear. But you must be brave, and you must be strong. You and the other women have a lot of work to do tending the animals."

"We're trying, father, but there are hundreds of cows, and some of the women are getting discouraged. They cry and complain that all of their work is a wasted effort."

"No, you must tell them to carry on as usual. Tell them not to get discouraged. We'll be released soon, I know it. Tell the women to, at least, milk the cows. It makes the men sad to hear the bellowing of the cows."

"Yes, father, but there are so many of them."

"All of the women must pitch in. All of them. I'm sure Madame Boudro will help you, too," said Benedict.

"I can't do such work," said Madame Boudro, removing her hand and pouting.

"Now, I'm sure you can do a little," said Benedict.

"No, I can't," said madame. "My thighs are too big!"

Benedict looked helplessly at Evangéline. Evangéline shook her head denying all responsibility. It wasn't me! She hadn't repeated Benedict's criticism of Madame Boudro's size. Benedict searched the ground trying to remember if he had made the same remark to one of his friends, to Basil perhaps. At any rate, it didn't matter now. It was his own fault. He should have known that the village's gossip network would have found his unkind remark too irresistible. He let go of Evangéline's hand, took Madame Boudro's in his, and said, "Next week, we'll be out of this foolish custody and I'll go to your house for supper; that is, if you still remember how to cook."

With a nod of her head and a simper, Madame Boudro said, "I'll be watching for you in the window." She looked at Evangéline. "And I think I'll be able to milk a few cows."

"Merci, madame," said Benedict.

Benedict and Madame Boudro moved aside to let the young lovers have their place again. As Gabriel slipped his hand through the fence, he scraped the raw wood and a splinter pierced his little finger. "Ouch!"

"Oh, let me see," said Evangéline. She used her fingernails and quickly removed the splinter.

"Is there anything that you *can't* do?"

"I can't shoe a horse. Yet. But if it would make you love me more, I could learn. How much do you love me?" asked Evangéline.

"From here to Halifax," said Gabriel, smiling.

"Is that all?" asked Evangéline.

"And back again," whispered Gabriel.

"Time's up!" yelled Captain Osgood. "All prisoners back inside!"

Gabriel raised Evangéline's hand to his mouth, kissed it, and whispered, "Until tomorrow. And remember: no fence, no unconditional oaths, no army in the world can keep us apart for long."

Another day's visit was over.

Chapter Twenty-eight

Uncommon Motions

September 9, 1755

Colonel Winslow wrote in his journal on September 9,

> "The French this morning discovered some uncommon motions among themselves which I did not like. Called my officers together and communicated to them what I had observed and after debating matters it was determined … that it would be best to divide the prisoners … that fifty men of the French inhabitants be embarked on board each of the five vessels taking first of all their young men…."

That morning, the 'uncommon motions' Winslow had observed in one corner of the enclosed churchyard involved a small group of young prisoners listening intently to a moving speech by one of the older men. The older man, oddly enough, was Basil, the one Acadian who normally was too bashful to speak in public. He made very few public speeches and, whenever he did, he had regrets later. He would go home, relive the experience, and perspire profusely as he concluded that everything he said had been prompted by his own vanity. He then would vow never to speak again in public. This particular morning, however, was different. He felt obliged to say something because no one else was speaking up. Anxiety and anger had made the others mute.

Since the group's arrest four days earlier, Benedict, the most verbal of the elders, had not said a word. He had lost some of his credibility with the men and was now re-evaluating his own position. He could be heard mumbling to himself, his voice quivering, "I was wrong. I was wrong." Basil had decided, then, to take Benedict's place in offering advice to the younger men. "We must always remember who we are," Basil said. "I've noticed over the years that it's when people forget who they are and how valuable they are to others, especially to members of their own families, that they get into trouble. No matter what happens to us, always remember that you are Acadians and be proud. Remember that we are all members of the same family. We are like threads and we are all woven into a single garment. And if that garment should be torn apart by those who don't understand us, we must have the strength to mend it and to sew it together again. And although months, or years, and even the ocean may divide us, we can reunite some day if we remember. And if it's not possible for *us* to reunite, then our children will if we teach them to remember who they are, if we teach them to remember us and Acadia, the land of their fathers and grandfathers, the land of their home in Grand Pré."

Basil's speech produced a variety of responses. Some of the listeners fell to tears, and some sat quietly spellbound, while a few others grew agitated at the thought of painful separation and stood, shouted, and clenched their fists in defiance. It was the sight of the clenched fists that had caught Colonel Winslow's eye, and these 'uncommon motions' forced his hand. "Divide the prisoners into two groups, Captain Adams. Put the younger men together on the left and the older, married men on the right," said Winslow. "We can no longer tolerate the presence of these men here on shore. Tell Mister Landry to come forward and translate my orders." Monsieur Landry stepped forward from the group of prisoners.

Word spread quickly through the village that something terrible was about to happen. Even the sick and the infirm, the young children and the feeble great-grandparents made their way to the churchyard and stood waiting, crying, and praying. The children, sensing the instability of the adults, began to whimper and whine.

"Six abreast, Captain Adams," shouted Winslow. "Translate, if you please, Mister Landry." Adams arranged the men in rows of six.

"Now, march!" shouted Winslow. Landry translated. No one moved.

"The women and children are making such a racket, sir, that the prisoners can't hear the order," said Captain Adams.

Winslow clenched both fists. He walked to the head of the line. "Mister Landry, *tell* these men to march!"

"They say they will not march, sir," said Landry.

"Will not march?" shouted Winslow.

"Yes, sir. They say they will not march unless they are accompanied by their fathers who are in the other group."

"Tell them, sir, that is a word I do not understand for the king's command to me is absolute and should be absolutely obeyed. I do not love to use harsh measures but there is no time for parleys (sic) or delays."

Landry translated.

Still no one budged.

Winslow turned towards his soldiers. "Fix bayonets! Advance!" The English troops advanced to within one foot of the prisoners. The prisoners stared straight ahead. One of them mumbled, "Notre Pere qui êtes aux cieux—"* Winslow's hands trembled as he stood seething beside Pierre in the first row. He reached out and, seizing the back of Pierre's shirt, placed the cold point of a bayonet on his neck. "Now, march!" Pierre limped forward and the rest of the men followed. Some of the prisoners then began to sing a hymn. Others recited the *Hail Mary*. The women, the old folk, and the children walked alongside the prisoners praying, singing, screaming, shrieking, and falling to their knees too distraught, in some cases, to proceed.

When the first group of younger men had passed by, Berthe Commo caught sight of Oliver in the second group of prisoners. "How thin and weak he looks!" she said. Then, as he passed in front of her, she stretched out her hand and touched his arm. "Oliver! Oh, my Oliver! Are you well? You look—" An English soldier stepped between them. Berthe struggled to hold on, but the soldier, not putting up with any nonsense, knocked Berthe to the ground.

"March!" the soldier shouted. The prisoners walked on.

When they reached the shore, the soldiers prodded them hurriedly into longboats and rowed them to the waiting ships. It took two hours to complete the transfer of eighty prisoners to each ship.

This troublesome task accomplished, Winslow turned from the shore and walked slowly, under armed guard, in the direction of the church. The armed escort was unnecessary since only old men, women, and children

---

* "Our Father who art in Heaven..."

under ten now remained on shore. But all of them, in a stony silence, stared at him. Winslow needed the escort, not to avoid physical assault, but to shield himself from the looks of anger, disbelief, and contempt in all those wide, unblinking eyes.

****

With the idea that it might comfort their men, many of the wives and girlfriends decided to stay down by the shore that night. Perhaps their husbands and boyfriends would be able to see them from the ships. To make their place visible and, coincidentally, to keep themselves warm in the cool September air, the women built a huge fire on the beach. No curfew would send them home tonight; with all of the able-bodied men under arrest, it would not be necessary.

When the sun went down, the air grew chilly. The heavy dew dampened the women's shawls. Feet grew cold, teeth chattered, and noses ran. The fire blazed. But when the women's faces overheated, their backs froze; and when they turned around to warm their backs, their foreheads and cheeks cooled.

At midnight, a bitter wind blew, and one of the oldest women announced that it would do her husband no good if she were to catch pneumonia. Some of her contemporaries agreed and left with her for home.

About two a.m., a middle-aged woman decided that, while her three young children at home were probably fast asleep, she couldn't be certain. They were, after all, still children and naturally irresponsible. A few of the other women with children at home left with her.

By the time the sun rose, only Evangéline and ten other young girlfriends still huddled, shivering and sniffling, on the beach. Their fresh young love was stronger than their ability to rationalize their way to a warmer place. However, just Evangéline and the only older woman to stay, Berthe Commo, lost without her Oliver, had stayed awake all night to keep the beach fire going. Their eyes were now inflamed from the smoke and their tears.

Chapter Twenty-nine

The Assault on the French Women

The Morning of September 13, 1755

Although John Winslow realized that the treatment of the Acadians would be deemed brutal by some, he did not consider himself a brute, and to prove it, he allowed twenty prisoners at a time to spend one night at home with their families. Such a policy would show some heart and, more importantly, might avert an open revolt. As insurance against escape, he made the prisoners responsible for one another's return. The angriest and most impatient men went home first - the English guards glad to be rid of them for the next twenty-four hours - and the older men stoically waited their turn.

Upon his release, Paul Richard found it puzzling that his wife, Héloise, and his twin daughters, Céleste and Cécile, had not arrived at the shore to escort him home. It was odd because all the mothers and daughters of the other released men had come down to the beach. Paul began to worry. Was his wife sick? He hurried across the meadow taking the shortest route home.

When he came within sight of his house, he saw no one outside in the yard. A nauseous lump formed in his stomach. He started to run. When he reached the door, he paused to catch his breath. Then, he slowly opened the door and peered inside.

He heaved a sigh of relief when he caught sight of his twin daughters, but was disturbed that they had not jumped up to greet him; in fact, they both had their backs to him, even now. Céleste sat in a chair near the fireplace, rocking back and forth, back and forth, her thin, fragile arms wrapped around her drawn-up knees. She stared straight ahead. The chair was not a rocking chair. "Céleste?" he said. Without turning, Céleste continued to rock. In the opposite corner of the room, Paul saw Cécile. Oblivious to his presence, she sat on a cot rubbing her bare inner thighs with a dark washcloth. She moaned, as though quietly chanting, and her glassy eyes were open, but they did not see.

Then Paul saw blood. Cécile's skinny, left inner thigh was bruised, bleeding, and shining with lymph. The washcloth's friction had produced a raw patch of red plaid just below the first wispy sprouts of pubic hair. He reached down and touched Cécile's hand. She flinched in terror. Then she began to wash herself again, rubbing the plaid harder, and moaning louder.

Other sounds came from above. Paul flew up the stairs and found his wife bound and gagged on the floor, her eyes blackened, and her left cheek and lower lip crusted with dried blood. "What happened?" Paul cried, as he loosened the gag from Heloise's mouth.

"Six of them!" she gasped. "Six of the drunken bastards! First on Céleste and then on Cécile!" Héloise sobbed and buried her face in her husband's chest. "Oh, mes filles! Oh, mes petites filles!"[*] Then, out of relief at seeing her husband, and realizing that her nightmare captivity was over, she took a deep breath, screamed at the horror of it all, struggled to her feet, and dashed downstairs to comfort her abused children.

When Colonel Winslow received the report of the assault, he immediately gave his men new orders.

> No party or person will be permitted to go out after calling
> the roll on any account whatever, as many bad things have been
> done lately in the night, to the distressing of the distressed (sic)
> French inhabitants in this neighborhood.

****

"What news now, Mr. Osgood?"
"None, I'm afraid, sir. No one seems to know who did it, sir."

---

[*] "Oh, my girls! Oh, my little girls!"

"Why am I not surprised to hear that?" said Winslow, sarcastically. "Have you any suspicions? You know most of these men, don't you?"

"One of the men, sir, says that he saw half a dozen Mi'kmaqs in the village late last night," said Osgood.

Winslow had not considered the Mi'kmaqs as the possible rapists, and he strongly suspected the notion to be a subterfuge. However, he had to investigate every imputation. "Bring me that young Indian boy, the one who plays with the Acadian children."

"The Joseph boy, sir?"

"Yes, that's the one. And tell the boy to bring his father with him. Assure him that no harm will come to anyone and that his father will receive a gift for coming here."

"And what about a translator, sir?"

"I understand that the boy speaks a little French, so we will need Mister Landry as well," said Winslow.

"Very good, sir."

****

Two hours later, the barefoot Mi'kmaq boy stood with his father before Colonel Winslow. It surprised Winslow that Matthew Joseph, one of the oldest sons of Grand Chief Jean Baptiste Cope, was a handsome bronze-skinned young man with penetrating, bright brown eyes, and a permanent smile. Up close, he didn't look at all savage, and had it not been for his ridiculous felt hat adorned with drooping feathers and porcupine quills, and his European blanket trimmed with squirrel tails he could have passed for a prince of Egypt on a visit to the New World. A large rosary with fat, black, wooden beads circled his neck. The rosary's crucifix was missing. Winslow looked down and discovered that the missing crucifix was attached by a piece of string to a leather bracelet on Matthew's left wrist. The crucifix dangled and jingled against three brass rings and two keys for locks that were now - who knows where? After the awkward bows and the gingerly handshakes, Matthew handed Winslow some sweet-grass. Winslow frowned and asked Landry, "What is *this* all about?"

"Sweet-grass is sacred to the Mi'kmaq. It's a peace offering."

"Grass?" Winslow snarled. Then he turned and tossed the sweet-grass on his desk. "Tell the boy to ask his father if he knows which of his brothers assaulted and raped the French women last night."

Landry spoke to the boy in French who, in turn, asked his father the question in Mi'kmaq. The smile on Matthew's face vanished. He raised his arm as his signal to speak. Then, he set his jaw and said firmly, "Mu Mi'kmaq na tela'taqiti'kw. Wantaqo'ltiek teleyek. Mu wen weji ajkneywaqitk. Ki'lew Aklasie'wk ne'kaw matntultioq. Emteskayatultioq, aqq winaknimtultioq. Kilew kmutnesk aqq ewla'tioq. Keskeltma'tioq. Mu wen welmituk keskmna'q na'tu koqoey menueket apaji iknmuksin. Mu na ninen kmutnesk. 'Kemutnemk,' na klusuaqn mu ewe'muek etlewistu'tiek. Weskunk wen wpkesikn pipnaqan, ali ktpi'ataq wikmaq."[*]

Hearing the translation, Winslow bristled. This boldfaced Indian was calling him a thief and a liar! "Ask this rascal if he or his brothers are in the habit of stealing sex from French women!"

When his son had finished translating, the young Mi'kmaq leader smiled again and said, "Mu Mi'kmaq wipemaqik e'pijik naqitkelsultijik ta'n pasik tett wetapeksij."[**]

"Tell him that six of his braves were seen prowling around the Richard house late last night," Winslow said.

Landry hesitated. "But that would be unlikely, Monsieur Winslow. The Mi'kmaq are very superstitious. They believe that evil spirits walk about at night. They rarely leave their campsites after dark."

Realizing he was on the wrong trail, Winslow fumed. The rapists obviously were members of his own tribe. Thwarted once again, he sighed, then reached over and took from his desk an open package containing a new dagger with an ornate dudgeon handle, and two brightly colored scarves. He handed the package as a gift to Matthew who looked at it, smiled, and said, "Wlaiknmatimkewey, Aklasie'w mnueketew na't koqoey apaji iknmuksin. Mu na ketloqo iknmatimkewey."[***]

"Is he refusing my gift?" asked Winslow.

"It appears that way," said Landry, amused.

"But why? I don't understand," said Winslow.

---

[*] "The Mi'kmaq do not do such things. We live peaceably. We do not hurt one another. You white men always fight among yourselves. You are envious of one another, and you slander one another. You are thieves and deceivers. You are not generous. You are not kind unless you want something in return. We are not thieves. 'Stealing' is not a word we use in our language. If we have a morsel of bread, we share it with our neighbor."

[**] "The Mi'kmaq do not lie down with unwilling females of any color."

[***] "For this gift, white man will want something in return. It is not a true gift."

"Siawi anko'te'n, aqq iknmuitisk jijuaqa elmi'knik, tliaq jel mu tali nuta'nuk," said Matthew. "Na Mi'kmaw tla'tekes."*

Early the next morning, Landry knocked on Winslow's office door. "What news?" asked Winslow.

"Chief Matthew is waiting outside the village this morning," said Landry.

"Why? Has he discovered the identity of the rapists?"

"No, sir. He wants to know if you are feeling generous this morning."

"'Generous this morning?' I don't understand."

"He wants to know if today is the day that you'll be giving him his gift for no reason at all."

Winslow felt like the butt of a joke. "No, I am not feeling at all generous this morning! Tell *that* to the scoundrel, Mister Landry!"

"Yes, sir. But he also said that if you're not feeling generous today, he'll come back again tomorrow morning."

"I see," said Winslow, realizing he could not win this small battle that was bound to resume every morning for the next God-only-knows-how-many. Shaking his head, he walked to his desk, picked up the package with the dagger and the scarves, and threw it at Landry. "Here! Give him the damn things and tell him to be off!"

Landry grinned and said, "Yes, sir."

A week later Winslow wrote in his journal,

'I should be glad a strict enquiry might be made for those persons that assaulted the French women which happened in the first of the evening … one of the women being now under the Doctor's hand, and her life precarious.' [1]

---

* "Save it, and give it to me sometime in the future for no reason at all," said Matthew. "That is what a Mi'kmaw would do."

Chapter Thirty

Cracking Under Pressure

Colonel Winslow heard a knock and said, "Enter, Mr. Osgood."

"Captain Davis of the *Neptune* is here, sir."

"Concerning what, Mr. Osgood?"

"Captain Davis, sir, is the man we discussed yesterday, the one who has been allowing the Acadian women extra time with the prisoners aboard his vessel."

Colonel Winslow, thoroughly frustrated by the long wait for the supply ships, and the nuisance of having to send food daily to the four hundred men on the five ships in the harbor, had decided to allow the womenfolk to row themselves out to the ships and to feed their husbands and sons on board.

"More than an hour a day?"

"More than an hour. On Tuesday, sir, the women were aboard all afternoon," said Osgood.

"Very well. Send him in."

"Sir, there's something else."

"Something else? What might that be, Osgood?"

Osgood lowered his voice to a whisper. "He has been taking French lessons from the prisoners, sir."

"I see. Send him in here."

Captain Jonathan Davis was a mild-mannered man who, up until now, had made his living as a transporter of goods, not people. While he was not an educated man, he had acquired a certain sophistication from his travels around the world. Like many sea captains of that time, he usually traveled with his wife and children. He and his wife were their children's tutors, teaching them to read and write, to calculate, and most importantly, to navigate their way through rough waters. For this trip, he was told to leave his family at home. He had not been told why. Now he knew. He was, at the moment, caught in rough seas himself, and was not certain of finding a safe - and honorable - passage home. This commission turned out to be a dirty job for money, a job of transporting men, women, and children - families like his own - against their will to secret destinations. "You wanted to see me, sir?" asked Davis.

"Yes, Mr. Davis. I understand that you have not been observing the time regulation regarding the women's visits on your vessel. Are you aware of the time regulation, the one-hour limit on your ship's visitors?"

"Yes sir, I am aware of it, and I do follow the regulation … most of the time, sir," said Davis.

"*Mos*t of the time, sir? Why not *all* of the time?"

"Well, I don't see the harm, sir, in allowing the women—"

"There is a great deal of harm, sir, in not following orders. If we all do as you are doing, sir, we will have chaos here." Winslow looked at Davis who lowered his head and did not reply. Winslow asked more quietly, "What is the matter, Mr. Davis? Something is bothering you."

"It's … it's—"

"It's what? Out with it, man!"

"It's the women's tears, sir. I cannot abide the women's tears."

"Now, now, Davis, we mustn't give in to this sort of weakness. This is weakness, plain and simple. We have jobs to do and we must do them as men. This task is unpleasant for me and for all of my men. Of course, I can't share with you my secret orders, but I can assure you that these people will not lose their lives under our care. A year from now they will all be fine and well-adjusted to their new condition. No need for you to fret on their part. Go now, sir. Return to your ship and do your duty. Our assignment will be over soon, and then we can all return to our own families," said Winslow. Davis, slightly calmer now, rose to go. "Oh, and one more thing."

"What is that, sir?"

"What is all this nonsense about your taking French lessons from the prisoners on your ship?"

"Just a few words, sir, you know, to help with the general communication of orders."

"But you have an interpreter on board, do you not?"

"Yes, sir."

"Well then, there's no need for you to complicate matters, is there?"

Davis paused and then said, "No, sir, I suppose not."

"Fine, then. Let us allow the interpreter to do his job, and we shall do ours."

Captain Davis walked to the door, then turned, and said, "My ship may not make it, sir."

"Not make it? And why is that?" asked Winslow.

"My anchor, sir. The chain on my anchor is damaged. I'm not certain my ship will be seaworthy."

"A small matter, Mr. Davis. One of my officers is an engineer. He will have your anchor chain repaired in a day or two. I shall inform him."

Davis looked helplessly at Winslow. He wanted to protest further but didn't know what else to say. "Yes, sir. Thank you, sir." He walked towards the door but then he remembered the letter. "I almost forgot to give this to you, sir."

"What is it?"

"It's a letter to you from the prisoners, sir."

Winslow, looking both surprised and apprehensive, opened the letter and read.

> "At the sight of the evils that seem to threaten us on every side, we are obliged to implore your protection and to beg of you to intercede with His Majesty, that he may have a care for those amongst us who have inviolably kept the fidelity and submission promised to His Majesty. "As you have given us to understand that the King has ordered us to be transported out of this province, we beg of you that, if we must forsake our lands, we may at least be allowed to go to places where we shall find fellow-countrymen, all expenses being defrayed by ourselves, and that we may be granted a suitable length of time therefore, and all the more because, by this means we shall be able to preserve our religion, which we have deeply at heart, and for which we are content to sacrifice our property."

Winslow folded the letter and stuck it in the pages of his journal. "Thank you, Davis. You may go."

Winslow watched in the window as Davis slouched down to the shore. He began to worry. Men like Davis were beginning to crack under the pressure, as was he. "We need those transport vessels!" he said, gritting his teeth and pounding his fist on the windowsill. "Damn you, Mr. Saul, bring me those transports!"

Captain Davis returned to his ship, the *Neptune*. On board, he spent the rest of the day and evening, locked in his private quarters, drinking rum.

"Must be missing his wife tonight," whispered the first mate to his companion that evening as they listened outside the captain's door. "Keeps mumbling something about a woman's tears."

Chapter Thirty-one

The Escape

October 7, 1755

"All right, all French whores must leave the ship at once!" yelled the first mate of the *Leopard*. "All whores off the ship! Your time is up for today!" The other English crew members laughed heartily at the first mate's vulgarity. Most of the Acadians did not understand his remark although they understood by the guffaws that they were being verbally abused again. It was nothing new. The wives, daughters, and girlfriends of the fifty prisoners aboard the *Leopard* rose to re-board the longboats that would take them to shore. The brief visit with their menfolk had once again sped by.

The wife of François Hébert suddenly looked shocked at what her husband had just whispered in her ear. "But François, why?" she asked.

"I don't have time to explain now. Just do as I say! Bring me one of your dresses the next time you come." Madame Hébert wore a blank look. "And tell the other women to bring one of theirs, too. Hide them in the bottom of your lunch baskets." Madame Hébert's face asked 'why' again. "Please, don't forget."

She climbed down the side of the ship on the rope ladder. When she got halfway down she looked up at her husband and asked, "You do still love me, don't you, François?"

"Hurry now, you French hussies! Hurry!" yelled the first mate. An elderly woman with snow-white hair and with a face as wrinkled as the skin of a baked apple passed in front of him. "Hey, Higgins!" he shouted to one of his youngest officers. "Take a look at her! How'd you like to wake up some morning and see *that* on the pillow next to yours?" He laughed loudly at his own joke as he held the old woman back for young Higgins to see.

"To be perfectly honest, sir, if I had married that lady fifty years ago, my face would now be as wrinkled as hers," replied the well-mannered young man. The first mate frowned at Higgins and then released the old woman from his grasp.

The women filled the longboats and rowed back to their empty lives on shore.

Many of the dresses didn't fit the men who wanted them. It took about five days of smuggling to outfit those prisoners convincingly. "You look beautiful!" said François to Jean Arsenault, one of the burliest men on board.

"You go to hell!" said Jean, blushing as he adjusted the white, Norman, milkmaid's bonnet to his large, balding head.

Later that afternoon, François Hébert and twenty-three other prisoners dressed as women, cautiously mingled with the other men on board and waited for the usual insulting invitation to disembark. While mingling, they hid their faces from the ship's crew. At last, the first mate yelled, "All right, ladies, it's time to say goodbye. Let's go! Hurry now!" François and the other men in dresses and aprons, sidled slowly, heads down, towards the rope ladders. One of the prisoners in an over-sized bonnet and a wrinkled blue gingham dress limped slightly. A crew member noticed the limp. Then he looked away. The limping lady climbed gingerly over the side and slipped into the waiting longboat. "Until tomorrow, bitches!" shouted the first mate, and the crew members roared with laughter as the last longboat rowed to shore.

****

About eleven o'clock the next morning there was nothing to laugh about when Colonel Winslow screamed in the faces of the first mate and seven of his 'blind' crew. "Eight of you, and not one of you even heard a splash? Were you all so drunk last night? Captain Church, have you any explanation for this escape?"

"No, sir. I'm sorry. It won't happen again, sir," mumbled the captain of the *Leopard*.

"How do we know it won't happen again, sir, if we don't know how it happened in the first place?"

"Pardon me, sir, but if it's any help I do suspect that a prisoner named François Hébert may have been a contriver and abettor in the escape. He has been one of the surliest and most uncooperative of my prisoners, sir," said Church.

"Get out of my sight, all of you. Out! Out!" Winslow paced the floor. Suddenly he turned to his interpreter, "Mr. Landry, I want those prisoners back on the *Leopard* within the next forty-eight hours. Spread the word! Do you understand me?" Landry nodded. "Fine, then. Now take me to the house of Mr. François Hébert!"

Half an hour later, two English officers stood with lighted torches outside the Hébert home. Captain Adams stood in front of Hébert's house, and Captain Hobbs in front of his barn. Madame Hébert and her two small boys looked on, shaking with terror, while a small crowd of women and children gathered, staring with open mouths. "Mr. Landry, tell everyone present that this is what will happen to everyone else's property if the prisoners have not returned to their ship within the next two days!" Landry spoke the threat in the French language. The crowd gasped. Winslow nodded to the officers with the torches, and within minutes the Hébert house and barn were engulfed in flames.

Landry made no attempt to conceal his outrage. "And if the prisoners do return, what guarantee will they have that their houses will not be burnt?" he asked.

"I give you my word of honor that nothing will happen to their property," said Winslow.

"But how can they be *assured* of that?" Landry persisted.

"I have given you my word of honor!" answered Winslow sharply, as he turned and walked away.

"The word of honor of an arsonist!" Landry mumbled to himself. "I understand English, but I will never understand the English!"

When Winslow returned to his headquarters, he said to Hobbs, "Row out to the ships and tell each ship captain to move his vessel farther away from the others. If the escapees retaliate by burning one ship, at least they won't all go up in flames."

****

Around ten the next morning, François and twenty-one other men walked sheepishly out of the woods and gave themselves up to Colonel Winslow.

Two prisoners remained at large.

"Mr. Osgood," said Winslow to his right-hand man, "send a patrol of six into the woods near River Canards. I understand that the Canards area is a favorite hiding place of local scoundrels."

"Yes, sir. Right away, sir," said Osgood.

Captain Osgood himself went to River Canards and took five other experienced soldiers with him.

After patrolling for two hours, Osgood and his men smelled smoke from a campfire. "Be careful," whispered Osgood. "It could be Indians." The six men crept along the ground on their stomachs and then, peering through some alder bushes, spied the last two escapees brazenly cooking over an open fire. A twig snapped under one soldier's elbow. In a flash, the two escapees mounted their horses and galloped off. "Shoot the bastards!" bellowed Captain Osgood.

In the gunfire, one of the escapees fell from his horse. The other rode off safely into the woods.

Osgood walked cautiously up to the fallen man who was lying face down. Blood oozed from the escapee's left temple and ran down his cheek. "Well, this one definitely needed a horse," said Osgood pointing to the dead man's feet. The dead man, with blood coursing through his mass of black shiny curls, wore one regular shoe, and one shoe with a two-inch sole and a three-inch heel.

The other escapee who galloped off into the woods was never heard from again.

However, Winslow, perhaps remembering the screams of Madame Hébert and her children, could not follow through with his dire threat.

At least, not for now.

Chapter Thirty-two

Losing His Anchor

October 13, 1755

"You sent for me, sir?" asked Captain Davis of the *Neptune*.

"Yes. Come in," said Winslow. "Be seated, sir."

Captain Davis had lost weight. His red eyes stood out against his pale cheeks. He reeked of stale rum and vomit. "Now, what's all this nonsense about a missing anchor?" asked Winslow.

"Well, it's a mystery to me, sir. It's gone."

"Gone? Gone? And where, pray tell, could your anchor have gone, Mr. Davis?" groaned Winslow.

"Well, that's just it, sir, I don't know where it is."

"That is a very disturbing development, Captain Davis, very disturbing, indeed."

"Yes, sir, it disturbs me greatly," said Davis.

"Was it not your anchor, Mr. Davis, that my engineer repaired recently?" asked Winslow.

"Yes, sir, the chain, sir, and now the whole anchor is missing."

"Where is it?"

"I don't have any idea, sir," said Davis.

"But you have not gone anywhere, Mr. Davis. Your ship has been in the harbor for over a month!"

Davis began to shake. He ached for a drink. "It's a mystery, sir," he said.

"No, Mr. Davis, it is not a mystery!" said Winslow rising and closing in on him. Beads of sweat dotted Davis' forehead. "It is not a mystery; it is sabotage, sir." Davis looked at Winslow, squirmed in his chair, and wiped his brow. "And do you know what happens to men who commit sabotage to a vessel commissioned in the King's service?"

Davis broke down. "I cannot, sir, I cannot."

"You cannot what, sir?"

"I cannot be a part of this, sir. I have a wife and children of my own."

Winslow reached down, grabbed his lapels, and pulled Davis to his feet. "And do you suppose that this disagreeable business is an easy task for me, sir? Do you not realize that I, too, have a family, that we all have families? This troublesome affair is more grievous to me than any service I was ever employed in." Davis's rank breath was too much for Winslow and he released him. Davis slumped again into the chair. "Now, listen to me, sir. You will return to your ship, and you will find your anchor, and you will re-attach it to your vessel. Do you hear me?" Davis did not respond. "If you do not do as ordered, sir, I will have you placed under military arrest, and it will be ten years before you see your wife and children again! Do you understand me now, Mr. Davis?" roared Winslow.

Davis whispered, "Yes, sir. I understand." He gathered himself together and left the room.

Winslow stood in the window and watched Davis as he trudged, head down, back to his ship. Winslow understood the man's feelings, but he couldn't allow sympathy to factor into the increasingly touchy situation. Right now, what most irked him was that, in Piziquid Harbor, only five leagues away, sat the other vessels he needed to complete his task. A small gray patch of fog developed on the windowpane as he fumed, "What in God's name is delaying those damned transports!"

The next morning the mysterious anchor re-appeared and was re-attached to the *Neptune*.

By noon, Captain Davis was so drunk he couldn't stand.

Chapter Thirty-three

Confusion, Despair, and Desolation

October 26, 1755

Mr. Saul's supply ships and the transports that Winslow had been chafing for - nineteen in all - sloops, barques, brigantines, and three-masted schooners - sailed into Minas Basin and dropped anchor.* Three frigates (the armed escort) also arrived: the *Nightingale* under the command of Captain Diggs, the *Warren* under Captain Adams, and the *Halifax* under Captain Taggart. The sight of the ships, especially the three huge frigates fortified with serious cannon, and bobbing at their moorings like impatient aquatic steeds anxious to bolt, terrified the villagers and silenced the last of the optimists among them.

Then, on the morning of October 26, eighty soldiers stood at ease chatting leisurely on the shore. Suddenly an officer shouted, "Here they come! Here they come!"

A long line of Acadians was slowly and obediently making its way, on its own, across the great meadow, 585 women, elderly men, and children. Although not a shot had been fired, they already looked like a sad caravan of war-torn refugees. The slow zigzag spread itself over a mile and a half. A raw dampness thickened the air. Puffy cauliflower clouds joined forces

---

* The first of these ships arrived on October 10. The others followed, two or three a day, until the 26th. Some were already filled with Acadians from the Beauséjour-Amherst area.

overhead and created an oppressive, gray canopy. Women pulled wagons piled high with household goods; Colonel Winslow had made it clear that he didn't want the beach area clogged with draft animals. Wagons also carried the feeble, the sick, and the blind. Healthy children, arms full of toys, walked beside the wains, shivering. Governor Lawrence had ordered the Acadians to take only essential items and "no useless rubbish". Unable to distinguish, they carried, pulled, pushed, and dragged almost everything they owned. Every few yards, some woman fell to her knees and prayed, "Mon, Dieu! Mon Dieu! Sauvez-nous! Sauvez-nous!"* It was amazing that many could still produce tears; they had been weeping for fifty-two consecutive days.

In his journal, Winslow himself later described the scene:

> "... the women with great lamentations upon their knees .... It was a scene of confusion, despair and desolation."

Patient at first, and hoping to avoid open rebellion, Winslow allowed the men already imprisoned on the ships to come ashore and to re-board with their families. However, by afternoon, frustrated by this time-consuming method, he loaded the remaining vessels indiscriminately. Some families would, therefore, sail together; others would not.

Evangéline was one of the lucky ones. Her father came ashore and she ran to greet him. "Oh, mon père, mon père!" she shouted and threw her arms around his neck. "What have they done to you?" Benedict, out of breath, couldn't speak. "Come and sit for a minute. Rest yourself." She sat him down on her cedar chest, the chest that held her trousseau. Benedict placed his hand over his racing heart. Disoriented and confused, he mumbled. Evangéline put her ear to his mouth. "What is it, father? What are you trying to say?"

Benedict panted, coughed, and fought for breath. "I was wrong," he said. "I was wrong ... I told ... everyone ... that this would never happen... we were all wrong. We came here many years ago and... we settled on a salty marshland ... a place no one else wanted because for part of each day it belonged to the ocean tides. But we were wrong in thinking that ... that no one else would want this land. The English now want it. They want ... everything. They want it all. I ... I was wrong." Like a dazed prizefighter on his corner stool, Benedict, arms flailing, threw wild punches at a phantom

---

* "My God! My God! Save us! Save us!"

assailant before gracelessly sliding from the cedar chest and crumpling in a heap on the sand.

"Mon père!" she screamed. "Mon père! Mon père!"

A soldier's shiny boots appeared. "What's the matter with him?" The soldier stooped. "Oh, oh! Captain Osgood, looks as if we've got a dead one here!"

"Who is she?" asked Osgood.

"Must be his daughter," said the soldier.

"This is a fine mess. Well, we'll have to bury him. Get two men to help you and take him and the daughter away. And be quick about it!" shouted Osgood.

"Gabriel, où es-tu? Gabriel, où es-tu?"* Evangéline screamed. "Gabriel! Gabriel!"

An English officer responsible for loading the ships bellowed names. "Alin, Apigne, Aucoine! Line up here! Babin, Belmerre, Belfontaine, Benois, Blanchard, Blana, Bobin, Boudro, Bouer, Bouns, Bourg, Bourquette, Brane, Brans, Brasseux, Brassin, Braux! *In single file, you idiots!*"

*"Où allons-nous?"***

Berthe Commo, utterly confounded without her Oliver and already overwhelmed by memories, stood at the shoreline, perfectly still, in a catatonic daze. Evangéline called to her, "Madame Commo! Madame Commo!" The tide was rising and Berthe, knee-deep in the frigid water, gave no response. In strong gusts of wind the whitecap mist, like unraveling lace, swirled and coiled around her.

Infected now with panic, Evangéline screamed again, "Gabriel, où es-tu? Où es-tu?"

"Come along now, girl!" barked one of the three soldiers carrying her father's body up the embankment.

Back on the beach, the English officers who at first had only nudged and gently guided their prisoners, now with the quickly rising tide, jostled, shoved, prodded, and butted them with their rifles into the longboats. They snarled their baffling English orders into French ears, convinced that foreign-language comprehension came quicker with louder shouting. Both

---

* "Gabriel, where are you?"
** "Where are we going?"

Monsieur Landry and Monsieur Le Blanc, the interpreters, grew hoarse bellowing their translations.

"Line up here! Over *here*! Brune, Capierre, Caretter, Célestine, Celve, Chard, Cleland, Clémenson, Cloatre, Choc, Chelle, Commo, Cotoe! Hurry up! Daigre, David, Doiron, Doucet, Doulet, Duon! What's the matter with you? Hurry! Can't you move any faster?"

A different officer began shouting more names. "Over here! Dupuis, Dupiers, Duzoy, Forest, Gotro, Gouitin, Granger, Hébert, Landry, Le Blanc, Laurent, Lebare, Labous, Lapierre, Le Prince, Le Sour! Come along now! Majet, Massier, Melanson, Munier, Mengean!"

They buried Benedict in a shallow grave. "But we can't leave him here alone! We need a priest! We need a priest to—"

"There are no priests, girl! They've all been sent away! Come along now. Back to join the others."

"Oh, mon Pere, forgive me! Forgive me!"

When Evangéline returned to the beach, she had no idea which ship held Gabriel. "Come along, girl. No more time to waste. In the longboat you go. Don't worry. You're all going to the same place, you know," said a soldier trying to calm her with one of Mr. Morris's anti-panic strategies.

"Noalis, Pitre, Richard, Rous! This way! Over here! Sapin, Semer, Sonier, Sorere, Sosonier, Terriot, Tibodo, Trahan, Trahase, Tunour, Vincent! Hurry up now!"

*"Où est-ce qu'ils nous emmenent?"**

The tide rose higher and noisy breakers lashed the embankments. Chunks of copper clay gave way and slid into the sea. Evangéline stepped into the longboat. She prayed. "Dear God. Let them take me to Gabriel's ship."

Minutes later, she climbed a slippery brine-sodden ladder.

"Gabriel's on the *Leopard*," said little Simon Aucoine, one of the children Evangéline and Pierre had tutored in the schoolhouse. "*That* one!" he said pointing to a ship two hundred yards to their left.

"Gabriel! Gabriel!" she shouted in the direction of the *Leopard* and waved her arms frantically. Dozens waved back. It was useless.

"What's the name of *our* ship?" asked Simon as he stood on the deck holding Evangéline's hand.

---

* "Where are they taking us?"

"I don't know," she replied.

"What's *that*?" someone shouted.

"What's what?"

"That noise!"

Then everyone asked, "Yes, what *is* making that horrible noise?"

"Sounds like thunder," someone said. The rumble grew louder, and louder, and louder. "It isn't thunder." Whatever it was, it was coming from the land. All heads turned.

"Look, Evangéline! Look! Father Chauvreulx told us they wouldn't ever come back, but they have. They've come back!" said Simon, pulling at her skirt.

"Who has come back, Simon? Who?"

"The animals! The animals in the flames!"

Evangéline looked towards the village. High above the beach and across the great meadow, hundreds of wild-eyed horses, cows, sheep, and goats were stampeding away from the flames. Her eyes opened wider as she gazed in the direction of her newly-constructed home. Stabs of red flame pierced the thatched roof from within, and thousands of yellow sparks spewed haphazardly into the air. An order had been given to burn all of the Acadians' houses, barns, tool sheds, sawmills, and churches.[1] The demolition was intended to demoralize the residents and to discourage any thoughts they might have of returning to Grand Pré. The arson order had, of course, been issued by Governor Lawrence.[2]

Evangéline and Simon watched in silence as the old Mi'kmaw's incomplete scroll slowly materialized in the distance, this time complete with the cross atop the steeple of St. Charles Des Mines straining, unsuccessfully, to detach itself from the savagery below.

"Pourquoi nous font-ils ça? Pourquoi? Pourquoi?"*

Its anchor weighed, its mainsail set, the ship lurched, throwing Evangéline and Simon off balance. Sheets of canvas whip-slapped in their ears, and the fumigating reek of tar stung their nostrils. She looked to her left, then ran along the railing towards the ship's quarterdeck. As she ran, she noticed Charles Le Blanc who stood and stared at his burning workshop. "Oh, Charles," she said, "all of your designs! Your wheels!"

Then she saw that the *Leopard* had turned and was already under full sail; in fact, the entire 27-ship convoy was now underway creating

---

* "Why are they doing this to us? Why? Why?"

a sight of terrible beauty, a breathtaking seascape of cruel magnificence in the skimming spindrift. Evangéline stood still and pressed her hands together in prayer. Facing the *Leopard,* she then parted her hands slightly, and proceeded to spread her arms as widely as she could. She whispered softly, "From here to Avignon, my Gabriel. From here to Avignon and back again."

With the tide at its fullest, Evangéline sailed away to an unknown destination on a dangerously overloaded ship whose name she didn't even know.

Overseeing the entire spectacle from the high pine branches on the southern ridge were the ever-vigilant Mi'kmaq sentinels. They gazed calmly down on the twenty-seven small specks on the horizon until they vanished completely. The older Mi'kmaq warrior sighed. Then he spoke to his companion in their ancient language, as ancient as the yearning in the salmon's upstream journey, "Na wulias pasik nike' Aklasie'wk nkitmi'tij kmitki'nu," he said, "Kjisaqmaw Klu'skap [3] kisi apaja'sis wmitki Wko'qekji'jk."[*]

And together they swore to remember all of the old Mi'kmaq ways.

****

Halifax, November 9, 1755 (Two Weeks Later)

"A letter for you, sir," said Lawrence's adjutant, Mr. Stone, as he entered the governor's office. "It appears to be from London, sir."

Lawrence looked at the letter and hesitated as though fearful of its contents. Slowly he opened the wax seal and scanned the long message until his eyes focused on the last paragraph:

> 'It cannot, therefore, be too much recommended to you, to use the greatest caution and prudence in your conduct towards these Neutrals, and to assure such of them, as may be trusted, specially upon their taking the oath, that they may remain in the quiet possession of their settlements under proper regulations.
>
> 'Thomas Robinson,
> Secretary of State,
> 13 August, 1755
> London, England'

---

[*] "And now if only the English would leave our land, the great god Klu'skap could return to his home on Blomidon."

"This letter was written three months ago. Why am I receiving it only now?" asked Lawrence.

Mr. Stone replied, "The young man who delivered it a few minutes ago, a Captain Innes, said that his ship, the *Otter*, was detained for the past few weeks in Newfoundland. Some sort of repair work being done on the jib boom, I believe he said."

"Well," said Lawrence with a heavy sigh.

Mr. Stone waited for a more detailed reply. Then he asked, "Well, sir?"

"Well, indeed, Mr. Stone. Well, well, well, well!"

****

All was quiet now in Grand Pré, and icy blasts of northern air strode through the desolate village like brash new money come to town. The days grew shorter and the darkness came even earlier when the November afternoon skies, in a dry cough, sputtered out the first few snowflakes of the season. The sap froze in the evergreens so that they creaked and cracked like brittle, arthritic bones when they swayed on their trunks in the night. No moon shone now like diamonds on a black velvet sea, and the gleam in the retreating feline's eyes had slunk away and disappeared. Icy gusts, like howling madmen, raced across the great meadow and tossed about the ashes of the burnt houses in a grisly game of catch.

And the apple tree, under which the young lovers had kissed, shook like a shadowy, sickened, fallen angel, and its gnarled branches, in impotent spasms, fluttered and pointed his black, bony wingtips towards a distant and imperceptible horizon.

PART TWO

Introduction

Since few facts have been documented about the Acadians' faithful quest for their loved ones in the American colonies, we must be content with a continuation of her story that can only be, at best, a probable extension. We can reconstruct the rest of her life by inference, speculate with some accuracy, and safely assume a few things. We do know of the treatment - good and bad - that many of the Acadian exiles received in the colonies. We also know that Evangéline was beautiful, young, and innocent, and we all know what happens, in any era, to beautiful, young, innocent girls: they are admired by some and placed on pedestals; and they are coveted and preyed upon by others, their pedestals and their lives shattered.

Therefore, using the few threads which are available, we can continue to stitch together the remaining patches in the priceless quilt of *Evangéline*. Some of the following patches may appear less colorful and less vivid in their pastel depiction of characters and events. A few patches may even seem, to some, badly mismatched. But we must extend the one segment with which we are familiar in order to attach the final square, the breathtaking end-piece that is, without doubt, one of the most poignant conclusions in the long history of love itself.

Chapter Thirty-four

On the Auction Block

Evangéline leaned against the teak railing of the *Seaflower*, [1] the schooner on which she had journeyed for the past fifteen days, as it slid slowly into Boston Harbor. The ship had been overloaded, carrying 206 passengers instead of 182 for a 91-ton vessel. She and some other passengers stood on deck enjoying the fresh air. Prisoners, fifty at a time, had permission to walk the decks for two hours, once a day. With her emerald green eyes, underlined now with dark half-circles, she surveyed the foreign scene. She focused, not on the unpainted wooden warehouses at dockside, nor on the busy muddy streets of colonial Boston, but on the other ships that were either docked or that lay at anchor farther out in the bay. Although dismayed by the great number of ships, she realized that the quantity also increased her possibilities that Gabriel could be on one of them.

These hopes, however, had very little foundation. Governor Lawrence had already made certain of that.

To avoid information leaks concerning the deportation, Lawrence (with the help of Charles Morris, the young provincial surveyor) had arranged with Colonel Winslow to give the ships' captains their secret sailing orders with their proposed destination points only after they had set sail. Each captain, therefore, knew only his own destination and not the destinations of any of the other deportation vessels.

Also leaning on the teak railing, about fifteen yards to her right, were the twins, Cécile and Céleste. They looked without interest on Boston, simply staring down into the icy November water. They had not spoken a word since their rape by the soldiers. Then, without breathing a word, and as though on some undetectable cue, each simultaneously let her rosary slip from her fingers. The two strings of green and black beads barely made a ripple on the water's surface as though nothing of any significance had fallen. Evangéline watched helplessly. Such gestures of despair were common sights now. The prisoners had to decide which ones they would allow to disturb them most. They could pick and choose.

Then Evangéline turned her gaze upon the growing town.

It is difficult now to imagine the Boston of 1755. Of the remarkable Boston that we know today - the proud city still carried forward by its traditions, the elderly yet vigorous city, ever competitive with its elegant hotels, its prestigious colleges, its state-of-the-art hospitals, and its world-class traffic congestion - only its pride and its competitive spirit flourished in 1755.

Evangéline peered down at the streets and docks swarming with the spasmodic steps of city dwellers moving like ants to and fro, on missions of mysterious purpose. Among the pedestrians, however, she couldn't see anyone that resembled Gabriel.

Evangéline, at this time, made the first of her many bargains with God. "Please God," she whispered as she knelt at the railing, "if I can be reunited with Gabriel, I promise that I will never commit another sin for the rest of my life." It was, in a way, a poor bargain for God since, up to now, she had never committed a sin intriguing enough to catch His Divine attention. Nevertheless, it was her sincere promise that counted.

All of a sudden, the captain of her ship, Captain Nathaniel Downall, a middle-aged man from the Territory of Maine, rushed past her, descended the gangplank, and spoke to a distinguished gray-haired gentleman. The dapper elderly man wore a stylish royal-blue dress-coat over an immaculate white shirt with ruffles at the cuffs. The two men then began shouting at each other. Evangéline couldn't understand what they were saying since their ravings were in English. Raving, she concluded, must be both the Canadian and American form of English communication.

She didn't recognize the well-dressed man although some of her neighbors might have - those who had been delegates to Halifax and subsequent prisoners on George's Island. The man in the fashionable blue coat was Mr. Benjamin Green, one of the members of Governor Lawrence's council. Mr. Green, a former resident of Boston, was wealthy. Now, back in

Boston, he was nursing a bothersome guilty conscience. Irony ruled again because Green was, on this day, arguing with a fellow "Englishman" on behalf of the French Canadians he himself had helped deport. "But I need to unload these people now!" shouted the captain. "I have my old folks to see at home before I sail again in four days! I can't have my ship tied up here while you hold meetings with Boston politicians! Meetings with politicians can go on forever!"

"You can't release your prisoners just yet," said Green. "Arrangements must be made for them. The good people of Boston do not want 206 new beggars walking their streets, applying for public assistance, and filling up their charitable institutions. They have enough beggars of their own to feed!"

"Well, then, why can't I just take them back up the coast and drop them off at Portsmouth?"

"We have already asked the people of the New Hampshire Colony to cooperate and take some of these immigrants, but they have absolutely refused."

"Well, for how long must my ship be tied up here?"

"Until I meet with the town council of Boston and we come up with a plan to absorb these poor people into our society in a way that is as painless as possible for everyone concerned. Good day to you, now. I must be off to the council meeting," said Green walking away. Then he turned and said, "Be a little patient, sir, and you'll soon see your family again, unlike the poor devils you have transported here."

"Aye, and transported here upon your orders, eh, Mr. Green?" said the captain impudently.

Green flinched. "You should be on your way in a day or two." He turned again to go. "Oh … and provided, of course, that your passengers are disease-free."

"May God damn to the hottest council chamber in hell all bloody politicians!" shouted the captain, as he stormed back up the gangplank of his impounded vessel. "Disease-free, indeed!"

When he reached the deck of his ship, the captain saw Evangéline on her knees, and he shouted, "What's the matter with you? Are you sick, girl?" Evangéline didn't understand and looked up in fear at the captain. "Bah! What's the use!" he snorted and continued on his way.

The disease that Green and the captain were referring to, and the one feared most at that time, was typhus. People had good reason to fear this illness since it was deadly and highly contagious.

In typhus, microscopic organisms spread by common lice attack the small blood vessels of the body especially those of the skin and brain. The facial complexion is so affected that the victim becomes almost unrecognizable. The circulation of the blood through the facial vessels stagnates, causing unsightly swelling and discoloration. The dark discoloration gave it the name of 'black fever' in some countries. In addition, the victim's temperature rises and he fidgets violently and raves deliriously. As the fever rages, the victim, so desperate to cool off, might jump out a window or off a bridge. The sufferer all the while is in great pain and vomits, develops sores and gangrene, loses fingers, toes, and feet, and develops such a disgusting body odor that the doctor can detect it long before he enters the sickroom.*

Fortunately, typhus had not been a lethal passenger aboard Evangéline's ship. However, there had been seasickness which provided the high volume of vomit expected from farmers with no sea legs. Later reports, though, did confirm the presence of typhus aboard some of the other deportation vessels that had feverishly drifted on to more distant destinations. There had been, as we know now, many other vessels deployed for many other deportations after many other arrests. In his complete demoralization scheme, Governor Lawrence had multiplied his villainies by leaving in ashes many other Canadian villages besides Grand Pré.

****

One week later, the *Seaflower*, still fully loaded, knocked monotonously against the dock in Boston Harbor. Captain Downall paced furiously up and down the deck. The politicians were still working things out.

Evangéline and her compatriots, below deck, were doing all the things they had been doing for the past eighteen days: they prayed, coughed, shivered, wept silently, prayed again, then sobbed aloud, "Dear God, have mercy! Let all of our misery pass, and lead us away from here for we are strangers in this foreign land."

Benjamin Green was trying hard to right his wrong. However, he had his hands full and soon discovered, with a kind of dramatic justice, how difficult it was to confront a council whose mind was already made up. These New England council members were even more xenophobic than the

---

    *   The information in this description is taken from Cecil Woodham-Smith's *The Great Hunger*, Penguin, New York, 1989, p. 188 - 189.

Nova Scotia ones. Not only that, but they took their orders from a frugal, puritanical, no-nonsense, and strongly anti-Catholic populace. Yet, it was not so much that the Acadian immigrants were French-speaking, Catholic, new mouths to feed; they were, most of all, just new mouths to feed. Green understood well the puritan mind; "it liked to converse upon a page from the universal Bible, but it acted upon a page from the municipal ledger."[*] He spoke to the Boston city councilors, therefore, in purely financial terms and together they came up with a plan.

On the afternoon of the eighteenth day in Boston, Evangéline and her neighbors disembarked and stood on the dock at auction, like slaves or workhorses. Then, after a close and humiliating personal inspection they were handed over, either individually or in groups, to residents of Massachusetts who would take them and employ them. According to the plan, the local residents would immediately provide the immigrants with basic necessities for which they would be financially reimbursed by the government of Massachusetts. The council instructed employers to keep a strict written account of any goods they provided to their new employees.

With this procedure, however, the ledger pen was invested with a cruel power that became, in the next few years, mightier than the combined power of all other weapons used against the Acadians.[**] Some of the new English-speaking employers took deliberate and unfair financial advantage of them. Many petitions documenting such financial exploitation still exist.

Worst of all, the separation[2] of parents from children, wives from husbands, brothers from brothers, and sisters from sisters took place not only at *departure* sites like Grand Pré, but on the auction blocks at the ports of entry. Farmers needing strong arms for chores didn't know (because of the language barrier) that they were getting only part of a family when they accepted two or three strapping young boys, or one or two hardy, capable girls. Like salt in their wounds, this indentured service plan continued and extended the Acadians' punishment, and made their heartbreak even more unbearable. Moreover, their French language now became even more of a serious handicap. It alienated them from their new culture much more than it had from their old one in Nova Scotia.

In many ways, their hardships had just begun.

---

[*]   From Thomas Chandler Haliburton's *Historical and Statistical Account of Nova Scotia,* Halifax, 1829, p. 178.

[**]   Ibid

Evangéline was sent off to work on a Massachusetts farm nine miles out of Boston on the southern road to Roxbury and Wrentham.* (She never saw the twins again.) Sent along with her were François Hébert, Charles Le Blanc the creative wheelwright, Jude Le Blanc the notary's son, and an older man named Claude Trahan. She felt fortunate to be in the company of François Hébert. François was feisty and, as an independent thinker, he was not easily intimidated. He had lost, however, some of his defiance when, as a punishment for his part in the escape from the *Leopard*, (in addition to the burning of his home), he had been deliberately placed on a different ship from his wife and two children. Like Evangéline and so many others, his only mission now was to be reunited with his loved ones.

Young Jude would also prove to be a useful boy since his father had taught him to speak English. In fact, when his father was not available, Jude had occasionally interpreted for Colonel Winslow in Grand Pré. Moreover, certain suspicions had arisen over Jude's many visits to Winslow's quarters; but though the gossip flew, none of the scandalous allegations of 'spying for the English' proved well-founded. The simple fact was that any Acadian who spoke English was regarded as a suspicious character and a superficial francophone. This anti-English prejudice, perfectly justified in Grand Pré, now was plainly an unaffordable luxury in New England. From now on, in order to survive, every deported Acadian would have to try to learn, at least, *some* English. Evangéline didn't hesitate. If learning English would help her to locate Gabriel, so be it. She would even learn German if she had to. Even Irish, even Scottish!

---

* At this time Boston was a peninsula and the only road out led southward across "the neck" to Roxbury, Dedham, and Wrentham.

Chapter Thirty-five

The Kindly Mr. Black

The farm of Mr. Zackariah Black, nine miles out of Boston, was a prosperous one of two hundred acres. There were cows, pigs, sheep, horses, and chickens to care for and, come summer, there would be numerous vegetable gardens with potatoes, carrots, tomatoes, and peas to weed.

Mr. Black, although a grandfather, was still strong and energetic. With his silver hair and beard, and kindly, relaxed, smiling face, he looked like Santa Claus without the burdensome bowl full of jelly.

Mistress Black was even slimmer than her husband and slightly taller. She wore the look of the typical puritan female, her face a list of what might have been. Etched into her face, her repressions spoiled her natural beauty and muted her natural healthy passions; a face that could have been a gem – a sparkling ruby set in silver – was instead a piece of estate jewelry, a dull garnet buried in filigreed pewter.

Jude Le Blanc had heard some good things about Mr. Black and his wife, Elizabeth. "People say that they are the kindest folks around," reported Jude. "They are always taking orphans and other unwanted children into their home. They even take in crippled children and children who are silly in the head."

"That must be why they took you in, Jude," said Charles in fun.

Within weeks, Evangéline, François, Jude, Charles, and Claude settled in and became good dependable workers on the Black homestead. The four men built extensions on the farmhouse and the barns; and they waited for springtime when they would work the fields. Evangéline milked cows, fed chickens, did the household laundry and some kitchen chores. Every day she, François, Charles, and Claude learned a few more English words from Jude, and within months, they could speak clearly enough to be understood. The two older men learned more slowly because their resentment was greater, and their vexation at having to learn the tongue of Governor Lawrence and Colonel Winslow often spilled over onto Jude, their unappreciated tutor. Jude understood and did not take their verbal abuse personally.

Evangéline worked long hard hours and, although poorly paid, she didn't complain. It would all work out somehow in the end, she just knew it! She saved every shilling she earned. Someday soon, when she had saved enough, she would be able to travel the country in search of Gabriel. The only thing to do now was to work, and pray, and save.

She tried to make friends with the other farm girls though it was difficult because of the high turnover among the Blacks' foster children. They came and went quickly, sometimes so abruptly that it triggered her keen sense of loss and she found herself crying uncontrollably. Later, she would worry about the futures of those castoffs since many of them were sad cases. No one wanted to take in grown children, especially those who were lame, blind, deaf, or mentally unstable.

****

April 8, 1756

She was not in Boston on this particular morning to hear the church bells of King's Chapel. A wedding was taking place.

Less than six months after the deportation, Miss Abigail Allen and Mr. Jonathan Belcher were fulfilling their contract. After the honeymoon, they planned to move permanently to Halifax which, Jonathan swore, was now "safer than London." The whole province of Nova Scotia, he said, was much safer now that the "violent" French Acadians had all been deported. The land of Acadia was now populated only by "God-fearing, civilized Englishmen."

Ding, dong bell!

****

One day in early June, Mistress Black discovered that one of her foster daughters was pregnant. Mistress Black had no sympathy for a pregnant foster child. She took the pregnancy personally, as a sign of the girl's ingratitude and lack of appreciation for her kindness in taking the girl in. Whenever she was told of a pregnancy, she flew into a rage, swore up and down at the "selfish" girl, and put her and her baggage out on the highroad. "How could she do this to *me*!" was her regular response.

Evangéline heard about the pregnancy from one of the milkmaids who had leaned over her pail and whispered, "Have you heard about poor Mary Hawkins? She's got herself in the family way and Mistress Black has given her just two days' notice."

Evangéline was stunned. How could that happen to Mary? What young man would do such a thing? Mary Hawkins was a large, loud, laughing girl with flaming red hair and freckles flecking her pale complexion. Despite her homeliness, Mary was a delightful girl to have around because she was always happy, always smiling. The farm work was hard and the hours were long, but they could always depend upon Mary for a smile or an outsized giggle.

Evangéline had been assigned kitchen duties on this particular day and was scrubbing the floor of the pantry, just off the kitchen, when Mr. Black entered the back door with Mary Hawkins. "I've brought the girl."

"I can see that!" said Mistress Black coldly.

"The Acadian men will be here shortly. I've sent Tom to fetch them."

"The Acadian men?" thought Evangéline. What was this all about? Why were Francois, Claude, and Charles all being summoned to the farmhouse? This was highly unusual. Were they to be given extra work to do? Perhaps as a punishment? Or some special kind of work? Some secret work? Evangeline stood still, listening intently.

"Take that smirk off your face, girl!" snapped Mistress Black. Mary did look somewhat insolent standing there with her belly protruding, and smiling into the scowling face of Mistress Black. It was not Mary's intention, however, to look insolent. She was a simple girl and didn't understand the social implications of her maternal condition and couldn't figure out the cause of Mistress Black's hostility.

There was a brief awkward silence. Then Mr. Black said, "I'll just step out and see what is keeping Tom," and he hurried out the door before his wife could object.

Evangéline felt caught in the middle. She didn't know whether to leave the pantry or stay quietly where she was. Before she could decide, the kitchen door opened and her friends entered with Mr. Black. The three men looked nervous, but curious. Nothing had been explained to them.

Mistress Black took charge. She stood pointing at François Hébert and asked, "Mary, is this man the father of your child? You must tell us who the father is so that we can hold him financially accountable."

François heard and understood the accusation. He gasped and was about to protest when Mary said, "No, not him."

Elizabeth turned and pointed to Claude Trahan. "Is this the father?" Claude was confused. He was still struggling to understand English. He understood only that angry finger-pointing was not a good sign.

"Oh, no, Mistress Black!"

Elizabeth pointed to Charles Le Blanc. "Well, then, is he the one?"

"I don't know him at all," said Mary.

"Who is the father of your unborn child, then?"

Mary Hawkins stared down at the wide pine floorboards and refused to answer.

"Get out! All of you!" snarled Elizabeth.

Mary and the three men left.

Evangéline breathed a sigh of relief.

There was an awkward silence now as the husband and wife stood alone. Evangéline thought she heard a sob. Then Elizabeth said softly, "Another broken promise." Her husband made no response. "How many more? How many more must I endure?" Tension was building. "You loved *me* once."

"Oh, let us not bring up that old story again, Elizabeth. You have paid little attention to me for years."

"Is it any wonder after all the girls I've had to dismiss because of you?"

"You cast me aside first," said Zachariah coldly.

"I was ill."

"You were ill because you refused to take care of yourself. You still defy me and refuse to eat properly. To spite me."

"Well, anyone can see that Mary Hawkins has plenty of meat on her bones to please you."

"I grew tired of wearing the bruises from your bony embraces," said Zachariah cruelly.

"You grew tired of me because one female is not enough for your bottomless lust."

Zachariah had developed the strange idea that his wife's emaciated physique was a deliberate scheme of hers, a plot against him. Her skinny frame, he reasoned, was a reflection of an inner emotional deficiency, a deficiency willfully contrived to deprive him of his rightful masculine share of pleasure. She could have eaten more to put flesh on her bones; she could have felt about him more deeply, cared more deeply, loved him more deeply. It was just a matter of will, of wanting to. He was the victim here, he felt; she was the villain.

Hearing all of this malice, Evangéline stood frozen in place. She had never been exposed to such domestic turmoil. The coldness, the anger, the bitterness, the death of love between a man and wife – this was all new to her. She felt a chill in her blood. How is it possible for marital love to die in such a hateful manner?"

"I don't believe you *ever* loved me," said Zachariah.

"I don't believe you ever loved *me*," answered Elizabeth.

"You took interest in me only when another woman came along."

"You took an interest in me only when—"

Zachariah shouted, "Woman, for Heaven's sake, at least make up your own criticisms of me and stop hurling my criticisms of you back in my face!"

Elizabeth went silent for a moment. Then she said quietly, "I do not spend my time thinking up criticisms of you. I have made no list of *your* shortcomings. The only criticism I have is that you no longer love me as you once did. As you once *said* you did."

"You have only one love, Elizabeth, and that is your role as mistress of this prosperous farm. You love power, status, and control, not me. You oversee every aspect of this farm. You attend to every detail. You are a storehouse of pettiness. If you had paid half of the attention to me as you have to this farm, I would have been the happiest man in Massachusetts."

"So now I am petty because I take care of the farm business that you hate to handle. And what status, pray tell, does any woman have when she is considered a fool by women with faithful husbands? Status! Other women wonder why I remain with you!"

"You are free to leave at any time," said Zachariah with brutal detachment. She was, of course, not at all free to leave and he knew it. Nothing that they owned was in her name, not even the clothes on her back. In 1755, in the eyes of the law, women were minors. Elizabeth buried her head in her hands and sobbed.

Zachariah walked out and slammed the door behind him. Elizabeth rose and went upstairs to her bedroom.

Evangéline then tiptoed out of the farmhouse. She was horrified. She didn't know what to do, or where to go. She trembled with fear and outrage. "Dear God, the father of Mary's child is the kindly Mr. Black! Oh, God, help Mary! Oh, God, help her! And help me! Show me the way! Lead me away from this cruel place! Please, God, please!" She wanted to run away now as fast as she could, but to where? "Oh, please, God, please!"

The next day a rumor went round the farm that Mistress Black was so distraught that she had gone into Boston to see a doctor. "Perhaps she took Mary with her," said Evangéline to herself. After all, it was Mary who was more in need of a doctor.

Later that evening, Elizabeth Black returned from Boston. She had not seen a doctor after all, but had visited a friend, a Mr. Robert Edwards, a wealthy importer who lived with his aging mother on a newly developing back lane, a lane later called Beacon Street.

Elizabeth had taken charge once again. She had another messy clean-up campaign to run. It infuriated her that she had to clean up after her husband again. "Men are so childish!" she mumbled to herself. "They are always making messes! As boys, they mess their pants. As men, they mess other people's pants!"

Well, something had to be done, and she was the one who had to do it. In fact, two things had to be done: Mary Hawkins had to go, and so did Evangéline. Mistress Black no longer could give her reckless husband any chance of falling in love with one of his charges. Evangéline was too young, too beautiful, and too much of a temptation for her high-spirited spouse. An animal affair with a defenseless servant like Mary Hawkins was one thing; but a head-spinning love affair with a young, intelligent French beauty was quite out of the question.

The visit with Robert Edwards, then, had been to explore an option presented by his bedridden mother who needed a young French maid to assist her old, rheumatic French maid, a woman who had faithfully served Robert's mother for the past thirty years.

Evangéline had prayed for an escape and, within a day, her prayers were answered. Tomorrow she would travel into Boston and become a French maid in the luxurious home of Mistress Robert T. Edwards and her son and heir, the handsome, rich, and single, Mr. Robert T. Edwards Jr.

Chapter Thirty-six

I Am Very Rich

"This calls for a celebration. Get the brandy, Robert," said Mistress Edwards with a mischievous grin.

"But, mother, it's only eleven o'clock in the morning."

"Fetch the brandy, son. When you're eighty-five, and perpetually horizontal, it's never too early in the day for brandy." Evangéline's English still needed polishing but she understood enough of it to giggle at the old woman's decadence.

Although she was an invalid, Mistress Edwards had a positive attitude that gave her incredible energy and vivacity. And despite the fact that she was an English-speaking American, she demonstrated exactly the brand of irrepressible spunk Evangéline needed to cultivate at this point in her life. This elderly lady with bad habits set a good example. She had never given up on life even though it was obvious that her best days were all behind her.

Robert did as he was told and brought some brandy.

"Now, I suppose Marie has already told you your duties?"

"Some, madame, oui," said Evangéline.

"Good. It will take a little time to learn them all. Well, now we can have a little chat. Tell me about yourself, my child. Where do you come from?"

"From Acadia, in Nova Scotia, madame."

"Oh, yes, Nova Scotia. I visited Nova Scotia with my first husband many years ago. I can't really say I liked the place. Too far north and too cold for me. My husband liked it, though. But that was probably because he made a lot of money there. My husband - the sweetest, most generous man in all the world!" She paused to catch her breath and to empty her glass. "More brandy, Robert!" Her glass was bone-dry. "Oh, I am enjoying myself. Nothing I enjoy more than hearing about the lives of young people. My husband enjoyed that, too. Such a sweet man!" Robert handed her a second drink and, after taking a long slow swig, she exhaled and smirked as if to say, 'Oh, Lord, that was good!' Evangéline blinked in disbelief. "Now, tell me, what was it that you did back in Nova Scotia?"

"I lived on my father's farm, madame," said Evangéline.

"Oh, farm life is a lovely life! I grew up on a farm, too, a lovely big, sprawling farm down in Virginia. It makes me lonesome just thinking about it. Ah, those were the days," said Mistress Edwards. "Those were the days! It's so sad. Those days are gone forever,"

"My farm days were not so happy," said Evangéline.

"Well, come to think of it, mine were not all that happy either. So much work! So many chores! But I suppose we only remember the happy times, don't we? Ha! Ha! Ha! I did have some jolly old times back then! Ha! Ha! Ha!" The noontime brandy had hit its mark.

Mistress Edwards radiated all of the fascination that bold, big-city women have for bashful, country girls. At twenty-five or thirty, she must have been an attractive, statuesque creature with dark red hair, steely blue eyes, and a smile that could reanimate a dead man. For the more uxorious men in her life, she must have been an exhausting handful, with all of the treacherous charm of a spoiled, demanding courtesan.

But now, at eighty-five, except for the eyes, all of the physical beauty was gone - withered, shrunken, dried, spent. Her slender, bony body had that unsightly etiolated skin of the elderly, shiny and transparent, skin so loose it seemed that she could move around underneath it without disturbing its surface. It hung at the jowls and below the eyes in gray folds like tiny, crescent drapery swags.

Most remarkably, although she was still spoiled and still insatiable, those twinkling, laughing, bright blue eyes of hers could still beguile - almost seduce; but only briefly, for the selfishness behind them soon set her victim free.

Mistress Edwards babbled on for another hour before tiring. "Well, I would love to hear more about your life in Canada but it's time for my midday nap. We shall talk more later, my child. Would you tell Marie to come in here now?"

"Oui, madame," said Evangéline and went to fetch Marie.

"Ah, Marie, it's time for my nap. That young girl is such a polite, pretty thing, but she has me completely worn out with all her talk of Nova Scotia farm life. Don't forget to bring my tea at two."

"Oui, madame," said Marie as she closed the door behind her.

Evangéline was happy to be employed in a warm spacious mansion and removed from the company of the vile Mr. Black. And she had never seen such luxury! Carpets six yards long, real silverware - not pewter - cherry furniture from France, and pretty hand-painted dishes with blue, miniature, crab apple trees - all the way from China!

She enjoyed hearing Marie's Parisian French, and soon began to understand the English orders of Mistress Edwards.

And Robert was such a considerate man that he spoke to her one day saying, "Vous êtes très jolie, Evangéline,"* in his best textbook French.

****

The next day Evangéline told Mistress Edwards about Gabriel, and the old woman extended genuine sympathy, but mentally countered it by concluding that Evangéline would make a good wife for her son. This new maid of hers, though foreign and from common stock, was stunningly beautiful and refreshingly innocent. Innocence mattered a great deal because her son was a timid man. Experienced women rattled him. "Life is too short and too precious to waste waiting for the perfect man to come along," Mistress Edwards said. "You should enjoy every minute of your youth, my dear. Oh, when I think of how I made my two husbands suffer with all my coy, competitive games. I always toyed with their affections when I should have simply enjoyed their company. Well, my first husband's, anyway."

Evangéline replied, "But a young woman cannot give herself to any man who comes along, madame."

"Why not?" answered Mistress Edwards. Evangéline laughed, pleasantly scandalized. "An older woman like myself cares only that a man - *any* man, shows an interest - *any* interest in her. The sad thing about being eighty-five is that no man ever shows interest in you. Men don't look

---

*   "You are very pretty!"

at you anymore. They look past you. Life is very cold and empty, my dear, when no one ever touches you out of love and passion. These days the only one who touches me is my doctor! And he's as old as I am!"

For the sake of argument, Evangéline replied, "But a young girl never knows when a man's affection is sincere."

"And that's exactly why you should never refuse any of them! You never know which ones you could be hurting by your rejection." Evangéline laughed again. "Short-term affection is better than no affection at all, my dear. We women are always waiting for our prince to come along. But I shall tell you a secret: inside every man is a prince and it's up to a woman to bring out the prince in him. Yes, it's true, it's true! And a woman can bring out the prince in her man and keep him out by her love, acceptance, and approval." Then she sighed, "But any man with breath and strength enough to hold my hand would be a prince to me now."

Evangéline smiled, thought of her mother, then took the hand of Mistress Edwards and patted it. The old lady, so moved by this genuine gesture of affection, took a handsome gold cross from her neck and placed it around Evangéline's.

"Oh, no, I can't accept," protested Evangéline. "It's too valuable for me."

"You have suddenly become very valuable to me, my dear. I hope you will stay with me for a long, long time. I never expected to enjoy such wonderful new company at my age. Suddenly, I am very happy. I have plenty of money, I have my son - my only heir - and I now have a beautiful young companion. That cross was a little gift to me from my son. So, you see, it's a small treasure that we will all share, our little secret." Mistress Edwards winked like a wily conspirator.

Evangéline held the cross and stared at it. It was useless to protest further. "Merci beaucoup," she whispered. Perhaps someday it would bring her good luck.

****

"Fetch the brandy, Evangéline! It's time to have a little chat," said Mistress Edwards. It was noon, one week later. "Come and tell me how you are getting on with Marie. She's getting old and forgetful, you know. I'm getting old, too, and unfortunately, I remember *everything*!"

"Oui, madame," said Evangéline as she poured Mistress Edwards her noonday drink.

"You may have a small one, too, if you wish, my dear."

"No, merci, madame." Evangéline grinned at the old woman's noontime intemperance. Aristocrats were so fascinating! So independent! So spoiled! So irresponsible! They made their own rules.

"Well, now tell me, have you heard any news around town about your compatriots?"

"There's a lot of suffering among them," said Evangéline sadly. "Some have no warm clothes. And the people of Boston call them dirty names."

"Suffering, yes, yes, suffering. Well, I know all about suffering, my dear. I've suffered all my life. Life is nothing but a vale of tears. And just look at me now. An old invalid stuck in this bed all day long. God only knows how I've suffered! But they say God rewards those who suffer here on earth. Well, I only hope He's keeping a good eye on me!"

"Oui, madame."

"And have you heard any news about your fiancé? Has he arrived here in Boston yet?"

"No, madame, nothing. If he was here, one of my friends would have told me by now."

"Well, isn't that too bad! But where could he be?"

"I've heard that the English have sent my neighbors down the coast as far as Georgia."

"Ah, Georgia! I wish someone would take me to Georgia. I hear it's one of the most beautiful places on earth! I need some place that's beautiful and warm. Boston is such a cold damp town! A friend of mine moved to Georgia a few years ago and, do you know, she has never written me even the smallest letter to tell me about her life there? Some people are so thoughtless, I find."

"Oui, madame."

"Well, I hate to say this, but perhaps it's time you started looking for a new fiancé. There's no telling where Gabriel is now. He may be gone forever, my dear."

"No, madame, he's not gone forever. I will find him."

"It disturbs me to see a young pretty girl like you so unhappy, and pining away for a man you may never see again. You must not waste your life, you know. Life is too precious a thing to waste. Far, far too precious!"

"Oui, madame."

"It's terrible to grow old alone. You don't know how terrible it is. You are young and you think that you have plenty of time. But you don't, my dear. You must seize happiness wherever you find it. And," she winked and giggled, "catch, and hold fast to any man you can! Ha! Ha! Ha!" The brandy was again hitting its mark.

"Oui, madame."

"And I shall tell you another of life's secrets, my dear; it's terrible to grow old poor! A woman needs security. Yes, she does, especially when she loses her looks! I tell you, life is very hard on old women! Financial security is a woman's only consolation." Mistress Edwards paused for a moment. "Tell me, my child, - and of course, it's none of my business - but does your fiancé have a lot of money?"

"No, madame, he does not. He's a blacksmith."

"Hmmm. I thought so. A blacksmith! Well, of course, it's up to you. If you want to wait for a poor man who may never arrive, that's entirely up to you. But you should start thinking about your own future. You mustn't wait too long. A girl's pretty face doesn't last forever, you know. I was beautiful once. But," she laughed, "God knows, that wasn't yesterday! Ha! Ha!"

"Oui, madame."

"Oh, it just wears me out trying to help other people! Fill up my glass again, will you, dear?"

"Oui, madame."

****

That evening, Marie instructed Evangéline in her evening duties. Up until now, Evangéline had cared for the old woman only during the day. She watched attentively as Marie bathed, powdered, perfumed, and dressed the old woman in a clean, *lace* nightgown. Then there was the clipping of the nails - all twenty – the oiling of the face and hands, and the brushing of the straw-and-pepper hair. Evangéline took everything in but was puzzled at the spreading of the hair. "Is it necessary," Evangéline asked Marie later in the hallway, "to spread out her long hair on her pillow?"

"Mais, oui," said Marie. "Once she gets into her bed for the night, she will lie on her back, and then you must fan out her hair on her pillow. She will be angry if you forget to do this."

"Is it *that* important?"

"Oui, oui, very important."

"But why?"

Marie winked and said, "It means that she is then ready to receive her husband."

"Receive her husband? But her husband is dead!"

"He is dead, yes. But her memory is not.

****

Although Robert, the son and heir of Mistress Edwards, was a handsome man, his good looks had not given him much self-confidence. He was one of those men with an inherent weakness, a timidity, an insecurity that propelled him, at times, into overcompensating actions. He would, at such times, and for no apparent reason, become surprisingly aggressive and assert himself as no truly confident man would. Especially when drinking, he would cast aside his normal reserve and make sudden and desperate attempts at affection, highly inappropriate displays that startled and unnerved the more unsuspecting ladies.

Evangéline, however, was wary. She understood that she was living in a house that also housed a man, a single wealthy man - a single wealthy Englishman. She, therefore, had several reasons to distrust him and she was, in fact, so wary that she always kept a small bag packed in case she needed to get away in a hurry.

As it turned out, having a bag already packed was a good idea.

****

One night, a few months later, she was sleeping soundly in her bed and dreaming of Gabriel so vividly that she could feel his closeness, his warm breath on the back of her neck, his strong arms holding her firmly, and his eager hands searching, touching, squeezing. She sighed in dreamy contentment. Gabriel felt so warm, so persistent with his strong fingers and the masculine, musky blend of tobacco and whiskey on his panting breath.

Tobacco? Whiskey?

Her dream dissolved and she awoke with a start. Robert, the meek son, with brandy and pipe tobacco on his breath, was sitting on a chair beside her bed. He had been leaning over and staring into her beautiful sleeping face. "Please don't scream and wake mother," he whispered. "It would upset her too much in her weak condition." As he continued, he raised his hand, gently stroked her hair and said, "I am very rich and I can give you a life of ease and comfort. You will want for nothing."

Though his sour breath filled her with nausea, she fought off panic. "Before I reply, sir, may I first get up to clean my mouth with peppermint … and to use … the commode?" she asked as sweetly as she could.

Thinking that her request was a trick to escape, Robert hesitated a moment. "You will live like a princess. You will have everything you wish for."

Then because liquor had given the timid man some confidence in his own personal charm, he patted her head as though she were the family pet, moved aside and allowed her to leave the room. He sat on the bed and waited for her to return.

Evangéline had slid demurely out of bed and taken the lantern Robert had brought into her room. She crept downstairs, went to the closet, put her coat over her nightgown, took out her packed bag, unlocked the front door heavily engraved with the proud family's coat-of-arms, and stepped quietly into the street.

Her first impulse was to run to the house of the local priest. But then she remembered that there were no Catholic priests in Boston. Upon penalty of death priests were forbidden, she had learned, to set foot on the puritan soil of Massachusetts.

She ran as fast as she could and then stopped at the next corner to catch her breath. She sobbed aloud, "This will make Robert's dear mother so unhappy, and I had grown to like her. I will miss the old woman. And now, because of me, she will discover her son's true character. May God forgive me if I did anything to encourage him." Mistress Edwards was already painfully aware of her son's weak character, but she would not tolerate criticism of it from anyone else.

Evangéline set off, then, for the only other place she could - the farm of Mr. Zackariah Black, nine miles out of town on the southern road to Wrentham.

****

Chapter Thirty-seven

Escape in a Leaky Boat

"And that is what happened," said Evangéline. "I hope that you will let me stay here again."

Elizabeth Black frowned. "Well, I suppose you can stay until I find you another placement. Perhaps you can go to Worcester. [1] I hear that they are even giving away land outright there to some of your friends. But, then, Worcester will take in anybody!" said Mistress Black disgustedly. "Go out to the barn now and help the other girls."

"Merci beaucoup … I mean, thank you," said Evangéline, hurrying away before Mistress Black could change her mind.

A few minutes later François and the others were telling Evangéline of their escape plans.

"We know a man who will sell us his old boat, and we plan to head south," said François.

"Why south?" asked Evangéline.

"Because," injected Jude, "I overheard Mr. Black telling his wife that all of the other ships sailed farther south than Boston."

"Well, that means Gabriel has gone south, too!" said Evangéline.

"He must have!" said Jude, confidently.

Charles added, "We can go to the Carolinas or to Georgia. Anyplace but here."

"But will Mr. Black let us leave his farm?" asked Evangéline.

"Mr. Black is a pig!" said big Claude.

"I know," said Evangéline.

"He has been cheating us out of our pay," sneered Charles. "François and Claude have been writing letters of appeal to the Massachusetts government asking for help in fighting Mr. Black."

"When can we leave?"

"I'm ready now," said Charles, "but François and Claude want to wait for news from the government."

"When will that be?"

"Who knows! But if we don't hear anything in a few months, we're all going to leave when the weather turns cold, perhaps in late October," said Jude.

"Isn't it wonderful, Evangéline?" Charles gushed. "We'll go to the warm south where we can sleep under the stars and pick fresh fruit off millions of orange trees and wild grape vines!"

"In October? That seems so far away," sighed Evangéline. "But, I can wait. Now I have new hope of finding Gabriel."

****

On the cold night of October 26, 1756, exactly one year after they had been deported, Evangéline, François, Claude, Charles, and Jude slipped away from the Massachusetts shore and began a perilous journey south. Over the next two years, this journey would endanger their lives, test their physical strength and moral courage and, most of all, challenge their faith. They would have to persevere, to endure, to hold on long enough to be reunited with their mothers, fathers, wives, husbands, lovers, brothers, sisters and other loved ones whose loss was now an agony, a nightmare that not only refused to end at dawn, but grew in intensity with each waking hour.

****

With money from Grand Pré they had kept hidden, they bought a boat, a clumsy ketch with a foremast no bigger than its mizzen-mast. It leaked, of course. They had expected that. They were beginning to expect the worst from everybody in every new situation. The Acadian inferiority complex that would, with good reason, continue to grow to crippling proportions was now only in its infancy. François and Claude repaired the leaks as best they could, and brought along two wooden milk pails for bailing purposes.

They set out, sailing close to the shoreline except when hostile colonists spied them and hurled stones to keep them offshore. However, when the coast was clear, they went ashore, set rabbit traps, and slept. When rested, they returned to the ketch, fished, ate their catch raw, and rowed on.

In Connecticut, they met other exiles who were being well treated. The legislature of that colony had issued orders that the 650 newly-arrived Acadians were to be "made welcome, helped and settled under the most advantageous conditions, or if they have to be sent away, measures be taken for their transfer." Some of the names of the exiles there were Babinot, Carsot, Caumeaux, Simon, Doucet, Granger, Martin, Michel, Brun, Braux, Fauret, Prejean, Bourgois, Savage, and Amiros.

François jumped for joy when he heard that other Héberts had landed there. However, he was disappointed to find only an elderly couple from the Fort Beauséjour area. His wife and two sons, then, were still missing.

New York, they learned, did not want them. Had they been able to read the newspaper there, they would have known that the members of the New York Assembly had been

> "… sitting for some days, in order to determine what to do with the French Neutrals brought here; and believe they are to be sent further. They are insolent rascals, talk in a high strain, call themselves subjects of the French king, owe* they were Neutrals, and that they took up arms against us, but allege for excuse, that Colonel Monckton** used them ill. They say they will settle here, if we allow them such privileges as they require, particularly the public exercise of their religion, with their priests etc., and unless we agree to their terms, they choose to be transported to some of the territories of the French king. They will not even upon any terms take the oath of allegiance. By this we may judge, what a pernicious gang they were in Nova Scotia." [2]

Evangéline and her friends later learned that the 250 who had initially been sent to New York were "sent further" to Santo Domingo. Wherever that was.

The New York *Mercury*, as well as many other American newspapers, ran ads for Acadians searching for their families.

---

*   admit
**   Lt. Col. Robert Monckton was the officer in charge of the Beauséjour-Piziquid-Annapolis deportations.

The five refugees drifted along bailing out their leaky boat. Evangéline wanted to stop at every seaside village to inquire about Gabriel. Whenever they did, they checked with the local authorities about recent visitors and recent deaths. In village after village, in town after town, they read names on hundreds of tombstones and makeshift crosses in dozens of cemeteries. And then they drifted on.

Unable to out-race the snow and icy winds, frozen and exhausted, they decided to spend the winter in Philadelphia where the kindhearted Quakers came to their rescue.

It was there, however, that they learned a terrible new English word - *smallpox*. The *Hannah* and the *Nightingale* had arrived there with passengers infected with that lethal disease. As a result, the two ships were immediately placed under quarantine and lay at anchor bobbing - fully loaded - in the harbor for the next forty days. Many died without ever stepping ashore.[*]

The truly Christian Quakers were the first to board those ships and offer help. They assisted in removing the dead and in distributing bread to the living. Later, they reported that they had found the exiles "crowded together, without socks, shirts, blankets or other necessary items," and immediately drafted a petition for public charity.

Evangéline and her friends were deeply disturbed by the sad news of the smallpox victims.

The good news was that neither of the infected ships was the *Leopard*.[3]

---

[*] The exact number of deaths is not known although estimates ran as high as 237. We do know that Pennsylvania's Governor Morris didn't want the Acadians. He said that Pennsylvania already had enough foreigners to deal with.

Chapter Thirty-eight

Remembering Is All I Ever Do

March, 1757

The winter dragged on, and although it snowed, the marrow-freezing Arctic blasts that always hit Grand Pré in February didn't reach Philadelphia. The Quakers gave shelter to the five refugees and Evangéline repaid them by helping to care for the old and the feeble in the Old Friends' Almshouse. The almshouse was a charity house built "in the interest of needy Friends," on property donated by the generous benefactor, John Martin.

****

The winter finally passed and one morning in late March, Charles announced to the other four, " I'm staying here. I don't want to go any farther south."

Evangéline was surprised and disappointed. "Why?" she asked.

"I'm tired of running. I'll have to stop somewhere and it might as well be here."

"I see," said Evangéline, not seeing at all.

"Everyday I see the city streets here filled with carts, and carriages, and wagons with wheels that in Grand Pré we stopped using years ago. I can make a fortune here. This is a land of opportunity!" No one said a word.

Then he turned to young Jude and said, "Stay in Philadelphia with me. I can teach you my trade and we can both get rich!"

"But what about your family?" asked cousin Jude. "Don't you want to find them?"

"I will find them faster when I have money!"

The offer was tempting. Jude and Claude were staring at the ground. Then François spoke, "I have to move on with Evangéline. I have to find my wife and children."

"Me, too," said Claude.

"Me, too," said Jude.

"May God keep you safe from harm, Charles," said Evangéline. "I hope your business dreams come true. And thank you for helping me get this far." Then she embraced him.

"God be with you all!" said Charles and, with tears in his eyes, he turned and walked briskly down the busy city street.

****

Maryland was friendly. Irish Catholics, veterans of political persecution, had settled there, and they welcomed the unwanted. An article in the *Annapolis Gazette* had earlier stated,

> "Four vessels of French Neutrals arrived here from Nova Scotia. This brings their number to more than 900 …. Since these poor people were stripped of their farms in Nova Scotia and sent here indigent and naked, for some political reason, Christian charity, the only sentiment common to humanity, is called upon from all to come to help, each according to his means, these human beings so worthy of our compassion."

In Maryland, Evangéline and her companions met many other Acadian exiles from other areas of Nova Scotia and from Isle St. Jean. But after months of searching unsuccessfully for their loved ones, they decided to move on still farther south.

****

"No, no, you don't! You can't land here! Keep moving! You're not wanted here!" The Virginians would not allow them to come ashore. Other Acadians who had earlier arrived there were detained at Williamsburg where hundreds died in an epidemic. A great deal of finger-pointing had taken place with Virginia's Governor, Robert Dinwiddie, blaming Charles Lawrence for not giving him sufficient warning of the coming of the immigrants. Those who survived the epidemic were shipped to England and held as prisoners of war.

The two Carolinas were equally unreceptive and were helpful only in booking passage for some Acadians on departing ships, and in supplying others with small boats for their return-trip home. Many of the latter perished at sea. The few who miraculously survived the Atlantic crossing and made it to Nova Scotia and Isle St. Jean were deported again, this time to places as far south as Georgia.

In the Georgia colony, the four friends could have stayed on, working the plantations. And it's hard to be sad when the sun's shining down on Georgia, and the hummingbirds, their tiny wings a blur, are plundering every blossom in sight. The bountiful sight of long healthy cotton fields and the fragrant smell of Cherokee roses prompted François to say, "Everyone in Georgia must be rich!"

Everywhere she went she heard the same remarks. "Ah, yes, Gabriel. Did you say Gabriel was his name? Yes, yes, we've seen him. He went west." "Oh, yes, Gabriel, the one with the beautiful blond hair! He went back to Isle St. Jean." "Did he have a reddish beard? Yes, I think he went north to Québec." "I heard he went to France!" "Lajeunesse? Someone named Lajeunesse went to Louisiana with his father."
"Louisiana? Is that north or south of here?"
"Just a little farther south and west."

****

Evangéline, François, Claude, and Jude hiked overland across Alabama and Mississippi until they reached the town of Natchez where they obtained a canoe and headed down the mighty Mississippi River. At Baton Rouge, they heard that some Acadians were living just west of there. So, they journeyed to Opelousas. "I'm sorry. I don't know anyone by that name. Try farther south."

Two nights later, Evangéline fell asleep under a huge oak and dreamt a wonderful dream. In her dream, Gabriel seemed near. She felt his presence strongly. She dreamt she was back in Grand Pré when all was beautiful and green. But when she awoke, her nightmare began again. She now remembered Grand Pré as brown, and red, and burning. She knew that no herds grazed there now, and from the church of St. Charles des Mines no Angelus sounded. No yellow lights gleamed from the cottage windows, and no friends ambled along the long winding road through the empty, ravaged town. Why, she asked herself, why? Why did it all have to happen? Why did our beautiful lives have to crumble? How can things like this happen to such good people? What did we ever do to deserve this? It isn't fair! It isn't fair! And why do things unloved seem to last forever? My whole life now is ashes, ashes. The best things in my life are now behind me, and remembering is all I ever do.

Then, pulling herself together, she said, "But, I know he's somewhere near. I can feel it! I can feel it!"

She made herself a mental note: "from now on, when I wake up, I must not think sad and spiteful thoughts; and I must always remember Father Chauvreulx's advice 'never to question the will of God'. He knows what He's doing. Yes, yes, I'm sure He does. He must. I'm certain of that!"

A stranger was staring down at her. An old man, a few feet away but still in the shadow of the oak tree, asked softly, "Are you all right, girl?"

Jude answered in English for her. "Yes, we're all right. But can you tell us where we are, sir?"

"I'm proud to tell you where you are, son. You are in the prettiest little place on earth. You're in St. Martin,* Louisiana!"

---

* St. Martin is the name Longfellow used.

Chapter Thirty-nine

On the Same Path

"Slowly they entered the Teche."* Day after day, their boat drifted through a strange and lovely wilderness where cotton trees nodded their stately plumed heads, and flocks of brown pelicans waded at noon past silvery sandbars in broad, shaded lagoons. But with this alien beauty came new, exotic threats like the arboreal reptiles that slithered without a sound along soft mossy boughs, their slender split tongues licking in the flying gnats just above her hair. Night after night, by their blazing fires, they camped on the bayou's borders and, trying to ignore the hooting owls, the whooping cranes, and the singing mosquitoes, slept badly beneath the sagging boughs of willows.

Then they saw it! A thin blue column of smoke rose above a large, low roof overshadowed by moss-covered oaks. A spacious veranda, wrapped in vines and wreathed in roses, extended around the house. Soft wooing and cooing could be heard at each end of the house where the dovecotes stood amid the flowers in the garden. Behind the house, and beyond the tangled grapevines, as far as her eyes could see, Evangéline gazed at a long stretch of flat land, a limitless prairie, and smiled. "He's here!" she said. "I know he's here!"

---

*   A line from Longfellow's poem.

205

A sudden blast from a hunting horn silenced all the birds. Mounted on his horse and sitting on his Spanish saddle, in gaiters and a leather vest, a herdsman stared down at the four travelers as they came towards him from the shore. Somehow the stranger looked familiar as he sprang from his horse and rushed to greet them. "Evangéline! And François! Claude! And little Jude! I am so happy to see you!" shouted the towering blacksmith, Basil Lajeunesse. He embraced each visitor heartily, and they all took turns laughing and shaking his huge hand. Then Basil asked, "If you came by the Atchafalaya, have you nowhere encountered my Gabriel's boat on the bayous?"

"Gone? Is he gone?" she asked.

"Cheer up, my dear! He had grown so moody and restless, always thinking of you, and always quiet except when he talked about you, that he became a little tedious, even to me. So I sent him off to Adayes to trade mules with the Spanish. Don't worry! He won't get far because the streams are against him. Tonight we'll feast and drink, and tomorrow we'll catch up with him and bring him back here. You need his love and I need his help. Oh, and here comes Michel, our own Acadian minstrel. He'll see that tonight we'll sing all of the old songs." Michel, the fiddler, embraced everybody twice, and the tears and the laughter flowed again. Michel looked a little older, his hair grayer. But he grinned happily because a new song was already taking shape in his head. Tonight he would again be the life of the party!

****

In the evening, after the coffee and oranges, the beef, the grapes, and the wine, Basil sat back and lit his pipe filled with sweet Natchitoches tobacco. "Did you know that the orange groves here bloom all year round? The lakes and rivers never freeze. The ground never hardens so that the plowshare runs always like a keel through water. The grass grows more in a single night than in a whole Canadian summer. Wild herds run unclaimed across that prairie out there. And did you know that land here may be had for the asking?" Basil paused. Then his fist closed and with a cloud of smoke erupting from his mouth, he pounded the table and shouted, "And here there is no King George of England and no Governor Lawrence to drive you away and burn your homestead!"

The four visitors sat listening, uncomfortably, to their host. Each was trying to think of a diplomatic counter-argument. None of them wanted to remain there.

Thank God for Michel's fiddle, thought François, as all eyes and ears turned to the next room of Basil's house where Michel was beginning to entertain. Basil's mood quickly changed, he smiled, and said, "All right, enough talk! It's time to sing and to dance the night away!"

Evangéline instead went outside to breathe the warm air. Such humidity! Breathing it in was like safely breathing water. She strolled along the path to the edge of the vast prairie. It felt good to walk the same path Gabriel had walked and to know that he had paced this path many times thinking of her. "Oh, dear God, give me patience!" she said. "At least until tomorrow!"

****

The sun's rays blazed brutally hot by eight in the morning. "We're off to find my Prodigal Son!" laughed Basil as he approached his boatmen who were waiting at the water's edge.

After three days of fast rowing, they found no trace of Gabriel. They inquired at the inn in the little Spanish town of Adayes. "He left here yesterday with horses and guides and companions. Said he was going to the West," the garrulous landlord told them.

"We'll be going north, then, Evangéline," announced François, reluctantly. Claude and Jude lowered their heads, nodding in agreement. "We have to head back. We must have passed our families somewhere along the way. Or perhaps they've returned to Canada."

"Oh, I was afraid that this would happen! But I suppose it had to happen someday. You must go your own way, I know." She embraced each friend. "I'll pray every day for you." They wept together, and then her three companions departed, waving their good-byes until they were out of sight.

Chapter Forty

Thistle Woman Tells Her Tales

Day after day, Evangéline and Basil, with their Indian guides, followed Gabriel's footsteps. Each day they felt certain they would overtake him. They crossed broad streams with swift currents and venomous moccasins; rivers with rapids where bears swiped salmon; hills so steep they slid down again; and ravines so deep that their interiors were dark at mid-day.

Sometimes they saw, or thought they saw from a distance, the smoke of Gabriel's campfire rise in the morning air. But by nightfall, when they reached the site of the smoky mirage, they found only embers and campfire stones, still warm. "He's hurrying because he is anxious to find me," she whispered to herself.

****

One evening as the searchers sat around their campsite, they were startled by the approach of a Shawnee woman. She strode casually, impassively out of the woods and, without speaking, stood by their fire to warm herself. Fire, it seemed, belonged to everyone. Although petite, she looked strong and apparently was, in her matter-of-fact way, fearless. She wore a sad expression that marred her handsome features although it made her condition all the more intriguing.

She had married, she told them, a man not of her tribe. He had recently been killed by the cruel Comanches near their settlement in Sawanogi. Now she was returning home to her people, west of here.

Evangéline felt an instant bond, welcomed her, and gave her meat.

Later that night when the men, worn by the day's long march, were sprawled around the quivering fire, Evangéline and Thistle Woman sat up, wide awake with the prospect of some sorely needed girl-talk. With the charm of her Indian accent, and in a soft low voice, the Shawnee woman told the tale of her love with all its pleasures, pains, and reversals. Evangéline cried to hear the story and to know that another heart like hers had loved and been disappointed. She, in turn, related her tale and all of its trials. Mute with wonder, the Shawnee woman sat and remained mute after Evangéline had finished. Then appearing excited, as though her brain had made some mysterious connection, the woman told her the eerie tale of Mowis. "Mowis, the bridegroom of snow, won and wedded a maiden, / But when morning came, arose and passed from the wigwam, / Fading and melting away and dissolving into the sunshine, / Till she beheld him no more, though she followed far into the forest."*

Evangéline's beautiful green eyes were wide and unblinking. When Thistle Woman seemed to be waiting for some response, Evangéline said proudly, "My Gabriel was certainly not made of snow. He was always burning with love for me."

The Shawnee woman paused, and then, not to be deterred, told another story. This time she told of "the fair Lilinau, who was wooed by a phantom, / that through the pines o'er her father's lodge, in the hush of twilight, / Breathed like the evening wind, and whispered love to the maiden, / Till she followed his green and waving plume through the forest, / And nevermore returned, nor was seen again by her people."

Evangéline didn't know whether to smile or to frown. The accuracy of the similarity amazed her, but the implied prediction for her future upset her. "My Gabriel is real and not a phantom. He is my breath, my blood, my life. And I will, with God's help, return some day to my people."

As if in agreement, the moon appeared from behind a cloud and shone its light as bright as day, and the women, talked-out for now, lay on their straw pallets and, though weary with travel, tried unsuccessfully to sleep. Thistle Woman lay seething with hate and plotting delicious revenge on the murdering Comanches, while Evangéline tossed and turned, as the

---

* The Indian tales of Mowis and Lilinau are directly taken from Longfellow's *Evangéline*.

message of Lilinau slowly sank in like the effect of a nauseating liquor. In her fatigue she began to question everything. Did Gabriel really exist? Was there really ever such a place as Grand Pré? It was all so long ago, like a phantom shape retreating. Was it a real memory, or merely the memory of a dream? Could she be, after all, foolishly chasing a...a—?

Oh, I shouldn't stay up this late, she thought. She then made herself a mental note: "get to sleep earlier from now on, and you won't have so many ridiculous thoughts swimming around in your head in the middle of the night!"

Then she covered her head to protect it from mosquitoes, said her prayers, and added, "Dear God, bring me good fortune. Help me to find my Gabriel."

Early the next morning they resumed their march. Then, later in the afternoon, the Shawnee woman excitedly pointed ahead of her and said, "Those mountains hide a village on their western slope. Many Christian tents. Home of Black Robe, chief of Jesuit Mission."

"A priest? Out here?"

"He teaches my people of Jesus and Mary."

"Let's hurry, then!"

Over the hills they scrambled all afternoon, and just as the sun went down, they saw a broad, green meadow by the bank of a river. There, an evening prayer service was taking place around a large crucifix fastened to the trunk of a huge oak. The travelers approached and joined in the evening devotions. It had been years since Evangéline heard the eternal Latin from the mouth of a priest, and she sighed, feeling safe and calm in the old attachment.

After the service and the benediction, the tall, thin, bearded Jesuit with deep, brown eyes welcomed them in French making them all feel at home. They feasted on corn cakes, slaked their thirst from water-gourds and, sitting on animal skins, told their story.

Then the priest said, "Five days ago, Gabriel sat here by my side and told me the same tale. He has gone far north to the hunting grounds but will return here in the autumn."

"May I remain here then, Father, and wait for him?" asked Evangéline.

"You are welcome, of course."

"And I must go back home," said Basil. "I've neglected my farm long enough. And I know," he said to Evangéline, "you will be in good hands now."

In the morning Basil, with his companions and Indian guides, turned homeward. Evangéline stayed behind at the Mission in the village of Thistle Woman's people, the Shawnee village of Long Tail.

****

Days and weeks and months passed, and the fields of corn that were springing green from the ground when she came were golden now. She gladly picked corn with the young Shawnee girls who laughed whenever they picked an ear with blood-red kernels, supposedly a sure sign that a new boyfriend would present himself in the near future. Evangéline found many of the blood-red ears, but Gabriel did not appear.

****

"Here, take this," said the Jesuit priest to Evangéline, as he handed her a flower with yellow petals.

"Merci beaucoup," said Evangéline.

"It is called a 'compass flower'. See how its leaves are turned to the north, just like a magnet? The Finger of God has planted it here to direct the traveler's journey, and if you have patience and faith in God, He will guide your Gabriel back to you."

"Oh, how beautiful!"

"Just look about you, my child, at the yellow blossoms, the golden fields of corn, and the colorful hills and you can see how the Finger of God touches our lives everywhere, every day."

Later that evening, two young Shawnee girls discussed in whispers the state of Evangéline's mental health. One said to the other, "Strange white girl! Going crazy! Lost her mind over her ghost boy."

"What she do now?" asked the other.

"She spend all day busy. Very busy. Fill her tepee with hundreds and hundreds of those smelly yellow weeds!"

****

The autumn passed and the winter, and when the crocus bloomed and the robins and the bluebirds again sang in the woods, there was still no sign of Gabriel. For the first time, she felt angry, cheated, abused. She stood amid the alien corn and wept bitter tears. She could not be consoled.

She didn't realize it then, but getting to know the Shawnee, at this point in her life, would prove a blessing in disguise. She was about to learn from them two very valuable lessons: to have a healthy disregard for time, and to learn to smile at almost everything.

It was an unending source of frustration for the Jesuit priest, but it was a comfort to her that the Shawnee were a nomadic tribe with an insatiable itch for travel, and who equated inertia with death and decay. In 1745, Cadwallader Colden, a Quaker, a scientist, and a friend of Benjamin Franklin, observed, "The Shawnees are the most restless of all the Indians." That was fine with Evangéline. She never knew exactly where she was going from day to day, but if Gabriel wasn't there, she was always content to go somewhere else.

Chapter Forty-one

Getting To Know the Shawnee

Although unmistakably nomadic, the entire Shawnee tribe seemed allergic to haste. They never hurried except when hunting. Hesitation was one of their minor virtues, delay their major. The opposite commands, "slow down!" and "hurry up!" elicited the same reaction - a brief look of confusion, and then a broad smile that seemed to say, "What a great joker you are!" Slowing down was for the elderly; rushing was for rivers.

When a decision was made to visit relatives, for example, departure and arrival times were anyone's guess. Early-late was a hyphenated concept. Visitors were always welcomed with open arms simply because neither the hosts nor the guests knew whether the visit was on schedule. In the Shawnee dictionary, the word *schedule* was unlisted. Guests might stay a day or a month. It all depended. Upon what, it was hard to say.

Besides, what was the point in hurrying anywhere? There was nowhere to go; and yet, there was everywhere. So, why rush? Furthermore, in rushing around, one might miss hearing the twitter-chatter of the sparrow, the signal-screeches of the hawk and the owl, or the ominous hint of gathering thunder among the distant hills. So, when on the move, the Shawnee ambled, sauntered, paused, ambled on again, strolled, hesitated, stopped dead as though on cue to listen - hushed and motionless - to nothing in particular sometimes for fifteen minutes or more; dawdled on again, paused, halted, faltered, lingered, loitered, and generally lagged along as though they were a royal family strolling the palace grounds. They could easily sit for an hour in total silence staring, mesmerized, at the sparkling of the sun on the ripples of a stream; and they could stand for half a morning appreciating the power of the sun to dissipate the overnight fog that had, like a vaporous lover, settled itself over the river at the bottom of the deep valley now slowly materializing before their all-absorbing eyes.

Now, *timing* was a different matter altogether. The Shawnee were masters of the art of timing. After all, a split-second could mean the difference between an empty stomach and a bellyful of fresh, warm deer meat. Shawnee arrows could nail unsuspecting rabbits in mid-leap. Shawnee children were taught the exact hour that berries were ripe enough before competitors, like the waxwing and the kingbird, swooped down to devour them all; and the exact minute that trout-meat would spoil. Timing was crucial; time was eternal.

Therefore, when they were not hunting or fishing, it would have been entirely unnecessary to tell the Shawnee, "Sit back, relax, and just take it easy." Such advice was beyond redundancy and, when foolishly offered, was casually received with the customary look of bewilderment followed by the happy grin as wide as all-outdoors. The Shawnee language had no equivalent for the expression *take your time*. The tribe even spoke in a kind of relaxed, slow drawl. "Shawnee" means "Southerners".

The Shawnee sense of time drove Evangéline almost to distraction at first. After all, she was on an urgent mission. She had to get places; the Shawnee, it seemed, were already there, wherever that happened to be. Daily agitation lead to exasperation which gave way to infuriation until she was exhausted and had to lie down. Although she tried hard to keep it all inside, so frantic was she at times that she broke down and cried openly. All that piddle-paddling through the woods was enough to make any reasonable woman scream. She simply didn't understand and would not begin to understand until she had lived with the Shawnee for over a year. She was to spend many years with the tribe, working on language with their children. She would teach them French and they would teach her Shawnee; and she would learn their sense of time.

What better way to learn a language than to learn it with children just learning it themselves. In a short time, she knew most of the Shawnee nouns, the names of things. And she began her French lessons by amusing the children with funny French songs. The Shawnee children smiled, giggled, and hooted when she sang:

Mon merle a perdu son bec [1]
Mon merle a perdu son bec
Un bec, deux becs, trois becs ah! oh!
Comment veux tu mon merl' chanter?

Mon merle a perdu son oeil
Un oeil, deux yeux, trois yeux,
Un bec, deux becs, trois becs, ah! Oh!

Mon merle a perdu sa tete
Un' tete, deux tet', trois tet'

Un oeil, deux yeux, trois yeux,
Un bec, deux becs, trois becs, ah! Oh!*

"Bec, bec, bec!" laughed the children.

It was through the children and their lessons that Evangéline finally caught on to the Shawnee slant on time.

Long after she had taught all the children the French words for 'good morning', 'good afternoon', and 'good evening', she began to doubt her teaching skills in observing that the children never seemed to get those terms straight. In the morning they often greeted her with 'Good evening, Miss Evangéline', and in the evening - sometimes after dark - they said, 'Good morning, Miss Evangéline.' It was funny, and a little eerie, but above all, frustrating. Surely *all* of the children could not be uniformly slow. Why could they not say 'good morning' in the morning and 'good evening' in the evening? She was willing to forget 'good afternoon' altogether.

Deciding to get to the bottom of it all, she gathered the children together one day and asked them the Shawnee words for 'good morning'. Nothing but blank expressions and giggles. "Then, how do you say 'good evening' in Shawnee?" More blank looks and louder giggles. "'Good afternoon?'" she asked. More of the same. It was baffling.

About a week later, she didn't understand why, but it suddenly dawned on her. What occurred to her was the fact that the Shawnee cared so little for time they simply had no expressions for dividing an ordinary day into three distinct categories. Only white men pressed for time needed such

---

*   Traditional children's song about a blackbird that has lost its beak, one eye, and its head.

divisions, people meeting deadlines like merchants with perishable goods on their hands, moneylenders charging interest by the day, and military men keeping time for the sake of making other military men keep time. The Shawnee, in fact, did not even have an equivalent for 'hello'. When meeting up with a friend, they simply waved their hands about, jumped for joy, and said something like, "Well, son of a gun, there you are!" They did say, 'Itah!' at times, which meant 'Good luck!' Therefore, she concluded, the mystery was solved; if *a day* were not particularly important, then why would the *divisions* of a day be important? And to have individual names for each separate division? What on earth for?

However, it took Evangéline almost two years to get this small inkling into the Shawnee sense of time and to begin to calm down. Her daily prayers for patience, it seemed, were being answered after all, an unseen Hand quelling her frustration and her tearful outbursts.

Besides their differing views on time, Evangéline and the Shawnee had other incompatibilities. Their lives were so simple; hers was a complicated mess. "It's that ghost in her head," they said behind her back. "She hunts everyday for a spirit. She should hunt rabbit." They smiled constantly; she seldom smiled, having lost everyone important in her life. They were so happy-go-lucky; she was intense, serious. Her intensity, however, turned out to be a godsend. For one thing, it kept the boys away.

According to the Shawnee, extreme seriousness was (fortunately for her) a symptom of mental instability. A very serious child was thought to be either mentally handicapped or emotionally disturbed - or both. Any seriousness in a Shawnee child, however, eventually wore off. Growing up surrounded by happy relatives who were in no hurry to change him or her, the child gradually unraveled into an easygoing, emotionally mature, grinning adult just like all the rest.

For a Shawnee to persist in his or her seriousness was both unwise and dangerous. Like most practical, nomadic tribes the Shawnee had little time or sympathy for the slow and the weak. While they didn't, however, leave the slow and the old behind to die on ice floes as did some northern tribes, they sometimes undertook journeys that only the strong and the healthy could survive. It was survival of the fittest by subtle elimination.

Naturally, then, it would have been a form of suicide for the elderly to sit around and moan about their aches and illnesses. Instead, the elderly, understandably, did their best to out-giggle the children and to be the most carefree of the tribal sub-groups.

Hence, for Evangéline, as bad as things were, they couldn't have been much better. In decoding the Shawnee idea of time she was able to relax and save some energy for the long journey west and north. And in persistently maintaining her seriousness, she unwittingly warded off the young braves. No young brave wanted a girl who was mentally unstable. Neither did he want a woman who was "ghost-haunted". Sadness was her savior since it also spoiled her looks. Her lack of attraction also inspired her Shawnee nickname, Lawanee Lo Tacketa: "the one who saved her gifts for another."

Fortunately, however, and for her own good, the intensity of her seriousness abated after the second year, thereby curtailing any tribal consideration of her "subtle elimination"; and she had developed that helpful, protective coating that made a lasting impression on the boys.

So far at least, things seemed to be, strangely enough, working out for the best.

****

Of course, it was dangerous to travel around America 250 years ago, but not as dangerous as one might think. Naturally there were mountain lions, snakes, wolves, and bears. But we now know that such animals do not attack humans unless they feel threatened, or feel that the safety of their young is threatened. Evangéline didn't know these things, but the Shawnee did. Chief Luther Standing Bear of the Oglala band of Sioux later explained,

> "We did not think of the great open plains, the beautiful rolling hills, and winding streams with tangled growth as 'wild'. Only to the white man was nature a 'wilderness' and only to him was the land 'infested' with 'wild' animals and 'savage' people. To us it was tame. Earth was bountiful and we were surrounded with the blessings of the Great Mystery. Not until the hairy man from the East came and with brutal frenzy heaped injustices upon us and the families we loved was it 'wild' for us. When the very animals of the forest began fleeing from his approach, then it was that for us the 'Wild West' began."*

---

* Chief Luther Standing Bear, *Land of the Spotted Eagle*, Houghton Mifflin, Boston and New York, 1933, pp. 192-197.

The biggest dangers of all involved the weather and the constant search for food and water, a daily task so time-consuming that it left room for little else. Occasionally in their travels, they came across a gutted deer carcass hanging from a tree branch. They understood that the meat belonged to another tribe, and would not dream of stealing it, feeling that the needs of its rightful owners could be greater than theirs.

"Where are we going this time?" was her usual question whenever the tribe again began to move.

"To visit our cousins."

"More cousins?"

"More cousins in Missouri, the Sac and the Fox!"

Months later, "Where to this time?"

"To visit cousins."

"More cousins?"

"More cousins in Illinois, the Kickapoo!"

Months later, "Cousins?"

"Yes, many cousins in Tippecanoe."

Tippecanoe must have been the home of their favorite cousins because they remained there for two whole years.

Evangéline continued to teach the children and the Native women were pleased to have such a willing nanny; but they complained that she hugged and kissed the children too much. The Native Peoples did not believe in spoiling their children; spoiling them was dangerous because it would make them too soft, too dependent. What nonsense, thought Evangéline. Don't they realize that it's love that makes us strong? The Native women did not agree and continued to complain. But the kissing and the hugging went on; she had to give her uncontainable affection to someone.

Her heart ached for a bit of good news. She had been surviving for too long on empty rumors and fading memories. Her blood felt thinner as though it lacked oxygen or some element that only fresh, nutritive news of her Gabriel could bring. But no news came, and the vast emptiness of the open Indiana countryside did not improve her mood. At first she was shocked, as most first-time easterners are, by the flatness of the land and the small number of trees. She had never seen so much sky, and under it, fields that flowed on for ten flat miles in every direction, a vast unchanging view. The dry grass swayed from side to side - negatively it seemed - and billowed on towards a horizon that mercilessly receded in giant steps, while she plodded on, in baby steps, lost, unbearably lost, stranded somewhere between insignificance and oblivion. "Such an empty place," she murmured. "Such a big empty place!"

She suffered, at this point, a serious case of homesickness. Weary of traveling in a big empty land, not knowing exactly where that land was, and not knowing where she was going, she missed the East. She missed the rolling hills covered with spruce, fir, cedar, and tall pine, the myriad rivers, ponds, and lakes, and the massive green Atlantic pounding salty white surf on Acadia's coppery shore. Oh, why did she have to be in this great flat, dry, tawny place! It would be good to be *anywhere* back East, at least some place where she could be indoors and out of the weather. For a white girl, so much fresh air was tiresome.

This primitive, nomadic life suddenly seemed intolerable and she desperately craved some permanence. She longed to see an established town, one with solid stone houses or, at least, with houses made of lumber cut smoothly at a sawmill. She was tired of living in portable leather triangles with holes in the roofs for chimneys, tired of greasing her face, arms, and legs with bears' oil to protect her from the sun, even if it was clarified oil, and tired of the way her dry hair reeked of campfire smoke. As she sat trying to untangle it with a fishbone comb, she mumbled, "I am so sick of makeshift things! This is not a real life! Everything I see is just a substitute!" It was true. Everything around her was rough-hewn, ill-fitted, raw-woven, knotted, braided, frayed, mended, or patched. There was not one single thing in her life now that did not squeak or leak! She was tired of freezing to death when she was not being baked by the brutal sun, and sick of dehydrating in the wind when not being drenched by the merciless rain. She hated waking in damp places. She yearned to sit in a warm room and watch flames dance in a proper stone fireplace; to sleep in a real bed in her own cozy bedroom; to bake bread cheerfully in a kitchen with curtains, and white spring flowers in an un-chipped jar on a windowsill painted yellow. She ached to see a *manufactured* item, perhaps a spinning wheel or a pewter plate. She pined for a product – any product - that had been engineered with precision, something smooth and sleek from Paris or Boston. "I have become as rough as my surroundings," she sighed.

Sometimes she spurned the bears' oil, and then her forehead, cheeks, and lips would become chapped, and would progress from peeling and flaking to hardening and caking. She had reached the point where she was ready to risk her life for one small portion of sweet-smelling soap! She looked down at her hands and remembered the tough feet of the little

Mi'kmaq boy who could walk on glass in the Grand Pré schoolyard. "I must leave this place soon," she mumbled aloud. "I must go back East soon, or I think I'll go mad!" She pulled the good-for-nothing fishbone comb from her painful scalp and threw it to the ground.

"Should braid hair, like Shawnee women," said Cornplanter, Thistle Woman's oldest brother. Although only in his thirties, tall, muscular, and soft-spoken, Cornplanter had the patience of an old chief. "You are sad today."

"I miss my home. I miss my people," she said. Then she pointed to the great empty flat land and, embarrassed to appear vulnerable and weak, said softly, "And I feel so lost."

"Lost? Lost? What is 'lost'?"

"'Lost' means that I don't know where I am."

Cornplanter looked puzzled, then smiled and said triumphantly as though he had made a great discovery, "You are here!"

"Yes, I know I'm *here*, but *where* is '*here*'?"

Cornplanter frowned. Then he grinned and repeated, "You are here. Not lost. You are here."

She understood his point of view that home was always 'here' but she was not consoled by it. "It's just that it's such an *empty* place, so big, so wide, and empty."

"Not empty. Full place. Holy place." Then Cornplanter spread out his arm with a wide sweep and said, "Much sacred place." He looked all around. "*Here* is where you can see the wind." She sat up a little straighter and peered into the distance seeing all there was to see - the panoramic vacancy – nothing but billions of blades of golden grass lazily waving for miles under a vast blue dome of sky.

Cornplanter was studying her expression because her face was relaxing with ripples of understanding. She smiled weakly and nodded. Not that she had actually seen the wind, but she was beginning to understand that if she were to look long enough she might see here a different kind of beauty from the beauty of the big green East. She nodded again, bent down, picked up the fishbone comb, and walked back to her tepee determined to be more patient.

To stay sane, she knew she had to adjust better to her surroundings, but her instincts were strongly resisting the adjustment. Adjusting to the new was risky, for would adjusting mean forgetting where she came from? And would it mean forgetting all of the people she had left behind?

As it turned out, Tippecanoe, would also become one of her favorite places because it was there that she heard, "Far to the north, in the Michigan forests, your man lives in his lodge on the banks of the Saginaw. But no Shawnee there, only Ottawas. Much danger. Ottawas sometimes friendly, but do not like uninvited guests. But I will go and my brothers will go, too. They are not afraid," said Thistle Woman. "Perhaps," she grinned, "we will see Comanches along the way and I can cut the throat of one."

With the permission of the Shawnee king, the Sachamahen,* they left the next day, Evangéline, Thistle Woman, and her three brothers, Cornplanter, Blackhoof, and Little Arrow.

Not until three months later, however, were they anywhere near the Saginaw River. Evangéline learned something interesting that few white people knew: Indians, too, did not always know exactly where they were going.

---

* In Harvey's book, this is the term for 'sachem'

Chapter Forty-two

The Cabin on the Saginaw

"There it is!" said Thistle Woman, as she pointed to a cabin on a river bank.

Evangéline looked up. Her mouth opened, her eyes widened, and her heart sank. A small log cabin stood in high grass with weeds and alders grown up to the windowsills and half way up the door. The door was ajar, and had been for so long that moss along the threshold now prevented its closing. Around the cabin, the acre that, at one time, was cleared had now been re-invaded by advancing aspens and maples. The forest was reclaiming, piece by piece, even the wood of the building. A section of the roof near the chimney had already fallen in on the cabin's earth floor. Crusted, scaly, pale, green lichen grew on the roof around the gaping hole.

"I want to go inside," said Evangéline.

"Not safe," replied Thistle Woman.

"I *have* to go inside!"

There was nothing in the cabin but a table, some shelves, and a toppled chair. It was impossible to see through the one unbroken windowpane, caked with neglect. Hundreds of dead flies, some of them separated from their dry, transparent wings littered the sill, and brown velvet spiders with plump creamy bellies occupied every webbed corner. Rabbit droppings littered the base of each wall, and the dust was everywhere. The dust itself was not disheartening, but the thickness of it.

"Silly girl!" said Little Arrow, Thistle Woman's youngest brother in his high-pitched voice. "Ne pane! Ne metsa!"* Little Arrow, impatient and immature, was only fourteen and quite effeminate. His older brothers had taken him along on the trip, not hoping to toughen him up, but because he was more accurate with a bow and arrow than they were. Before she met Little Arrow, Evangéline had thought that all young Indian braves were rough and tough. Little Arrow was neither. In fact, much of the time, he sulked and complained that he should have been left at home with the rest of the tribe. He was much happier weaving baskets with the girls, and he enjoyed braiding their hair far more than he enjoyed hunting and killing deer. "Ne pane! Ne metsa!" he repeated.

"Not for food," said Thistle Woman. "She is looking for a sign. For some message left behind by her man."

Evangéline appeared in the doorway. She looked down, searching the tall weeds for a trodden pathway. The Shawnee, sitting passively on a nearby knoll, stared at her. Then, Thistle Woman approached and asked her, "Anything?"

"Nothing."

****

"Go back south now," Thistle Woman said.

"South? I hoped we would go east," said Evangéline.

"Must go south first or we drown," laughed Blackhoof.

"Only great water to the east, he means. Must go south again before we go east," explained Thistle Woman.

"How far south?"

"To Wapakoneta."

"Cousins?"

The three brothers, in anticipation of another reunion, laughed like innocent children, their white teeth flashing against their mocha lips. "Many, many cousins in Wapakoneta. Come. We go now."

That night she slept badly. A disturbing dream disrupted her rest. She dreamt she was beneath an apple tree, an apple tree shaped like a large Y. The top-center of the tree seemed to have been cut away or pressed down towards the top of the trunk. The arms of the Y were covered with the green sleeves of a man's shirt. The shirtsleeves were Gabriel's, and from his

---

* "No bread! Nothing to eat."

arms hung shiny red apples. They looked delicious and she reached up to pick one. When she had the apple in her hand, she found that the back of it was covered with a spider's web. She let it fall to the ground and picked another but it, too, was half-covered with a spider's web. Then she saw every apple on the tree spoiled by a spider's web, and from every apple emerged a long, plump, cream-colored worm. Utterly repulsed by the apples, she stepped back, and as she did, she saw, surrounding each apple, large, dried, transparent wings that fluttered noiselessly, detaching the apples from the trees and carrying them high into the air and out of sight.

She awoke with a start and remained awake for the rest of the long, long night. With the dawn, they were off again, and within a week, encamped with many, many cousins in Wapakoneta, one of the largest Shawnee settlements they had visited. The cousins entertained them lavishly, and they feasted for the next ten days on delicacies they hadn't seen in months.

At the end of their stay, Evangéline asked, "Where to, now?"

"We go farther east to visit the Hathawekela."

"East?"

"East. Then we bring you to Big Tree. To Coaquannuck. East!" said Thistle Woman, waiting for Evangéline to appreciate the good news.

Evangéline had no idea where they were headed, but she mustered up a smile and said, "East, that's good. East is good."

Chapter Forty-three

A Daily Battle

To occupy her active mind, Evangéline asked Thistle Woman and her three brothers to teach her the medicinal properties of every flower, shrub, and tree they saw along the way. Learning something new helped her to fight off depression. Whenever she felt herself getting too despondent, she took up a new interest. Thus, Indian medicine became therapeutic in more ways than one.

The Indians, she learned, had herbal powders that could cure headaches, earaches, and toothaches. They also knew how to prepare tonics for promoting appetites, and diet drinks for curbing them. Mysteriously concocted poultices, salves, and balms were used to treat burns, infections, and skin cancers. With a mixture of roots, they made mashes for alleviating asthma, rheumatism, and kidney ailments. They knew various medicines for helping new-born babies with colic, teen-age girls with menstrual cramps, and middle-aged men with swollen prostates. Evangéline refused, however, to learn their abortion-inducing formula that would, allegedly, terminate an unwanted pregnancy at any stage.

Still, regardless of the distraction provided by her new pastime, the battle against depression was a daily one. The recurring thought that she might, after all, be wasting her life now plagued her night and day. Maybe it was true. Maybe she *was* wasting her life and throwing away her youth. Gabriel could be dead by now. It was possible. He could be lying at the bottom of a sluggish bayou poisoned by a water snake. He could be lying in a dark ravine with a murderous Comanche's arrow in his back. He could be in England, a prisoner of war. He could be lost at sea, or buried at sea having died of typhus or smallpox. Worst still, he could, impatient of her absence, be married to another.

Impossible! What nonsense! "There I go again," she huffed. "I must be tired. Fatigue always brings on despair. The Devil must be a very tired old boy!"

Recovering hope, she reasoned that for all her wandering around, she was not so different from other women who spent their lives restlessly travelling, searching for that elusive romance that would hand them a life of emotional ease and a permanent sense of tranquilized fulfillment. And was she any worse off than all of those single women staying in their own hometowns and never finding a man to love? At least she was getting to see the world! Was she any worse off than others, like Thistle Woman, whose husbands died young? And was she any worse off than a woman who finds her man, marries him, and later feels love slipping away, a woman who continues to clean and cook for a man, and to have lonely sex with him - a woman of snow - in a marriage that ended a short time after it had begun?

"No, my life is not that bad," she sighed. "Many women have lives more tragic than mine. God is good and true love lasts. Yes, yes, God is good and He will not forsake me. I will find my Gabriel in the East!"

And with such reasoning, condemned to a life of hope, she moved on.

Chapter Forty-four

Charred Remains

One afternoon, after they had traveled another week, Evangéline's companions abruptly stopped hiking and began to set up camp. "Why are we making camp now?" asked Evangéline. "It's only the middle of the afternoon."

"Beyond that hill are the Hathawekela. My brothers want to bring a gift. They will hunt this afternoon. Maybe tomorrow, too."

"What kind of gift?"

"Big buck is best," said Thistle Woman.

The three braves went hunting, but came back at sunset empty-handed. Exhausted, Cornplanter and Little Arrow lay down immediately and fell asleep. Evangéline pulled up tufts of grass to make herself a bed. Somewhere on that day's journey she had lost her straw pallet. Blackhoof, lying on the ground nearby, watched her for a few minutes. Then he said, "Let the earth touch you." [1]

"What?" she asked, startled. Blackhoof rarely spoke. She didn't speak to him either, a little afraid of him. Of all three braves he had the most 'savage' looks. His straight, shiny, black hair hung down in sharp points like onyx daggers on his forehead. He was living proof of the family's recessive gene for the Asian face. The high cheek bones stretched the facial skin and forced an Oriental slant in his sparkling, black eyes. A long, narrow nose, hooked like a hawk's beak, cast a shadow over his indented upper lip, and his small, inverted-triangle of a mouth never seemed to close, leaving his tiny baby teeth visible at all times. His small teeth were widely spaced as though they had been given room to grow but never did. His was the face that still shows up every now and then in every Native tribe in North America; the face that the early White men found most foreign, and that made them shiver and slyly reach for the security of their guns. However, despite his exotic looks - and fiercely handsome looks once she got used to them - Blackhoof was the least aggressive of the three braves.

"It is good to let the earth touch your skin," Blackhoof said. "The earth is our Mother. She wants to hold us in her arms. Let the earth touch you."

What a beautiful thought! So sweet! So touching! So impractical! Yet, it would be good to be held in *someone's* arms. She dropped the grass from her hands and lay down on the earth to sleep. The ground, however, was predictably hard, and after her friends had fallen asleep, she reached over and took just a handful of dry grass to put under her hip bone so that she could fall asleep on her side.

The arrows of the three Shawnee brothers landed on target two dawns later and, with the prize buck, the proud march over the eastern hill began.

A few hours later, on the downward slope of the hill, the three brothers stopped in their tracks. Evangéline and Thistle Woman stopped and stared, too. Something was not right with the village of the Hathawekela. No activity. All was still. Even the few tethered horses that could be seen were lying down, motionless. In the morning breeze, the flaps of the wigwam entrances, as though in angry protest, slapped shut and open like howling mouths. Here and there on the grass near the wigwams were perfectly square, bluish-gray patches.

The three men, empty-handed, slid down the hill while the women followed, dragging behind them the heavy buck draped over two birch poles. (Shawnee men provided food; Shawnee women carried it.)

When they reached the village, they discovered the identity of the bluish-gray patches - dozens and dozens of bodies of Hathawekela men, women, and children covered with English army blankets. The stench was unbearable. Bodies, bloated with gases, hissed as they lay rotting in the sun.

"Whatever you do," said Evangéline, "do not touch the blankets! The English have filled them with sickness!"

Evangéline was referring to the vile English practice of giving the Indians gifts of military blankets infected with smallpox.[2] The Indians, unsuspecting, and flattered by the gifts, accepted them in good faith. The childlike innocence of the Hathawekela was particularly obvious; the agents of their deaths became their ostentatious shrouds.

It took Evangéline hours to convince the three brothers that, for fear of contagion, they had to burn all of the bodies where they lay, not carry them off for burial. She finally succeeded and, that evening, dozens of patches glowed with murky, lurid lights that transformed the village of the Hathawekela into a monstrous crematory under the twinkling brightness of the indifferent stars.

The three braves then built a separate fire for the carcass of the buck they had brought to the village. After a long day, they were all weak with hunger. As Evangéline prepared some utensils for the evening meal, Thistle Woman whispered to her, "Ne metsa. Not to eat. Buck is for sacrifice."

That night, no one ate. The buck was offered up in a religious sacrifice and the men danced and chanted around the burnt offering.

After the buck's cremation, the three braves took pieces of charcoal from the fire and smeared their faces black. Evangéline did the same, although she found it odd to dirty her face deliberately. Cornplanter noticed, understood, and whispered, "Not dirt. Only ashes. Ashes to clean the spirit."

She had seen the mourning ritual before in other Shawnee villages, and the blackened faces that would, upon the death of a close relative, remain black for a full year. Although the Hathawekela were not close relatives, the deaths of so many victims, victims of such demented premeditation, produced a sense of ritual obligation, even in Evangéline. She blackened her face, then, for the Hathawekela and, belatedly, for the charred remains of all the homes that had been destroyed in her village of Grand Pré.

No one slept that night because of the many fires that still burned and flickered disturbing light in their eyes.

Chapter Forty-five

Precious Gems

Fatigue, dismay, and disgust combined to make her mumble, "Men! Swords, guns, smallpox, oaths, and wars! Bullies and haters! Aren't there any loving men left in this world?" She trudged along and sighed. "I am travelling towards some 'big tree' and another Indian village, this one named Coaquannuck! Dear God, help me. Please give me patience!"

It was lonely trudging along with the taciturn Shawnee. They seldom felt the need for words. They communicated by staring together at the same sunrise or at the same glint of moonlight on the river. They sat close to each other and studied, in silence, the progress of the clouds at noon and the stars at night. They sometimes quietly marveled as they ran their fingers appreciatively over multi-colored strata in a rock. They loved even the stones they walked on. Sometimes Evangéline spoke to break the monotony of peace only to hear, "Shhhh! You will scare away partridge!" Or, "Shhhh! Rabbit will hear you!" And when she looked, sure enough, there would be an animal nearby feeding itself, oblivious to its human spies.

One particular afternoon upon stopping by a stream to drink and rest, she noticed that, once again, Cornplanter had picked up and was examining some small banded stones. Like a born geologist, he seemed to have a special interest in rocks. Evangéline had seen him do this many times and she was curious. "Why are you always looking at rocks? What is so interesting about ordinary stones?"

"Things which are alike in their nature grow to look like one another. Old man married many years to old wife begins to look like her," he said with a grin.

Evangéline laughed and said, "Yes, I've noticed that, too."

"These stones are round like the sun and the moon," he continued.

"Round like the sun and the moon?"

"Yes, they have been lying here so long looking up at the sun and the moon that now they look like them." [1]

"How beautiful!" she whispered, and suddenly burst into tears. Cornplanter looked bewildered. "It's just that I've been selfish. Thinking only of myself all the time. You are right and the priest was right; there is evidence of God's beauty everywhere." And with a new respect in her voice, she asked, "May I hold them?" Cornplanter handed her two round gray stones the size of sand dollars. She took them as though they were now precious gems. "May I keep them?"

"They will be sad if you take them from their home. No need to take them. They are everywhere," he said and laughed.

"Oh, no," she said, "we mustn't do that. Where did you find them?"

"Here," he said pointing to two small indentations in the soil. She carefully set the stones back in their rightful places. From that day on, she never looked at ordinary rocks quite the same again.

Neither did she look again upon the great flat land as a lonely, empty place. She never did learn to see the wind, but gradually she began to appreciate the golds, tans, yellows, ochers, and siennas of the Midwest, and to abandon the idea that beauty had to include green pine forests and a great green ocean.

****

"You will find your man by Big Tree," said Thistle Woman.

"Do you think so?" asked Evangéline, vaguely.

"Big Tree by Coaquannuck. You will find him there. Or maybe another man. Better man who will not leave you."

"But I don't want another man. I only want Gabriel. And we were separated by the English. He didn't leave me!"

"You need some man soon!" she said, as though Evangéline's days were numbered.

"I know. I'm getting older every day. I'm afraid to look at my reflection in the water. I'm not so young anymore." Then she laughed and said, "Maybe I'll have to marry one of your brothers."

Evangéline didn't think her remark was that funny, but Thistle Woman laughed for five minutes. "One of my brothers! Ha! Ha! Ha! Ha! Ha!"

"Why is that funny?"

Thistle Woman stopped laughing for a minute and then said,

"You will have to marry white man, or lonely old Shawnee man!" She paused to laugh again. "Young Shawnee braves only like girls twelve, thirteen. No older. Ha! Ha! Ha!"

"Well, that's a relief!" said Evangéline, not feeling relieved at all. She didn't quite know how to take this bit of news. How does one welcome an insult? It was like being slapped across the face with a compliment. "Mon dieu! And to think that I worried all those nights for nothing!"

That night she made herself another mental note: "do not take seriously any advice on love matters from women who have no love lives of their own."

They walked for days. She didn't count how many, now numb to time like her Shawnee friends. Numb, also, were her feet, and her skin as tough and dry as spruce bark. Although she had good moccasins, she actually preferred going barefoot now. It was true that the touch of the earth was good. Besides, footwear did not always protect, and sometimes got in the way, especially when wet.

They came to a beautiful river and the three brothers built a small birchbark canoe. It was small, Thistle Woman told her, because the river was gentle and Coaquannuck was not far from there. They wanted to approach Coaquannuck by water because, as children, they had always done so with their parents.

The gently gliding river was so clean they could see the bottom twenty feet down. They cupped their hands and slurped its pristine sweetness. In the sun's warmth, Evangéline fell asleep in the stern as the men unhurriedly paddled towards their traditional landing site.

Late in the afternoon, Thistle Woman poked Evangéline awake and said, "There! There is Big Tree [2] by Coaquannuck! Many Bigknives[*] there."

Evangéline rubbed her eyes and gazed. She couldn't believe it! A town! A real town with proper houses! And shingled, too! And large stone public

---

[*] "Bigknives" was the Shawnee term for Englishmen.

buildings looking so permanent! And all those people walking about! White people! "This is Coaquannuck?"

"Coaquannuck," nodded Thistle Woman.

Evangéline smiled and said softly, "Thank you, God. Oh, thank you!"

Coaquannuck was Philadelphia!

Chapter Forty-six

On Unsteady Legs

Half an hour later, all five went ashore and into the streets of Philadelphia. The Shawnee were in no danger there. The City of Friends was friendly to everyone. The Christian genius, William Penn, seventy-five years earlier had paved the way for Christian charity to be shown to the Indians when he decreed that " ... no man shall, by any ways or means, in word or deed, affront or wrong an Indian, but he shall incur the same penalty of the law as if he had committed a wrong against his fellow planter." [1] By 1721, Penn's tolerance was so firmly implanted that the governor of Pennsylvania openly extended his hospitality to the Shawnee when he told them at a meeting " ... we desire that you will come to Philadelphia to visit our families and our children born there, where we can provide better for you and make you more welcome - for people always receive their friends best at their own houses." Moreover, at this point in Pennsylvania's history, " ... not a drop of Quaker blood was ever shed by Indians." [2]

As they ambled, strolled, sauntered, hesitated, and stopped to look at almost everything in the city streets, words of welcome, however, were not the first words they heard from passing pedestrians. "Good God, what a sight! Look at that!"

"What is the world coming to!"

"Disgraceful! Absolutely disgraceful!"

"Doesn't the girl have any sense of shame?"

"Shameful! Shame, shame, shame on her!"

"Scandalous!"

"So dirty!"

"Oh, the smell!"

"And a white girl, too!"

"White! No, she can't be!"

"Didn't you see her green eyes? I tell you, she's white!"

"What a disgrace!"

The words offended Evangéline and she hurried as fast as she could to Walnut Street, the location of the Quaker hospital she had worked at years earlier. Her Shawnee friends dawdled along behind her and when she finally reached the hospital, perspiring more from the humiliation than the heat, she inquired at the door for Friend Mary, the Quaker nurse who had formerly employed her. Friend Mary came to the door and didn't recognize her. Mary was startled by the appearance of this tangle-haired, green-eyed girl in moccasins and a deerskin dress. "Don't you recognize me? Has it been that long?" asked Evangéline.

"I'm sorry," said Friend Mary. "Have we met before?"

"I am Evangéline. I once worked for you here."

The nurse stared hard, straining for recognition. "The only Evangéline I ever knew was a white girl."

"But I *am* a white girl!" She ran her hand over her face as though to prove its whiteness. Then she looked down at her hand and saw the black ashes. "Oh, I forgot, we are all in mourning."

"Sweet God in Heaven!" said Mary, and she threw out her arms. "Evangéline! My poor, poor Evangéline! I'm sorry I didn't recognize you. It's just that your face is … is … so … so dirty."

Evangéline whispered confidentially, "It's not dirt. Only ashes." Then she took from her neck the gold cross that Mistress Edwards had given her, turned, and put it around Thistle Woman's neck. Thistle Woman was ecstatic. (She had had her eye on the cross for quite some time.) Then Evangéline asked Mary, "What day is it?"

"Why, it's Tuesday!"

"I mean, … what *day* is it?"

"Do you mean 'what month'? It's Tuesday, the twelfth of July."

"In what year?"

"Oh, dear God! Dear God!" With a tear of understanding gathering in her eye, Friend Mary answered, "It's July 12, 1762!" Hearing the date, Evangéline grew faint, and then collapsed in Friend Mary's arms.

She was immediately put to bed where she was washed and left to rest. In a kind of after-shock, she remained in bed for a full week waking only long enough to eat, and then slept again, the fatigue of seven long years subsiding like the echoes of passing thunder.

At the end of the week, Evangéline asked Friend Mary, "What has happened to my Shawnee friends?"

"They are gone. They were homesick, they said. We had to give them white man's clothing to wear as disguises. Philadelphia is not friendly to Indians these days. The British and the Americans are on bad terms, and each side is trying to use the Indians against the other. The Indians are getting caught in the middle of it all." Evangéline heard this depressing news, turned over in her bed, and stayed there for another two days.

At the end of the second day, Mary leaned over the bed and whispered, "Come now, my friend. It's time for you to get back on your feet. Good hard work will help you more than rest."

"Work?"

"Yes, I can find work for you at the City Hospital."[*]

"But why can't I remain here at the Old Friends' Almshouse and work for you as I did before?"

"We allowed you to stay here before because we knew you would stay only the winter. Now you will need more permanent employment."

"What kind of employment?"

"Well, you can find work at the City Hospital. They are always in need of good nurses there."

"The City Hospital?"

"Philadelphia now has a new hospital. This place is only for the old and the feeble, as you must have noticed. It is also a place only for old and feeble Quakers.[3] Others, especially strangers, are always cared for at the City Hospital," said Mary. "I know some people there who will give you work. You are still young and strong and you can do much good there."

Evangéline didn't feel young and strong. Now back in the land of the Bigknives - the English - the land of so many Charles Lawrences, she felt her old timidity return. Living with the easygoing Shawnee, she had forgotten the pressures and stresses of living in the predatory, ravenous white man's world where the strong and the competitive devoured the small and the weak. She had learned to love the Shawnee and they had civilized her. Now she was more unfit than ever to cope with life in a large,

---

[*]   The Pennsylvania Hospital

raw English city where she was female, French, emotionally damaged, and alone.

Nevertheless, she did as Friend Mary asked. On unsteady legs, she left her bed, dressed, and prepared to face the world. She had to press on though she knew she would never be a competitor. She was not the predatory, ravenous type. She had no desire to devour the weak. She was a dull little weapon in the land of the big sharp knives. Or a small, round, sun-shaped stone that had been taken from its home and buried deep into the dark earth, separated from the sun. Oh, she would survive. But she would go on existing in a hazardous new world, cut off forever from the two gentle worlds that had shaped her soul, the two phantom worlds that were now retreating, vanishing, slowly and irretrievably, behind her.

On this shaky ground, Evangéline began her long career in nursing[4] and social assistance in the friendly, fast-growing city of Philadelphia. She was drawn like a magnet to the love in the hearts of the Quakers. Employed by the City Hospital, half of her time was spent as a visiting nurse, walking back streets and alleyways, appeasing hunger, distress, neglect, and disease. German farmers on their way to market often saw her at dawn returning from another night vigil by another sickbed. Her natural warmth and kindness found a legitimate outlet and, rather than diminish as they would in the average person, her warmth and kindness grew with each passing year.

PART THREE

Chapter Forty-seven

The Brilliant Doctor Durveldt

May, 1771

"What are you reading?"

Evangéline was startled. She had not heard Dr. Durveldt approaching. "Oh, it's you, Dr. Durveldt."

"Did I startle you?" he asked with a boyish grin. "Well?"

"Well what, doctor?"

"What is it that you read?"

"Oh, just some poems that Friend Mary gave me," she replied. She was keeping the night watch in the hospital's main corridor where all was quiet except for the voice of the visiting doctor. "The poems are published in a newspaper. Isn't that wonderful? A newspaper with poems!"

"Most of the newspapers, unfortunately, have poems. Poems. Hmmm!" he groaned. "I was hoping you were reading something more sensible."

"I'm sorry," said Evangéline, although she really had nothing to be sorry for. Apologizing had again become a way of life because, even though she was in a friendly place, it was unmistakably an English place, and she had not forgotten her treatment by the English in Nova Scotia. Like many other Acadian exiles, she was acquiring that meekness of spirit that the child of irrational and abusive parents develops. A submissive posture, after all, seems the wisest one when dealing with irrational superiors, but one that is difficult to correct years later.

The doctor sat at the desk and scribbled in his casebook. He scribbled and spoke at the same time. He was a foreigner, too, a Dutchman who had come to America to visit relatives in New York and then decided to stay. One of his relatives, also a doctor, got him this job in Philadelphia. Like Evangéline, he spoke English with a thick accent. His Nordic blond hair was beginning, in his forties, to turn gray. Small and wiry, he had the alertness and the quick movements seen only in highly intelligent men and women. "You should be reading sensible things. Poetry is unscientific," he said.

"Is poetry supposed to be scientific?"

"Everything is supposed to be scientific; otherwise, it doesn't make any sense."

"Well," said Evangéline smiling, "these poems make sense to me, doctor."

The doctor continued to scratch away with his quill and ink. "Read one."

"Out loud?"

"Otherwise I shall not be able to hear it. Go ahead, read one. I'm listening."

Evangéline was embarrassed. "I can't read well in English."

"I'm certain you can. Please do."

"Well, let me see," said Evangéline, trying to select a sensible one. Then she read,

> The sun set in God's western sky
> Like blood and flames commingled—

"That's dust!" interrupted Doctor Durveldt without looking up.

"I beg your pardon, doctor?"

"That's just dust, my dear."

Evangéline made a quick check of her dress. "What dust, doctor?"

"The sunset, of course. The blood and the flames. That's just dust in the air. The setting sun reflects off the dust particles in the air making the sky appear red. It has nothing to do with blood, and very little to do with flames. Not a very scientific poem, I'm afraid," said Durveldt. "Read a different one." He continued to scratch away with his pen.

Evangéline didn't know what to think. She stared for a second at the gray-blond head. Then she tried again.

> In Heaven where I wish to go
> There is no hail or rain or snow

> But only meadows green and fair
> And flowers growing—

"Impossible!" interrupted the doctor again. Oh my, thought Evangéline, it is just as the other nurses had said; he *is* mad. And probably an atheist, too! "Impossible! Quite, quite impossible!"

"What is impossible, doctor? Heaven?"

"No, no, the green meadows and the flowers growing and all that! Can't have that, you know. I mean, it's simply not possible. If you don't have any rain or moisture of some kind in the place, then it's quite impossible to have green meadows and flowers growing. Not scientific, you know. Not at all scientific. Such a place couldn't exist, you see." He continued to write in his book as though he were the only one in the room.

Doctor Durveldt, one of those single-minded characters who believe that science is the only road in life worth travelling, had such unflinching faith in science that he regarded the world of emotion - that is, of unclear thinking - as a false doctrine to be vehemently opposed. As a result of his scientific obsession, he was intellectually advanced, but emotionally obtuse and, therefore, socially handicapped as well. His progressivism, so to speak, held him back. All this aside, he was harmless, and he had been married to a sweet, charming lady for twenty years.

However, it was common knowledge around the hospital that whenever he did become romantically heated (in scientific terms - during his rutting periods - which were infrequent) he assumed that his high temperature and other physiological responses were simultaneously being transmitted telepathically to the object of his affection. Then, when he discovered later that the poor girl had no idea what he was referring to, the brilliant, stupid man was invariably shocked and disappointed by the girl's insensitivity, and by the appallingly low number of psychic receptors in her hopelessly tiny brain. Suddenly, he stopped writing, looked up, and stared into space for a minute, then rose abruptly to go. "Well, I must be off to see my patients."

"Goodnight, doctor."

"And, Evangéline, my dear, tell Friend Mary that you want to read more sensible poems from now on."

"Yes, doctor. Goodnight, doctor." She watched Dr Durveldt as he walked, in his quick jaunty way, down the hospital corridor. "What a strange man!" she whispered.

The next night, the little wiry man who was too busy to look at her, appeared again and began writing furiously at the desk in the hospital corridor. "Still reading silly stuff, are we?" asked Dr. Durveldt.

Evangéline smiled and said, "Yes, doctor."

"What is it this time? More blood in the clouds?"

She smiled again and said, "No blood in the clouds, doctor. Just a lock and a key."

"A lock and a key. Well, that sounds intriguing. Let's hear it."

She looked down at the new poem she was currently enjoying, cleared her throat, and read,

> Love is the key that unlocks the door
> To the happiness of life and—

"More like Pandora's box, if you ask me."

"I beg your pardon, doctor?"

"I mean that love unlocks as much misery as it does happiness, I'm afraid. That poem is just sentimentality, my dear. Very unscientific. Just sentiment from unreliable emotions. Not scientific."

"But you do believe in love, don't you, doctor?"

"All glandular, I'm afraid. Love is not a scientific word, my dear. Love is just Mother Nature's word for reproducing herself. In fact, Mother Nature will go on reproducing herself whether there's any love involved or not. 'Love' is not a scientific word; 'reproduction' is." He paused to write something in his casebook. "And tell me, if I may be so bold, my dear, why is it that a healthy girl like you has not reproduced?"

A little shocked by the eccentric doctor's bluntness, she took a moment before replying. "I was separated from my fiancé, Gabriel Lajeunesse, in the deportation of 1755."

"Ah! you are one of those Acadian exiles?"

"Yes, doctor."

"I'm sorry. I didn't know. And you have not located your fiancé?"

"No, doctor. I've searched in vain for the past sixteen years." She paused and lowered her eyes. Then she asked, "Do you believe in superstitions, doctor?"

"It depends. Some superstitions have their basis in rare, but real human experiences."

She then told the doctor the Indian tales of Mowis, the bridegroom of snow, who vanished in the forest, and of Lilinau and her phantom lover.

"The Shawnee told me that I was pursuing a ghost, a phantom, and that I would never catch up with him. I don't believe that I've been chasing a ghost, do you?"

"Perhaps by now he is a ghost—"

"Oh no, doctor, he's not a ghost. He's not dead. I would know it in my heart."

"That is not what I mean. I mean that, by now, perhaps he is a ghost in your head."

"I don't understand, doctor."

"The real Gabriel is not the man now in your head. The idealized man is there and that man doesn't exist."

"Idealized man?"

"You were so young. You did not have time to get to know Gabriel's faults. You did not get to know the *real* Gabriel. You did not marry him and get to live with him. Therefore, you have built up in your mind the image of a man who does not exist. In your mind he's perfect, but believe me, my dear, as a doctor, I can tell you that there are no perfect men in this world. So, yes, in a sense, you are looking for a ghost."

The doctor's matter-of-fact comments upset and confused her. Part of what he said made sense, and part of it didn't. She would have to think it all over later. Besides, she was now finding it difficult to concentrate because the busy little man who never had time to look at her had stopped his scribbling and was staring quietly and deeply into her beautiful green eyes. "I must go now and tend to my patients. Good night," said the doctor.

"Good night, doctor."

Later that night, as she crawled into bed, she reached under her pillow for her white rosary beads that now were worn gray with prayers, and she thought about Doctor Durveldt's answer to her question about phantoms. His explanation intrigued her, but something about it didn't ring true. It sounded like one of those fancy medical theories that nurses often scoffed at. It made sense, but it was a little too clever, a little too neat, a little too perfect. It's too perfect, she thought, too perfect… too ideal. Yes, that's it! It's too ideal! It's too ideal an explanation and, therefore, it can't exist. If idealized people can't exist, then neither can idealized explanations. "Well, thank you, God!" she said aloud. "I'm glad You helped me to untangle that knot."

Satisfied, she nestled under the covers. Then she thought: "besides, what a ridiculous idea that I would begin to love Gabriel less after I got to know him better! Of course, I could only grow to love him more every day, every month, every year. Some people, like poor Doctor Durveldt, just don't know what true love is. It's sad, but true. They just don't know."

Then she began her formal nighttime prayer, "Dear God, it's me, Evangéline, and I just want to remind You of our bargain. I am keeping my side of it, and I know that You will keep yours. And, Dear God, if You are trying to test me by sending into my life people like Mistress Edwards, and Thistle Woman, and Doctor Durveldt to tempt me to give up my quest, (and with clever explanations, I might add), it won't work. I'll pass any test You put in my way. You, above all, should know that by now. Notre Pere, qui êtes aux cieux, que votre nom soit sanctifié—"

When she finished her prayers, she revised the mental note she had made on Thistle Woman: "remember also never to take any advice on love from men who don't know what real love is!"

Chapter Forty-eight

Cushioned Discomfort

Her blood froze! Someone, a man, behind her somewhere in the bustling traffic was shouting her name. "Evangéline! Evangéline! Wait! Wait!" She turned and saw a man leap from a horse-drawn carriage and run towards her. "Evangéline, I am happy to see you again!" Her heart pounded, her eyes lit up, and then she tried to hide a look of disappointment. "Oh, I'm sorry! You were expecting to see someone else," said Charles Le Blanc, the wheelwright, her old friend who, years earlier, had stayed behind in Philadelphia.

"Oh, no, Charles! I'm delighted to see you again!" Then she spoke to him in French, "Comment ça va, toi?"

"I'm very well, thank you," he replied in perfect English. "Oh, let's go some place where we can talk. Do you have time?"

"Of course. I'll always have time to talk to you, Charles."

"The Philadelphia Inn is just down the street. We can go there, have tea, and talk," said Charles.

"But I'm not dressed well enough for that place!" said Evangéline, looking at the shiny boots, and the handsome stylish suit Charles was wearing. Her dark green dress was plain, the bonnet she wore at least five years old, and her dust-covered brown shoes had not been fashionable even when new.

"Of course, you are. Besides I'm a regular customer there. They wouldn't dare turn us away," he said and laughed.

They walked down High Street* to the Philadelphia Inn, the city's most elegant hostelry. As they entered the carpeted lobby, Evangéline thought of the Edwards' mansion in Boston. Every table in the dining area had a bright white tablecloth and a small candelabrum. "How do they get those tablecloths so white?" whispered Evangéline.

A black, uniformed waiter served them tea. "And you have not found Gabriel anywhere?" asked Charles.

"No," said Evangéline.

"I'm sorry," said Charles. "Well, I guess you didn't need me after all. I mean, it's unlikely that my presence on the trip would have made a difference."

Evangéline found it hard to concentrate on the conversation. She was growing increasingly uncomfortable because a few well-dressed ladies at other tables were looking her up and down. She saw their flowery, satin-trimmed parasols leaning casually against their chairs and her heart sank. She didn't own a parasol. The place was elegant and everyone, except her, fashionably attired.

Something else made her uncomfortable: Charles continued to speak to her in English. "This was a wise move for me, Evangéline. I knew I would make money here, and I have. Plenty of it! I now have my own carriage shop and business is thriving."

"Your cushioned wheel has been a success here?"

"Well, not exactly. That was one of my old ideas. I later discovered that it was not the wheel that would do the best cushioning job, but the springs."

"Springs?"

"Yes, we put the extra cushioning on the cart itself, not on the wheels. Under the seat, or under the carriage itself, we now position powerful springs to help cushion the ride, and that has been the secret to our success. You must come out for a long ride with me one day in one of our newest carriages!"

"I would like that, Charles," she said, looking shyly into her lap.

"What's the matter?"

"People are staring at me. I'm not dressed well enough for this dining room," she whispered. "I have to go."

"But, you're—"

---

* Now Market Street

"Please, Charles!"

"Fine, then, we'll go."

Once outside, Evangéline asked, "Do you speak English all the time now, Charles?"

"It's better for my business. Most of my customers, except for a few Germans, speak English."

"But I'm not English."

"I know. But when I speak French for a day now, or even half a day, it sets me back, and I begin to speak English with a thick French accent again."

"Are you ashamed of your French accent?"

"It's not a matter of shame; it's just impractical. French is just not a part of the future, Evangéline. The world has become an English place."

"And we must *move on*?"

"Exactly, or we will be trampled and left behind."

Evangéline nodded and smiled an ironic smile. It was that same old refrain: give up, forget the past, move on, make a new life for yourself. She was sick of hearing it. "Well, I must be going," she said.

"Will you go for a ride with me on Sunday afternoon?" he asked.

"Of course," she said. "I'll look forward to that." She gave him her address, smiled, embraced him, and then hurried home.

****

Sunday came, and wearing a prettier dress of a lighter color, she went with Charles for a ride around the city streets. She thought that they'd be going for a ride in the country, but Charles was more interested in showing her the homes of Philadelphia's wealthiest citizens. They drove around Walnut, Spruce, and Prune* Streets oohing and aahing at the huge, new Georgian-style mansions.

At the corners of Sixth and Sassafras** Streets, he pointed to a not-so-elegant, red brick house and said, "And that's where *he* lives with his common-law wife!"

"No!" said Evangéline, in shock.

"It's true," said Charles. "Her name is Deborah Read, and she's really married to a Mr. Rogers who abandoned her and disappeared. And you know what that makes her children!"

---

*   Now Locust Street

**   Now Race Street

"What?"

"Well, they're not the children of Mr. Rogers, so they're bastards!" he said. Then, like a little boy, he giggled at his boldness.

They drove on past the inelegant red brick home of Mr. Benjamin Franklin and Evangéline said, "It's incredible! I don't believe it! But what if Mr. Rogers comes back?"

"Oh, he won't come back. He's probably dead by now. That was all thirty-five years ago. They certainly make an odd couple, though."

"Why do you say that?"

"Because he runs his own newspaper and people say that she can't read."

Evangéline shook her head disapprovingly and said, "Well, for a political leader here, don't you think he is setting a bad example?"

"I suppose he is," said Charles, smiling at her naiveté.

"And do you think a man living in a state of mortal sin and fathering... illegitimate children can still be a good leader of the people?"

"I don't know how, but he certainly is a good leader."

"Well, it would never happen in Grand Pré!"

"The Philadelphians seem to think a lot of him. He's intelligent, and extremely inventive," boasted Charles. "Did you know that he invented bifocals? And the lightening rod?"

"And he's very rich! Perhaps he's too rich for his own good," said Evangéline, preaching a little to Charles.

To change the subject, Charles reached into his pocket and pulled out a piece of crumpled paper. "Have you seen any of these notices?"

"What is it?"

"It's an invitation for us to return home. The various governors of the Canadian provinces have been sending invitations to the Acadians to return to Canada. They're promising free land and freedom of religious practice. This one is from Governor Murray[1] of Québec. Wasn't he the young captain who came with his troops to Grand Pré and confiscated all of our guns?"

"I don't remember, but I remember all those other promises they gave us," she said, handing back the crumpled invitation as though it were last month's newspaper. "Besides I now think I have a better chance of reuniting with Gabriel if I stay in one place. Someone will meet up with him somewhere and tell him where I am. It's not wise if both of us are always on the move."

"You're wise to stay here. The future is here, not back there!"

"You frighten me, Charles. I'm afraid you are completely forgetting your roots."

"Roots? Roots?"

"Yes, you sound as if you want to forget all about the past and where you came from."

"What is there to remember?"

"Oh, Charles, we must never forget our roots. It's not a wise thing - not a healthy thing to do."

Charles bristled. "Do you want to see our roots? Do you? I'll show you our roots! I'll show you!" he said, almost shouting.

He turned his carriage away from the fashionable part of town and drove quickly to the poorest section of Philadelphia, the dockside district by the big Delaware River. Small shabby shacks shared the streets with larger miserable tenements. He stopped the carriage in front of a squalid, wooden, three-story building. A dozen, ill-clad children argued loudly with each other in the street. Charles pointed to the house whose broken windows were covered with mismatched boards and he said, "Here are our roots! These are the roots that you want me to hold on to, and that I'm trying to forget! Miserable French-speaking paupers hiding in back pockets of large English cities like this one, holding on to their precious French language and their stifling Catholic religion! Begging Englishmen for a little food and a small place to die! Well, not me, my dear. Not me! I'm one Frenchman who is not terrified of change!"

"The people who live here are *French*?"

"Yes, I'm sorry to say. I suppose your English hospital employers don't send you to this part of town."

"Oh, Charles, don't say any more. I will pray hard for you. You're more in need of help than these poor people. You sound exactly like a Bigknife!"

"A Bigknife?"

"Never mind. Oh, Charles, we must help these people. Now I know why God gave you money, Charles. I've been asking myself that question, and now I know why. God works His wonders in mysterious ways, you know."

Charles didn't like the expensive sound of God's mysterious ways, but he said no more. Something deep inside him, something guilty, agreed with her. He knew the first time he had seen this pitiful house filled with Acadian exiles from the Fort Edward area at Piziquid that he had to offer some help. Until now, he hadn't known how. Evangéline could help them and help him. Using his money, she could ease their poverty and his conscience.

Charles nodded his head, looked at Evangéline with tears forming in his eyes, and said, "Work with them and just tell me what you need."

Evangéline squeezed his arm. "I knew you were still a good man, Charles."

Charles drove her home and began to feel much better about himself. Evangéline was a blessing in disguise. She would be his way out of his private hell. "Oh, by the way," he said as she stepped out of the carriage, "did you know that Mr. Franklin can speak a little French?"

"Is that true?"

"That's what they say."

She grinned. "Perhaps he's not such a bad man after all!"

****

She saw Charles mostly on a business basis after that. She reported to him on the needs of the French exiles, and he funded her projects on their behalf. There were forty-five immigrants from nine families crammed into the three-story building that had once been a single-family dwelling. Using Charles's wealth and her own meager savings, she first took care of the children, feeding and clothing them. Then, she bought warm clothes for the adults. Some months, she also paid the rent and counseled the tenants on the merits of thrift and sobriety, though she understood that the men drank mainly out of shame and frustration at being economically impotent. Most of all, she listened to their grievances and discovered that what they wanted most was to return to Canada. So, reluctant to be too generous with Charles's money, she sent each family home, one at a time, over the next two years.

She was grateful to Charles and she prayed for him. She knew that he was emotionally confused in struggling with his new identity. For all his wealth he, in a way, perhaps suffered more than did many other exiles. For the English-Americans he was too French, and for the French-Acadians he was too English. Evangéline became even more aware of Charles's inner turmoil when she learned that he had an English girlfriend whom he never introduced to any of his French associates, a lady friend that he kept hidden away like a bright new key. "It's none of my business," she told herself. All that she could do was pray that Charles would work things out for himself.

It was also comforting proof to her that everybody, even wealthy people like Charles, was searching for an elusive something in the world.

Chapter Forty-nine

What We Should Have Done

July 16, 1776

Charles had a free Sunday afternoon because his girlfriend was visiting a sick relative who was about to deliver. He called on Evangéline and took her for a ride in his most modern carriage, a fancy, cornflower-blue box buggy with a shiny, black leather top. "Have you read the *Gazette* this week?" he asked, holding up the latest edition of the *Pennsylvania Gazette*, Benjamin Franklin's controversial newspaper.

"No," said Evangéline, "I've been too busy this week to read anything. Why?"

"Here," he said, "read this. This is what we should have done in Nova Scotia. Perhaps if we had all listened more to Pierre Melanson we might have stood up to the British, too!"

"Where?"

"Right here. On the front page, if you don't mind! What courage! What guts!" said Charles.

Evangéline looked at the front page of the *Gazette* dated July 10, 1776. In the first column, she read:

'In Congress, July 4, 1776. A Declaration by the Representatives of the United States of America, in General Congress Assembled.

'When in the Course of human events, it becomes necessary for one people to dissolve the political bands which have connected them with another, and to assume among the powers of the earth, the separate and equal station to which the Laws of Nature and of Nature's God entitle them, a decent respect to the opinions of mankind requires that they should declare the causes which impel them to the separation. ---We hold these truths to be self-evident, that all men are created equal, that they are endowed by their Creator with certain unalienable Rights, that among these are Life, Liberty and the pursuit of Happiness. --- That to secure these rights, Governments are instituted among Men, deriving their just powers from the consent of the governed, --- That whenever any Form of Government becomes destructive of these ends, it is the Right of the People to alter or abolish it, and to institute new Government laying its foundation on such principles and organizing its powers in such form, as to them shall seem most likely to effect their Safety and Happiness.'

Evangéline stopped reading and asked, "Does this mean that the Americans are going to abolish the British government and set up their own?"

"Exactly! That's what we should have done, I tell you!"

Evangéline read on.

'The history of the present King of Great Britain is a history of repeated injuries and usurpations, all having in direct object the establishment of an absolute Tyranny over these states ... He has plundered our seas, ravaged our Coasts, burnt our towns, and destroyed the lives of our people. Our repeated Petitions have been answered only by repeated injury. A Prince, whose character is thus marked by every act which may define a Tyrant, is unfit to be the ruler of a free people.'

"Well!" said Evangéline, impressed.

"Isn't that the most courageous thing you've ever read? Imagine calling the king a tyrant on the front page of the newspaper!"

Looking at the signature at the end of the declaration, Evangéline asked, "Did this man, John Hancock, write this?"

"They all did, the men who have been meeting downtown at the state house. The men of the Continental Congress: John Adams, Thomas Jefferson, Benjamin Franklin, John Hancock and the others."

"Benjamin Franklin?"

"Yes."

"It's very dangerous to say such things about a king. Sounds to me like trouble is coming!"

"Yes, a big war. There's been some fighting already in Massachusetts - at Lexington, Concord, and Bunker Hill."

"Men and their fighting! I knew he would not be a good leader."

"Who?"

"That man living in sin with the married woman! Benjamin Franklin!"

"But he is a great leader, I tell you. This is all wonderful news. These Americans are standing up for what they believe in!"

"War is not wonderful, Charles. Mr. Franklin and his Continental friends are just getting themselves into the same trouble we got ourselves into."

"Oh no, dear, this is very different."

"I don't think so," said Evangéline firmly. "The same thing will happen to them!"

"What can happen to them?"

"The British will have them all deported! Just like us! You mark my words!"

****

The Revolutionary War came, of course, and the sword and the gun reigned once more. Evangéline became busier than ever. But this war was, in one way, good for her since it gave her no time to think about her personal problems. She was better off buried in her work. The war benefited Charles, too. He made another fortune selling military wagons to the army.

In 1783, the war officially ended and she was happy to be living in a freer country. She was glad that the members of the Second Continental Congress had not been deported after all. Philadelphia was a good place to be, an exciting, dynamic place, a place full of hope and optimism. If only she had her Gabriel with her to share the excitement!

****

And the years crawled by, one after another, after another, after another, seamlessly blending because time, as it was for the Shawnee, would be eternal until she could find her Gabriel. The only day, month, and year that would have any meaning for her would be the date of their reunion. Nothing else in the world mattered.

And each succeeding year stole a small measure of her beauty. Shadows cast by lines crossed her face, and then there came, like muffled insults, the first dreaded strands of gray above her forehead.

Chapter Fifty

Ideal Image

After all she had been through, nothing much shocked her, but she was somewhat shaken when, a mere hour after his wife's funeral, Doctor Durveldt told Evangéline that it was a sad blow but he was fortunate because he still had *her*. In the churchyard, just after the burial, she had said to him, "I'm sorry, Doctor, for your loss," and he had replied, "Thank you, but I'm fortunate because I still have you."

The remark didn't register as she continued on her way in the line of mourners, nor even later when she recalled what he had said. She simply passed it off as "the babble of the bereaved" as the saying went.

Three days later at the hospital, however, when he repeated those same words to her, his secret love unmistakably lurched into the bright light of day.

"But what do you mean, Doctor, that you 'still have' me?"

"I mean just what I say. I still have you, I will always have you because I've loved you from the moment I first saw you." He stared into her eyes. In amazement, she stared back into his and thought she recognized the look. She had seen that look before. It was the same look she used to see in Gabriel's eyes, that helpless gaze full of hungry longing. Feeling linked to Gabriel, she continued to look into the doctor's eyes. Then, she lowered her head and stared at the floor. It was the right gaze, but the wrong pair of eyes.

"I didn't know," she said.

"I didn't want you to know."

"Why?"

"I was afraid you might be offended. Or worse, that you would feel that I was pressuring you and that, as a result, you might move away, go somewhere else."

"Well, ..." she said, "I don't know what to say."

"You don't have to say anything."

There was an awkward pause. Then she asked, "But what do you mean that you will always have me?" She had understood perfectly, but she just wanted to hear the words again.

"I mean that I hope to always have you in my heart and in my mind. You have always been the image of perfection to me. You've been my reason for living, for going on, for surviving. If I hadn't had you here, I think I would have gone mad in this place."

"But your wife—"

"Our love faded many years ago."

"But you know that I'm waiting for another man. I've told you that," she said.

"Yes, and I understand that, and that's why I've never ... approached you, never ... touched you."

"Oh, Doctor!" sighed Evangéline.

"And you needn't worry. I will not touch you or push myself on you. I'd be too afraid that you would become real to me and then you would disappear." He grinned feebly, ashamed for being confessional. "I hope that you'll understand and that you will remain here where I can at least look at you and hear your voice." He lowered his eyes.

The brilliant idiot looked so miserable standing there with his head down and his sandy-gray hair growing thinner by the minute, so helpless, so powerless, disarmed by his own affection, waylaid by her beauty, a victim of her eyes, such a completely disabled aging man in love that she took pity on him, put her arms gently around him, and whispered, "Not very scientific, Doctor."

He laughed at her little joke which lightened the tone of their conversation, and feeling suddenly relieved, he said, "Well, I must see to my patients." Then he looked into her eyes again and said, "I hope you understand."

She smiled at him, nodded, and said, "I'll be here. I'm not going anywhere."

That night, after she had crawled into bed and said her prayers, she made herself two mental notes: "remember that what people say and what they do are two entirely different things; and remember that all human beings have love in their hearts, even the so-called smart ones!"

Chapter Fifty-one

The Return Of Blackhoof

Introduction

February 12, 1802

"The White people never cared for land or deer or bear. When we Indians kill meat, we eat it all up. When we dig roots, we make little holes. When we build houses, we make little holes. When we burn grass for grasshoppers, we don't ruin things. We shake down acorns and pine nuts. We don't chop down the trees. We only use dead wood. But the White people plow up the ground, pull down the trees, kill everything. The tree says, "Don't. I am sore. Don't hurt me." But they chop it down and cut it up. The spirit of the land hates them. They blast out trees and stir it up to its depths. They saw up the trees. That hurts them. The Indians never hurt anything, but the White people destroy all. They blast rocks and scatter them on the ground. The rock says, "Don't. You are hurting me." But the White people pay no attention. When the Indians use rocks, they take little round ones for their cooking …

How can the spirit of the earth like the White man? … Everywhere the White man has touched it, it is sore."*

---

* The words of an old Wintu woman from Dorothy Lee, *Freedom and Culture*, Prentice-Hall, Englewood Cliffs, New Jersey, 1959, pp. 163-164.

****

"In the year 1802, a deputation of Shawnees, of which the chief, Blackhoof, was one, and several of the Delaware chiefs in company with him on their way to Washington City; in order to renew their acquaintance with their old friends, the Quakers, they visited Philadelphia." [1]

****

Evangéline was out attending to the poor and missed seeing him when Blackhoof came to visit her at the City Hospital. (Friend Mary had told him where to find her.) She did see him, however, when he stopped by the hospital on his return trip home. Evangéline was delighted to see one of the braves who had helped to guide her back to Philadelphia years earlier.

Blackhoof was now in his fifties, and looked distinguished with his graying hair, the sharp onyx bangs now striated with silver. He had been the toughest-looking of the three brothers, but he appeared more mellow now. His voice was softer, more resigned. He wore a large gold chain around his neck, and after she had embraced him, she said, "You have a beautiful chain! Is it real gold?"

Blackhoof shrugged and with a cynical smile said, "Maybe. Who knows? Henry Dearborn, a Bigknife in Washington, gave it to me. I want to believe it is gold. Gave me this, too." He handed her a fancy scroll tied with a gold ribbon. She unrolled the paper stamped with President Jefferson's seal, and read aloud:

> "'To the chiefs of the Delawares and Shawnee Nations of Indians.
> 'The Secretary of War of the United States sends greeting.
>
> 'Friends and brothers: ... your Father, the President, instructs me to assure you on behalf of your nation, that he will pay the most sacred regard to existing treaties between your respective nations and ours, and protect your whole territory against all intrusions that may be attempted by white people.
>
> That all encouragement shall be given to you in your just pursuits and laudable progress toward comfort and happiness, by the introduction of useful arts. That all persons, who shall offend against your treaties, or against any of the laws made for

your protection, shall be brought to justice, or if this should be impossible, that a faithful remuneration shall be made to you, and that he never will abandon his beloved Delawares and Shawnees, nor their children, so long as they shall act justly toward white people and their red brethren.

'This is all that he requires from you for his friendship and protection; he trusts you will not force him to recede from these determinations by improper or unjust change of conduct, but that you will give him abundant course to increase, if possible, his desire to see you happy and contented under the fostering care of the United States.

'I send you a chain (which is made of pure gold) by your beloved chiefs; it will never rust, and I pray the Great Spirit to assist us in keeping the chain of friendship (of which this gold chain is an emblem) bright for a long succession of years. 'Given under my hand and seal of the war office of the United States, the ninth day of February, one thousand eight hundred and two.

'Signed:
Henry Dearborn,
Secretary of War.'" [2]

"I hope that you will get more than a gold chain for all of the land you have given the American government," said Evangéline.

"The White Men think that by stealing the land they will become richer, but stealing it will only make them poorer. They have agreed to let us stay on our land along the Miami River in Ohio and to give us one thousand dollars a year. We must accept because too many white men here now, and our tribes too small to fight back. The future of our land is in the hands of the Bigknives now.

"Many years ago, the White Man came to our land with Bibles. Now the Shawnee have the Bibles, and the White Man has our land."

Evangéline nodded. She understood perfectly. "And how are my other friends - your sister, Thistle Woman, and your two brothers, Little Arrow and Cornplanter?"

"Cornplanter is dead. In a treaty with the White Man, we were given land that belonged to the Wyandot.[3] The Bigknives showed cunning. They set our two tribes against each other fighting for the same piece of land. In the fight, Cornplanter was killed by a Wyandot arrow."

"That makes me sad." She paused for a minute and then asked. "And Thistle Woman?"

"Thistle Woman is old and crippled now. Little Arrow cooks for her and takes good care of her."

She took his hand and squeezed it. "Thank you for coming to see me. I will keep you in all of my prayers."

Blackhoof smiled and said, "Itah, nitcap!"*

"Itah!" she replied.

She saw Blackhoof turn and walk away down the long corridor, a disturbing sight, an incongruous sight in moccasins, assorted feathers, and a gray gift blanket. That once-tough, fiercely independent Native was now strangely out of place in his own country with nothing to show for his losses but a gold chain of uncertain value, and a piece of Washington parchment of even more dubious value. She knew instinctively that she was witnessing more than the dark, retreating shape of one good friend.

---

*   "Good luck, friend!"

Chapter Fifty-two

The Name of a Place

July 16, 1803

It was the Feast Day of Our Lady of Mount Carmel. Evangéline slid out of bed, said her morning prayers, ate a light breakfast, and set off for work at the hospital. She felt at home now in Philadelphia where many other Acadian exiles had taken refuge. The gentle Christianity of the compassionate Quakers reminded her of the old Acadian country where all were brothers and sisters, where all were equals. She could breathe easier here and no longer felt the urge to move. Still lonely but uncomplaining, she worked and prayed, worked and prayed. There was nothing else she could do, and Philadelphia's atmosphere of tolerance soothed her thoughts and her tired feet.

Every morning she whispered, "Thy will be done." It was no longer just a line from the *Our Father*. Nor was it an admission of defeat, nor another submissive posture. It was, instead, an expression of her evolving acceptance of God's will in all things. "*Thy* will be done."

Acceptance had not come easy. Her days of darkest despair were now behind her, but it was not so long ago that she had been seen "screaming at the sky", as the other nurses testified. From time to time, she had been seen in the hospital courtyard, looking skyward with her arms raised, and screaming, "O Lord, how long! I am weary with my groaning; I water my couch with my tears."

But lately, as though a veil or a heavy mist had lifted, she began to see the world a little more clearly. No doubt the world was a place of loneliness and sorrow; but one could always light one's pathway with faith, with love, and with hope that was, for all its empty promises, a life-extending investment in itself.

This did not mean, of course, that Gabriel was forgotten. His image was imprinted on her soul. In her mind, he was still young, still handsome, still untouched by time. Over his memory the years had no power. And it was not true as many women, so many times, had whispered behind her back that thoughts of Gabriel had spoiled her chance of a happy marriage to someone else. Rather it was all those thoughts of him that had lengthened her life and made her suffering more bearable.

A deadly epidemic of yellow fever[1] broke out in the city and took the lives of the rich as well as the poor. The homeless died in the streets or came crawling to die in the hospital. Day and night, Evangéline went to her post and comforted the sick.

Before dawn on this particular morning in July, Evangéline walked the city streets, deserted and silent, until she came to the hospital gate. In the courtyard she stopped to pick some flowers. Their fragrance and beauty would bring a little joy to the dying. She loved all of the flowers and had a hard time deciding which would serve best as life's ambassadors. She liked the homely marigolds, inspired by their struggle to be more golden. "You are not very golden, but you are good for cleaning wounds," she said. "Oh, you smell so good!" she said to the tall, proud, aromatic lavender. And to the smaller, purplish-white buds of sweet marjoram she whispered, "And I don't know what our feverish patients would do without you." Once in a while she touched a rose and was always amazed at the dusty velour of its petals. Sometimes, too, when battling the demon of self-pity, she would deliberately prick her finger on a rose thorn as if to impale the beast within. A drop of her blood on a rose petal served to remind her that, in this world, thorns are sometimes more of an advantage than soft pretty petals. "Now, let me see. 'Marigold's for cleaning wounds. Marjoram's for fever.' How does the rest of it go? Oh, yes! 'Lavender's for pains and sprains ... Dee dum dee dum dee dever.' Now I'm getting silly. Can't remember the rest of it. My memory now, I'm afraid, is just a memory."

Two nurses entered the gate behind her and she overheard one whispering to the other, "There's poor Evangéline! Talking to the flowers again." Evangéline simply smiled her gnostic smile and cast a knowing wink at her co-conspirators, the daisies, nodding their complicity in the breeze beside the shady garden wall.

"I suppose I am getting a little eccentric in my old age," she said aloud, and her mouth flashed a wide Shawnee grin. "Goodness! I've reached the age when I'm talking to myself." She slowly climbed the steps to the hospital dormitory and was short of breath when she reached the top.

Then she heard the chimes from the belfry of Christ Church and hymns being sung by the Swedish congregation in their church at Wicaco.

A sudden calm fell on her as though from descending wings. She peered around to see if some large bird had actually landed near-by. A voice inside her seemed to be saying, "Your trials have ended." She didn't understand the voice, but with a new lightness in her step she entered the dormitory, every bed of which held a dying patient.

Other nurses were moving noiselessly from bed to bed, moistening feverish lips and burning foreheads, closing the sightless eyes of the dead and covering their faces. For some patients, Evangéline's presence was like a ray of sunshine on a prison wall, and they raised their heads from their pillows when she passed. She had an aura, they said, that could calm a frantic mind. She was also beginning to understand that death, in some forms, could be a blessing when it came.

She scanned the room and noticed that some of the familiar patients had disappeared in the night and that their beds were filled already by strangers. "We have many new faces this morning," she whispered to one of the elderly nurses on duty.

"Many more for thee to care for," said the old nurse.

Evangéline smiled. She liked being addressed by the Quaker nurses with the archaic pronoun 'thee'. It made her feel a little younger. "Such sad victims," she whispered. "They are dying homeless and nameless."

"Not all nameless," said the old nurse, pointing. "A new one down there at the end has managed to write his name proudly on a piece of dirty paper."

"How strange!" said Evangéline.

"Yes, and a strange name it is. More like the name of a place."

Something inside Evangéline began to stir, something deep, seismic, and unnerving. Oh no, she thought, not that old tugging at my heart! Hope, that persistent gigolo, is rearing his tiresome head again! And just when I thought I was so mature. Oh, these jolts to my heart will be the death of me!

Trying to compose herself, she stiffened her spine, stood more erect, and asked, "The name of a place?"

"Yes," said the old nurse, "I think so. A foreign name. It begins with the letter 'A'. Sounds like Analon, or Aragon, or something like that. Or perhaps it was—" The old nurse faltered because Evangéline's cheeks were turning pale, and the flowers she had picked slid from her hands to the floor.

"Oh, mon Dieu!" she whispered. And suddenly she was running, running like a mad woman, frenzied and reckless, racing to see the face of the new patient lying in the last bed at the end of the hall.

Out of breath, she reached the last bed in the room, bent down at the foot, and saw a dirty piece of paper pinned to the bed sheet. She struggled for air as an uncomfortable pain spread through her chest. One word was printed in large letters. "Avignon!" she gasped. Above it, in smaller letters that had gone unnoticed by the other nurses, three other words, "From here to."

On the narrow pallet before her was the frame of an old man. Though gray hair covered his temples, he still retained the handsome looks of his earlier years. His cheeks were flushed with fever and his spirit was slowly sinking.

Echoes. Echoes. The dying man could hear echoes, the echoes of a long cry of pain as in a dream. Then at his ear, a sweet voice whispered, "Gabriel! Oh, my beloved!"

In that voice he heard the cry of hungry gulls and the soft surge of white sea foam on a distant northern shore.

Opening his eyes, he saw before him the vision of his dream. Evangéline knelt by his bed and she understood by the motion of his lips that he was trying to whisper her name. Gabriel moved to raise himself, but seeing his struggle, she leaned closer. After forty-eight years - long, weary years - the reunited lovers kissed and closed their eyes. And as she placed her lower lip between the two of his, suddenly they were home again, home under their own apple blossoms beside their own house, near the copper-colored beach in the shadow of Blomidon at Grand Pré, lying together in the fresh green grass at the end of the great meadow that stretched on and on.

After a moment, the pressure from his lips subsided. She lifted her head and saw that his eyes were closed in peace.

All was over now, all the fears, and all the restless, unsatisfied longing. Even the dull pain of patience was retreating.

Although no visible ring encircled her finger, the circle of her life was now complete. Her journey was over. She pressed his head to her breast and said, "Heavenly Father, I thank You."

And despite a life of separation, she was *sincerely* thankful for a life that had promised her an undiminished love and that, over the years, had kept that promise fresh, and strong, and true. The slim chance of finding her perfect mate was always preferable to settling for a suitable substitute. She sat and stared at Gabriel's handsome face as a great pain and a frightening tension squeezed her chest and made her wince. "I'm afraid I have the heart of my mother *and* my father," she whispered. To ease her pain and to catch her breath, she leaned forward and laid her head on Gabriel's shoulder. And yet, no matter how deeply she inhaled, she couldn't draw a full, satisfying breath as though each of her lungs had developed a small puncture.

She rested for a minute, then reached into the pocket of her apron and took out a letter. "I wrote this letter to you, mon trésor, but I didn't know where to send it. I didn't know where you were. It doesn't matter now. I've found you." She laid her head again on his shoulder, and with her pain slowly subsiding, she relaxed and simply fell asleep.

She never woke again.

From a short distance down the aisle, the older nurse and her companion watched the spectacle of the reunited lovers. They stood and stared in amazement, not knowing what to do at first. Then curiosity drove them closer. The older nurse stooped and picked up the letter from the floor. She read, but didn't fully understand.

> 'Oh Gabriel, my love, what strange lives we've led when all we ever wanted was to be left alone to love one another in a small place that we could call our own. It seems that in this big world of competing ambitions, we were asking a little too much. And I'm not certain that we would ever have found peace, even here in America, because of the many Bigknives here, too. The future, it seems, is now in the hands, not of the English Bigknives, but of the American ones.
>
> 'I can see, at last, that Pierre was right, and that you were right in defending him. We had too many fears, and our fears made

us timid. We should have fought, and fought hard. Pierre understood that everything is tied to politics. It's sad, but in this confused world, lovers can't just love, they also have to fight. They have to fight even if it's only to fight for their own neutrality, to fight for their own quiet spot where they can lie down safely somewhere between the knives. The world has too many haters seeking to befoul the world with their hatred.

'And so, goodbye, my dearest love. I loved you faithfully all of my life. No man ever took your place. You were the promise I depended upon. You were the dream that kept me strong.

'And when we meet again, this time we'll stand together and fight for our right to live, and our right to love one another, in our own clean house, on our own rightful land, in our own sweet country, Canada.

Forever,

Evangéline'

And today in Nova Scotia, along the misty Atlantic shores, live Acadians whose forefathers from exile wandered back to their native land to die and to be buried in its sacred soil. There, the story of Evangéline is still heard by the evening fire, a story that can never be too often told.

The epilogue follows.

EPILOGUE

Five years after he had deported the Acadians, Charles Lawrence collapsed at a banquet at Government House in Halifax. He never regained consciousness and died eight days later on October 19, 1760. (King George II died the same year.) Lawrence was fifty and unmarried. It was said that "he enjoyed the company of his soldiers." He left no money or property behind although, in 1754, he inherited £10,000 from an uncle in Southhampton, John Harding, Esq. (his mother's brother), and to his credit he paid one-half the cost of the erection of the new Government House built in Halifax in 1758, and the entire cost of the furnishings.

He was born for the military life. His father, John, was an army man, and "his mother, a Harding of Southhampton, came from a family that for generations had provided commanders to the army and navy of Britain." Both Charles and his father had been wounded in battles with the French. His father's injuries were so serious that he was already living on a disability pension when Charles was born. The Montagu family ties to George Montagu Dunk, 2nd Earl of Halifax, probably helped Charles to become governor, and accounted for his confidence and possibly for some of his arrogance in taking the expulsion of the Acadians into his own hands. (Another relative, Montagu Wilmot, became governor of Nova Scotia eight years later.)

At his funeral on October 25 with the Reverend Doctor Breynton presiding, Lawrence was given full Masonic honors; 4,400 military personnel attended along with hundreds of Halifax citizens. His body rests today in a vault in St. Paul's Anglican Church on Barrington Street in downtown Halifax, the first person to be so honored there. At his funeral, Belcher delivered the eulogy saying, " … he had every admirable quality and exerted his uncommon abilities with unwearied application. He encouraged the industrious, rewarded the deserving, excited the indolent, protected the oppressed, and relieved the needy. His affability and masterly address endeared him to all ranks of people, and a peculiar greatness of soul made him superior to vanity, envy, avarice or revenge. In him Halifax and the Province have lost the guide and guardian of their interests." (This eulogy contains the same stock phrases commonly used during this period at the funeral of any public official: "excited the indolent", "relieved the needy", etc.) Fort Lawrence, outside Amherst, Nova Scotia, Lawrencetown outside Dartmouth, N. S., and Lawrencetown west of Middleton, N.S., still bear his name today. It would be no exaggeration to add that if a modern governor, say in 1945, had done what Lawrence did in 1755 (burned the homes and ruined the lives of over 7,000 residents), he would undoubtedly have been tried as a war criminal.

Jonathan Belcher, who succeeded Lawrence as the next lieutenant-governor, and who continued the expulsion that Lawrence began, is also buried in St. Paul's Church. He died March 30, 1776. He was sixty-five. His wife (née Abigail Allen) and seven children - five boys and two girls, only two of whom (a boy and a girl) lived to adulthood - are buried a few blocks away in the upper right-hand corner of the Old Burial Grounds at the corners of Barrington Street and Spring Garden Road in Halifax. (Abigail died at the age of forty-four.) Jonathan was a regular churchgoer who, in his later years, gave Bibles, free of charge, to anybody who wanted one. (Atonement?)

Belcher's father was the governor of New Jersey, and helped establish the Ivy League college, Princeton, although he himself was once described as 'an angry, ignorant man.' (Princeton's original name was The College of New Jersey.) Jonathan's grandmother was the sister of Deputy-Governor Danforth, one of the men involved in the Salem Witch Trials, and one of the characters in Arthur Miller's play, *The Crucible*. Large portraits of Belcher and his wife (by John Singleton Copley) hang today in the Beaverbrook Art Gallery in Fredericton, New Brunswick. Belchertown, Massachusetts, was later named for Jonathan's father who, although invited, never set foot in the town.

John Winslow of Marshfield, Massachusetts was born in 1702. Described as "good-natured", he was quoted in the *New York Gazette* (August 25, 1755) as having said, "If we can accomplish this noble and great project (the deportation), it will have been one of the greatest deeds the English in America have ever achieved." So much for "good nature". He was also "a zealous upholder of Great Britain." (See Shortt & Doughty, p. 95.) He "got a poor education and could never write a literate letter without a scribe's aid." (Note the redundant wording of his order written after the assault on the French women.) Nevertheless, the Winslow name is still famous in Massachusetts, and some very literate family members later gained prominence; Charlotte, the mother of the modern poet Robert Lowell, was a Winslow.

In 1752, three years before he went to Grand Pré, Colonel John had been stationed at Fort Halifax, Maine. In 1771, Fort Halifax changed its name to Winslow to honor him. He was married twice, first to Mary Little, and later to Bethiah Johnson of Hingham, Massachusetts. Mary gave him two sons, Pelham and Isaac. Like his father, Pelham was a military man and a Loyalist who went to Halifax in 1776 with the army. Isaac became a doctor. In his later years, Colonel John complained that he "never received adequate remuneration, and to the end of his life submitted fruitless claims to the colonies and to Great Britain for pay or preferment. Nevertheless, after his death, his name remained on the half-pay lists, presumably for his widow's benefit, until 1787." He died in Hingham in 1774. His portrait now hangs in the Plymouth Historical Society, Plymouth, Massachussetts. A copy of this portrait can also be seen in the Winslow House Museum in Marshfield. He kept a journal of his daily activities in Grand Pré, and this journal, in his own handwriting, is available for viewing today in the Massachusetts Historical Society on Tremont Street in Boston, and in the Nova Scotia Provincial Archives, Robie Street, Halifax.

Although Governor Peregrine Thomas Hopson "was already seriously ill," he must have recovered at least some of his eyesight because on November 10, 1758, three years after the deportation, he sailed as commander of the English forces against the French on the sugar islands of Martinique and Guadaloupe. However, he died at Basse-Terre in Guadaloupe on February 27, 1759, at one o'clock in the morning. "He died of the fevers which had more than decimated his idle troops." Unmarried, he left his fortune to Lydia Goodall, a niece who lived with him in Berry, England, and to two sisters, Grace Hopson and Anne Bennett. He was a key character because he appreciated the value of the Acadian farmers and, had he been a healthy man, it is likely that Charles Lawrence would never have succeeded him, and there might never have been an expulsion of the Acadians.

Charles Morris, the provincial surveyor responsible for the logistics of the deportation, is buried near Mrs. Belcher and her children in the Old Burial Grounds. Some say that he is buried in Windsor, N. S., (Piziquid) but there doesn't appear to be any evidence to support this claim. As early as 1751, "Morris believed that the presence of the Indians and French on the north shore of the Bay of Fundy and Chignecto made effective British settlement impossible, and he recommended that the Acadians be removed 'by some stratagem...the most effectual way is to destroy all these settlements by burning down all the houses, cutting the dykes, and destroying the grain now growing.'" In 1764, he and John Collier were appointed assistant judges to Chief Justice Belcher although neither man had any official legal training. Morris Street, on which stands the old Halifax Infirmary, bears his name as does Morristown, south of Aylesford in the Annapolis Valley. Morris founded a dynasty of provincial surveyors; his son, Charles II; his grandson, Charles III; and his great grandson, John Spry Morris all followed in his footsteps.

Abbé Le Loutre really did have asthma, escape capture at the siege of Fort Beauséjour, pay Mi'kmaqs for English scalps, burn down his own church, and garner a price on his head. Moreover, having possessed such a volatile personality, it is safe to assume that spanking young ladies was the least of his faux pas. After the loss of Beauséjour, he tried to escape (in a woman's dress*) to France but his ship, the brigantine *Swan*, was captured at sea by the *H. M. S. Ambuscade* belonging to Sir Edward Hawke's squadron. He was traveling under the alias J. L. Deprez, but was discovered anyway. (His father's name was Jean Maurice Le Loutre, Sieur Despré.) He was taken to England and imprisoned at Elizabeth Castle on the Island of Jersey. The Church disowned him and (in a fate similar to John Winslow's) he had to write letters to the French government pleading for financial aid. The French government responded and gave him a small pension.

While in prison, Le Loutre wrote a self-inflating autobiography (available in the N. S. Archives) in which he fudged statistics: he claimed that the price on his head of £100 (offered by Governor Cornwallis on January 13, 1750) was six thousand, and that the price he was offered to give up his subversive activities was the highly unlikely sum of £100,000, an amount that today would be roughly twenty million dollars. Governor Cornwallis called him "a villain, and a good for nothing scoundrel as ever

---

* This may not be true. Alleged cowards were routinely accused of escaping in women's clothing.

lived." However, in his autobiography (written in the third person) Le Loutre said of himself, "... always passed for an honest man, did nothing not in keeping with his office of missionary, committed no crime contrary to the laws of Great Britain." (With his elastic reasoning, perhaps what he meant was that he didn't acknowledge the validity of the laws of Great Britain in French Acadia.) He died suddenly, possibly of a heart attack, in Nantes, France in 1772. He was sixty-one.

Abbé Maillard, Le Loutre's mentor, did write a small Mi'kmaq dictionary and he translated the Roman Catholic liturgy into the Mi'kmaq language. He was so conciliatory that, while spending the last two years of his life in Halifax, he was given a pension, not by the French Government, but by the British Government for "urging his people and the Mi'kmaq to submit to British rule." (There is evidence that he was given living quarters in the Halifax Citadel.)

One French historian said that having Maillard in Nova Scotia in the 1750's was "the equivalent of having, in the heat of battle, a general who sends for reinforcements, and they send him the Dalai Lama." Most astonishing (for today's Roman Catholics, at least) is the fact that "in the presence of almost all the gentlemen in Halifax and a very numerous assembly of French and Indians" he was given an Anglican burial service and burial in St. Paul's Anglican Cemetery. He died in August 1762. He was fifty-five. His Mi'kmaq book of hieroglyphics can be seen at the Art Museum of Nova Scotia on Hollis Street, Halifax.

Vice-Admiral Edward Boscawen died of typhoid fever in Hatchlands, Surrey, England, in January, 1761, three months after the death of Charles Lawrence. He was forty-nine. He left a wife, Fannie, whose letters (available in the National Archives in Ottawa) attest to a loving relationship. They had five children. "He commanded the fleet that carried General Amherst and Colonel Wolfe for the siege and capture of Louisboug, which in turn led to the capture of Quebec in 1759 and all Canada the following year." His odd habit of cocking his head to the right was actually caused by a neck injury he had received in a battle with the French at Cape Finisterre. The Boscawen family distinguished itself right into the twentieth century with Sir Winston Churchill; Edward's maternal grandmother was Arabella Churchill, the Duke of Marlborough's sister.

Rear-Admiral Savage Mostyn died September 16, 1757, just two years after the expulsion. He was about forty-five years old. It may tempt some present-day Acadians to conclude that his Christian name was an apt epithet, but it was simply his grandmother's maiden name.

The taunt he received, "All's well, Mr. Mostyn, sir. There's no Frenchman in the way," was first hurled at him in the Portsmouth Dockyard, quite possibly by rowdy students from the recently established Naval Academy nearby. He never got over the shame of his court martial, and some believed that the real cause of his death was suicide.

His death was certainly hastened by another personal disgrace that he faced on March 14, six months earlier. His ship, the *H.M.S. Monarch*, was used as the place of execution (by firing squad) for another "alleged"* coward, Admiral John Byng. Byng, in 1756, had sailed away from Minorca abandoning a garrison of English soldiers who were trying to hold off an attacking French fleet. For this inexcusable retreat to safer waters, he was court-martialed and sentenced to death. The British authorities, fed up with dishonor in high places, thought that the *Monarch* was the most appropriate site for Byng's execution since the ship, with Mostyn at the helm, was already a disgrace to the British navy. (Byng's execution "inspired Voltaire's remark in *Candide* that in England it was sometimes necessary to shoot an admiral 'pour encourager les autres'." See Chapter 23 of *Candide*.) Compounding their disgrace was the fact that Byng's father was an admiral of the fleet, and Mostyn's father had been a Member of Parliament. Both Mostyn and his uncle, Daniel Finch, are conspicuously omitted from *The Oxford Companion To Ships and the Sea*, a popular reference book now used in British naval training schools. A portrait of Mostyn in early youth was engraved by Thomas Worlidge.

There was a Charles Le Blanc who became very wealthy in Philadelphia and died there in 1816. In fact, his estate, in the millions, has still not been settled, his true heirs legally undetermined.

René Leblanc, the notary public, his wife (née Anne Bourgeois) and their two youngest children were shipped to New York. Seventeen others

---

* The word "alleged" is used here because to this day there are Byng supporters who believe that his court martial and execution were simply the result of dirty politics. (His epitaph states this.) Even Voltaire, the famous French writer, in a generous gesture of fair play, defended Byng by pointing out that French admirals behave the same way and they are not tried and executed by their French superiors.

of his extended family sailed on a different ship and were later discovered in Philadelphia.

In South Carolina, one branch of the Lanneau family became Protestants and gave two ministers to the Presbyterian church: the Reverend John Lanneau who went as a missionary to Jerusalem, and the Reverend Basil Lanneau who became Hebrew tutor in the theological seminary at Columbia.

Today, in the oldest cemetery in Philadelphia, which now forms a part of Washington Park, lie the remains of many deported Acadians. (According to one source, 237 of them lie there, most of these the victims of smallpox they contracted while waiting on board their ships in Philadelphia's harbor.) Since the graves are unmarked, the names of those buried there will never be known.

In 1829 the Catholic Emancipation Act of Canada permitted Catholics to hold public office. However, the Coronation Oath was not recinded until 1910.

The Grand Pré National Park in Nova Scotia receives thousands of visitors from all over the world every summer. Among these are hundreds of Acadian descendants who visit the museum there, stroll the coppery beach, and gaze across the water at Cape Blomidon, burning with curiosity to know more about their Acadian roots.

The story isn't over. It just goes on, and on, and on.

NOTES

Chapter 1: The Kiss

1. W. J. Eccles on page 172 of his *The Canadian Frontier* writes, "... (Lawrence) had no desire to fight the French with some 10,000 Acadians in his midst who might very well support an invading army."

Chapter Three: The Replacement

1. A scene similar to this one probably took place a year earlier. On November 1, 1753, Governor Hopson sailed for England on the *Torrington* taking a medical leave of absence.

Chapter Ten: Two Hundred Hunters

1. It was the attempt by the British, under General Thomas Gage, to confiscate guns at Lexington and Concord that helped to set off the American Revolution. (No doubt the Americans had learned a thing or two from the Acadian expulsions at places like Grand Pré twenty years earlier.) This attempt to disarm citizens is also what prompted the Second Amendment to the American Constitution (the Right to Bear Arms), the amendment which today is America's defense against tougher gun control laws. Gagetown, New Brunswick, the site chosen in 1952 for the Canadian Forces Base, was named for General Gage.

Chapter Eleven: The Murdering Priest

1. It was Nicolas Denys, the early entrepreneur, who reported that he had seen a Mi'kmaq who was 140 years old.

Chapter Twelve: Hieroglyphics on the Wall

1. Abbé Maillard's Mi'kmaq book of hieroglyphics can be seen today in the Art Museum of Nova Scotia in Halifax.

Chapter Seventeen: Belligerent Neutrals

1. Lawrence had probably seen copies of these lawsuits, but Naomi Griffiths in her superb *Contexts of Acadian History 1686 – 1784* (page 73) tells us that "… land claims by Acadians were registered and suits between Acadians about land were judged by the officials at Annapolis Royal." She gives as one example the *"Petition of Reny and Francois Leblancs Against Antoin Landry"*.
2. Lawrence's invitation to the admirals read in part, "I am to acquaint you that it is both agreable (sic) to the Instructions I have received from His Majesty, and the earnest Request of his Council for this Province, that I beg the honour of your Company and Asistance (sic) at our Consultation." (*Collections of the Nova Scotia Historical Society: 3-351.*)
3. The minutes of the July 15 meeting read in part, "Both the said Admirals approved of the said Proceedings, and gave it as their Opinion, that it was now the properest (sic) time to oblige the said Inhabitants to take the Oath of Allegiance to His Majesty or quit the Country." And in a later paragraph of the same minutes, "And then the Question was proposed whether it would not be absolutely necessary for the good of His Majesty's Service, and the Security of this His Province, to retain in pay the Two Thousand New England Troops now under the Command of Lieutenant Colonel Monckton on the Isthmus of Chignecto. It was unanimously the Opinion of His Majesty's Council and all present that they should be retained at least until the Augmentation was completed, or further Orders should be received from England; and it was Resolved that the Transports should be immediately discharged to avoid any unnecessary Expence." (sic)

Moncton, New Brunswick, is named for Robert Monckton, the commander of the British expedition against Fort Beausejour in 1755. For some interesting information on the city's name, see *Place Names of Atlantic Canada, p.* 104.

Chapter Eighteen: If That Be the Case…

1. These are supposed to be Boscawen's own words as reported in the *Pennsylvania Gazette*, September 11, 1755. He was reacting to Braddock's defeat.

2. George's Island has been proposed as a restoration project. According to the Parks Canada website, "it is not open to the public due to the fragile condition of resources. Parks Canada is now preparing this heritage site for future visitation."

Chapter Nineteen: No Priest, No Wedding

1. The arrest of the priests completely eliminates Longfellow's fictitious character, Father Felicien. With his *happy* name, Father Felicien was merely a literary device employed by Longfellow to allow Evangéline to move, later in the story, from place to place unmolested.

Chapter Twenty: Enter Colonel John Winslow

1. The "English" ships of Colonel Winslow, Colonel Winslow himself, and his men were American. However, they were, in effect, "English" since the Americans in 1755 (twenty-one years before their revolution) were loyal English or British citizens and were carrying out the deportation orders on behalf of the British Government's representative in Halifax. There were no real Americans, as we know them, until after 1776, the year they broke away from England. In fact, Winslow must have preached loyalty to England in his own home because his son, Pelham, later refused to revolt against England and moved to Canada as a United Empire Loyalist. It would be safe to assume, then, that in 1755 most, if not all, Americans were good "Empire Loyalists" because they had, at that point, no reason not to be. Furthermore, as early as October 14,1747, Sir Thomas Robinson, the British Secretary of State

wrote to Governor Shirley of Massachusetts, "His Majesty bids you study carefully how this project can best be executed, the opportune time for its execution, and what precautions should be taken to avoid the inconveniences which are to be expected, general revolt, etc. " (See Dudley Le Blanc's book, p. 52.) Later, in July of 1751, four years before the expulsion, Governor Shirley went to London to seek advice on the Acadian problem. And yet, after Longfellow's *Evangéline* brought the brutal deportations to the world's attention, some loyal English sympathizers, like Charles G. D. Roberts in his book *The Land of Evangéline and the Gateways Thither*, (page 7) tried to exonerate the English by writing, "The expulsion of the Acadians was not a wanton piece of cruelty on the part of England. It was done to satisfy New England; and it was carried out by New Englanders." Will R. Bird also makes the same remark in his book, *Done At Grand Pré*. Roberts, Bird, and Sir Adams G. Archibald, another pro-British writer, all offer the same unconvincing denial of British responsibility.

To put it even more plainly, William Shirley was not an American. He was, according to the historian Francis Parkman, "an English barrister who had come to Massachusetts in 1731 to practise his profession and seek his fortune. After filling various offices with credit, he was made governor of the province in 1741, and had discharged his duties with both tact and talent. He was able, sanguine, and a sincere well-wisher to the province, though gnawed by an insatiable hunger for distinction. He thought himself a born strategist, and was possessed by a propensity for contriving military operations, which finally cost him dear."

Chapter Twenty-three: A Loving Ritual

1. The early historians of Acadian life were Jesuits who, to put it kindly, wrote *inspirational* histories. Warts-and-all accounts they were not. According to the Abbé Raynal, for example, no Acadian ever smoked, drank, or became pregnant before marriage. While pre-nuptial pregnancies were rare because most girls married at fifteen, it's still unlikely that there was complete peace in the valley because we do have evidence of both smoking and drinking. We know that the Acadians smoked because their clay pipes have been unearthed by archaeologists. As for drinking, Naomi Griffiths in her excellent *Contexts of Acadian History*

mentions that "one ecclesiastic...complained of too much Acadian drinking in taverns during Sunday mass." However, this depiction by the ecclesiastic of bohemian Sunday-morning-hair-of-the-dog parties is perhaps just as fanciful as Raynal's depiction of the no-dogs-at-all parties in Kings County's Garden of Eden. The truth probably lies somewhere in between. Beer and brandy were common and every ship that came to town carried barrels of rum to sell. Nicolas Denys, one hundred years *earlier*, complained about the bad effects of rum on the Mi'kmaqs.

Chapter Twenty-nine: The Assault on the French Women

1. In his journal, Winslow mentions "the assault on the French women" but he does not say how many women were involved. Two, therefore, is the minimum. It is also quite possible that there were more sexual assaults than he records since the village's women and girls were completely unprotected and at the mercy of foreign soldiers from September 5 to December 20 when the *Race Horse* and the *Ranger*, the last two deportation ships, left Grand Pré.

Chapter Thirty-three: Confusion, Despair, and Desolation

1. Bona Arsenault, on page 147 of his *History of the Acadians,* one of the best and most readable books on the Acadians, gives these statistics: "six hundred and eighty-six houses, eleven mills and two churches were set on fire in the two villages of Grand Pré and Rivière aux Canards alone."

2. Although scorched-earth policies were standard even then,(the ancient Greeks and Romans had implemented them), the Acadians had never been on the receiving end of one. And why now? No official declaration of war had been made. There was, therefore, something malicious in applying this war-time practice to Grand Pré, and something fiendish in its premeditation. It also sent a clear message that there was nothing to return to, should the Acadians ever consider returning home.

3. The Mi'kmaq god, Klu'skap, was said to have left his home on Cape Blomidon in despair at the approach of the White Man, and he would return only when the last White Man left.

Chapter Thirty-four: On the Auction Block

1. The *Seaflower* was one of the ships that carried exiles to Boston.
2. The New York *Mercury* of November 30, 1762, told of deliberate separation of husbands from wives and fathers from their children.

Chapter Thirty-seven: Escape in a Leaky Boat

1. Eleven exiles were sent to Worcester. One of them, an elderly lady, died there. The other ten returned to Canada.
2. This news story also appeared in the *Pennsylvania Gazette* on December 15, 1755.
3. The *Leopard*, Gabriel's ship in the story, was one of the ships that actually went to Maryland.

Chapter Forty-one: Getting To Know the Shawnee

1. My blackbird has lost its beak My blackbird has lost its beak One beak, two beaks, three beaks ah! oh! How do you want my blackbird to sing? My blackbird has lost its eye One eye, two eyes, three eyes One beak, two beaks, three beaks ah! oh!

    My blackbird has lost its head One head, two heads, three heads One eye, two eyes, three eyes, One beak, two beaks, three beaks ah! Oh!

Chapter Forty-four: Charred Remains

1. Chief Luther Standing Bear, *Land of the Spotted Eagle*, Houghton Mifflin, Boston and New York, 1933.
2. Germ warfare apparently is a time-honored strategy. The English officer whose name is frequently associated with "the vile practice" is General Jeffrey Amherst. One source says that he didn't *give* the infected blankets away, but *sold* them to the Indians. In 1763 he wrote to Colonel Henry Bouquet, the chief British officer in Pennsylvania, "Could it not be contrived to send the smallpox among those disaffected tribes of Indians? We must, on this occasion, use every stratagem in our power to reduce them." (See Oldstone's book, p. 33.) Bouquet

responded, "I will try to inoculate the Indians with some blankets that may fall in their hands and take care not to get the disease myself." *The Dictionary of Canadian Biography* states that Amherst hated Indians and devised for them the "most disgraceful means of revenge," and even advised "the use of bloodhounds to track them down... His failure with the Indians was not strange, for he committed the great fault of despising his enemy... Yet, though not a great man, he deserves a very honorable position amongst English soldiers and statesmen of the last (18th) century." Amherst was also the commander at Louisbourg, and it was he who gave the order to destroy the Acadian homes on Prince Edward Island (then under Louisbourg's jurisdiction) after the 1758 expulsion there. Also, it was in that expulsion that 673 Acadians drowned when two ships, the *Violet* and the *Duke William*, bound for France, sank shortly after departure from Charlottetown, or Port Lajoie as it was then called. Accusations of sabotage proliferated since one of these vessels sank because of an explosion. In 1760, to put "a spin" on Amherst's soiled reputation, Francis Hayman painted *The Humanity of General Amherst,* a commissioned work that shows Amherst offering aid and comfort to the poor. This painting hangs today in the Beaverbrook Art Gallery in Fredericton, New Brunswick. Another portrait of him, by Gainsborough, hangs today in the National Portrait Gallery. Amherst, Nova Scotia, is named for General Amherst as are towns in Prince Edward Island, Ontario, Quebec, Newfoundland, Maine, New Hampshire, Massachusetts, Ohio, Virginia, and Colorado.

Chapter Forty-five: Precious Gems

1. Densmore, Frances, *Teton Sioux Music*, Bulletin 61, Bureau of American Ethnology, Washington, D.C., 1918.
2. Big Tree, at that time, was Kensington, a suburb of Philadelphia, and a tribal meeting place. It is now simply North Philadelphia.

Chapter Forty-six: On Unsteady Legs

1. William Penn was a man far ahead of his time. In 1725, he even had the idea that defendants should be tried before a *racially-balanced* jury of their peers.

2. This statement and all of the information on the Shawnee can be found in Henry Harvey's *History of the Shawnee Indians*.

3. It is true that the Old Friends' Almshouse, the "hospital" in Longfellow's poem, could not have taken Gabriel in because it was a senior citizens' home for elderly Quakers.

4. Evangéline's occupation was supposedly that of a nurse. Longfellow called her a "Sister of Mercy", a euphemism for a nurse in his time. But the word "sister" was mistakenly interpreted by some (perhaps even by Longfellow himself) to mean "nun". However, if by the term "Sister of Mercy" Longfellow meant only that she was a nurse, then many of the illustrators of the various editions of *Evangéline* certainly *thought* he meant nun. Howard Chandler Christy, M. L. Kirk, F.O.C. Darley, H. Hirshaver, and Frank Dicksee all drew portraits of Evangéline wearing a nun's habit. The habit in each case, however, indicated a different religious order, and in one of them, Darley's grotesque creation, the habit of an order yet to be established, and hopefully never.

   For the purpose of his plot, Longfellow may also have been thinking of Hamlet's command to Ophelia, "Get thee to a nunnery!" If so, then for Evangéline and Ophelia, the real notion being implied was "Get thee to a nunnery until I can get back to you later," nuns-on-hold, so to speak, until such time as it was more convenient for them to leave the convent and marry their lovers. It was a common practice in Europe, and had been since the Middle Ages, for a woman to rent a room in a convent while awaiting her husband's or lover's return. (An infamous example in 1781 was the wife of the Marquis de Sade who was awaiting her husband's release from prison. She waited in vain.) Moreover, if in 1762 Catholic priests could lose their lives for setting foot in Massachusetts, it is highly unlikely that there were well established convents in Philadelphia which was then the city only of Protestant Brotherly Love. (The first nuns to arrive in Philadelphia were the Sisters of Charity and they did not arrive until 1814, and then only to work with orphans.) Therefore, Evangéline might have been a Sister of Mercy, that is, a nurse, but definitely not a nursing nun.

Chapter Forty-eight: Cushioned Discomfort

1. Charles here is referring to the only Murray he had met. But, like several Acadian historians, he has the wrong Murray. It was Captain Alexander Murray who had confiscated their guns at Grand Pré,

while it was James Murray, one of Wolfe's brigadiers at the capture of Québec, who became the first British governor of Québec.

Chapter Fifty-one: The Return of Blackhoof

1. A Shawnee named Blackhoof did go to Washington in 1802.
2. From *History of the Shawnee Indians.* (Pages 129-131)
3. The Catawbas were the fiercest enemies of the Shawnee, but it was the Wyandots (Huron-Iroquois) with whom they fought over land rights.

Chapter Fifty-two: The Name of a Place

1. Philadelphia's worst yellow fever epidemic occurred in 1793.

Bibliography

Albert, Renaud S., Editor, *Chansons de Chez-Nous*, National Materials Development Centre French and Portuguese, Bedford, N. H., 1978.

Arsenault, Bona, *History of the Acadians*, Editions Fides, Saint-Laurent, Québec, 1994.

Bailey, A. G., *Conflict of European and Eastern Algonkian Cultures*, Tribune Press, Sackville, New Brunswick, 1937.

Bird, Will R., *Done At Grand Pré*, Ryerson Press, Toronto, 1955.

Chief Luther Standing Bear, *Land of the Spotted Eagle*, Houghton Mifflin, Boston and New York, 1933, pp. 192-197.

Clarke, George Frederic, *Expulsion of the Acadians: The True Story (Documented),* Brunswick Press, Fredericton, N. B., 1955.

Daigle, Jean, ed., *The Acadians of the Maritimes: Thematic Studies*, Centre For Acadian Studies, Moncton, 1982.

Densmore, Frances, *Teton Sioux Music*, Bulletin 61, Bureau of American Ethnology, Washington, D.C., 1918, pp. 207-208.

Dictionary of American Biography, Scribner's, New York, 1936.

Dictionary of Canadian Biography, University of Toronto Press, 1974.

Doughty, Arthur, G., *The Acadian Exiles*, Glasgow, Brook & Company, Toronto, 1916.

Eccles, William, J., *The Canadian Frontier 1534 - 1760*, Holt, Rinehart & Winston, Toronto, 1969.

Enquiry into the Conduct Of Captain Mostyn, W. Webb, London, 1745. (Microfilm, Courtesy of Harvard University.)

Griffiths, Naomi, E. S., *The Acadian Deportation: Deliberate Perfidy or Cruel Necessity,* Copp Clark, Toronto, 1969.

Griffiths, Naomi, E., S., *The Contexts of Acadian History 1686 - 1784*, McGill-Queens University Press, Montreal, 1992.

Haliburton, Thomas Chandler, *Historical and Statistical Account of Nova Scotia, Halifax,* 1829.

Hamilton, William B., *Place Names of Atlantic Canada*, University of Toronto Press, Toronto, 1996.

Harvey, Henry, *History of the Shawnee Indians From the Year 1681 to 1884,* Ephraim Morgan & Sons, Cincinnati, 1855, and Kraus Reprint Co., New York, 1971.

Hawthorne, Manning & Dana, Henry Wadsworth Longfellow, *The Origin and Development of Evangéline,* Anthoensen Press, Portland, Maine, 1947, Copyright 1947, The Bibliographical Society of America.

Herbin, John Frederic, *History of Grand Pré*, Barnes & Company, Saint John, New Brunswick, 1905.

Lacey, Laurie, *Mi'kmaq Medicines*, Nimbus Publishing Limited, Halifax, N. S., 1993.

Le Blanc, Dudley, J., *The True Story of the Acadians*, Lafayette, Louisiana, 1937.

Lee, Dorothy, *Freedom and Culture*, Prentice-Hall, Englewood Cliffs, New Jersey, 1959, pp. 163-164. Excerpt (p. 265) reprinted by permission of the author.

Le Loutre, Jean-louis, *Autobiography of Abbé Le Loutre*, Public Archives of Nova Scotia.

Lewis, Michael, *England's Sea-Officers: the Story of the Naval Profession*, George Allen & Unwin Ltd., London, 1939. (Courtesy of the University of Massachusetts Library at Amherst.)

"*Life and Administration of Governor Charles Lawrence 1749 - 1760,*" Collections of the Nova Scotia Historical Society, Vol. Xii, McAlpine Publishing Company, Halifax, 1905.

Longfellow, Henry Wadsworth, *Evangéline*, Grosset & Dunlap, New York, 1847.

Looney, Robert F., *Old Philadelphia in Early Photographs 1839 – 1914,* from The Free Library and published by Dover Publications, Inc., New York, 1976.

Morison, Samuel Eliot, ed., *The Francis Parkman Reader*, Little, Brown, Boston, 1955.

Oldstone, Michael, B. A., *Viruses, Plagues, & History*, Oxford University Press, New York, 1998.

Oxford Companion to Ships and the Sea edited by Peter Kemp, Oxford University Press, 1976.

Parkman, Francis, *A Half Century of Conflict*, Little, Brown & Company, Boston, 1892.

Pennsylvania Gazette, 1755, the Philadelphia Historical Society.

Poirier, Pascal, *Des Acadiens deportes a Boston, en 1755 - (Un episode du Grand Dérangement)* Des Memoires De Le Societe Royale Du Canada, Vol. Ll, 1908.

Raymond, W. O., *Nova Scotia Under British Rule: From the Capture of Port Royal to the Conquest of Canada, 1710 - 1760*, Royal Society of Canada, 1910.

Reid, John G., *Six Crucial Decades: Times of Change in the History of the Maritimes*, Nimbus Publishing Limited, Halifax, N. S., 1987.

Roberts, Charles, G. D., *The Land of Evangéline and the Gateways Thither*, Dominion Atlantic Railway Company, Kentville, N.S., 1922.

Ross, Sally, & Deveau, Alphonse, *The Acadians of Nova Scotia, Past and Present*, Nimbus Publishing, Halifax, 1992.

Shortt, Adam & Doughty, Arthur G., Editors, *Canada and Its Provinces*, Edinburgh University Press for the Publishers Association of Canada Limited, Toronto, 1914.

Smelser, Marshall, *The Campaign for the Sugar Islands, 1759: A study of Amphibious Warfare*, University of North Carolina Press, Chapel Hill, 1955.

Swanton, John R., *The Indian Tribes of North America*, Smithsonian Institution Press, Washington, D. C., 1952.

Voltaire, *Candide*.

Voorhies, Felix, *Acadian Reminicences*, New Iberia, Louisiana, 1907.

Webster, John Clarence, *Career of Abbé Le Loutre in Nova Scotia*, privately printed, Shediac, New Brunswick, 1933.

Webster, John Clarence, *Life of Thomas Pichon*, Public Archives of Nova Scotia, 1937.

Westcott, Thompson, *Historical Mansions of Philadelphia*, Porter & Coates, Philadelphia, 1877.

Winslow, John, *Journal of John Winslow*, Collections of the Nova Scotia Historical Society, Vol. III. Also available in the Massachusetts Historical Society, Boyleston Street, Boston.

Winzerling, O. W., *Acadian Odyssey*, Louisiana State University Press, Baton Rouge, 1955.

Woodham-Smith, Cecil, *The Great Hunger*, Old Town Books, New York, 1962, by arrangement with Harper & Row, now Harper Collins Publishers, 10 East 53rd Street, 22nd Floor, New York, N. Y., 10022-5299